The Rivals
of Sherlock Holmes

The Rivals of
SHERLOCK HOLMES
EARLY DETECTIVE STORIES

EDITED AND INTRODUCED BY

HUGH GREENE

PANTHEON BOOKS
New York

FOR
CHRISTOPHER
AND
TIMOTHY

Compilation Copyright © 1970
by Sir Hugh Greene

Originally published in a hardcover edition in Great Britain by The Bodley
Head Ltd., and in the United States by Pantheon Books, a division of
Random House, Inc., in 1970.
Library of Congress Cataloging in Publication Data
Main entry under title:

The Rivals of Sherlock Holmes.

Originally published: 1970.
1. Detective and mystery stories, English. I. Greene, Hugh, Sir.
[PR1309.D4R47   1983]   823′.0872′08   82-22520
ISBN 0-394-71487-3 (pbk.)

Manufactured in the United States of America
First Pantheon Paperback Edition

CONTENTS

Acknowledgments

Introduction

I. The Ripening Rubies, *Max Pemberton*, 21

II. The Case of Laker, Absconded, *Arthur Morrison*, 41

III. The Duchess of Wiltshire's Diamonds, *Guy Boothby*, 70

IV. The Affair of the 'Avalanche Bicycle and Tyre Co. Ltd,' *Arthur Morrison*, 99

V. The Assyrian Rejuvenator, *Clifford Ashdown*, 127

VI. Madame Sara, *L. T. Meade* and *Robert Eustace*, 145

VII. The Submarine Boat, *Clifford Ashdown*, 176

VIII. The Secret of the Fox Hunter, *William Le Queux*, 194

IX. The Mysterious Death on the Underground Railway, *Baroness Orczy*, 217

X. The Moabite Cipher, *R. Austin Freeman*, 238

XI. The Woman in the Big Hat, *Baroness Orczy*, 268

XII. The Horse of the Invisible, *William Hope Hodgson*, 294

XIII. The Game Played in the Dark, *Ernest Bramah*, 325

ACKNOWLEDGMENTS

For permission to reprint some of these stories my thanks are due to: The Estate of Max Pemberton and Ward Lock and Co. Ltd for *The Ripening Rubies*; The Estate of Arthur Morrison and Ward Lock and Co. Ltd for *The Case of Laker, Absconded* and *The Affair of the 'Avalanche Bicycle & Tyre Co. Ltd'*; The Estate of Clifford Ashdown and Ward Lock and Co. Ltd for *The Assyrian Rejuvenator*; The Estate of Clifford Ashdown for *The Submarine Boat*; The Estate of Baroness Orczy for *The Mysterious Death on the Underground Railway*; The Estate of R. Austin Freeman and Hodder and Stoughton Ltd for *The Moabite Cipher*; The Estate of Baroness Orczy and Cassell & Co. Ltd for *The Woman in the Big Hat*; Mrs Watt and Methuen and Co. Ltd for *The Game Played in the Dark*.

I am very grateful to Mrs Petra Lewis of A. D. Peters and Co. and Miss J. Houlgate, the BBC Reference Librarian, for their help on biographical research. I should also acknowledge the help of Mr Bruce M. Brown, the Librarian of Colgate University, Hamilton N.Y. which owns the Arthur Morrison correspondence from which I have quoted in the introduction.

All the stories included here are on my shelves either in book or magazine form or both. I have, however, found it necessary to check bibliographical details with *Victorian Detective Fiction* by Dorothy Glover and Graham Greene (Bodley Head, 1966), *The Detective Short Story* by Ellery Queen (Boston: Little, Brown and Company, 1942) and *Queen's Quorum* by Ellery Queen (Gollancz, 1953).

Introduction

1. *The Stories*

The rivals of Sherlock Holmes have remained for too long in the shadow of the master.

Some were honest men: some were crooks: all were formidable. From Holborn and the Temple in the east, to Richmond in the west, they dominated the criminal underworld of late Victorian and Edwardian London, sometimes rescuing their clients, sometimes eliminating them. It was a fortunate man who, in his hour of need, knocked on the door of Martin Hewitt or Dr Thorndyke. If he was diverted to the office of Dorrington and Hicks he would be lucky to escape with his life.

The years between 1891, when the 'Adventures of Sherlock Holmes' began to appear in the *Strand Magazine*, and 1914 were a great period for the writers of detective short stories. All the necessary economic circumstances existed for the encouragement of talent: an eager readership and plenty of outlets. The *Strand Magazine* did not stand alone. There were also *Pearson's, Cassell's, Harmsworth's*, the *Windsor* and the *Royal Magazine* competing for stories.

In book form the leading publisher of detective short stories for more than a decade was Ward Lock, usually with illustrations by such masters as Stanley L. Wood, Sidney Paget, Gordon Browne, Sydney Cowell, Fred Barnard and Harold Piffard. Some of the original Ward Lock editions, such as Max Pemberton's *Jewel Mysteries I Have Known*, shining in blue, silver and gold pictorial cloth, are beautiful examples of book production, and the cheap editions in brightly coloured pictorial boards must have made the railway bookstalls of those years a delight to the eye.

In the best of these stories, particularly those by Arthur Morrison, Austin Freeman and Clifford Ashdown, the London of the time comes alive. The action takes place in real streets resounding to the clatter of horses' hoofs, the characters are concerned with petty crime, with small seedy businesses in back streets in the City and off the Strand, the dividing line between crook and detective is a narrow one. The railway is the quickest means of travel and, in case of emergency, a special train* can always be ordered to some country station: time-tables are reliable and for a train to be seven minutes late is cause for alarm.

The setting of most of these stories is much closer to Raymond Chandler's 'mean streets' down which Philip Marlowe walked than to the unreal country house, ye olde English village, world of the English detective story in the years between the wars when Agatha Christie, Margery Allingham, Ngaio Marsh and Dorothy Sayers exercised their monstrous regiment of women. There are only two women writers in this collection, both determinedly metropolitan, and Baroness Orczy, the creator of the Scarlet Pimpernel was, surprisingly, much more down to earth when she wrote detective stories.

In one of these stories, by William Hope Hodgson, the sound of a horse's hoofs does not ring in a city street. That is a reminder that this was also the great era of the ghost story.

---

* In those days an engine to draw a special train always seemed to be available at short notice at the main London termini 'with steam up in the shed'. In Richard Marsh's mystery novel *The Beetle*, published in 1897, 50 minutes or less is regarded as a reasonable time for a run by special train from St Pancras to Bedford. Few expresses do it in that time today.

Introduction

In this collection I have restricted myself to stories in which the detectives have identifiable, or nearly identifiable, addresses in the London of the day. This gives the characters, I think, something of the closeness and reality which still clings to No. 221b Baker Street. King's Bench Walk, Bedford Street, 33 Furnival's Inn (on the left as you enter from Holborn) and the Norfolk Street, Strand, branch of the Aerated Bread Company* also have, or have had, their ghosts.

2. *The Writers*

Max Pemberton, the author of *Jewel Mysteries I Have Known*, was born in 1863 and lived until 1950. He was one of the now, I suppose, almost extinct breed of clubman journalist, a bit of a dandy (Lord Northcliffe admired his 'fancy vests') moving gaily and elegantly between Fleet Street and the Savage Club. He edited *Chums*, a very fine boys' magazine in its heyday and later, from 1896 to 1906, *Cassell's Magazine*. He published early stories by Austin Freeman, Clifford Ashdown, William Le Queux—and Max Pemberton. Among his immense output two books may be remembered, *The Iron Pirate* (published in 1893), the story of a great gas-driven iron-clad which could outpace the navies of the world and terrorized the Atlantic, and its sequel, *Captain Black* (published in 1911). He founded the London School of Journalism in 1920, wrote a life of Lord Northcliffe and was knighted.

Arthur Morrison, the author of the Martin Hewitt stories and *The Dorrington Deed-Box*, is a much more interesting writer, who has fallen into undeserved oblivion. He was

* Ever since I first read the 'Old Man in the Corner' stories I have wondered what 'aerated bread' was. I am indebted to the Aerated Bread Company Limited (which was founded in 1862) for the information that the company was named after a type of bread made by it at the time which did not contain yeast but was manufactured by an 'aerated' process.

born in the same year as Max Pemberton and died in 1945. Apart from his detective stories he wrote a number of novels and short stories about the East End of London and the Essex countryside. The first of his books which he wanted to have remembered was *Tales of Mean Streets* published in 1894. *A Child of the Jago* (1896) and *The Hole in the Wall* (1902) have occasionally been reprinted. The latter, a thriller about a child's adventures in mid-nineteenth-century Dockland, deserves to survive as a minor classic. In a letter to a friend written in the early nineteenthirties Arthur Morrison made a somewhat cryptic reference to his earlier books: '*Tales of Mean Streets* was not the first volume I published—you already know of a pot-boiling compilation of my youth, which I wished forgotten.' He went on to say that the books he valued and was not ashamed to own began with *Tales of Mean Streets*. Until recently I had assumed that the 'pot-boiling compilation' must be the first collection of Martin Hewitt stories, *Martin Hewitt, Investigator*, which, like *Tales of Mean Streets*, appeared in 1894 and was followed by *The Chronicles of Martin Hewitt* and *The Adventures of Martin Hewitt*. Recently, however, I came across a little book in grey card wrappers, *Shadows Around Us, Authentic Tales of the Supernatural* by Arthur Morrison. The second edition, which I have, was published in 1891, at the price of one shilling, by Hay Nisbet & Co. of London and Glasgow. This is much more of a pot-boiler than the first three volumes of Martin Hewitt stories: a later collection, *The Red Triangle*, which appeared in 1903, was very inferior. Arthur Morrison nearly achieved his ambition that *Shadows Around Us* should be forgotten. The one bibliography of his books which I know of does not mention it. Morrison worked on W. E. Henley's *National Observer* with Rudyard Kipling, J. M. Barrie, R. L. Stevenson and Thomas Hardy and expected, one feels, that his books would live with those of his colleagues. He was a collector of Chinese and Japanese paintings which he sold to the British Museum, and he was proud of the fact that, as Chief Inspector of Special Constabulary in Epping Forest, he telephoned the first warning of the first Zeppelin raid on London in May 1915.

Guy Boothby is remembered, if at all, for his 'Dr Nikola' thrillers. He was born in Adelaide in 1867, where he wrote unsuccessful plays and was secretary to the Mayor. He settled in England in 1894 and between then and his death from influenza in Bournemouth in 1905 turned out more than 50 books of which, so far as I know, only four are detective stories.

Clifford Ashdown is a pseudonym used at the beginning of his writing career by R. Austin Freeman, the creator of Dr Thorndyke and, in my opinion, one of the best detective story writers of all time. Two series of Romney Pringle stories by Clifford Ashdown appeared in *Cassell's Magazine* in 1902 and 1903, and were written in collaboration with Dr James Pitcairn, a prison medical officer. The first series, *The Adventures of Romney Pringle*, was published in book form by Ward Lock in 1902 and is one of the rarest of all detective books. The second series, from which I have taken *The Submarine Boat*, has never appeared in book form at all. Clifford Ashdown made one more appearance in *Cassell's Magazine* between December 1904 and May 1905 with a series of six medical crime stories, *From a Surgeon's Diary*, very much in the style of Mrs L. T. Meade. This series, too, was never published in book form. Austin Freeman in later life seems either to have forgotten, or been unnecessarily ashamed of, his first efforts as Clifford Ashdown. In the entry he wrote for *Twentieth Century Authors* he said that he turned to writing in 1904 as a full-time occupation because of ill-health, having previously published nothing except for a book of African travels. This leaves another unexplained oddity. In 1902* R. Austin Freeman contributed to *Cassell's Magazine* under his own name three short stories of a mildly humorous character and an article on the coastwise lights of England. The stories were infinitely inferior to the Romney Pringle adventures appearing at the same time under the name of Clifford Ashdown. One wonders whether his obscure collaborator Dr Pitcairn, about whom I have been able to discover nothing apart from his profession contributed more than one will ever know to the development of R. Austin Freeman into a great writer of detective stories.

Mrs L. T. Meade, the author of *The Sorceress of the Strand*, was born the daughter of a rector in County Cork in 1854 and died in 1914. She was one of the most prolific of all writers of detective short stories in the eighteen-nineties and the early years of this century, usually with a medical or scientific subject and in collaboration with medical men. One can hardly open any of the magazines of the period without finding examples of her work, which are always readable without reaching the heights. In the original *Strand Magazine* publication of *The Sorceress of the Strand*, but not in the book, Robert Eustace is given credit as her collaborator. Robert Eustace is a mysterious figure. He was already collaborating with Mrs Meade in the eighteen-nineties, went on to work with Edgar Jepson on a famous short story, 'The Tea Leaf', which is included in Dorothy Sayers' Everyman Anthology *Tales of Detection*, and collaborated with Dorothy Sayers herself on *The Documents in the Case* in 1930, an extraordinarily long span of playing

---

* R. Austin Freeman had, in fact, appeared in *Cassell's Magazine* even earlier, in August 1900, with a story called *Caveat Emptor: The Story of a Pram* about a waterman and a bargee—a very feeble imitation of W. W. Jacobs.

second fiddle. His real identity* and the facts of his life have proved remarkably elusive. He was Dr. Eustace Robert Barton, M.R.C.S., L.R.C.P., who led a wandering and undistinguished medical life, partly in Portugal. He died in 1945 at the age of seventy-five at Newport in Wales while acting as an assistant medical officer in a mental hospital. He left a total estate of just over £128, and there is no mention whatever in his will that he had been a writer. There is, however, a strange echo of the medical detective stories on which he had collaborated: His macabre instructions for the treatment of his body after death show that he had a horror of being buried alive. Mrs Meade, who was married to Alfred Toulmin-Smith, was also, on her own, a prolific writer of books for girls, with such titles as *A World of Girls, Sweet Girl Graduate, Bashful Fifteen* and *Girls of Merton College* (a prophetic title). I am grateful to a second-hand bookseller who thought *The Sorceress of the Strand* was a book for girls, put it on the wrong shelf, and thus enabled me to acquire a first edition for a few shillings.

William Le Queux (who was born in 1864 and died in 1927) must have been one of the most prolific writers of all time. Edgar Wallace was hardly in the same class. I have 60 books of his on my shelves (with the imprints of 15 different publishers) and I doubt whether I have one book in four of his total output. All, he claimed, were written in his own hand: he never dictated or used a typewriter. After a discouraging start (the publishers of one of his first books, the Tower Publishing Company, went into liquidation) his books sold well. One of his admirers was Princess, later Queen, Alexandra and perhaps in some forgotten corner the Royal Family still has an unrivalled collection of his inscribed first editions. At the height of his fame early in the century he had villas in Florence and in Signa in the foothills of the Apennines, a house in London

---

*I owe most of the facts about Robert Eustace to Dr. Trevor H. Hall's detective work, in which I helped to a small extent.

and a house near Peterborough. In London he was Chargé
d'Affaires of the Republic of San Marino, a pleasant sine-
cure, which helped to bring him a chestful of decorations.
Espionage was his passion and the danger of an invasion of
England the bee which was constantly buzzing around in
his bonnet. Perhaps his best book is *The Great War in
England in 1897* (published in 1894 with an endorsement
by Lord Roberts) which describes the invasion of England
by France and Russia with Germany and Italy coming to
England's aid. He followed this up in 1899 with *England's
Peril* in which war with France is only just averted and in
1906 with *The Invasion of 1910* (again endorsed by Lord
Roberts) in which the invader is Germany. William Le
Queux took himself very seriously as a sort of amateur
international secret agent and friend of crowned heads
(mainly of the Balkan variety of which there was then a
rich selection) as his autobiography *Things I Know* shows.
(One of the curiosities of publishing is Le Queux's biography
by N. St Barbe Sladen in which chapter after chapter con-
sists of large slabs of the autobiography transferred from
the first to the third person.) Le Queux was an early motor-
ing enthusiast and later a wireless pioneer (I have some
letters from him to another wireless amateur written in
1921). Just as among his early titles one finds *The Mystery
of a Motor Car* and *The Lady in the Car,* so towards the end
of his career come *Tracked by Wireless* and *The Voice from
the Void.* It is curious that this writer of fantastic stories
who carried so much fantasy into his own life was, as a
young journalist in Paris, and again in London after his
early failure, encouraged to persevere as a novelist by Zola.

Emmuska, Baroness Orczy was born in 1865 at Tarna-
Örs in Hungary of, according to her own account, a noble
family which could trace its ancestry back to the entry of
Arpad and his knights into Hungary nearly 200 years before

the Norman Conquest. In 1867 her father's peasants, resenting the introduction of farm machinery, set fire to his crops and farm buildings, and the family moved first to Budapest, then to Brussels and finally, when Baroness Orczy was eight years old, to London. It is no wonder that Emmuska's imagination, at any rate in her historical novels, particularly the Scarlet Pimpernel series, was always rather over-heated. Her *Old Man in the Corner* detective stories are much more sober and were a genuine innovation in their indirect method of narration. Their publishing history is a mystery. The first series of *Old Man in the Corner* stories appeared in the *Royal Magazine* in 1901 and 1902, the story I have chosen dating from 1901. They were not published in book form until 1909. Meanwhile a second—and much inferior—series had also appeared in the *Royal Magazine* and been published in book form in 1905 under the colourless title of *The Case of Miss Elliott*. There is no sign that Baroness Orczy realized that in *The Old Man in the Corner* she had created a minor classic of detective fiction. She much preferred (Lud, Sir) Sir Percy Blakeney, and indeed he brought her much more fame and money. She died in November 1947 a fortnight after the publication of her memoirs *Links in the Chain of Life*, which is almost as much a biography of the Scarlet Pimpernel as an autobiography of his creator. She mentions the *Old Man in the Corner* twice and Lady Molly not at all but claims that the creation of the Scarlet Pimpernel was directly inspired by God.

Richard Austin Freeman, emerging from the very talented Clifford Ashdown, created, as Conan Doyle did, a world. Dr John Thorndyke, his friend, Dr Jervis, his laboratory assistant, Mr Polton, and the solid policeman who so often turned to them for advice, Superintendent Miller of Scotland Yard, still haunt King's Bench Walk where Thorndyke had his chambers and his laboratory. Thorndyke, a barrister and expert in medical jurisprudence, is a more realistic figure than Sherlock Holmes. One can believe with no difficulty in his existence as a police, and private, consultant. Austin Freeman, who was born in 1862, was a surgeon by profession and, after being house physician at Middlesex Hospital, went to the Gold Coast in 1897 as Assistant Colonial Surgeon. He had a distinguished career there both medically and politically (he was a member of an Anglo-German boundary commission) before he was invalided out of the service after a bout of blackwater fever. For a time he was Medical Officer at Holloway prison, worked for the Port of London Authority (one can see traces of that in some of his stories) and in private practice was an ear, nose and throat specialist. His first Thorndyke book, after he devoted himself full time to writing, was *The Red Thumb Mark*, which appeared in 1907. Immediately on the first page Thorndyke is there, alive, as Holmes is in *A Study in Scarlet*. It is, perhaps, no coincidence that Austin Freeman, like Conan Doyle, modelled his leading character on a former teacher, a professor of medical jurisprudence, and he maintained a laboratory in which he worked out every experiment described in his books. Austin Freeman lived until 1943 and almost every year, without ever reaching a very large public, produced a new Thorndyke book, maintaining an astonishingly high standard. Always Thorndyke and Jervis seem to be walking through the gas-lit streets of a timeless Edwardian London, though by the time their creator died bombs were falling on the Temple.

William Hope Hodgson was born in 1877 and was killed on the Western Front, a second-lieutenant of 40, on April 17th 1918. As a young man he spent several years in the Merchant Navy and first became known as a writer of weird sea stories. He was an athlete, a boxer and a strong swimmer, who was awarded the Royal Humane Society's Medal for saving life at sea. *Carnacki the Ghost-Finder* is his one collection of detective stories and one can feel in it his admiration of courage at moments of extreme danger. When war broke out in 1914 he was living in the south of France. He returned immediately to England, joined the University of London O.T.C. and was commissioned in the Royal Field Artillery. As a result of a serious accident in training he was gazetted out of the army in 1916, but he was determined to get himself fit and he was commissioned again in March 1917. Just over a year later while on duty as an Observation Officer he was killed. His Commanding Officer wrote: 'He was the life and soul of the mess, always willing and cheery. He was always volunteering for dangerous duty and it is owing to his entire lack of fear that he probably met his death.'

Ernest Bramah Smith (to give him his full name) was born at Hulme in Lancashire in 1868 (it is curious that only two writers represented in this collection were not born in the sixties) and died in 1942. His second name, which was his mother's maiden name, is spelt Brammah on his birth certificate. Not for nothing is he described in one work of reference as 'one of the most self-effacing of modern authors'. His first book, published in 1894, was called *English Farming and Why I Turned It Up*. He went on to create the characters of Kai Lung and Max Carrados, the blind detective, about whom he wrote three volumes of short stories. Otherwise all he seems to have left behind him is a description of himself as a 'small bald man with twinkly black eyes' and a reputation for immense kindness of heart.

And that brings us to the end of our cast of authors.

3. *Detectives' Directory*

Carnacki: Cheyne Walk, Chelsea.

Max Carrados: 'The Turrets', Richmond.

Dorrington and Hicks: Bedford Street, Covent Garden.

Duckworth Drew: Guilford Street, Bloomsbury.

Martin Hewitt: Off the Strand—about 30 yards from Charing Cross station.

Klimo alias Simon Carne: 1, Belverton Terrace, Park Lane (next door to Porchester House).

Lady Molly: Scotland Yard.

Old Man in the Corner: A.B.C. tea-shop, Norfolk Street, Strand.

Romney Pringle: 33, Furnival's Inn (on the left as you enter from Holborn).

Bernard Sutton (jewel dealer): Bond Street.

Dr John Thorndyke: King's Bench Walk.

Eric Vandeleur (Police Surgeon for the Westminster District): 192, Victoria Street.

I

The Ripening Rubies

Max Pemberton

'The plain fact is,' said Lady Faber, 'we are entertaining thieves. It positively makes me shudder to look at my own guests, and to think that some of them are criminals.'

We stood together in the conservatory of her house in Portman Square, looking down upon a brilliant ballroom, upon a glow of colour, and the radiance of unnumbered gems. She had taken me aside after the fourth waltz to tell me that her famous belt of rubies had been shorn of one of its finest pendants; and she showed me beyond possibility of dispute that the loss was no accident, but another of those amazing thefts which startled London so frequently during the season of 1893. Nor was hers the only case. Though I had been in her house but an hour, complaints from other sources had reached me. The Countess of Dunholm had lost a crescent brooch of brilliants; Mrs Kenningham-Hardy had missed a spray of pearls and turquoise; Lady Hallingham made mention of an emerald locket which was gone, as she thought, from her necklace; though, as she confessed with a truly feminine doubt, she was not positive that her maid had given it to her. And these misfortunes, being capped by the abstraction of Lady Faber's pendant, compelled me to believe that of all the startling stories of thefts which the season had known the story of this dance would be the most remarkable.

These things and many more came to my mind as I held the mutilated belt in my hand and examined the fracture, while my hostess stood, with an angry flush upon her face, waiting for my verdict. A moment's inspection of the bauble revealed to me at once its exceeding value, and the means whereby a pendant of it had been snatched.

'If you will look closely,' said I, 'you will see that the gold chain here has been cut with a pair of scissors. As we don't know the name of the person who used them, we may describe them as pickpocket's scissors.'

'Which means that I am entertaining a pickpocket,' said she, flushing again at the thought.

'Or a person in possession of a pickpocket's implements,' I suggested.

'How dreadful,' she cried, 'not for myself, though the rubies are very valuable, but for the others. This is the third dance during the week at which people's jewels have been stolen. When will it end?'

'The end of it will come,' said I, 'directly that you, and others with your power to lead, call in the police. It is very evident by this time that some person is socially engaged in a campaign of wholesale robbery. While a silly delicacy forbids us to permit our guests to be suspected or in any way watched, the person we mention may consider himself in a terrestrial paradise, which is very near the seventh heaven of delight. He will continue to rob with impunity, and to offer up his thanks for that generosity of conduct which refuses us a glimpse of his hat, or even an inspection of the boots in which he may place his plunder.'

'You speak very lightly of it,' she interrupted, as I still held her belt in my hands. 'Do you know that my husband values the rubies in each of those pendants at eight hundred pounds?'

'I can quite believe it,' said I; 'some of them are white as these are, I presume; but I want you to describe it for me, and as accurately as your memory will let you.'

'How will that help to its recovery?' she asked, looking at me questioningly.

'Possibly not at all,' I replied; 'but it might be offered for sale at my place, and I should be glad if I had the means of restoring it to you. Stranger things have happened.'

'I believe,' said she sharply, 'you would like to find out the thief yourself.'

'I should not have the smallest objection,' I exclaimed frankly; 'if these robberies continue, no woman in London will wear real stones; and I shall be the loser.'

'I have thought of that,' said she; 'but, you know, you are not to make the slightest attempt to expose any guest in my house; what you do outside is no concern of mine.'

'Exactly,' said I, 'and for the matter of that I am likely to do very little in either case; we are working against clever heads; and if my judgment be correct, there is a whole gang to cope with. But tell me about the rubies.'

'Well,' said she, 'the stolen pendant is in the shape of a rose. The belt, as you know, was brought by Lord Faber from Burmah. Besides the ring of rubies, which each drop has, the missing star includes four yellow stones, which the natives declare are ripening rubies. It is only a superstition, of course; but the gems are full of fire, and as brilliant as diamonds.'

'I know the stones well,' said I; 'the Burmese will sell you rubies of all colours if you will buy them, though the blue variety is nothing more than the sapphire. And how long is it since you missed the pendant?'

'Not ten minutes ago,' she answered.

'Which means that your next partner might be the thief?' I suggested. 'Really, a dance is becoming a capital entertainment.'

'My next partner is my husband,' said she, laughing for the first time, 'and whatever you do, don't say a word to him. He would never forgive me for losing the rubies.'

When she was gone, I, who had come to her dance solely in the hope that a word or a face there would cast light upon the amazing mystery of the season's thefts, went down again where the press was, and stood while the dancers were pursuing the dreary paths of a 'square'. There before me were the hundred types one sees in a London ball-room —types of character and of want of character, of age aping youth, and of youth aping age, of well-dressed women and ill-dressed women, of dandies and of the bored, of fresh girlhood and worn maturity. Mixed in the dazzling *mêlée*, or swaying to the rhythm of a music-hall melody, you saw the lean form of boys; the robust forms of men; the pretty figures of the girls just out; the figures, not so pretty, of the matrons, who, for the sake of the picturesque, should long ago have been in. As the picture changed quickly, and fair faces succeeded to dark faces, and the coquetting eyes of pretty women passed by with a glance to give place to the uninteresting eyes of the dancing men, I asked myself what hope would the astutest spy have of getting a clue to the mysteries in such a room; how could he look for a moment to name one man or one woman who had part or lot in the astounding robberies which were the wonder of the town? Yet I knew that if nothing were done, the sale of jewels in London would come to the lowest ebb the trade had known, and that I, personally, should suffer loss to an extent which I did not care to think about.

I have said often, in jotting down from my book a few of the most interesting cases which have come to my notice, that I am no detective, nor do I pretend to the smallest gift of foresight above my fellow men. Whenever I have busied myself about some trouble it has been from a personal motive which drove me on, or in the hope of serving someone who henceforth should serve me. And never have I brought to my aid other weapon than a certain measure of common sense. In many instances the purest good chance has given to me my only clue; the merest accident has set me straight when a hundred roads lay before me. I had come to Lady Faber's house hoping that the sight of some stranger, a chance word, or even an impulse might cast light upon the darkness in which we had walked for many weeks. Yet the longer I stayed in the ball-room the more futile did the whole thing seem. Though I knew that a nimble-fingered gentleman might be at my very elbow, that half-a-dozen others might be dancing cheerfully about me in that way of life to which their rascality had called them, I had not so much as a hand-breadth of suspicion; saw no face that was not the face of the dancing ass, or the smart man about town; did not observe a single creature who led me to hazard a question. And so profound at last was my disgust that I elbowed my way from the ball-room in despair; and went again to the conservatory where the palms waved seductively, and the flying corks of the champagne bottles made music harmonious to hear.

There were few people in this room at the moment— old General Sharard, who was never yet known to leave a refreshment table until the supper table was set; the Rev. Arthur Mellbank, the curate of St Peter's, sipping tea; a lean youth who ate an ice with the relish of a schoolboy; and the ubiquitous Sibyl Kavanagh, who has been vulgarly described as a garrison hack. She was a woman of many partialities, whom every one saw at every dance, and then asked how she got there—a woman with sufficient personal attraction left to remind you that she was *passée*, and sufficient wit to make an interval tolerable. I, as a rule, had danced once with her, and then avoided both her pro-gramme and her chatter; but now that I came suddenly upon her, she cried out with a delicious pretence of artlessness, and ostentatiously made room for me at her side.

'*Do* get me another cup of tea,' she said; 'I've been talking for ten minutes to Colonel Harner, who has just come from the great thirst land, and I've caught it.'

'You'll ruin your nerves,' said I, as I fetched her the cup, 'and you'll miss the next dance.'

'I'll sit it out with you,' she cried gushingly; 'and as for nerves, I haven't got any; I must have shed them with my first teeth. But I want to talk to you—you've heard the news, of course! Isn't it dreadful?'

She said this with a beautiful look of sadness, and for a moment I did not know to what she referred. Then it dawned upon my mind that she had heard of Lady Faber's loss.

'Yes,' said I, 'it's the profoundest mystery I have ever known.'

'And can't you think of any explanation at all?' she asked, as she drank her tea at a draught. 'Isn't it possible to suspect some one just to pass the time?'

'If you can suggest any one,' said I, 'we will begin with pleasure.'

'Well, there's no one in this room to think of, is there?' she asked with her limpid laugh; 'of course you couldn't search the curate's pockets, unless sermons were missing instead of rubies?'

'This is a case of "sermons in stones",' I replied, 'and a very serious case. I wonder you have escaped with all those pretty brilliants on your sleeves.'

'But I haven't escaped,' she cried; 'why, you're not up to date. Don't you know that I lost a marquise brooch at the Hayes's dance the other evening? I have never heard the last of it from my husband, who will not believe for a minute that I did not lose it in the crowd.'

'And you yourself believe——'

'That it was stolen, of course. I pin my brooches too well to lose them—some one took it in the same cruel way that Lady Faber's rubies have been taken. Isn't it really awful to think that at every party we go to thieves go with us? It's enough to make one emigrate to the shires.'

She fell to the flippant mood again, for nothing could keep her from that; and as there was obviously nothing to be learnt from her, I listened to her chatter sufferingly.

'But we were going to suspect people,' she continued suddenly, 'and we have not done it. As we can't begin with the curate, let's take the slim young man opposite. Hasn't he what Sheridan calls—but there, I mustn't say it; you know—a something disinheriting countenance?'

'He eats too many jam tarts and drinks too much lemonade to be a criminal,' I replied; 'besides, he is not occupied, you'll have to look in the ball-room.'

'I can just see the top of the men's heads,' said she, craning her neck forward in the effort. 'Have you noticed that when a man is dancing, either he stargazes in ecstasy, as though he were in heaven, or looks down to his boots— well, as if it were the other thing?'

'Possibly,' said I; 'but you're not going to constitute yourself a *vehmgericht* from seeing the top of people's heads.'

'Indeed,' she cried, 'that shows how little you know; there is more character in the crown of an old man's head than is dreamt of in your philosophy, as what's-his-name says. Look at that shining roof bobbing up there, for instance; that is the halo of port and honesty—and a difficulty in dancing the polka. Oh! that mine enemy would dance the polka—especially if he were stout.'

'Do you really possess an enemy?' I asked, as she fell into a vulgar burst of laughter at her own humour; but she said:

'Do I possess one? Go and discuss me with the other

women—that's what I tell all my partners to do; and they come back and report to me. It's as good as a play!'

'It must be,' said I, 'a complete extravaganza. But your enemy has finished his exercise, and they are going to play a waltz. Shall I take you down?'

'Yes,' she cried, 'and don't forget to discuss me. Oh, these crushes!'

She said this as we came to the press upon the corner of the stairs leading to the ball-room, a corner where she was pushed desperately against the banisters. The vigour of the polka had sent an army of dancers to the conservatory, and for some minutes we could neither descend nor go back; but when the press was somewhat relieved, and she made an effort to progress, her dress caught in a spike of the iron-work, and the top of a panel of silk which went down one side of it was ripped open and left hanging. For a minute she did not notice the mishap; but as the torn panel of silk fell away slightly from the more substantial portion of her dress, I observed, pinned to the inner side of it, a large crescent brooch of diamonds. In the same instant she turned with indescribable quickness, and made good the damage. But her face was scarlet in the flush of its colour; and she looked at me with questioning eyes.

'What a miserable accident,' she said. 'I have spoilt my gown.'

'Have you?' said I sympathetically, 'I hope it was not my clumsiness—but really there doesn't seem much damage done. Did you tear it in front?'

There was need of very great restraint in saying this. Though I stood simply palpitating with amazement, and had to make some show of examining her gown, I knew that even an ill-judged word might undo the whole good of the amazing discovery, and deprive me of that which appeared to be one of the most astounding stories of the year. To put an end to the interview, I asked her laughingly if she would not care to see one of the maids upstairs; and she jumped at the excuse, leaving me upon the landing to watch her hurriedly mounting to the bedroom storey above.

When she was gone, I went back to the conservatory and drank a cup of tea, always the best promotor of clear thought; and for some ten minutes I turned the thing over in my mind. Who was Mrs Sibyl Kavanagh, and why had she sewn a brooch of brilliants to the inside of a panel of her gown—sewn it in a place where it was as safely hid from sight as though buried in the Thames? A child could have given the answer—but a child would have over-looked many things which were vital to the development of the unavoidable conclusion of the discovery. The brooch that I had seen corresponded perfectly with the crescent of which Lady Dunholme was robbed—yet it was a brooch which a hundred women might have possessed; and if I had simply stepped down and told Lady Faber, 'the thief you are entertaining is Mrs Sibyl Kavanagh', a slander action with damages had trodden upon the heels of the folly. Yet I would have given a hundred pounds to have been allowed full inspection of the whole panel of the woman's dress—and I would have staked an equal sum that there had been found in it the pendant of the ripening rubies; a pendant which seemed to me the one certain clue that would end the series of jewel robberies, and the colossal mystery of the year. Now, however, the woman had gone upstairs to hide in another place whatever she had to hide; and for the time it was unlikely that a sudden searching of her dress would add to my knowledge.

A second cup of tea helped me still further on my path. It made quite clear to me the fact that the woman was the recipient of the stolen jewels, rather than the actual taker of them. She, clearly, could not use the scissors which had severed Lady Faber's pendant from the ruby belt. A skilful man had in all probability done that—but

which man, or perhaps men? I had long felt that the
season's robberies were the work of many hands. Chance
had now marked for me one pair; but it was vastly more
important to know the others. The punishment of the
woman would scarce stop the widespread conspiracy; the
arrest of her for the possession of a crescent brooch, hid
suspiciously it is true, but a brooch of a pattern which
abounded in every jeweller's shop from Kensington to
Temple Bar, would have been consummate lunacy. Of
course, I could have taken cab to Scotland Yard, and have
told my tale; but with no other support, how far would
that have availed me? If the history of the surpassingly
strange case were to be written, I knew that I must write
it, and lose no moment in the work.

I had now got a sufficient grip upon the whole situation
to act decisively, and my first step was to re-enter the
ball-room, and take a partner for the next waltz. We had
made some turns before I discovered that Mrs Kavanagh
was again in the room, dancing with her usual dash, and
seemingly in no way moved by the mishap. As we passed
in the press, she even smiled at me, saying, 'I've set full
sail again'; and her whole bearing convinced me of her
belief that I had seen nothing.

At the end of my dance my own partner, a pretty little
girl in pink, left me with the remark, 'You're awfully
stupid to-night! I ask you if you've seen *Manon Lescaut*,
and the only thing you say is, "The panel buttons up, I
thought so".' This convinced me that it was dangerous to
dance again, and I waited in the room only until the supper
was ready, and Mrs Kavanagh passed me, making for the
dining-room, on the arm of General Sharard. I had loitered
to see what jewels she wore upon her dress; and when I
had made a note of them, I slipped from the front door of
the house unobserved, and took a hansom to my place in
Bond Street.

At the second ring of the bell my watchman opened the door to me; and while he stood staring with profound surprise, I walked straight to one of the jewel cases in which our cheaper jewels are kept, and took therefrom a spray of diamonds, and hooked it to the inside of my coat. Then I sent the man up stairs to awaken Abel, and in five minutes my servant was with me, though he wore only his trousers and his shirt.

'Abel,' said I, 'there's good news for you. I'm on the path of the gang we're wanting.'

'Good God, sir!' cried he, 'you don't mean that!'

'Yes,' said I, 'there's a woman named Sibyl Kavanagh in it to begin with, and she's helped herself to a couple of diamond sprays, and a pendant of rubies at Lady Faber's to-night. One of the sprays I know she's got; if I could trace the pendant to her, the case would begin to look complete.'

'Whew!' he ejaculated, brightening up at the prospect of business. 'I knew there was a woman in it all along—but this one, why, she's a regular flier, ain't she, sir?'

'We'll find out her history presently. I'm going straight back to Portman Square now. Follow me in a hansom, and when you get to the house, wait inside my brougham until I come. But before you do that, run round to Marlborough Street police-station and ask them if we can have ten or a dozen men ready to mark a house in Bayswater some time between this and six o'clock to-morrow morning.'

'You're going to follow her home then?'

'Exactly, and if my wits can find a way I'm going to be her guest for ten minutes after she quits Lady Faber's. They're sure to let you have the men either at Marlborough Street or at the Harrow Road station. This business has been a disgrace to them quite long enough.'

'That's so, sir; King told me yesterday that he'd bury his head in the sand if something didn't turn up soon. You haven't given me the exact address though.'

'Because I haven't got it. I only know that the woman lives somewhere near St Stephen's Church—she sits under, or on, one of the curates there. If you can get her address from her coachman, do so. But go and dress and be in Portman Square at the earliest possible moment.'

It was now very near one o'clock, indeed the hour struck as I passed the chapel in Orchard Street; and when I came into the square I found my own coachman waiting with the brougham at the corner by Baker Street. I told him, before I entered the house, to expect Abel; and not by any chance to draw up at Lady Faber's. Then I made my way quietly to the ball-room and observed Mrs Kavanagh—I will not say dancing, but hurling herself through the last figure of the lancers. It was evident that she did not intend to quit yet awhile; and I left her to get some supper, choosing a seat near to the door of the dining-room, so that any one passing must be seen by me. To my surprise, I had not been in the room ten minutes when she suddenly appeared in the hall, unattended, and her cloak wrapped round her; but she passed without perceiving me; and I, waiting until I heard the hall door close, went out instantly and got my wraps. Many of the guests had left already, but a few carriages and cabs were in the square, and a linkman seemed busy in the distribution of unlimited potations. It occurred to me that if Abel had not got the woman's address, this man might give it to me, and I put the plain question to him.

'That lady who just left,' said I, 'did she have a carriage or a cab?'

'Oh, you mean Mrs Kevenner,' he answered thickly, 'she's a keb, she is, allus takes a hansom, sir; 192, Westbourne Park; I don't want to ask when I see her, sir.'

'Thank you,' said I, 'she has dropped a piece of jewellery in the hall, and I thought I would drive round and return it to her.'

He looked surprised, at the notion, perhaps, of any one returning anything found in a London ball-room; but I left him with his astonishment and entered my carriage. There I found Abel crouching down under the front seat, and he met me with a piteous plea that the woman had no coachman, and that he had failed to obtain her address.

'Never mind that,' said I, as we drove off sharply, 'what did they say at the station?'

'They wanted to bring a force of police round, and arrest every one in the house, sir. I had trouble enough to hold them in, I'm sure. But I said that we'd sit down and watch if they made any fuss, and then they gave in. It's agreed now that a dozen men will be at the Harrow Road station at your call till morning. They've a wonderful confidence in you, sir.'

'It's a pity they haven't more confidence in themselves— but anyway, we are in luck. The woman's address is 192, Westbourne Park, and I seem to remember that it is a square.'

'I'm sure of it,' said he; 'it's a round square in the shape of an oblong, and one hundred and ninety two is at the side near Durham something or other; we can watch it easily from the palings.'

After this, ten minutes' drive brought us to the place, and I found it as he had said, the 'square' being really a triangle. Number one hundred and ninety-two was a big house, its outer points gone much to decay, but lighted on its second and third floors; though so far as I could see, for the blinds of the drawing-room were up, no one was moving. This did not deter me, however, and, taking my stand with Abel at the corner where two great trees gave us perfect shelter, we waited silently for many minutes, to the astonishment of the constable upon the beat, with whom I soon settled; and to his satisfaction.

'Ah,' said he, 'I knew they was rum 'uns all along; they

owe fourteen pounds for milk, and their butcher ain't paid; young men going in all night, too—why, there's one of them there now.'

I looked through the trees at his word, and saw that he was right. A youth in an opera hat and a black coat was upon the doorstep of the house; and as the light of a street lamp fell upon his face, I recognized him. He was the boy who had eaten of the jam-tarts so plentifully at Lady Faber's—the youth with whom Sibyl Kavanagh had pretended to have no acquaintance when she talked to me in the conservatory. And at the sight of him, I knew that the moment had come.

'Abel,' I said, 'it's time you went. Tell the men to bring a short ladder with them. They'll have to come in by the balcony—but only when I make a sign. The signal will be the cracking of the glass of that lamp you can see upon the table there. Did you bring my pistol?'

'Would I forget that?' he asked; 'I brought you two, and look out! for you may want them.'

'I know that,' said I, 'but I depend upon you. Get back at the earliest possible moment, and don't act until I give the signal. It will mean that the clue is complete.'

He nodded his head, and disappeared quickly in the direction where the carriage was; but I went straight up to the house, and knocked loudly upon the door. To my surprise, it was opened at once by a thick-set man in livery, who did not appear at all astonished to see me.

'They're upstairs, sir, will you go up?' said he.

'Certainly,' said I, taking him at his word. 'Lead the way.'

This request made him hesitate.

'I beg your pardon,' said he, 'I think I have made a mistake—I'll speak to Mrs Kavanagh.'

Before I could answer he had run up the stairs nimbly; but I was quick after him; and when I came upon the landing, I could see into the front drawing-room, where there sat the woman herself, a small and oldish man with long black whiskers, and the youth who had just come into the room. But the back room which gave off from the other with folding-doors, was empty; and there was no light in it. All this I perceived in a momentary glance, for no sooner had the serving-man spoken to the woman, than she pushed the youth out upon the balcony, and came hurriedly to the landing, closing the door behind her.

'Why, Mr Sutton,' she cried, when she saw me, 'this is a surprise; I was just going to bed.'

'I was afraid you would have been already gone,' said I with the simplest smile possible, 'but I found a diamond spray in Lady Faber's hall just after you had left. The footman said it must be yours, and as I am going out of town to-morrow, I thought I would risk leaving it to-night.'

I handed to her as I spoke the spray of diamonds I had taken from my own show-case in Bond Street; but while she examined it she shot up at me a quick searching glance from her bright eyes, and her thick sensual lips were closed hard upon each other. Yet, in the next instant, she laughed again, and handed me back the jewel.

'I'm indeed very grateful to you,' she exclaimed, 'but I've just put my spray in its case; you want to give me someone else's property.'

'Then it isn't yours?' said I, affecting disappointment. 'I'm really very sorry for having troubled you.'

'It is I that should be sorry for having brought you here,' she cried. 'Won't you have a brandy and seltzer or something before you go?'

'Nothing whatever, thanks,' said I. 'Let me apologize again for having disturbed you—and wish you "Goodnight".'

She held out her hand to me, seemingly much reassured;

and as I began to descend the stairs, she re-entered the drawing-room for the purpose, I did not doubt, of getting the man off the balcony. The substantial lackey was then waiting in the hall to open the door for me; but I went down very slowly, for in truth the whole of my plan appeared to have failed; and at that moment I was without the veriest rag of an idea. My object in coming to the house had been to trace, and if possible to lay hands upon the woman's associates, taking her, as I hoped, somewhat by surprise; yet though I had made my chain more complete, vital links were missing; and I stood no nearer to the forging of them. That which I had to ask myself, and to answer in the space of ten seconds, was the question, 'Now, or to-morrow?'—whether I should leave the house without effort, and wait until the gang betrayed itself again; or make some bold stroke which would end the matter there and then. The latter course was the one I chose. The morrow, said I, may find these people in Paris or in Belgium; there never may be such a clue again as that of the ruby pendant—there never may be a similar opportunity of taking at least three of those for whom we had so long hunted. And with this thought a whole plan of action suddenly leaped up in my mind; and I acted upon it, silently and swiftly, and with a readiness which to this day I wonder at.

I now stood at the hall-door, which the lackey held open. One searching look at the man convinced me that my design was a sound one. He was obtuse, patronizing—but probably honest. As we faced each other I suddenly took the door-handle from him, and banged the door loudly, remaining in the hall. Then I clapped my pistol to his head (though for this offence I surmise that a judge might have given me a month), and I whispered fiercely to him:

'This house is surrounded by police; if you say a word I'll give you seven years as an accomplice of the woman upstairs, whom we are going to arrest. When she calls out, answer that I'm gone, and then come back to me for instructions. If you do as I tell you, you shall not be charged —otherwise, you go to jail.'

At this speech the poor wretch paled before me, and shook so that I could feel the tremor all down the arm of his which I held.

'I—I won't speak, sir,' he gasped. 'I won't, I do assure you—to think as I should have served such folk.'

'Then hide me, and be quick about it—in this room here, it seems dark. Now run upstairs and say I'm gone.'

I had stepped into a little breakfast-room at the back of the dining-room, and there had gone unhesitatingly under a round table. The place was absolutely dark, and was a vantage ground, since I could see therefrom the whole of the staircase; but before the footman could mount the stairs, the woman came half-way down them, and, looking over the hall, she asked him:

'Is that gentleman gone?'

'Just left, mum,' he replied.

'Then go to bed, and never let me see you admit a stranger like that again.'

She went up again at this, and he turned to me, asking:

'What shall I do now, sir? I'll do anything if you'll speak for me, sir; I've got twenty years' kerecter from Lord Walley; to think as she's a bad 'un—it's hardly creditable.'

'I shall speak for you,' said I, 'if you do exactly what I tell you. Are any more men expected now?'

'Yes, there's two more; the capting and the clergymin, pretty clergymin he must be, too.'

'Never mind that; wait and let them in. Then go up-stairs and turn the light out on the staircase as if by accident. After that you can go to bed.'

'Did you say the police was 'ere?' he asked in his hoarse whisper; and I said:

'Yes, they're everywhere, on the roof, and in the street, and on the balcony. If there's the least resistance, the house will swarm with them.'

What he would have said to this I cannot tell, for at that moment there was another knock upon the front door, and he opened it instantly. Two men, one in clerical dress, and one, a very powerful man, in a Newmarket coat, went quickly upstairs, and the butler followed them. A moment later the gas went out on the stairs; and there was no sound but the echo of the talk in the front drawing-room.

The critical moment in my night's work had now come. Taking off my boots, and putting my revolver at the half-cock, I crawled up the stairs with the step of a cat, and entered the back drawing-room. One of the folding doors of this was ajar, so that a false step would probably have cost me my life—and I could not possibly tell if the police were really in the street, or only upon their way. But it was my good luck that the men talked loudly, and seemed actually to be disputing. The first thing I observed on looking through the open door was that the woman had left the four to themselves. Three of them stood about the table whereon the lamp was; the dumpy man with the black whiskers sat in his arm-chair. But the most pleasing sight of all was that of a large piece of cotton-wool spread upon the table and almost covered with brooches, lockets, and sprays of diamonds; and to my infinite satisfaction I saw Lady Faber's pendant of rubies lying conspicuous even amongst the wealth of jewels which the light showed.

There then was the clue; but how was it to be used? It came to me suddenly that four consummate rogues such as these would not be unarmed. Did I step into the room, they might shoot me at the first sound; and if the police had not come, there would be the end of it. Had opportunity been permitted to me, I would, undoubtedly, have waited five or ten minutes to assure myself that Abel was in the street without. But this was not to be. Even as I debated the point, a candle's light shone upon the staircase; and in another moment Mrs Kavanagh herself stood in the doorway watching me. For one instant she stood, but it served my purpose; and as a scream rose upon her lips, and I felt my heart thudding against my ribs, I threw open the folding doors, and deliberately shot down the glass of the lamp which had cast the aureola of light upon the stolen jewels.

As the glass flew, for my reputation as a pistol shot was not belied in this critical moment, Mrs Kavanagh ran in a wild fit of hysterical screaming to her bedroom above—but the four men turned with loud cries to the door where they had seen me; and as I saw them coming, I prayed that Abel might be there. This thought need not have occurred to me. Scarce had the men taken two steps when the glass of the balcony windows was burst in with a crash, and the whole room seemed to fill with police.

*   *   *

I cannot now remember precisely the sentences which were passed upon the great gang (known to police history as the Westbourne Park gang) of jewel thieves; but the history of that case is curious enough to be worthy of mention. The husband of the woman Kavanagh—he of the black whiskers—was a man of the name of Whyte, formerly a manager in the house of James Thorndike, the Universal Provider near the Tottenham Court Road. Whyte's business had been to provide all things needful for dances; and, though it astonishes me to write it, he had even found dancing men for ladies whose range of acquaintance was narrow. In the course of business, he set up for himself eventually; and as he worked, the bright idea came to him, why not find as guests men who may snap up, in the heat and the security of the dance, such unconsidered trifles as sprays, pendants, and lockets. To this end he married, and his wife being a clever woman who fell in with his idea, she—under the name of Kavanagh—made the acquaintance of a number of youths whose business it was to dance; and eventually wormed herself into many good houses. The trial brought to light the extraordinary fact that no less than twenty-three men and eight women were bound in this amazing conspiracy, and that Kavanagh acted as the buyer of the property they stole, giving them a third of the profits, and swindling them outrageously. He, I believe, is now taking the air at Portland; and the other young men are finding in the exemplary exercise of picking oakum, work for idle hands to do.

As for Mrs Kavanagh, she was dramatic to the end of it; and, as I learnt from King, she insisted on being arrested in bed.

II

The Case of Laker, Absconded

Arthur Morrison

There were several of the larger London banks and insurance offices from which Hewitt held a sort of general retainer as detective adviser, in fulfilment of which he was regularly consulted as to the measures to be taken in different cases of fraud, forgery, theft, and so forth, which it might be the misfortune of the particular firms to encounter. The more important and intricate of these cases were placed in his hands entirely, with separate commissions, in the usual way. One of the most important companies of the sort was the General Guarantee Society, an insurance corporation which, among other risks, took those of the integrity of secretaries, clerks, and cashiers. In the case of a cash-box elopement on the part of any person guaranteed by the society, the directors were naturally anxious for a speedy capture of the culprit, and more especially of the booty, before too much of it was spent, in order to lighten the claim upon their funds, and in work of this sort Hewitt was at times engaged, either in general advice and direction or in the actual pursuit of the plunder and the plunderer.

Arriving at his office a little later than usual one morning, Hewitt found an urgent message awaiting him from the

General Guarantee Society, requesting his attention to a robbery which had taken place on the previous day. He had gleaned some hint of the case from the morning paper, wherein appeared a short paragraph, which ran thus:

SERIOUS BANK ROBBERY.—In the course of yesterday a clerk employed by Messrs Liddle, Neal & Liddle, the well-known bankers, disappeared, having in his possession a large sum of money, the property of his employers—a sum reported to be rather over £15,000. It would seem that he had been entrusted to collect the money in his capacity of 'walk-clerk' from various other banks and trading concerns during the morning, but failed to return at the usual time. A large number of the notes which he received had been cashed at the Bank of England before suspicion was aroused. We understand that Detective-Inspector Plummer, of Scotland Yard, has the case in hand.

The clerk, whose name was Charles William Laker, had, it appeared from the message, been guaranteed in the usual way by the General Guarantee Society, and Hewitt's presence at the office was at once desired in order that steps might quickly be taken for the man's apprehension and in the recovery, at any rate, of as much of the booty as possible.

A smart hansom brought Hewitt to Threadneedle Street in a bare quarter of an hour, and there a few minutes' talk with the manager, Mr Lyster, put him in possession of the main facts of the case, which appeared to be simple. Charles William Laker was twenty-five years of age, and had been in the employ of Messrs Liddle, Neal & Liddle for something more than seven years—since he left school, in fact—and until the previous day there had been nothing in his conduct to complain of. His duties as walk-clerk consisted in making a certain round, beginning at about half-past ten each morning. There were a certain number of the more important banks between which and Messrs Liddle, Neal & Liddle there were daily transactions, and a few smaller semi-private banks and merchant firms acting as financial agents with whom there was business intercourse of less importance and regularity; and each of these, as necessary, he visited in turn, collecting cash due on bills and other instruments of a like nature. He carried a wallet, fastened securely to his person by a chain, and this wallet contained the bills and the cash. Usually at the end of his round, when all his bills had been converted into cash, the wallet held very large sums. His work and responsibilities, in fine, were those common to walk-clerks in all banks.

On the day of the robbery he had started out as usual—possibly a little earlier than was customary—and the bills and other securities in his possession represented considerably more than £15,000. It had been ascertained that he had called in the usual way at each establishment on the round, and had transacted his business at the last place by about a quarter-past one, being then, without doubt, in possession of cash to the full value of the bills negotiated. After that, Mr Lyster said, yesterday's report was that nothing more had been heard of him. But this morning there had been a message to the effect that he had been traced out of the country—to Calais, at least, it was thought. The directors of the society wished Hewitt to take the case in hand personally and at once, with a view of recovering what was possible from the plunder by way of salvage; also, of course, of finding Laker, for it is an important moral gain to guarantee societies, as an example, if a thief is caught and punished. Therefore Hewitt and Mr Lyster, as soon as might be, made for Messrs Liddle, Neal & Liddle's, that the investigation might be begun.

The bank premises were quite near—in Leadenhall Street. Having arrived there, Hewitt and Mr Lyster made their way to the firm's private rooms. As they were passing an outer waiting-room, Hewitt noticed two women. One, the elder, in widow's weeds, was sitting with her head bowed in her hand over a small writing-table. Her face was not visible, but her whole attitude was that of a person over-come with unbearable grief; and she sobbed quietly. The other was a young woman of twenty-two or twenty-three. Her thick black veil revealed no more than that her features were small and regular and that her face was pale and drawn. She stood with a hand on the elder woman's shoulder, and she quickly turned her head away as the two men entered.

Mr Neal, one of the partners, received them in his own room. 'Good-morning, Mr Hewitt,' he said, when Mr Lyster had introduced the detective. 'This is a serious business—very. I think I am sorrier for Laker himself than for anybody else, ourselves included—or, at any rate, I am sorrier for his mother. She is waiting now to see Mr Liddle, as soon as he arrives—Mr Liddle has known the family for a long time. Miss Shaw is with her, too, poor girl. She is a governess, or something of that sort, and I believe she and Laker were engaged to be married. It's all very sad.'

'Inspector Plummer, I understand,' Hewitt remarked, 'has the affair in hand, on behalf of the police?'

'Yes,' Mr Neal replied; 'in fact, he's here now, going through the contents of Laker's desk, and so forth; he thinks it possible Laker may have had accomplices. Will you see him?'

'Presently. Inspector Plummer and I are old friends. We met last, I think, in the case of the Stanway cameo, some months ago. But, first, will you tell me how long Laker has been a walk-clerk?'

'Barely four months, although he has been with us altogether seven years. He was promoted to the walk soon after the beginning of the year.'

'Do you know anything of his habits—what he used to do in his spare time, and so forth?'

'Not a great deal. He went in for boating, I believe, though I have heard it whispered that he had one or two more expensive tastes—expensive, that is, for a young man in his position,' Mr Neal explained, with a dignified wave of the hand that he peculiarly affected. He was a stout old gentleman, and the gesture suited him.

'You have had no reason to suspect him of dishonesty before, I take it?'

'Oh, no. He made a wrong return once, I believe, that went for some time undetected, but it turned out, after all, to be a clerical error—a mere clerical error.'

'Do you know anything of his associates out of the office?'

'No, how should I? I believe Inspector Plummer has been making inquiries as to that, however, of the other clerks. Here he is, by the bye, I expect. Come in!'

It was Plummer who had knocked, and he came in at Mr Neal's call. He was a middle-sized, small-eyed, impenetrable-looking man, as yet of no great reputation in the force. Some of my readers may remember his connection with that case, so long a public mystery, that I have elsewhere fully set forth and explained under the title of 'The Stanway Cameo Mystery'. Plummer carried his billy-cock hat in one hand and a few papers in the other. He gave Hewitt good-morning, placed his hat on a chair, and spread the papers on the table.

'There's not a great deal here,' he said, 'but one thing's plain—Laker had been betting. See here, and here, and here'—he took a few letters from the bundle in his hand—'two letters from a bookmaker about settling—wonder he trusted a clerk—several telegrams from tipsters, and a letter from some friend—only signed by initials—asking Laker to put a sovereign on a horse for the friend "with

his own ". I'll keep these, I think. It may be worth while
to see that friend, if we can find him. Ah, we often find it's
betting, don't we, Mr Hewitt? Meanwhile, there's no news
from France yet.'

'You are sure that is where he is gone?' asked Hewitt.

'Well, I'll tell you what we've done as yet. First, of
course, I went round to all the banks. There was nothing
to be got from that. The cashiers all knew him by sight,
and one was a personal friend of his. He had called as usual,
said nothing in particular, cashed his bills in the ordinary
way, and finished up at the Eastern Consolidated Bank
at about a quarter-past one. So far there was nothing
whatever. But I had started two or three men meanwhile
making inquiries at the railway stations, and so on. I had
scarcely left the Eastern Consolidated when one of them
came after me with news. He had tried Palmer's Tourist
Office, although that seemed an unlikely place, and there
struck the track.'

'Had he been there?'

'Not only had he been there, but he had taken a tourist
ticket for France. It was quite a smart move, in a way.
You see it was the sort of ticket that lets you do pretty
well what you like; you have the choice of two or three
different routes to begin with, and you can break your
journey where you please, and make all sorts of variations.
So that a man with a ticket like that, and a few hours'
start, could twist about on some remote branch route,
and strike off in another direction altogether, with a new
ticket, from some out-of-the-way place, while we were
carefully sorting out and inquiring along the different
routes he *might* have taken. Not half a bad move for a new
hand; but he made one bad mistake, as new hands always
do—as old hands do, in fact, very often. He was fool enough
to give his own name, C. Laker! Although that didn't
matter much, as the description was enough to fix him.

There he was, wallet and all, just as he had come from the Eastern Consolidated Bank. He went straight from there to Palmer's, by the bye, and probably in a cab. We judge that by the time. He left the Eastern Consolidated at a quarter-past one, and was at Palmer's by twenty-five-past —ten minutes. The clerk at Palmer's remembered the time because he was anxious to get out to his lunch, and kept looking at the clock, expecting another clerk in to relieve him. Laker didn't take much in the way of luggage, I fancy. We inquired carefully at the stations, and got the porters to remember the passengers for whom they had been carrying luggage, but none appeared to have had any dealings with our man. That, of course, is as one would expect. He'd take as little as possible with him, and buy what he wanted on the way, or when he'd reached his hiding-place. Of course, I wired to Calais (it was a Dover to Calais route ticket) and sent a couple of smart men off by the 8.15 mail from Charing Cross. I expect we shall hear from them in the course of the day. I am being kept in London in view of something expected at headquarters, or I should have been off myself.'

'That is all, then, up to the present? Have you anything else in view?'

'That's all I've absolutely ascertained at present. As for what I'm going to do'—a slight smile curled Plummer's lip—'well, I shall see. I've a thing or two in my mind.'

Hewitt smiled slightly himself; he recognized Plummer's touch of professional jealousy. 'Very well,' he said, rising, 'I'll make an inquiry or two for myself at once. Perhaps, Mr Neal, you'll allow one of your clerks to show me the banks, in their regular order, at which Laker called yesterday. I think I'll begin at the beginning.'

Mr Neal offered to place at Hewitt's disposal anything or anybody the bank contained, and the conference broke up. As Hewitt, with the clerk, came through the rooms separating Mr Neal's sanctum from the outer office, he fancied he saw the two veiled women leaving by a side door.

The first bank was quite close to Liddle, Neal & Liddle's. There the cashier who had dealt with Laker the day before remembered nothing in particular about the interview. Many other walk-clerks had called during the morning, as they did every morning, and the only circumstances of the visit that he could say anything definite about were those recorded in figures in the books. He did not know Laker's name till Plummer had mentioned it in making inquiries on the previous afternoon. As far as he could remember, Laker behaved much as usual, though really he did not notice much; he looked chiefly at the bills. He described Laker in a way that corresponded with the photograph that Hewitt had borrowed from the bank; a young man with a brown moustache and ordinary-looking fairly regular face, dressing much as other clerks dressed— tall hat, black cutaway coat, and so on. The numbers of the notes handed over had already been given to Inspector Plummer, and these Hewitt did not trouble about.

The next bank was in Cornhill, and here the cashier was a personal friend of Laker's—at any rate, an acquaintance —and he remembered a little more. Laker's manner had been quite as usual, he said; certainly he did not seem preoccupied or excited in his manner. He spoke for a moment or two—of being on the river on Sunday, and so on—and left in his usual way.

'Can you remember *everything* he said?' Hewitt asked. 'If you can tell me, I should like to know exactly what he did and said to the smallest particular.'

'Well, he saw me a little distance off—I was behind there, at one of the desks—and raised his hand to me, and said, "How d'ye do?" I came across and took his bills, and dealt with them in the usual way. He had a new umbrella lying on the counter—rather a handsome umbrella

—and I made a remark about the handle. He took it up to show me, and told me it was a present he had just received from a friend. It was a gorse-root handle, with two silver bands, one with his monogram, C.W.L. I said it was a very nice handle, and asked him whether it was fine in his district on Sunday. He said he had been up the river, and it was very fine there. And I think that was all.'

'Thank you. Now about this umbrella. Did he carry it rolled? Can you describe it in detail?'

'Well, I've told you about the handle, and the rest was much as usual, I think; it wasn't rolled—just flapping loosely, you know. It was rather an odd-shaped handle, though. I'll try and sketch it, if you like, as well as I can remember.' He did so, and Hewitt saw in the result rough indications of a gnarled crook, with one silver band near the end, and another, with the monogram, a few inches down the handle. Hewitt put the sketch in his pocket, and bade the cashier good-day.

At the next bank the story was the same as at the first— there was nothing remembered but the usual routine. Hewitt and the clerk turned down a narrow paved court, and through into Lombard Street for the next visit. The bank—that of Buller, Clayton, Ladds & Co.—was just at the corner at the end of the court, and the imposing stone entrance-porch was being made larger and more imposing still, the way being almost blocked by ladders and scaffold-poles. Here there was only the usual tale, and so on through the whole walk. The cashiers knew Laker only by sight, and that not always very distinctly. The calls of walk-clerks were such matters of routine that little note was taken of the persons of the clerks themselves, who were called by the names of their firms, if they were called by any names at all. Laker had behaved much as usual, so far as the cashiers could remember, and when finally the

Eastern Consolidated was left behind, nothing more had been learnt than the chat about Laker's new umbrella.

Hewitt had taken leave of Mr Neal's clerk, and was stepping into a hansom, when he noticed a veiled woman in widow's weeds hailing another hansom a little way behind. He recognized the figure again, and said to the driver: 'Drive fast to Palmer's Tourist Office, but keep your eye on that cab behind, and tell me presently if it is following us.'

The cabman drove off, and after passing one or two turnings, opened the lid above Hewitt's head, and said: 'That there other keb *is* a-follerin' us, sir, an' keepin' about even distance all along.'

'All right; that's what I wanted to know. Palmer's now.'

At Palmer's the clerk who had attended to Laker remembered him very well and described him. He also remembered the wallet, and *thought* he remembered the umbrella—was practically sure of it, in fact, upon reflection. He had no record of the name given, but remembered it distinctly to be Laker. As a matter of fact, names were never asked in such a transaction, but in this case Laker appeared to be ignorant of the usual procedure, as well as in a great hurry, and asked for the ticket and gave his name all in one breath, probably assuming that the name would be required.

Hewitt got back to his cab, and started for Charing Cross. The cabman once more lifted the lid and informed him that the hansom with the veiled woman in it was again following, having waited while Hewitt had visited Palmer's. At Charing Cross Hewitt discharged his cab and walked straight to the lost property office. The man in charge knew him very well, for his business had carried him there frequently before.

'I fancy an umbrella was lost in the station yesterday,' Hewitt said. 'It was a new umbrella, silk, with a gnarled gorse-root handle and two silver bands, something like this sketch. There was a monogram on the lower band—"C. W. L." were the letters. Has it been brought here?'

'There was two or three yesterday,' the man said; 'let's see.' He took the sketch and retired to a corner of his room. 'Oh, yes—here it is, I think; isn't this it? Do you claim it?'

'Well, not exactly that, but I think I'll take a look at it, if you'll let me. By the way, I see it's rolled up. Was it found like that?'

'No; the chap rolled it up what found it—porter he was. It's a fad of his, rolling up umbrellas close and neat, and he's rather proud of it. He often looks as though he'd like to take a man's umbrella away and roll it up for him when it's a bit clumsy done. Rum fad, eh?'

'Yes; everybody has his little fad, though. Where was this found—close by here?'

'Yes, sir; just there, almost opposite this window, in the little corner.'

'About two o'clock?'

'Ah, about that time, more or less.'

Hewitt took the umbrella up, unfastened the band, and shook the silk out loose. Then he opened it, and as he did so a small scrap of paper fell from inside it. Hewitt pounced on it like lightning. Then, after examining the umbrella thoroughly, inside and out, he handed it back to the man, who had not observed the incident of the scrap of paper.

'That will do, thanks,' he said. 'I only wanted to take a peep at it—just a small matter connected with a little case of mine. Good-morning.'

He turned suddenly and saw, gazing at him with a terrified expression from a door behind, the face of the woman who had followed him in the cab. The veil was lifted, and he caught but a mere glance of the face ere it was suddenly withdrawn. He stood for a moment to allow the woman time to retreat, and then left the station and walked toward his office, close by.

Scarcely thirty yards along the Strand he met Plummer.

'I'm going to make some much closer inquiries all down the line as far as Dover,' Plummer said. 'They wire from Calais that they have no clue as yet, and I mean to make quite sure, if I can, that Laker hasn't quietly slipped off the line somewhere between here and Dover. There's one very peculiar thing,' Plummer added confidentially. 'Did you see the two women who were waiting to see a member of the firm at Liddle, Neal & Liddle's?'

'Yes. Laker's mother and his *fiancée*, I was told.'

'That's right. Well, do you know that girl—Shaw her name is—has been shadowing me ever since I left the Bank. Of course I spotted it from the beginning—these amateurs don't know how to follow anybody—and, as a matter of fact, she's just inside that jeweller's shop door behind me now, pretending to look at the things in the window. But it's odd, isn't it?'

'Well,' Hewitt replied, 'of course it's not a thing to be neglected. If you'll look very carefully at the corner of Villiers Street, without appearing to stare, I think you will possibly observe some signs of Laker's mother. She's shadowing *me*.'

Plummer looked casually in the direction indicated, and then immediately turned his eyes in another direction.

'I see her,' he said; 'she's just taking a look round the corner. That's a thing not to be be ignored. Of course, the Lakers' house is being watched—we set a man on it at once, yesterday. But I'll put some one on now to watch Miss Shaw's place too. I'll telephone through to Liddle's—probably they'll be able to say where it is. And the women themselves must be watched, too. As a matter of fact, I had a notion that Laker wasn't alone in it. And it's just possible, you know, that he has sent an accomplice off with his tourist ticket to lead us a dance while he looks after himself in another direction. Have you done anything?'

'Well,' Hewitt replied, with a faint reproduction of the secretive smile with which Plummer had met an inquiry of his earlier in the morning, 'I've been to the station here, and I've found Laker's umbrella in the lost property office.'

'Oh! Then probably he *has* gone. I'll bear that in mind, and perhaps have a word with the lost property man.'

Plummer made for the station and Hewitt for his office. He mounted the stairs and reached his door just as I myself, who had been disappointed in not finding him in, was leaving. I had called with the idea of taking Hewitt to lunch with me at my club, but he declined lunch. 'I have an important case in hand,' he said. 'Look here, Brett. See this scrap of paper. You know the types of the different newspapers—which is this?'

He handed me a small piece of paper. It was part of a cutting containing an advertisement, which had been torn in half.

> oast.   You 1st.   Then to-
> 3rd L.   No.197 red bl. straight
> time.

'I *think*,' I said, 'this is from the *Daily Chronicle*, judging by the paper. It is plainly from the "agony column", but all the papers use pretty much the same type for these advertisements, except the *Times*. If it were not torn I could tell you at once, because the *Chronicle* columns are rather narrow.'

'Never mind—I'll send for them all.' He rang, and sent Kerrett for a copy of each morning paper of the previous day. Then he took from a large wardrobe cupboard a decent but well-worn and rather roughened tall hat. Also a coat a little worn and shiny on the collar. He exchanged these for his own hat and coat, and then substituted an old necktie for his own clean white one, and encased his legs in mud-spotted leggings. This done, he produced a very large and thick pocket-book, fastened by a broad elastic band, and said, 'Well, what do you think of this? Will it do for Queen's taxes, or sanitary inspection, or the gas, or the water-supply?'

'Very well indeed, I should say,' I replied. 'What's the case?'

'Oh, I'll tell you all about that when it's over—no time now. Oh, here you are, Kerrett. By the bye, Kerrett, I'm going out presently by the back way. Wait for about ten minutes or a quarter of an hour after I am gone, and then just go across the road and speak to that lady in black, with the veil, who is waiting in that little foot-passage opposite. Say Mr Martin Hewitt sends his compliments, and he advises her not to wait, as he has already left his office by another door, and has been gone some little time. That's all; it would be a pity to keep the poor woman waiting all day for nothing. Now the papers. *Daily News*, *Standard*, *Telegraph*, *Chronicle*—yes, here it is, in the *Chronicle*.'

The whole advertisement read thus:

YOB.—H.R. Shop roast.   You 1st.   Then to-night.   02.   2nd top 3rd L.   No.197 red bl. straight mon.   One at a time.

'What's this,' I asked, 'a cryptogram?'

'I'll see,' Hewitt answered. 'But I won't tell you anything about it till afterwards, so you get your lunch. Kerrett, bring the directory.'

This was all I actually saw of this case myself, and I have written the rest in its proper order from Hewitt's information, as I have written some other cases entirely.

To resume at the point where, for the time, I lost sight of the matter. Hewitt left by the back way and stopped an empty cab as it passed. 'Abney Park Cemetery' was his direction to the driver. In little more than twenty minutes the cab was branching off down the Essex Road on its way to Stoke Newington, and in twenty minutes more Hewitt stopped it in Church Street, Stoke Newington. He walked through a street or two, and then down another, the houses of which he scanned carefully as he passed. Opposite one which stood by itself he stopped, and, making a pretence of consulting and arranging his large pocket-book, he took a good look at the house. It was rather larger, neater, and more pretentious than the others in the street, and it had a natty little coach-house just visible up the side entrance. There were red blinds hung with heavy lace in the front windows, and behind one of these blinds Hewitt was able to catch the glint of a heavy gas chandelier.

He stepped briskly up the front steps and knocked sharply at the door. 'Mr Merston?' he asked, pocket-book in hand, when a neat parlourmaid opened the door.

'Yes.'

'Ah!' Hewitt stepped into the hall and pulled off his hat; 'it's only the meter. There's been a deal of gas running away somewhere here, and I'm just looking to see if the meters are right. Where is it?'

The girl hesitated. 'I'll—I'll ask master,' she said.

'Very well. I don't want to take it away, you know— only to give it a tap or two, and so on.'

The girl retired to the back of the hall, and without taking her eyes off Martin Hewitt, gave his message to some invisible person in a back room, whence came a growling reply of 'All right'.

Hewitt followed the girl to the basement, apparently looking straight before him, but in reality taking in every detail of the place. The gas meter was in a very large lumber cupboard under the kitchen stairs. The girl opened the door and lit a candle. The meter stood on the floor, which was littered with hampers and boxes and odd sheets of brown paper. But a thing that at once arrested Hewitt's attention was a garment of some sort of bright blue cloth, with large brass buttons, which was lying in a tumbled heap in a corner, and appeared to be the only thing in the place that was not covered with dust. Nevertheless, Hewitt took no apparent notice of it, but stooped down and solemnly tapped the meter three times with his pencil, and listened with great gravity, placing his ear to the top. Then he shook his head and tapped again. At length he said:

'It's a bit doubtful. I'll just get you to light the gas in the kitchen a moment. Keep your hand to the burner, and when I call out shut it off *at once*; see?'

The girl turned and entered the kitchen, and Hewitt immediately seized the blue coat—for a coat it was. It had a dull red piping in the seams, and was of the swallow-tail pattern—livery coat, in fact. He held it for a moment before him, examining its pattern and colour, and then rolled it up and flung it again into the corner.

'Right!' he called to the servant. 'Shut off!'

The girl emerged from the kitchen as he left the cupboard.

'Well,' she asked, 'are you satisfied now?'

'Quite satisfied, thank you,' Hewitt replied.

'Is it all right?' she continued, jerking her hand toward the cupboard.

'Well, no, it isn't; there's something wrong there, and I'm glad I came. You can tell Mr Merston, if you like, that I expect his gas bill will be a good deal less next quarter.' And there was a suspicion of a chuckle in Hewitt's voice as he crossed the hall to leave. For a gas inspector is pleased when he finds at length what he has been searching for.

Things had fallen out better than Hewitt had dared to expect. He saw the key of the whole mystery in that blue coat; for it was the uniform coat of the hall porters at one of the banks that he had visited in the morning, though which one he could not for the moment remember. He entered the nearest post-office and despatched a telegram to Plummer, giving certain directions and asking the inspector to meet him; then he hailed the first available cab and hurried toward the City.

At Lombard Street he alighted, and looked in at the door of each bank till he came to Buller, Clayton, Ladds & Co.'s. This was the bank he wanted. In the other banks the hall porters wore mulberry coats, brick-dust coats, brown coats, and what not, but here, behind the ladders and scaffold poles which obscured the entrance, he could see a man in a blue coat, with dull red piping and brass buttons. He sprang up the steps, pushed open the inner swing door, and finally satisfied himself by a closer view of the coat, to the wearer's astonishment. Then he regained the pavement and walked the whole length of the bank premises in front, afterwards turning up the paved passage at the side, deep in thought. The bank had no windows or doors on the side next the court, and the two adjoining houses were old and supported in place by wooden shores. Both were empty, and a great board announced that tenders would be received in a month's time for the purchase of the old materials of which they were constructed; also that some part of the site would be let on a long building lease.

Hewitt looked up at the grimy fronts of the old buildings. The windows were crusted thick with dirt—all except the bottom window of the house nearer the bank, which was fairly clean, and seemed to have been quite lately washed.

The door, too, of this house was cleaner than that of the other, though the paint was worn. Hewitt reached and fingered a hook driven into the left-hand doorpost about six feet from the ground. It was new, and not at all rusted; also a tiny splinter had been displaced when the hook was driven in, and clean wood showed at the spot.

Having observed these things, Hewitt stepped back and read at the bottom of the big board the name, 'Winsor & Weekes, Surveyors and Auctioneers, Abchurch Lane'. Then he stepped into Lombard Street.

Two hansoms pulled up near the post-office, and out of the first stepped Inspector Plummer and another man. This man and the two who alighted from the second hansom were unmistakably plain-clothes constables—their air, gait, and boots proclaimed it.

'What's all this?' demanded Plummer, as Hewitt approached.

'You'll soon see, I think. But, first, have you put the watch on No. 197, Hackworth Road?'

'Yes; nobody will get away from there alone.'

'Very good. I am going into Abchurch Lane for a few minutes. Leave your men out here, but just go round into the court by Buller, Clayton & Ladds's, and keep your eye on the first door on the left. I think we'll find something soon. Did you get rid of Miss Shaw?'

'No, she's behind now, and Mrs Laker's with her. They met in the Strand, and came after us in another cab. Rare fun, eh! They think we're pretty green! It's quite handy, too. So long as they keep behind me it saves all trouble of watching *them*.' And Inspector Plummer chuckled and winked.

'Very good. You don't mind keeping your eye on that door, do you? I'll be back very soon,' and with that Hewitt turned off into Abchurch Lane.

At Winsor & Weekes's information was not difficult to

obtain. The houses were destined to come down very shortly, but a week or so ago an office and a cellar in one of them was let temporarily to a Mr Westley. He brought no references; indeed, as he paid a fortnight's rent in advance, he was not asked for any, considering the circumstances of the case. He was opening a London branch for a large firm of cider merchants, he said, and just wanted a rough office and a cool cellar to store samples in for a few weeks till the permanent premises were ready. There was another key, and no doubt the premises might be entered if there were any special need for such a course. Martin Hewitt gave such excellent reasons that Winsor & Weekes's managing clerk immediately produced the key and accompanied Hewitt to the spot.

'I think you'd better have your men handy,' Hewitt remarked to Plummer when they reached the door, and a whistle quickly brought the men over.

The key was inserted in the lock and turned, but the door would not open; the bolt was fastened at the bottom. Hewitt stooped and looked under the door.

'It's a drop bolt,' he said. 'Probably the man who left last let it fall loose, and then banged the door, so that it fell into its place. I must try my best with a wire or a piece of string.'

A wire was brought, and with some manoeuvring Hewitt contrived to pass it round the bolt, and lift it little by little, steadying it with the blade of a pocket-knife. When at length the bolt was raised out of the hole, the knife-blade was slipped under it, and the door swung open.

They entered. The door of the little office just inside stood open, but in the office there was nothing, except a board a couple of feet long in a corner. Hewitt stepped across and lifted this, turning it downward face toward Plummer. On it, in fresh white paint on a black ground, were painted the words

"BULLER, CLAYTON, LADDS & CO.,

TEMPORARY ENTRANCE."

Hewitt turned to Winsor & Weekes's clerk and asked, 'The man who took this room called himself Westley, didn't he?'

'Yes.'

'Youngish man, clean-shaven, and well-dressed?'

'Yes, he was.'

'I fancy,' Hewitt said, turning to Plummer, 'I *fancy* an old friend of yours is in this—Mr Sam Gunter.'

'What, the "Hoxton Yob"?'

'I think it's possible he's been Mr Westley for a bit, and somebody else for another bit. But let's come to the cellar.'

Winsor & Weekes's clerk led the way down a steep flight of steps into a dark underground corridor, wherein they lighted their way with many successive matches. Soon the cellar corridor made a turn to the right, and as the party passed the turn, there came from the end of the passage before them a fearful yell.

'Help! help! Open the door! I'm going mad—mad! O my God!'

And there was a sound of desperate beating from the inside of the cellar door at the extreme end. The men stopped, startled.

'Come,' said Hewitt, 'more matches!' and he rushed to the door. It was fastened with a bar and padlock.

'Let me out, for God's sake!' came the voice, sick and hoarse, from the inside. 'Let me out!'

'All right!' Hewitt shouted. 'We have come for you. Wait a moment.'

The voice sank into a sort of sobbing croon, and Hewitt tried several keys from his own bunch on the padlock. None fitted. He drew from his pocket the wire he had used for the bolt of the front door, straightened it out, and made a sharp bend at the end.

'Hold a match close,' he ordered shortly, and one of the men obeyed. Three or four attempts were necessary, and several different bendings of the wire were effected, but in the end Hewitt picked the lock, and flung open the door.

From within a ghastly figure fell forward among them fainting, and knocked out the matches.

'Hullo!' cried Plummer. 'Hold up! Who are you?'

'Let's get him up into the open,' said Hewitt. 'He can't tell you who he is for a bit, but I believe he's Laker.'

'Laker! What, here?'

'I think so. Steady up the steps. Don't bump him. He's pretty sore already, I expect.'

Truly the man was a pitiable sight. His hair and face were caked in dust and blood, and his finger-nails were torn and bleeding. Water was sent for at once, and brandy.

'Well,' said Plummer hazily, looking first at the unconscious prisoner and then at Hewitt, 'but what about the swag?'

'You'll have to find that yourself,' Hewitt replied. 'I think my share of the case is about finished. I only act for the Guarantee Society, you know, and if Laker's proved innocent——'

'Innocent! How?'

'Well, this is what took place, as near as I can figure it. You'd better undo his collar, I think'—this to the men. 'What I believe has happened is this. There has been a very clever and carefully prepared conspiracy here, and Laker has not been the criminal, but the victim.'

'Been robbed himself, you mean? But how? Where?'

'Yesterday morning, before he had been to more than three banks—here, in fact.'

'But then how? You're all wrong. We *know* he made

the whole round, and did all the collection. And then Palmer's office, and all, and the umbrella; why—'

The man lay still unconscious. 'Don't raise his head,' Hewitt said. 'And one of you had best fetch a doctor. He's had a terrible shock.' Then turning to Plummer he went on, 'As to *how* they managed the job, I'll tell you what I think. First it struck some very clever person that a deal of money might be got by robbing a walk-clerk from a bank. This clever person was one of a clever gang of thieves —perhaps the Hoxton Row gang, as I think I hinted. Now you know quite as well as I do that such a gang will spend any amount of time over a job that promises a big haul, and that for such a job they can always command the necessary capital. There are many most respectable persons living in good style in the suburbs whose chief business lies in financing such ventures, and taking the chief share of the proceeds. Well, this is their plan, carefully and intelligently carried out. They watch Laker, observe the round he takes, and his habits. They find that there is only one of the clerks with whom he does business that he is much acquainted with, and that this clerk is in a bank which is commonly second in Laker's round. The sharpest man among them—and I don't think there's a man in London could do this as well as young Sam Gunter— studies Laker's dress and habits just as an actor studies a character. They take this office and cellar, as we have seen, *because it is next door to a bank whose front entrance is being altered*—a fact which Laker must know from his daily visits. The smart man—Gunter, let us say, and I have other reasons for believing it to be he—makes up precisely like Laker, false moustache, dress, and everything, and waits here with the rest of the gang. One of the gang is dressed in a blue coat with brass buttons, like a hall-porter in Buller's bank. Do you see?'

'Yes, I think so. It's pretty clear now.'

'A confederate watches at the top of the court, and the moment Laker turns in from Cornhill—having already been, mind, at the only bank where he was so well known that the disguised thief would not have passed muster— as soon as he turns in from Cornhill, I say, a signal is given, and that board'—pointing to that with the white letters—'is hung on the hook in the doorpost. The sham porter stands beside it, and as Laker approaches says, "This way in, sir, this morning. The front way's shut for the alterations". Laker suspecting nothing, and supposing that the firm have made a temporary entrance through the empty house, enters. He is seized when well along the corridor, the board is taken down and the door shut. Probably he is stunned by a blow on the head—see the blood now. They take his wallet and all the cash he has already collected. Gunter takes the wallet and also the umbrella, since it has Laker's initials, and is therefore distinctive. He simply completes the walk in the character of Laker, beginning with Buller, Clayton & Ladds's just round the corner. It is nothing but routine work, which is quickly done, and nobody notices him particularly—it is the bills they examine. Meanwhile this unfortunate fellow is locked up in the cellar here, right at the end of the underground corridor, where he can never make himself heard in the street, and where next him are only the empty cellars of the deserted house next door. The thieves shut the front door and vanish. The rest is plain. Gunter, having completed the round, and bagged some £15,000 or more, spends a few pounds in a tourist ticket at Palmer's as a blind, being careful to give Laker's name. He leaves the umbrella at Charing Cross in a conspicuous place right opposite the lost property office, where it is sure to be seen, and so completes his false trail.'

'Then who are the people at 197, Hackworth Road?'

'The capitalist lives there—the financier, and probably

the directing spirit of the whole thing. Merston's the name
he goes by there, and I've no doubt he cuts a very imposing
figure in chapel every Sunday. He'll be worth picking up—
this isn't the first thing he's been in, I'll warrant.'

'But—but what about Laker's mother and Miss Shaw?'

'Well, what? The poor women are nearly out of their
minds with terror and shame, that's all, but though they
may think Laker a criminal, they'll never desert him.
They've been following us about with a feeble, vague sort
of hope of being able to baffle us in some way or help him
if we caught him, or something, poor things. Did you ever
hear of a real woman who'd desert a son or a lover merely
because he was a criminal? But here's the doctor. When
he's attended to him will you let your men take Laker
home? I must hurry and report to the Guarantee Society,
I think.'

'But,' said the perplexed Plummer, 'where did you
get your clue? You must have had a tip from some one,
you know—you can't have done it by clairvoyance. What
gave you the tip?'

'The *Daily Chronicle.*'

'The *what*?'

'The *Daily Chronicle*. Just take a look at the "agony
column" in yesterday morning's issue, and read the
message to "Yob"—to Gunter, in fact. That's all.'

By this time a cab was waiting in Lombard Street, and
two of Plummer's men, under the doctor's directions,
carried Laker to it. No sooner, however, were they in the
court than the two watching women threw themselves
hysterically upon Laker, and it was long before they could
be persuaded that he was not being taken to gaol. The
mother shrieked aloud, 'My boy—my boy! Don't take
him! Oh, don't take him! They've killed my boy! Look
at his head—oh, his head!' and wrestled desperately with
the men, while Hewitt attempted to soothe her, and

promised to allow her to go in the cab with her son if she would only be quiet. The younger woman made no noise, but she held one of Laker's limp hands in both hers.

Hewitt and I dined together that evening, and he gave me a full account of the occurrences which I have here set down. Still, when he was finished I was not able to see clearly by what process of reasoning he had arrived at the conclusions that gave him the key to the mystery, nor did I understand the 'agony column' message, and I said so.

'In the beginning,' Hewitt explained, 'the thing that struck me as curious was the fact that Laker was said to have given his own name at Palmer's in buying his ticket. Now, the first thing the greenest and newest criminal thinks of is changing his name, so that the giving of his own name seemed unlikely to begin with. Still, he *might* have made such a mistake, as Plummer suggested when he said that criminals usually make a mistake somewhere —as they do, in fact. Still, it was the least likely mistake I could think of—especially as he actually didn't wait to be asked for his name, but blurted it out when it wasn't really wanted. And it was conjoined with another rather curious mistake, or what would have been a mistake, if the thief were Laker. Why should he conspicuously display his wallet—such a distinctive article—for the clerk to see and note? Why rather had he not got rid of it before showing himself? Suppose it should be somebody personating Laker? In any case I determined not to be prejudiced by what I had heard of Laker's betting. A man may bet without being a thief.

'But, again, supposing it *were* Laker? Might he not have given his name, and displayed his wallet, and so on, while buying a ticket for France, in order to draw pursuit after himself in that direction while he made off in another, in another name, and disguised? Each supposition was plausible. And, in either case, it might happen that whoever was laying this trail would probably lay it a little farther. Charing Cross was the next point, and there I went. I already had it from Plummer that Laker had not been recognized there. Perhaps the trail had been laid in some other manner. Something left behind with Laker's name on it, perhaps? I at once thought of the umbrella with his monogram, and, making a long shot, asked for it at the lost property office, as you know. The guess was lucky. In the umbrella, as you know, I found the scrap of paper. That, I judged, had fallen in from the hand of the man carrying the umbrella. He had torn the paper in half in order to fling it away, and one piece had fallen into the loosely flapping umbrella. It is a thing that will often happen with an omnibus ticket, as you may have noticed. Also, it was proved that the umbrella *was* unrolled when found, and rolled immediately after. So here was a piece of paper dropped by the person who had brought the umbrella to Charing Cross and left it. I got the whole advertisement, as you remember, and I studied it. "Yob" is back-slang for "boy", and is often used in nicknames to denote a young smooth-faced thief. Gunter, the man I suspect, as a matter of fact, is known as the "Hoxton Yob". The message, then, was addressed to some one known by such a nickname. Next, "H.R. shop roast". Now, in thieves' slang, to "roast" a thing or a person is to watch it or him. They call any place a shop—notably, a thieves' den. So that this meant that some resort—perhaps the "Hoxton Row shop"—was watched. "You 1st then to-night" would be clearer, perhaps, when the rest was understood. I thought a little over the rest, and it struck me that it must be a direction to some other house, since one was warned of as being watched. Besides, there was the number, 197, and "red bl.", which would be extremely likely to mean "red blinds", by way of clearly distinguishing the house. And then the plan of the thing was plain. You have noticed, probably, that the map of London which accompanies the Post Office Directory is divided, for convenience of reference, into numbered squares?'

'Yes. The squares are denoted by letters along the top margin and figures down the side. So that if you consult the directory, and find a place marked as being in D 5, for instance, you find vertical divisions D, and run your finger down it till it intersects horizontal division 5, and there you are.'

'Precisely. I got my Post Office Directory, and looked for "0 2". It was in North London, and took in parts of Abney Park Cemetery and Clissold Park; "2nd top" was the next sign. Very well, I counted the second street intersecting the top of the square—counting, in the usual way, from the left. That was Lordship Road. Then "3rd L". From the point where Lordship Road crossed the top of the square, I ran my finger down the road till it came to "3rd L", or, in other words, the third turning on the left —Hackworth Road. So there we were, unless my guesses were altogether wrong. "Straight mon" probably meant "straight moniker"—that is to say, the proper name, a thief's *real* name, in contradistinction to that he may assume. I turned over the directory till I found Hackworth Road, and found that No. 197 was inhabited by a Mr Merston. From the whole thing I judged this. There was to have been a meeting at the "H.R. shop", but that was found, at the last moment, to be watched by the police for some purpose, so that another appointment was made for this house in the suburbs. "You 1st. Then to-night"— the person addressed was to come first, and the others in the evening. They were- to ask for the householder's "straight moniker"—Mr Merston. And they were to come one at a time.

'Now, then, what was this? What theory would fit it?

Suppose this were a robbery, directed from afar by the advertiser. Suppose, on the day before the robbery, it was found that the place fixed for division of spoils were watched. Suppose that the principal thereupon advertised (as had already been agreed in case of emergency) in these terms. The principal in the actual robbery—the "Yob" addressed—was to go first with the booty. The others were to come after, one at a time. Anyway, the thing was good enough to follow a little further, and I determined to try No. 197 Hackworth Road. I have told you what I found there, and how it opened my eyes. I went, of course, merely on chance, to see what I might chance to see. But luck favoured, and I happened on that coat—brought back rolled up, on the evening after the robbery, doubtless by the thief who had used it, and flung carelessly into the handiest cupboard. *That* was this gang's mistake.'

'Well, I congratulate you,' I said. 'I hope they'll catch the rascals.'

'I rather think they will, now they know where to look. They can scarcely miss Merston, anyway. There has been very little to go upon in this case, but I stuck to the thread, however slight, and it brought me through. The rest of the case, of course, is Plummer's. It was a peculiarity of my commission that I could equally well fulfil it by catching the man with all the plunder, or by proving him innocent. Having done the latter, my work was at an end, but I left it where Plummer will be able to finish the job handsomely.'

Plummer did. Sam Gunter, Merston, and one accomplice were taken—the first and last were well known to the police—and were identified by Laker. Merston, as Hewitt had suspected, had kept the lion's share for himself, so that altogether, with what was recovered from him and the other two, nearly £11,000 was saved for Messrs Liddle, Neal & Liddle. Merston, when taken, was in the act of packing up to take a holiday abroad, and there cash his notes, which were found, neatly packed in separate thousands, in his portmanteau. As Hewitt had predicted, his gas bill *was* considerably less next quarter, for less than half-way through it he began a term in gaol.

As for Laker, he was reinstated, of course, with an increase of salary by way of compensation for his broken head. He had passed a terrible twenty-six hours in the cellar, unfed and unheard. Several times he had become insensible, and again and again he had thrown himself madly against the door, shouting and tearing at it, till he fell back exhausted, with broken nails and bleeding fingers. For some hours before the arrival of his rescuers he had been sitting in a sort of stupor, from which he was suddenly aroused by the sound of voices and footsteps. He was in bed for a week, and required a rest of a month in addition before he could resume his duties. Then he was quietly lectured by Mr Neal as to betting, and, I believe, dropped that practice in consequence. I am told that he is 'at the counter' now—a considerable promotion.

III

The Duchess of Wiltshire's Diamonds

Guy Boothby

To the reflective mind the rapidity with which the inhabitants of the world's greatest city seize upon a new name or idea, and familiarize themselves with it, can scarcely prove otherwise than astonishing. As an illustration of my meaning let me take the case of Klimo—the now famous private detective, who has won for himself the right to be considered as great as Lecocq, or even the late lamented Sherlock Holmes.

Up to a certain morning London had never even heard his name, nor had it the remotest notion as to who or what he might be. It was as sublimely ignorant and careless on the subject as the inhabitants of Kamtchatka or Peru. Within twenty-four hours, however, the whole aspect of the case was changed. The man, woman, or child who had not seen his posters, or heard his name, was counted an ignoramus unworthy of intercourse with human beings.

Princes became familiar with it as their trains bore them to Windsor to luncheon with the Queen; the nobility noticed and commented upon it as they drove about the town; merchants, and business men generally, read it as they made their ways by omnibus or underground, to

[70]

their various shops and counting-houses; street boys called each other by it as a nickname; music hall artists introduced it into their patter, while it was even rumoured that the Stock Exchange itself had paused in the full flood tide of business to manufacture a riddle on the subject.

That Klimo made his profession pay him well was certain, first from the fact that his advertisements must have cost a good round sum, and, second, because he had taken a mansion in Belverton Street, Park Lane, next door to Porchester House, where, to the dismay of that aristocratic neighbourhood, he advertised that he was prepared to receive and be consulted by his clients. The invitation was responded to with alacrity, and from that day forward, between the hours of twelve and two, the pavement upon the north side of the street was lined with carriages, every one containing some person desirous of testing the great man's skill.

I must here explain that I have narrated all this in order to show the state of affairs in Belverton Street and Park Lane when Simon Carne arrived, or was supposed to arrive, in England. If my memory serves me correctly, it was on Wednesday, the 3rd of May, that the Earl of Amberley drove to Victoria to meet and welcome the man whose acquaintance he had made in India under such peculiar circumstances, and under the spell of whose fascination he and his family had fallen so completely.

Reaching the station, his lordship descended from his carriage, and made his way to the platform set apart for the reception of the Continental express. He walked with a jaunty air, and seemed to be on the best of terms with himself and the world in general. How little he suspected the existence of the noose into which he was so innocently running his head!

As if out of compliment to his arrival, the train put in an appearance within a few moments of his reaching the platform. He immediately placed himself in such a position that he could make sure of seeing the man he wanted, and waited patiently until he should come in sight. Carne, however, was not among the first batch; indeed, the majority of passengers had passed before his lordship caught sight of him.

One thing was very certain, however great the crush might have been, it would have been difficult to mistake Carne's figure. The man's infirmity and the peculiar beauty of his face rendered him easily recognisable. Possibly, after his long sojourn in India, he found the morning cold, for he wore a long fur coat, the collar of which he had turned up round his ears, thus making a fitting frame for his delicate face. On seeing Lord Amberley he hastened forward to greet him.

'This is most kind and friendly of you,' he said, as he shook the other by the hand. 'A fine day and Lord Amberley to meet me. One could scarcely imagine a better welcome.'

As he spoke, one of his Indian servants approached and salaamed before him. He gave him an order, and received an answer in Hindustani, whereupon he turned again to Lord Amberley.

'You may imagine how anxious I am to see my new dwelling,' he said. 'My servant tells me that my carriage is here, so may I hope that you will drive back with me and see for yourself how I am likely to be lodged?'

'I shall be delighted,' said Lord Amberley, who was longing for the opportunity, and they accordingly went out into the station yard together to discover a brougham, drawn by two magnificent horses, and with Nur Ali, in all the glory of white raiment and crested turban, on the box, waiting to receive them. His lordship dismissed his Victoria, and when Jowur Singh had taken his place beside his fellow servant upon the box, the carriage rolled out of the station yard in the direction of Hyde Park.

'I trust her ladyship is quite well,' said Simon Carne politely, as they turned into Gloucester Place.

'Excellently well, thank you,' replied his lordship. 'She bade me welcome you to England in her name as well as my own, and I was to say that she is looking forward to seeing you.'

'She is most kind, and I shall do myself the honour of calling upon her as soon as circumstances will permit,' answered Carne. 'I beg you will convey my best thanks to her for her thought of me.'

While these polite speeches were passing between them they were rapidly approaching a large hoarding, on which was displayed a poster setting forth the name of the now famous detective, Klimo.

Simon Carne, leaning forward, studied it, and when they had passed, turned to his friend again.

'At Victoria and on all the hoardings we meet I see an enormous placard, bearing the word "Klimo". Pray, what does it mean?'

His lordship laughed.

'You are asking a question which, a month ago, was on the lips of nine out of every ten Londoners. It is only within the last fortnight that we have learned who and what "Klimo" is.'

'And pray what is he?'

'Well, the explanation is very simple. He is neither more nor less than a remarkably astute private detective, who has succeeded in attracting notice in such a way that half London has been induced to patronize him. I have had no dealings with the man myself. But a friend of mine, Lord Orpington, has been the victim of a most audacious burglary, and, the police having failed to solve the mystery, he has called Klimo in. We shall therefore see what he can do before many days are past. But, there, I expect you will soon know more about him than any of us.'

'Indeed! And why?'

'For the simple reason that he has taken No. 1, Belverton Terrace, the house adjoining your own, and sees his clients there.'

Simon Carne pursed up his lips, and appeared to be considering something.

'I trust he will not prove a nuisance,' he said at last. 'The agents who found me the house should have acquainted me with the fact. Private detectives, on however large a scale, scarcely strike one as the most desirable of neighbours—particularly for a man who is so fond of quiet as myself.'

At this moment they were approaching their destination. As the carriage passed Belverton Street and pulled up, Lord Amberley pointed to a long line of vehicles standing before the detective's door.

'You can see for yourself something of the business he does,' he said. 'Those are the carriages of his clients, and it is probable that twice as many have arrived on foot.'

'I shall certainly speak to the agent on the subject,' said Carne, with a shadow of annoyance upon his face. 'I consider the fact of this man's being so close to me a serious drawback to the house.'

Jowur Singh here descended from the box and opened the door in order that his master and his guest might alight, while portly Ram Gafur, the butler, came down the steps and salaamed before them with Oriental obsequiousness. Carne greeted his domestics with kindly condescension, and then, accompanied by the ex-Viceroy, entered his new abode.

'I think you may congratulate yourself upon having secured one of the most desirable residences in London,' said his lordship ten minutes or so later, when they had explored the principal rooms.

'I am very glad to hear you say so,' said Carne. 'I trust

your lordship will remember that you will always be welcome in the house as long as I am its owner.'

'It is very kind of you to say so,' returned Lord Amberley warmly. 'I shall look forward to some months of pleasant intercourse. And now I must be going. Tomorrow, perhaps, if you have nothing better to do, you will give us the pleasure of your company at dinner. Your fame has already gone abroad, and we shall ask one or two nice people to meet you, including my brother and sister-in-law, Lord and Lady Gelpington, Lord and Lady Orpington, and my cousin, the Duchess of Wiltshire, whose interest in china and Indian art, as perhaps you know, is only second to your own.'

'I shall be most glad to come.'

'We may count on seeing you in Eaton Square, then, at eight o'clock?'

'If I am alive you may be sure I shall be there. Must you really go? Then good-bye, and many thanks for meeting me.'

His lordship having left the house, Simon Carne went upstairs to his dressing-room, which it was to be noticed he found without inquiry, and rang the electric bell, beside the fireplace, three times. While he was waiting for it to be answered he stood looking out of the window at the long line of carriages in the street below.

'Everything is progressing admirably,' he said to himself. 'Amberley does not suspect any more than the world in general. As a proof he asks me to dinner tomorrow evening to meet his brother and sister-in-law, two of his particular friends, and above all Her Grace of Wiltshire.'

At this moment the door opened, and his valet, the grave and respectable Belton, entered the room. Carne turned to greet him impatiently.

'Come, come, Belton,' he said, 'we must be quick. It is twenty minutes to twelve, and if we don't hurry, the folk next door will become impatient. Have you succeeded in doing what I spoke to you about last night?'

'I have done everything, sir.'

'I am glad to hear it. Now lock that door and let us get to work. You can let me have your news while I am dressing.'

Opening one side of a massive wardrobe, that completely filled one end of the room, Belton took from it a number of garments. They included a well-worn velvet coat, a baggy pair of trousers—so old that only a notorious pauper or a millionaire could have afforded to wear them— a flannel waistcoat, a Gladstone collar, a soft silk tie, and a pair of embroidered carpet slippers upon which no old clothes man in the most reckless way of business in Petticoat Lane would have advanced a single halfpenny. Into these he assisted his master to change.

'Now give me the wig, and unfasten the straps of this hump,' said Carne, as the other placed the garments just referred to upon a neighbouring chair.

Belton did as he was ordered, and then there happened a thing the like of which no one would have believed. Having unbuckled a strap on either shoulder, and slipped his hand beneath the waistcoat, he withdrew a large *papier-mâché* hump, which he carried away and carefully placed in a drawer of the bureau. Relieved of his burden, Simon Carne stood up as straight and well-made a man as any in Her Majesty's dominions. The malformation, for which so many, including the Earl and Countess of Amberley, had often pitied him, was nothing but a hoax intended to produce an effect which would permit him additional facilities of disguise.

The hump discarded, and the grey wig fitted carefully to his head in such a manner that not even a pinch of his own curly locks could be seen beneath it, he adorned his cheeks with a pair of *crépu*-hair whiskers, donned the flannel vest and the velvet coat previously mentioned, slipped his feet in the carpet slippers, placed a pair of smoked glasses upon his nose, and declared himself ready to proceed about his business. The man who would have known him for Simon Carne would have been as astute as, well, shall we say, as the private detective—Klimo himself.

'It's on the stroke of twelve,' he said, as he gave a final glance at himself in the pier-glass above the dressing-table, and arranged his tie to his satisfaction. 'Should any one call, instruct Ram Gafur to tell them that I have gone out on business, and shall not be back until three o'clock.'

'Very good, sir.'

'Now undo the door and let me go in.'

Thus commanded, Belton went across to the large wardrobe which, as I have already said, covered the whole of one side of the room, and opened the middle door. Two or three garments were seen inside suspended on pegs, and these he removed, at the same time pushing towards the right the panel at the rear. When this was done a large aperture in the wall between the two houses was disclosed. Through this door Carne passed, drawing it behind him.

In No. 1, Belverton Terrace, the house occupied by the detective, whose presence in the street Carne seemed to find so objectionable, the entrance thus constructed was covered by the peculiar kind of confessional box in which Klimo invariably sat to receive his clients, the rearmost panels of which opened in the same fashion as those in the wardrobe in the dressing-room. These being pulled aside, he had but to draw them to again after him, take his seat, ring the electric bell to inform his house-keeper that he was ready, and then welcome his clients as quickly as they cared to come.

Punctually at two o'clock the interviews ceased, and Klimo, having reaped an excellent harvest of fees, returned to Porchester House to become Simon Carne once more.

The Duchess of Wiltshire's Diamonds

Possibly it was due to the fact that the Earl and Countess of Amberley were brimming over with his praise, or it may have been the rumour that he was worth as many millions as you have fingers upon your hand that did it; one thing, however, was self evident, within twenty-four hours of the noble earl's meeting him at Victoria Station, Simon Carne was the talk, not only of fashionable, but also of unfashionable London.

That his household were, with one exception, natives of India, that he had paid a rental for Porchester House which ran into five figures, that he was the greatest living authority upon china and Indian art generally, and that he had come over to England in search of a wife, were among the smallest of the *canards* set afloat concerning him.

During dinner next evening Carne put forth every effort to please. He was placed on the right hand of his hostess and next to the Duchess of Wiltshire. To the latter he paid particular attention, and to such good purpose that when the ladies returned to the drawing-room afterwards, Her Grace was full of his praises. They had discussed china of all sorts, Carne had promised her a specimen which she had longed for all her life, but had never been able to obtain, and in return she had promised to show him the quaintly carved Indian casket in which the famous necklace, of which he had, of course, heard, spent most of its time. She would be wearing the jewels in question at her own ball in a week's time, she informed him, and if he would care to see the case when it came from her bankers on that day, she would be only too pleased to show it to him.

As Simon Carne drove home in his luxurious brougham afterwards, he smiled to himself as he thought of the success which was attending his first endeavour. Two of the guests, who were stewards of the Jockey Club, had heard with delight his idea of purchasing a horse, in order to have an interest in the Derby. While another, on hearing that he desired to become the possessor of a yacht, had offered to propose him for the R.C.Y.C. To crown it all, however, and much better than all, the Duchess of Wiltshire had promised to show him her famous diamonds.

'But satisfactory as my progress has been hitherto,' he said to himself, 'it is difficult to see how I am to get possession of the stones. From what I have been able to discover, they are only brought from the bank on the day the Duchess intends to wear them, and they are taken back by His Grace the morning following.

'While she has got them on her person it would be manifestly impossible to get them from her. And as, when she takes them off, they are returned to their box and placed in a safe, constructed in the wall of the bedroom adjoining, and which for the occasion is occupied by the butler and one of the under footmen, the only key being in the possession of the Duke himself, it would be equally foolish to hope to appropriate them. In what manner, therefore, I am to become their possessor passes my comprehension. However, one thing is certain, obtained they must be, and the attempt must be made on the night of the ball if possible. In the meantime I'll set my wits to work upon a plan.'

Next day Simon Carne was the recipient of an invitation to the ball in question, and two days later he called upon the Duchess of Wiltshire, at her residence in Belgrave Square, with a plan prepared. He also took with him the small vase he had promised her four nights before. She received him most graciously, and their talk fell at once into the usual channel. Having examined her collection, and charmed her by means of one or two judicious criticisms, he asked permission to include photographs of certain of her treasures in his forthcoming book, then little by little he skilfully guided the conversation on to the subject of jewels.

'Since we are discussing gems, Mr Carne,' she said, 'perhaps it would interest you to see my famous necklace. By good fortune I have it in the house now, for the reason that an alteration is being made to one of the clasps by my jewellers.'

'I should like to see it immensely,' answered Carne. 'At one time and another I have had the good fortune to examine the jewels of the leading Indian princes, and I should like to be able to say that I have seen the famous Wiltshire necklace.'

'Then you shall certainly have the honour,' she answered with a smile. 'If you will ring that bell I will send for it.'

Carne rang the bell as requested, and when the butler entered he was given the key of the safe and ordered to bring the case to the drawing-room.

'We must not keep it very long,' she observed while the man was absent. 'It is to be returned to the bank in an hour's time.'

'I am indeed fortunate,' Carne replied, and turned to the description of some curious Indian wood carving, of which he was making a special feature in his book. As he explained, he had collected his illustrations from the doors of Indian temples, from the gateways of palaces, from old brass work, and even from carved chairs and boxes he had picked up in all sorts of odd corners. Her Grace was most interested.

'How strange that you should have mentioned it,' she said. 'If carved boxes have any interest for you, it is possible my jewel case itself may be of use to you. As I think I told you during Lady Amberley's dinner, it came from Benares, and has carved upon it the portraits of nearly every god in the Hindu Pantheon.'

'You raise my curiosity to fever heat,' said Carne.

A few moments later the servant returned, bringing with him a wooden box, about sixteen inches long, by twelve wide, and eight deep, which he placed upon a table beside his mistress, after which he retired.

'This is the case to which I have just been referring,' said the Duchess, placing her hand on the article in question. 'If you glance at it you will see how exquisitely it is carved.'

Concealing his eagerness with an effort, Simon Carne drew his chair up to the table, and examined the box.

It was with justice she had described it as a work of art. What the wood was of which it was constructed Carne was unable to tell. It was dark and heavy, and, though it was not teak, closely resembled it. It was literally covered with quaint carving, and of its kind was an unique work of art.

'It is most curious and beautiful,' said Carne when he had finished his examination. 'In all my experience I can safely say I have never seen its equal. If you will permit me I should very much like to include a description and an illustration of it in my book.'

'Of course you may do so; I shall be only too delighted,' answered Her Grace. 'If it will help you in your work I shall be glad to lend it to you for a few hours, in order that you may have the illustration made.'

This was exactly what Carne had been waiting for, and he accepted the offer with alacrity.

'Very well, then,' she said. 'On the day of my ball, when it will be brought from the bank again, I will take the necklace out and send the case to you. I must make one proviso, however, and that is that you let me have it back the same day.'

'I will certainly promise to do that,' replied Carne.

'And now let us look inside,' said his hostess.

Choosing a key from a bunch she carried in her pocket, she unlocked the casket, and lifted the lid. Accustomed as Carne had all his life been to the sight of gems, what he then saw before him almost took his breath away. The inside of the box, both sides and bottom, was quilted with the softest Russia leather, and on this luxurious couch reposed the famous necklace. The fire of the stones when the light caught them was sufficient to dazzle the eyes, so fierce was it.

As Carne could see, every gem was perfect of its kind, and there were no fewer than three hundred of them. The setting was a fine example of the jeweller's art, and last, but not least, the value of the whole affair was fifty thousand pounds, a mere fleabite to the man who had given it to his wife, but a fortune to any humbler person.

'And now that you have seen my property, what do you think of it?' asked the Duchess as she watched her visitor's face.

'It is very beautiful,' he answered, 'and I do not wonder that you are proud of it. Yes, the diamonds are very fine, but I think it is their abiding place that fascinates me more. Have you any objection to my measuring it?'

'Pray do so, if it is likely to be of any assistance to you,' replied Her Grace.

Carne therefore produced a small ivory rule, ran it over the box, and the figures he thus obtained he jotted down in his pocket-book.

Ten minutes later, when the case had been returned to the safe, he thanked the Duchess for her kindness and took his departure, promising to call in person for the empty case on the morning of the ball.

Reaching home he passed into his study, and, seating himself at his writing table, pulled a sheet of note paper towards him and began to sketch, as well as he could remember it, the box he had seen. Then he leant back in his chair and closed his eyes.

'I have cracked a good many hard nuts in my time,' he said reflectively, 'but never one that seemed so difficult at first sight as this. As far as I see at present, the case

stands as follows: the box will be brought from the bank
where it usually reposes to Wiltshire House on the morning
of the dance. I shall be allowed to have possession of it,
without the stones of course, for a period possibly ex-
tending from eleven o'clock in the morning to four or five,
at any rate not later than seven, in the evening. After the
ball the necklace will be returned to it, when it will be
locked up in the safe, over which the butler and a footman
will mount guard.

'To get into the room during the night is not only too
risky, but physically out of the question; while to rob
Her Grace of her treasure during the progress of the dance
would be equally impossible. The Duke fetches the casket
and takes it back to the bank himself, so that to all intents
and purposes I am almost as far off the solution as
ever.'

Half an hour went by and found him still seated at his
desk, staring at the drawing on the paper, then an hour.
The traffic of the streets rolled past the house unheeded.
Finally Jowur Singh announced his carriage, and, feeling
that an idea might come to him with a change of scene,
he set off for a drive in the park.

By this time his elegant mail phaeton, with its magnificent horses and Indian servant on the seat behind,
was as well-known as Her Majesty's state equipage, and
attracted almost as much attention. To-day, however, the
fashionable world noticed that Simon Carne looked preoccupied. He was still working out his problem, but so
far without much success. Suddenly something, no one
will ever be able to say what, put an idea into his head.
The notion was no sooner born in his brain than he left
the park and drove quickly home. Ten minutes had scarcely
elapsed before he was back in his study again, and had
ordered that Wajib Baksh should be sent to him.

When the man he wanted put in an appearance, Carne

handed him the paper upon which he had made the drawing of the jewel case.

'Look at that,' he said, 'and tell me what thou seest there.'

'I see a box,' answered the man, who by this time was well accustomed to his master's ways.

'As thou say'st, it is a box,' said Carne. 'The wood is heavy and thick, though what wood it is I do not know. The measurements are upon the paper below. Within, both the sides and bottom are quilted with soft leather, as I have also shown. Think now, Wajib Baksh, for in this case thou wilt need to have all thy wits about thee. Tell me is it in thy power, oh most cunning of all craftsmen, to insert such extra sides within this box that they, being held by a spring, shall lie so snug as not to be noticeable to the ordinary eye? Can it be so arranged that, when the box is locked, they will fall flat upon the bottom, thus covering and holding fast what lies beneath them, and yet making the box appear to the eye as if it were empty. Is it possible for thee to do such a thing?'

Wajib Baksh did not reply for a few moments. His instinct told him what his master wanted, and he was not disposed to answer hastily, for he also saw that his reputation as the most cunning craftsman in India was at stake.

'If the Heaven-born will permit me the night for thought,' he said at last, 'I will come to him when he rises from his bed and tell him what I can do, and he can then give his orders as it pleases him.'

'Very good,' said Carne. 'Then to-morrow morning I shall expect thy report. Let the work be good, and there will be many rupees for thee to touch in return. As to the lock and the way it shall act, let that be the concern of Hiram Singh.'

Wajib Baksh salaamed and withdrew, and Simon Carne for the time being dismissed the matter from his mind.

Next morning, while he was dressing, Belton reported that the two artificers desired an interview with him. He ordered them to be admitted, and forthwith they entered the room. It was noticeable that Wajib Baksh carried in his hand a heavy box, which, upon Carne's motioning him to do so, he placed upon the table.

'Have ye thought over the matter?' he asked, seeing that the men waited for him to speak.

'We have thought of it,' replied Hiram Singh, who always acted as spokesman for the pair. 'If the Presence will deign to look, he will see that we have made a box of the size and shape such as he drew upon the paper.'

'Yes, it is certainly a good copy,' said Carne condescendingly, after he had examined it.

Wajib Baksh showed his white teeth in appreciation of the compliment, and Hiram Singh drew closer to the table.

'And now, if the Sahib will open it, he will in his wisdom be able to tell if it resembles the other that he has in his mind.'

Carne opened the box as requested, and discovered that the interior was an exact counterfeit of the Duchess of Wiltshire's jewel case, even to the extent of the quilted leather lining which had been the other's principal feature. He admitted that the likeness was all that could be desired.

'As he is satisfied,' said Hiram Singh, 'it may be that the Protector of the Poor will deign to try an experiment with it. See, here is a comb. Let it be placed in the box, so—now he will see what he will see.'

The broad, silver-backed comb, lying upon his dressing-table, was placed on the bottom of the box, the lid was closed, and the key turned in the lock. The case being securely fastened, Hiram Singh laid it before his master.

'I am to open it, I suppose?' said Carne, taking the key and replacing it in the lock.

'If my master pleases,' replied the other.

Carne accordingly turned it in the lock, and, having done so, raised the lid and looked inside. His astonishment was complete. To all intents and purposes the box was empty. The comb was not to be seen, and yet the quilted sides and bottom were, to all appearances, just the same as when he had first looked inside.

'This is most wonderful,' he said. And indeed it was as clever a conjuring trick as any he had ever seen.

'Nay, it is very simple,' Wajib Baksh replied. 'The Heaven-born told me that there must be no risk of detection.'

He took the box in his own hands and running his nails down the centre of the quilting, divided the false bottom into two pieces; these he lifted out, revealing the comb lying upon the real bottom beneath.

'The sides, as my lord will see,' said Hiram Singh, taking a step forward, 'are held in their appointed places by these two springs. Thus, when the key is turned the springs relax, and the sides are driven by others into their places on the bottom, where the seams in the quilting mask the join. There is but one disadvantage. It is as follows: When the pieces which form the bottom are lifted out in order that my lord may get at whatever lies concealed beneath, the springs must of necessity stand revealed. However, to any one who knows sufficient of the working of the box to lift out the false bottom, it will be an easy matter to withdraw the springs and conceal them about his person.'

'As you say that is an easy matter,' said Carne, 'and I shall not be likely to forget. Now one other question. Presuming I am in a position to put the real box into your hands for say eight hours, do you think that in that time you can fit it up so that detection will be impossible?'

'Assuredly, my lord,' replied Hiram Singh with conviction. 'There is but the lock and the fitting of the springs to be done. Three hours at most would suffice for that.'

'I am pleased with you,' said Carne. 'As a proof of my satisfaction, when the work is finished you will each receive five hundred rupees. Now you can go.'

According to his promise, ten o'clock on the Friday following found him in his hansom driving towards Belgrave Square. He was a little anxious, though the casual observer would scarcely have been able to tell it. The magnitude of the stake for which he was playing was enough to try the nerve of even such a past master in his profession as Simon Carne.

Arriving at the house he discovered some workmen erecting an awning across the footway in preparation for the ball that was to take place at night. It was not long, however, before he found himself in the boudoir, reminding Her Grace of her promise to permit him an opportunity of making a drawing of the famous jewel case. The Duchess was naturally busy, and within a quarter of an hour he was on his way home with the box placed on the seat of the carriage beside him.

'Now,' he said, as he patted it good-humouredly, 'if only the notion worked out by Hiram Singh and Wajib Baksh holds good, the famous Wiltshire diamonds will become my property before very many hours are passed. By this time to-morrow, I suppose, London will be all agog concerning the burglary.'

On reaching his house he left his carriage, and himself carried the box into the study. Once there he rang his bell and ordered Hiram Singh and Wajib Baksh to be sent to him. When they arrived he showed them the box upon which they were to exercise their ingenuity.

'Bring the tools in here,' he said, 'and do the work under my own eyes. You have but nine hours before you, so you must make the most of them.'

The men went for their implements, and as soon as they were ready set to work. All through the day they

[87]

were kept hard at it, with the result that by five o'clock
the alterations had been effected and the case stood ready.
By the time Carne returned from his afternoon drive in the
Park it was quite prepared for the part it was to play in
his scheme. Having praised the men, he turned them out
and locked the door, then went across the room and unlocked a drawer in his writing table. From it he took a
flat leather jewel case, which he opened. It contained a
necklace of counterfeit diamonds, if anything a little
larger than the one he intended to try to obtain. He had
purchased it that morning in the Burlington Arcade for
the purpose of testing the apparatus his servants had made,
and this he now proceeded to do.

Laying it carefully upon the bottom he closed the lid
and turned the key. When he opened it again the necklace
was gone, and even though he knew the secret he could
not for the life of him see where the false bottom began
and ended. After that he reset the trap and tossed the
necklace carelessly in. To his delight it acted as well as on
the previous occasion. He could scarcely contain his satisfaction. His conscience was sufficiently elastic to give him
no trouble. To him it was scarcely a robbery he was plan-
ning, but an artistic trial of skill, in which he pitted
his wits and cunning against the forces of society in
general.

At half-past seven he dined, and afterwards smoked a
meditative cigar over the evening paper in the billiard room.
The invitations to the ball were for ten o'clock, and at
nine-thirty he went to his dressing-room.

'Make me tidy as quickly as you can,' he said to Belton
when the latter appeared, 'and while you are doing so
listen to my final instructions.

'To-night, as you know, I am endeavouring to secure
the Duchess of Wiltshire's necklace. To-morrow morning
all London will resound with the hubbub, and I have been

making my plans in such a way as to arrange that Klimo shall be the first person consulted. When the messenger calls, if call he does, see that the old woman next door bids him tell the Duke to come personally at twelve o'clock. Do you understand?'

'Perfectly, sir.'

'Very good. Now give me the jewel case, and let me be off. You need not sit up for me.'

Precisely as the clocks in the neighbourhood were striking ten Simon Carne reached Belgrave Square, and, as he hoped, found himself the first guest.

His hostess and her husband received him in the ante-room of the drawing-room.

'I come laden with a thousand apologies,' he said as he took Her Grace's hand, and bent over it with that cere-monious politeness which was one of the man's chief characteristics. 'I am most unconscionably early, I know, but I hastened here in order that I might personally return the jewel case you so kindly lent me. I must trust to your generosity to forgive me. The drawings took longer than I expected.'

'Please do not apologise,' answered Her Grace. 'It is very kind of you to have brought the case yourself. I hope the illustrations have proved successful. I shall look forward to seeing them as soon as they are ready. But I am keeping you holding the box. One of my servants will take it to my room.'

She called a footman to her, and bade him take the box and place it upon her dressing-table.

'Before it goes I must let you see that I have not damaged it either externally or internally,' said Carne with a laugh. 'It is such a valuable case that I should never forgive my-self if it had even received a scratch during the time it has been in my possession.'

So saying he lifted the lid and allowed her to look inside.

To all appearance it was exactly the same as when she had lent it to him earlier in the day.

'You have been most careful,' she said. And then, with an air of banter, she continued: 'If you desire it, I shall be pleased to give you a certificate to that effect.'

They jested in this fashion for a few moments after the servant's departure, during which time Carne promised to call upon her the following morning at 11 o'clock, and to bring with him the illustrations he had made and a queer little piece of china he had had the good fortune to pick up in a dealer's shop the previous afternoon. By this time fashionable London was making its way up the grand staircase, and with its appearance further conversation became impossible.

Shortly after midnight Carne bade his hostess good-night and slipped away. He was perfectly satisfied with his evening's entertainment, and if the key of the jewel case were not turned before the jewels were placed in it, he was convinced they would become his property. It speaks well for his strength of nerve when I record the fact that on going to bed his slumbers were as peaceful and untroubled as those of a little child.

Breakfast was scarcely over next morning before a hansom drew up at his front door and Lord Amberley alighted. He was ushered into Carne's presence forthwith, and on seeing that the latter was surprised at his early visit, hastened to explain.

'My dear fellow,' he said, as he took possession of the chair the other offered him, 'I have come round to see you on most important business. As I told you last night at the dance, when you so kindly asked me to come and see the steam yacht you have purchased, I had an appointment with Wiltshire at half-past nine this morning. On reaching Belgrave Square, I found the whole house in confusion. Servants were running hither and thither with scared faces, the butler was on the borders of lunacy, the Duchess was well-nigh hysterical in her boudoir, while her husband was in his study vowing vengeance against all the world.'

'You alarm me,' said Carne, lighting a cigarette with a hand that was as steady as a rock. 'What on earth has happened?'

'I think I might safely allow you fifty guesses and then wager a hundred pounds you'd not hit the mark; and yet in a certain measure it concerns you.'

'Concerns me? Good gracious! What have I done to bring all this about?'

'Pray do not look so alarmed,' said Amberley. 'Personally you have done nothing. Indeed, on second thoughts, I don't know that I am right in saying that it concerns you at all. The fact of the matter is, Carne, a burglary took place last night at Wiltshire House, *and the famous necklace has disappeared.*'

'Good heavens! You don't say so?'

'But I *do*. The circumstances of the case are as follows: When my cousin retired to her room last night after the ball, she unclasped the necklace, and, in her husband's presence, placed it carefully in her jewel case, which she locked. That having been done, Wiltshire took the box to the room which contained the safe, and himself placed it there, locking the iron door with his own key. The room was occupied that night, according to custom, by the butler and one of the footmen, both of whom have been in the family since they were boys.

'Next morning, after breakfast, the Duke unlocked the safe and took out the box, intending to convey it to the Bank as usual. Before leaving, however, he placed it on his study-table and went upstairs to speak to his wife. He cannot remember exactly how long he was absent, but he feels convinced that he was not gone more than a quarter of an hour at the very utmost.

'Their conversation finished, she accompanied him downstairs, where she saw him take up the case to carry it to his carriage. Before he left the house, however, she said: "I suppose you have looked to see that the necklace is all right?" "How could I do so?" was his reply. "You know you possess the only key that will fit it."

'She felt in her pockets, but to her surprise the key was not there.'

'If I were a detective I should say that that is a point to be remembered,' said Carne with a smile. 'Pray, where did she find her keys?'

'Upon her dressing-table,' said Amberley. 'Though she has not the slightest recollection of leaving them there.'

'Well, when she had procured the keys, what happened?'

'Why, they opened the box, and, to their astonishment and dismay, *found it empty. The jewels were gone!*'

'Good gracious! What a terrible loss! It seems almost impossible that it can be true. And pray, what did they do?'

'At first they stood staring into the empty box, hardly believing the evidence of their own eyes. Stare how they would, however, they could not bring them back. The jewels had, without doubt, disappeared, but when and where the robbery had taken place it was impossible to say. After that they had up all the servants and questioned them, but the result was what they might have foreseen, no one from the butler to the kitchenmaid could throw any light upon the subject. To this minute it remains as great a mystery as when they first discovered it.'

'I am more concerned than I can tell you,' said Carne. 'How thankful I ought to be that I returned the case to Her Grace last night. But in thinking of myself I am forgetting to ask what has brought you to me. If I can be of any assistance I hope you will command me.'

'Well, I'll tell you why I have come,' replied Lord Amberley. 'Naturally, they are most anxious to have the mystery solved and the jewels recovered as soon as possible. Wiltshire wanted to send to Scotland Yard there and then, but his wife and I eventually persuaded him to consult Klimo. As you know, if the police authorities are called in first, he refuses the business altogether. Now, we thought, as you are his next door neighbour, you might possibly be able to assist us.'

'You may be very sure, my lord, I will do everything that lies in my power. Let us go in and see him at once.'

As he spoke he rose and threw what remained of his cigarette into the fireplace. His visitor having imitated his example, they procured their hats and walked round from Park Lane into Belverton Street to bring up at No. 1. After they had rung the bell the door was opened to them by the old woman who invariably received the detective's clients.

'Is Mr Klimo at home?' asked Carne. 'And if so, can we see him?'

The old lady was a little deaf, and the question had to be repeated before she could be made to understand what was wanted. As soon, however, as she realized their desire, she informed them that her master was absent from town, but would be back as usual at twelve o'clock to meet his clients.

'What on earth's to be done?' said the Earl, looking at his companion in dismay. 'I am afraid I can't come back again, as I have a most important appointment at that hour.'

'Do you think you could entrust the business to me?' asked Carne. 'If so, I will make a point of seeing him at twelve o'clock, and could call at Wiltshire House afterwards and tell the Duke what I have done.'

'That's very good of you,' replied Amberley. 'If you are sure it would not put you to too much trouble, that would be quite the best thing to be done.'

'I will do it with pleasure,' Carne replied. 'I feel it my duty to help in whatever way I can.'

'You are very kind,' said the other. 'Then, as I understand it, you are to call upon Klimo at twelve o'clock, and afterwards to let my cousins know what you have succeeded in doing. I only hope he will help us to secure the thief. We are having too many of these burglaries just now. I must catch this hansom and be off. Good-bye, and many thanks.'

'Good-bye,' said Carne, and shook him by the hand.

The hansom having rolled away, Carne retraced his steps to his own abode.

'It is really very strange,' he muttered as he walked along, 'how often chance condescends to lend her assistance to my little schemes. The mere fact that His Grace left the box unwatched in his study for a quarter of an hour may serve to throw the police off on quite another scent. I am also glad that they decided to open the case in the house, for if it had gone to the bankers' and had been placed in the strong room unexamined, I should never have been able to get possession of the jewels at all.'

Three hours later he drove to Wiltshire House and saw the Duke. The Duchess was far too much upset by the catastrophe to see any one.

'This is really most kind of you, Mr Carne,' said His Grace when the other had supplied an elaborate account of his interview with Klimo. 'We are extremely indebted to you. I am sorry he cannot come before ten o'clock to-night, and that he makes this stipulation of my seeing him alone, for I must confess I should like to have had some one else present to ask any questions that might escape me. But if that's his usual hour and custom, well, we must abide by it, that's all. I hope he will do some good, for this is the greatest calamity that has ever befallen me. As I told you just now, it has made my wife quite ill. She is confined to her bedroom and quite hysterical.'

'You do not suspect any one, I suppose?' inquired Carne.

'Not a soul,' the other answered. 'The thing is such a mystery that we do not know what to think. I feel convinced, however, that my servants are as innocent as I am. Nothing will ever make me think them otherwise. I wish I could catch the fellow, that's all. I'd make him suffer for the trick he's played me.'

Carne offered an appropriate reply, and after a little further conversation upon the subject, bade the irate nobleman good-bye and left the house. From Belgrave Square he drove to one of the clubs of which he had been elected a member, in search of Lord Orpington, with whom he had promised to lunch, and afterwards took him to a ship-builder's yard near Greenwich, in order to show him the steam yacht he had lately purchased.

It was close upon dinner time before he returned to his own residence. He brought Lord Orpington with him, and they dined in state together. At nine the latter bade him good-bye, and at ten Carne retired to his dressing-room and rang for Belton.

'What have you to report,' he asked, 'with regard to what I bade you do in Belgrave Square?'

'I followed your instructions to the letter,' Belton replied. 'Yesterday morning I wrote to Messrs Horniblow and Jimson, the house agents in Piccadilly, in the name of Colonel Braithwaite, and asked for an order to view the residence to the right of Wiltshire House. I asked that the order might be sent direct to the house, where the Colonel would get it upon his arrival. This letter I posted myself in Basingstoke, as you desired me to do.

'At nine o'clock yesterday morning I dressed myself as much like an elderly army officer as possible, and took a cab to Belgrave Square. The caretaker, an old fellow of close upon seventy years of age, admitted me immediately upon hearing my name, and proposed that he should show

me over the house. This, however, I told him was quite
unnecessary, backing my speech with a present of half a
crown, whereupon he returned to his breakfast perfectly
satisfied, while I wandered about the house at my own
leisure.

'Reaching the same floor as that upon which is situated
the room in which the Duke's safe is kept, I discovered
that your supposition was quite correct, and that it would
be possible for a man, by opening the window, to make
his way along the coping from one house to the other,
without being seen. I made certain that there was no one
in the bedroom in which the butler slept, and then arranged
the long telescope walking-stick you gave me, and fixed one
of my boots to it by means of the screw in the end. With
this I was able to make a regular succession of footsteps
in the dust along the ledge, between one window and the
other.

'That done, I went downstairs again, bade the caretaker
good-morning, and got into my cab. From Belgrave Square
I drove to the shop of the pawnbroker whom you told me
you had discovered was out of town. His assistant inquired
my business, and was anxious to do what he could for me.
I told him, however, that I must see his master personally,
as it was about the sale of some diamonds I had had left
me. I pretended to be annoyed that he was not at home,
and muttered to myself, so that the man could hear, something about its meaning a journey to Amsterdam.

'Then I limped out of the shop, paid off my cab, and,
walking down a by-street, removed my moustache, and
altered my appearance by taking off my great coat and
muffler. A few streets further on I purchased a bowler
hat in place of the old-fashioned topper I had hitherto
been wearing, and then took a cab from Piccadilly and
came home.'

'You have fulfilled my instructions admirably,' said

Carne. 'And if the business comes off, as I expect it will, you shall receive your usual percentage. Now I must be turned into Klimo and be off to Belgrave Square to put His Grace upon the track of this burglar.'

Before he retired to rest that night Simon Carne took something, wrapped in a red silk handkerchief, from the capacious pocket of the coat Klimo had been wearing a few moments before. Having unrolled the covering, he held up to the light the magnificent necklace which for so many years had been the joy and pride of the ducal house of Wiltshire. The electric light played upon it, and touched it with a thousand different hues.

'Where so many have failed,' he said to himself, as he wrapped it in the handkerchief again and locked it in his safe, 'it is pleasant to be able to congratulate oneself on having succeeded.'

Next morning all London was astonished by the news that the famous Wiltshire diamonds had been stolen, and a few hours later Carne learnt from an evening paper that the detectives who had taken up the case, upon the supposed retirement from it of Klimo, were still completely at fault.

That evening he was to entertain several friends to dinner. They included Lord Amberley, Lord Orpington, and a prominent member of the Privy Council. Lord Amberley arrived late, but filled to overflowing with importance. His friends noticed his state, and questioned him.

'Well, gentlemen,' he answered, as he took up a commanding position upon the drawing-room hearthrug, 'I am in a position to inform you that Klimo has reported upon the case, and the upshot of it is that the Wiltshire Diamond Mystery is a mystery no longer.'

'What do you mean?' asked the others in a chorus.

'I mean that he sent in his report to Wiltshire this afternoon, as arranged. From what he said the other night, after being alone in the room with the empty jewel case and a magnifying glass for two minutes or so, he was in a position to describe the *modus operandi*, and, what is more, to put the police on the scent of the burglar.'

'And how *was* it worked?' asked Carne.

'From the empty house next door,' replied the other. 'On the morning of the burglary a man, purporting to be a retired army officer, called with an order to view, got the caretaker out of the way, clambered along to Wiltshire House by means of the parapet outside, reached the room during the time the servants were at breakfast, opened the safe, and abstracted the jewels.'

'But how did Klimo find all this out?' asked Lord Orpington.

'By his own inimitable cleverness,' replied Lord Amberley. 'At any rate it has been proved that he was correct. The man *did* make his way from next door, and the police have since discovered that an individual answering to the description given, visited a pawnbroker's shop in the city about an hour later, and stated that he had diamonds to sell.'

'If that is so it turns out to be a very simple mystery after all,' said Lord Orpington as they began their meal.

'Thanks to the ingenuity of the cleverest detective in the world,' remarked Amberley.

'In that case here's a good health to Klimo,' said the Privy Councillor, raising his glass.

'I will join you in that,' said Simon Carne. 'Here's a very good health to Klimo and his connection with the Duchess of Wiltshire's diamonds. May he always be equally successful!'

'Hear, hear to that,' replied his guests.

IV

The Affair of the 'Avalanche Bicycle and Tyre Co., Limited'

Arthur Morrison

1

Cycle companies were in the market everywhere. Immense fortunes were being made in a few days and sometimes little fortunes were being lost to build them up. Mining shares were dull for a season, and any company with the word 'cycle' or 'tyre' in its title was certain to attract capital, no matter what its prospects were like in the eyes of the expert. All the old private cycle companies suddenly were offered to the public, and their proprietors, already rich men, built themselves houses on the Riviera, bought yachts, ran racehorses, and left business for ever. Sometimes the shareholders got their money's worth, sometimes more, sometimes less—sometimes they got nothing but total loss; but still the game went on. One could never open a newspaper without finding, displayed at large, the prospectus of yet another cycle company with capital expressed in six figures at least, often in seven. Solemn old dailies, into whose editorial heads no new thing ever

found its way till years after it had been forgotten elsewhere, suddenly exhibited the scandalous phenomenon of
'broken columns' in their advertising sections, and the
universal prospectuses stretched outrageously across half
or even all the page—a thing to cause apoplexy in the
bodily system of any self-respecting manager of the old
school.

In the midst of this excitement it chanced that the firm
of Dorrington & Hicks were engaged upon an investigation
for the famous and long-established 'Indestructible Bicycle
and Tricycle Manufacturing Company', of London and
Coventry. The matter was not one of sufficient intricacy
or difficulty to engage Dorrington's personal attention,
and it was given to an assistant. There was some doubt
as to the validity of a certain patent having reference to
a particular method of tightening the spokes and truing
the wheels of a bicycle, and Dorrington's assistant had
to make inquiries (without attracting attention to the
matter) as to whether or not there existed any evidence,
either documentary or in the memory of veterans, of the
use of this method, or anything like it, before the year
1885. The assistant completed his inquiries and made his
report to Dorrington. Now I think I have said that, from
every evidence I have seen, the chief matter of Dorrington's
solicitude was his own interest, and just at this time he had
heard, as had others, much of the money being made in
cycle companies. Also, like others, he had conceived a
great desire to get the confidential advice of somebody
'in the know'—advice which might lead him into the
'good thing' desired by all the greedy who flutter about
at the outside edge of the stock and share market. For
this reason Dorrington determined to make this small
matter of the wheel patent an affair of personal report.
He was a man of infinite resource, plausibility and good-
companionship, and there was money going in the cycle

trade. Why then should he lose an opportunity of making himself pleasant in the inner groves of that trade, and catch whatever might come his way—information, syndicate shares, directorships, anything? So that Dorrington made himself master of his assistant's information, and proceeded to the head office of the 'Indestructible' company on Holborn Viaduct, resolved to become the entertaining acquaintance of the managing director.

On his way his attention was attracted by a very elaborately fitted cycle shop, which his recollection told him was new. 'The Avalanche Bicycle and Tyre Company' was the legend gilt above the great plate-glass window, and in the window itself stood many brilliantly enamelled and plated bicycles, each labelled on the frame with the flaming red and gold transfer of the firm; and in the midst of all was another bicycle covered with dried mud, of which, however, sufficient had been carefully cleared away to expose a similar glaring transfer to those that decorated the rest—with a placard announcing that on this particular machine somebody had ridden some incredible distance on bad roads in very little more than no time at all. A crowd stood about the window and gaped respectfully at the placard, the bicycles, the transfers, and the mud, though they paid little attention to certain piles of folded white papers, endorsed in bold letters with the name of the company, with the suffix 'limited' and the word 'prospectus' in bloated black letter below. These, however, Dorrington observed at once, for he had himself that morning, in common with several thousand other people, received one by post. Also half a page of his morning paper had been filled with a copy of that same prospectus, and the afternoon had brought another copy in the evening paper. In the list of directors there was a titled name or two, together with a few unknown names—doubtless the 'practical men'. And below this list there were such positive

promises of tremendous dividends, backed up and proved
beyond dispute by such ingenious piles of business-like
figures, every line of figures referring to some other line
for testimonials to its perfect genuineness and accuracy,
that any reasonable man, it would seem, must instantly
sell the hat off his head and the boots off his feet to buy
one share at least, and so make his fortune for ever. True,
the business was but lately established, but that was just
it. It had rushed ahead with such amazing rapidity (as
was natural with an avalanche) that it had got altogether
out of hand, and orders couldn't be executed at all; where-
fore the proprietors were reluctantly compelled to let the
public have some of the luck. This was Thursday. The
share list was to be opened on Monday morning and closed
inexorably at four o'clock on Tuesday afternoon, with a
merciful extension to Wednesday morning for the candi-
dates for wealth who were so unfortunate as to live in the
country. So that it behoved everybody to waste no time
lest he be numbered among the unlucky whose subscription-
money should be returned in full, failing allotment. The
prospectus did not absolutely say it in so many words,
but no rational person could fail to feel that the directors
were fervently hoping that nobody would get injured in
the rush.

Dorrington passed on and reached the well-known
establishment of the 'Indestructible Bicycle Company'.
This was already a limited company of a private sort, and
had been so for ten years or more. And before that the
concern had had eight or nine years of prosperous experience. The founder of the firm, Mr Paul Mallows, was
now the managing director, and a great pillar of the cycling
industry. Dorrington gave a clerk his card, and asked to
see Mr Mallows.

Mr Mallows was out, it seemed, but Mr Stedman, the
secretary, was in, and him Dorrington saw. Mr Stedman

was a pleasant, youngish man, who had been a famous amateur bicyclist in his time, and was still an enthusiast. In ten minutes business was settled and dismissed, and Dorrington's tact had brought the secretary into a pleasant discursive chat, with much exchange of anecdote. Dorrington expressed much interest in the subject of bicycling, and, seeing that Stedman had been a racing man, particularly as to bicycling races.

'There'll be a rare good race on Saturday, I expect,' Stedman said. 'Or rather,' he went on, 'I expect the fifty miles record will go. I fancy our man Gillett is pretty safe to win, but he'll have to move, and I quite expect to see a good set of new records on our advertisements next week. The next best man is Lant—the new fellow, you know— who rides for the "Avalanche" people.'

'Let's see, they're going to the public as a limited company, aren't they?' Dorrington asked casually.

Stedman nodded, with a little grimace.

'You don't think it's a good thing, perhaps,' Dorrington said, noticing the grimace. 'Is that so?'

'Well,' Stedman answered, 'of course I can't say. I don't know much about the firm—nobody does, as far as I can tell—but they seem to have got a business together in almost no time; that is, if the business is as genuine as it looks at first sight. But they want a rare lot of capital, and then the prospectus—well, I've seen more satisfactory ones, you know. I don't say it isn't all right, of course, but still I shan't go out of my way to recommend any friends of mine to plunge on it.'

'You won't?'

'No, I won't. Though no doubt they'll get their capital, or most of it. Almost any cycle or tyre company can get subscribed just now. And this "Avalanche" affair is both, and it is well advertised, you know. Lant has been winning on their mounts just lately, and they've been booming it for all they're worth. By jove, if they could only screw him up to win the fifty miles on Saturday, and beat our man Gillett, that *would* give them a push! Just at the correct moment too. Gillett's never been beaten yet at the distance, you know. But Lant can't do it—though, as I have said, he'll make some fast riding—it'll be a race, I tell you.'

'I should like to see it.'

'Why not come? See about it, will you? And perhaps you'd like to run down to the track after dinner this evening and see our man training—awfully interesting, I can tell you, with all the pacing machinery and that. Will you come?'

Dorrington expressed himself delighted, and suggested that Stedman should dine with him before going to the track. Stedman, for his part, charmed with his new acquaintance—as everybody was at a first meeting with Dorrington—assented gladly.

At that moment the door of Stedman's room was pushed open and a well-dressed, middle-aged man, with a shaven, flabby face, appeared. 'I beg pardon,' he said, 'I thought you were alone. I've just ripped my finger against the handle of my brougham door as I came in—the screw sticks out. Have you a piece of sticking plaster?' He extended a bleeding finger as he spoke. Stedman looked doubtfully at his desk.

'Here is some court plaster,' Dorrington exclaimed, producing his pocket-book. 'I always carry it—it's handier than ordinary sticking plaster. How much do you want?'

'Thanks—an inch or so.'

'This is Mr Dorrington, of Messrs Dorrington & Hicks, Mr Mallows,' Stedman said. 'Our managing director, Mr Paul Mallows, Mr Dorrington.'

Dorrington was delighted to make Mr Mallows' acquaintance, and he busied himself with a careful strapping of the damaged finger. Mr Mallows had the large frame of a man of strong build who had had much hard bodily work, but there hung about it the heavier, softer flesh that told of a later period of ease and sloth. 'Ah, Mr Mallows,' Stedman said, 'the bicycle's the safest thing, after all! Dangerous things these broughams!'

'Ah, you younger men,' Mr Mallows replied, with a slow and rounded enunciation, 'you younger men can afford to be active. We elders——'

'Can afford a brougham,' Dorrington added, before the managing director began the next word. 'Just so—and the bicycle does it all; wonderful thing the bicycle!'

Dorrington had not misjudged his man, and the oblique reference to his wealth flattered Mr Mallows. Dorrington went once more through his report as to the spoke patent, and then Mr Mallows bade him good-bye.

'Good-day, Mr Dorrington, good-day,' he said. 'I am extremely obliged by your careful personal attention to this matter of the patent. We may leave it with Mr Stedman now, I think. Good-day. I hope soon to have the pleasure of meeting you again.' And with clumsy stateliness Mr Mallows vanished.

2

'So you don't think the "Avalanche" good business as an investment?' Dorrington said once more as he and Stedman, after an excellent dinner, were cabbing it to the track.

'No, no,' Stedman answered, 'don't touch it! There's better things than that coming along presently. Perhaps I shall be able to put you in for something, you know, a bit later; but don't be in a hurry. As to the "Avalanche", even if everything else were satisfactory, there's too much "booming" being done just now to please me. All sorts of rumours, you know, of their having something "up their sleeve", and so on; mysterious hints in the papers, and all that, as to something revolutionary being in hand with the "Avalanche" people. Perhaps there is. But why they don't fetch it out in view of the public subscription for shares is more than I can understand, unless they don't want too much of a rush. And as to that, well they don't look like modestly shrinking from anything of that sort up to the present.'

They were at the track soon after seven o'clock, but Gillett was not yet riding. Dorrington remarked that Gillett appeared to begin late.

'Well,' Stedman explained, 'he's one of those fellows that afternoon training doesn't seem to suit, unless it is a bit of walking exercise. He just does a few miles in the morning and a spurt or two, and then he comes on just before sunset for a fast ten or fifteen miles—that is, when he is getting fit for such a race as Saturday's. To-night will be his last spin of that length before Saturday, because to-morrow will be the day before the race. To-morrow he'll only go a spurt or two, and rest most of the day.'

They strolled about inside the track, the two highly 'banked' ends whereof seemed to a near-sighted person in the centre to be solid erect walls, along the face of which the training riders skimmed, fly-fashion. Only three or four persons beside themselves were in the enclosure when they first came, but in ten minutes' time Mr Paul Mallows came across the track.

'Why,' said Stedman to Dorrington, 'here's the Governor! It isn't often he comes down here. But I expect he's anxious to see how Gillett's going, in view of Saturday.'

'Good evening, Mr Mallows,' said Dorrington. 'I hope the finger's all right? Want any more plaster?'

'Good evening, good evening,' responded Mr Mallows heavily. 'Thank you, the finger's not troubling me a bit.'

He held it up, still decorated by the black plaster. 'Your plaster remains, you see—I was a little careful not to fray it too much in washing, that was all.' And Mr Mallows sat down on a light iron garden-chair (of which several stood here and there in the enclosure) and began to watch the riding.

The track was clear, and dusk was approaching when at last the great Gillett made his appearance on the track. He answered a friendly question or two put to him by Mallows and Stedman, and then, giving his coat to his trainer, swung off along the track on his bicycle, led in front by a tandem and closely attended by a triplet. In fifty yards his pace quickened, and he settled down into a swift even pace, regular as clockwork. Sometimes the tandem and sometimes the triplet went to the front, but Gillett neither checked nor heeded as, nursed by his pacers, who were directed by the trainer from the centre, he swept along mile after mile, each mile in but a few seconds over the two minutes.

'Look at the action!' exclaimed Stedman with enthusiasm. 'Just watch him. Not an ounce of power wasted there! Did you ever see more regular ankle work? And did anybody ever sit a machine quite so well as that? Show me a movement anywhere above the hips!'

'Ah,' said Mr Mallows, 'Gillett has a wonderful style—a wonderful style, really!'

The men in the enclosure wandered about here and there on the grass, watching Gillett's riding as one watches the performance of a great piece of art—which, indeed, was what Gillett's riding was. There were, besides Mallows, Stedman, Dorrington and the trainer, two officials of the Cyclists' Union, an amateur racing man named Sparks, the track superintendent and another man. The sky grew darker, and gloom fell about the track. The machines became invisible, and little could be seen of the riders across the ground but the row of rhythmically working legs and the white cap that Gillett wore. The trainer had just told Stedman that there would be three fast laps and then his man would come off the track.

'Well, Mr Stedman,' said Mr Mallows, 'I think we shall be all right for Saturday.'

'Rather!' answered Stedman confidently. 'Gillett's going great guns, and steady as a watch!'

The pace now suddenly increased. The tandem shot once more to the front, the triplet hung on the rider's flank, and the group of swishing wheels flew round the track at a 'one-fifty' gait. The spectators turned about, following the riders round the track with their eyes. And then, swinging into the straight from the top bend, the tandem checked suddenly and gave a little jump. Gillett crashed into it from behind, and the triplet, failing to clear, wavered and swung, and crashed over and along the track too. All three machines and six men were involved in one complicated smash.

Everybody rushed across the grass, the trainer first. Then the cause of the disaster was seen. Lying on its side on the track, with men and bicycles piled over and against it, was one of the green painted light iron garden-chairs that had been standing in the enclosure. The triplet men were struggling to their feet, and though much cut and shaken, seemed the least hurt of the lot. One of the men of the tandem was insensible, and Gillett, who from his position had got all the worst of it, lay senseless too, badly cut and bruised, and his left arm was broken.

The trainer was cursing and tearing his hair. 'If I knew who'd done this,' Stedman cried, 'I'd *pulp* him with that chair!'

'Oh, that betting, that betting!' wailed Mr Mallows, hopping about distractedly; 'see what it leads people into doing! It can't have been an accident, can it?'

'Accident? Skittles! A man doesn't put a chair on a track in the dark and leave it there by accident. Is anybody getting away there from the outside of the track?'

'No, there's nobody. He wouldn't wait till this; he's clear off a minute ago and more. Here, Fielders! Shut the outer gate, and we'll see who's about.'

But there seemed to be no suspicious character. Indeed, except for the ground-man, his boy, Gillett's trainer, and a racing man, who had just finished dressing in the pavilion, there seemed to be nobody about beyond those whom everybody had seen standing in the enclosure. But there had been ample time for anybody, standing unnoticed at the outer rails, to get across the track in the dark, just after the riders had passed, place the obstruction, and escape before the completion of the lap.

The damaged men were helped or carried into the pavilion, and the damaged machines were dragged after them. 'I will give fifty pounds gladly—more, a hundred,' said Mr Mallows, excitedly, 'to anybody who will find out who put the chair on the track. It might have ended in murder. Some wretched bookmaker, I suppose, who has taken too many bets on Gillett. As I've said a thousand times, betting is the curse of all sport nowadays.'

'The governor excites himself a great deal about betting and bookmakers,' Stedman said to Dorrington, as they walked toward the pavilion, 'but, between you and me, I believe some of the "Avalanche" people are in this. The betting bee is always in Mallows' bonnet, but as a matter of fact there's very little betting at all on cycle races, and what there is is little more than a matter of half-crowns or at most half-sovereigns on the day of the race. No bookmaker ever makes a heavy book first. Still there *may* be something in it this time, of course. But look at the "Avalanche" people. With Gillett away their man can certainly win on Saturday, and if only the weather keeps fair he can almost as certainly beat the record; just at present the fifty miles is fairly easy, and it's bound to go soon. Indeed, our intention was that Gillett should pull it down on Saturday. He was a safe winner, bar accidents, and it was good odds on his altering the record, if the weather were any good at all. With Gillett out of it Lant is just about as certain a winner as our man would be if all were well. And there would be a boom for the "Avalanche" company, on the very eve of the share subscription! Lant, you must know, was very second-rate till this season, but he has improved wonderfully in the last month or two, since he has been with the "Avalanche" people. Let him win, and they can point to the machine as responsible for it all. "Here", they will say in effect, "is a man who could rarely get in front, even in second-class company, till he rode an "Avalanche". Now he beats the world's record for fifty miles on it, and makes rings round the topmost professionals!" Why, it will be worth thousands of capital to them. Of course the subscription of capital won't hurt us, but the loss of the record may, and to have Gillett knocked out like this in the middle of the season is serious.'

'Yes, I suppose with you it is more than a matter of this one race.'

'Of course. And so it will be with the "Avalanche" company. Don't you see, with Gillett probably useless for the rest of the season, Lant will have it all his own way at anything over ten miles. That'll help to boom up the shares and there'll be big profit made on trading in them. Oh, I tell you this thing seems pretty suspicious to me.'

'Look here,' said Dorrington, 'can you borrow a light for me, and let me run over with it to the spot where the smash took place? The people have cleared into the pavilion and I could go alone.'

'Certainly. Will you have a try for the governor's hundred?'

'Well, perhaps. But anyway there's no harm in doing you a good turn if I can, while I'm here. Some day perhaps you'll do me one.'

'Right you are—I'll ask Fielders, the ground-man.'

A lantern was brought, and Dorrington betook himself to the spot where the iron chair still lay, while Stedman joined the rest of the crowd in the pavilion.

Dorrington minutely examined the grass within two yards of the place where the chair lay, and then, crossing the track and getting over the rails, did the same with the damp gravel that paved the outer ring. The track itself was of cement, and unimpressionable by footmarks, but nevertheless he scrutinized that with equal care, as well as the rails. Then he turned his attention to the chair. It was, as I have said, a light chair made of flat iron strip, bent to shape and riveted. It had seen good service, and its present coat of green paint was evidently far from being its original one. Also it was rusty in places, and parts had been repaired and strengthened with cross-pieces secured by bolts and square nuts, some rusty and loose. It was from one of these square nuts, holding a cross-piece that stayed the back at the top, that Dorrington secured some object—it might have been a hair—which he carefully transferred to his pocket-book. This done, with one more glance round, he betook himself to the pavilion.

A surgeon had arrived, and he reported well of the chief patient. It was a simple fracture, and a healthy subject. When Dorrington entered, preparations were beginning for setting the limb. There was a sofa in the pavilion, and the surgeon saw no reason for removing the patient till all was made secure.

'Found anything?' asked Stedman in a low tone of Dorrington.

Dorrington shook his head. 'Not much,' he answered at a whisper. 'I'll think over it later.'

Dorrington asked one of the Cyclists' Union officials for the loan of a pencil, and, having made a note with it, immediately, in another part of the room, asked Sparks, the amateur, to lend him another.

Stedman had told Mr Mallows of Dorrington's late employment with the lantern, and the managing director now said quietly, 'You remember what I said about rewarding anybody who discovered the perpetrator of this outrage, Mr Dorrington? Well, I was excited at the time, but I quite hold to it. It is a shameful thing. You have been looking about the grounds, I hear. I hope you have come across something that will enable you to find something out. Nothing will please me more than to have to pay you, I'm sure.'

'Well,' Dorrington confessed, 'I'm afraid I haven't seen anything very big in the way of a clue, Mr Mallows; but I'll think a bit. The worst of it is, you never know who these betting men are, do you, once they get away? There are so many, and it may be anybody. Not only that, but they may bribe anybody.'

'Yes, of course—there's no end to their wickedness, I'm afraid. Stedman suggests that trade rivalry may have had something to do with it. But that seems an uncharitable view, don't you think? Of course we stand very high, and there are jealousies and all that, but this is a thing I'm sure no firm would think of stooping to, for a moment. No, it's betting that is at the bottom of this, I fear. And I hope, Mr Dorrington, that you will make some attempt to find the guilty parties.'

Presently Stedman spoke to Dorrington again. 'Here's something that may help you,' he said. 'To begin with, it must have been done by some one from the outside of the track.'

'Why?'

'Well, at least every probability's that way. Everybody inside was directly interested in Gillett's success, excepting the Union officials and Sparks, who's a gentleman and quite above suspicion, as much so, indeed, as the Union officials. Of course there was the ground-man, but he's all right, I'm sure.'

'And the trainer?'

'Oh, that's altogether improbable—altogether. I was going to say——'

'And there's that other man who was standing about; I haven't heard who he was.'

'Right you are. I don't know him either. Where is he now?'

But the man had gone.

'Look here, I'll make some quiet inquiries about that man,' Stedman pursued. 'I forgot all about him in the excitement of the moment. I was going to say that although whoever did it could easily have got away by the gate before the smash came, he might not have liked to go that way in case of observation in passing the pavilion. In that case he could have got away (and indeed he could have got into the grounds to begin with) by way of one of those garden walls that bound the ground just by where the smash occurred. If that were so he must either live in one of the houses, or he must know somebody that does. Perhaps you might put a man to smell about along the road—it's only a short one; Chisnall Road's the name.'

'Yes, yes,' Dorrington responded patiently. 'There might be something in that.'

By this time Gillett's arm was in a starched bandage and secured by splints, and a cab was ready to take him home. Mr Mallows took Stedman away with him, expressing a desire to talk business, and Dorrington went home by himself. He did not turn down Chisnall Road. But he

walked jauntily along toward the nearest cab-stand, and
once or twice he chuckled, for he saw his way to a delightfully lucrative financial operation in cycle companies,
without risk of capital.

The cab gained, he called at the lodgings of two of his
men assistants and gave them instant instructions. Then
he packed a small bag at his rooms in Conduit Street, and
at midnight was in the late fast train for Birmingham.

3

The prospectus of the 'Avalanche Bicycle and Tyre Company' stated that the works were at Exeter and Birmingham. Exeter is a delightful old town, but it can scarcely be
regarded as the centre of the cycle trade; neither is it in
especially easy and short communication with Birmingham.
It was the sort of thing that any critic anxious to pick
holes in the prospectus might wonder at, and so one of
Dorrington's assistants had gone by the night mail to
inspect the works. It was from this man that Dorrington,
in Birmingham, about noon on the day after Gillett's
disaster, received this telegram—

> *Works here old disused cloth-mills just out of town.
> Closed and empty but with big new signboard and notice
> that works now running are at Birmingham. Agent says
> only deposit paid—tenancy agreement not signed.—
> Farrish.*

The telegram increased Dorrington's satisfaction, for
he had just taken a look at the Birmingham works. They
were not empty, though nearly so, nor were they large; and
a man there had told him that the chief premises, where
most of the work was done, were at Exeter. And the
hollower the business the better prize he saw in store for
himself. He had already, early in the morning, indulged

in a telegram on his own account, though he had not signed it. This was how it ran—

> *Mallows, 58, Upper Sandown Place,*
> *London, W.*
> *Fear all not safe here. Run down by 10.10 train with-*
> *out fail.*

Thus it happened that at a little later than half-past eight Dorrington's other assistant, watching the door of No. 58, Upper Sandown Place, saw a telegram delivered, and immediately afterwards Mr Paul Mallows in much haste dashed away in a cab which was called from the end of the street. The assistant followed in another. Mr Mallows dismissed his cab at a theatrical wig-maker's in Bow Street and entered. When he emerged in little more than forty minutes' time, none but a practised watcher, who had guessed the reason for the visit, would have recognized him. He had not assumed the clumsy disguise of a false beard. He was 'made up' deftly. His colour was heightened, and his face seemed thinner. There was no heavy accession of false hair, but a slight crepe-hair whisker at each side made a better and less pronounced disguise. He seemed a younger, healthier man. The watcher saw him safely off to Birmingham by the ten minutes past ten train, and then gave Dorrington note by telegraph of the guise in which Mr Mallows was travelling.

Now this train was timed to arrive at Birmingham at one, which was the reason that Dorrington had named it in the anonymous telegram. The entrance to the 'Avalanche' works was by a large gate, which was closed, but which was provided with a small door to pass a man. Within was a yard, and at a little before one o'clock Dorrington pushed open the small door, peeped, and entered. Nobody was about in the yard, but what little noise could be heard came from a particular part of the building on the right.

[115]

A pile of solid 'export' crates stood to the left, and these Dorrington had noted at his previous call that morning as making a suitable hiding-place for temporary use. Now he slipped behind them and awaited the stroke of one. Prompt at the hour a door on the opposite side of the yard swung open, and two men and a boy emerged and climbed one after another through the little door in the big gate. Then presently another man, not a workman, but apparently a sort of overseer, came from the opposite door, which he carelessly let fall-to behind him, and he also disappeared through the little door, which he then locked. Dorrington was now alone in the sole active works of the 'Avalanche Bicycle and Tyre Company, Limited'.

He tried the door opposite and found it was free to open. Within he saw in a dark corner a candle which had been left burning, and opposite him a large iron enamelling oven, like an immense safe, and round about, on benches, were strewn heaps of the glaring red and gold transfer which Dorrington had observed the day before on the machines exhibited in the Holborn Viaduct window. Some of the frames had the label newly applied, and others were still plain. It would seem that the chief business of the 'Avalanche Bicycle and Tyre Company, Limited', was the attaching of labels to previously nondescript machines. But there was little time to examine further, and indeed Dorrington presently heard the noise of a key in the outer gate. So he stood and waited by the enamelling oven to welcome Mr Mallows.

As the door was pushed open Dorrington advanced and bowed politely. Mallows started guiltily, but, remembering his disguise, steadied himself, and asked gruffly, 'Well, sir, and who are you?'

'I,' answered Dorrington with perfect composure, 'I am Mr Paul Mallows—you may have heard of me in connection with the "Indestructible Bicycle Company".'

Mallows was altogether taken aback. But then it struck him that perhaps the detective, anxious to win the reward he had offered in the matter of the Gillett outrage, was here making inquiries in the assumed character of the man who stood, impenetrably disguised, before him. So after a pause he asked again, a little less gruffly, 'And what may be your business?'

'Well,' said Dorrington, 'I did think of taking shares in this company. I suppose there would be no objection to the managing director of another company taking shares in this?'

'No,' answered Mallows, wondering what all this was to lead to.

'Of course not; I'm sure *you* don't think so, eh?' Dorrington, as he spoke, looked in the other's face with a sly leer, and Mallows began to feel altogether uncomfortable. 'But there's one other thing,' Dorrington pursued, taking out his pocket-book, though still maintaining his leer in Mallow's face—'one other thing. And by the way, *will* you have another piece of court plaster now I've got it out? Don't say no. It's a pleasure to oblige you, really.' And Dorrington, his leer growing positively fiendish, tapped the side of his nose with the case of court plaster.

Mallows paled under the paint, gasped, and felt for support. Dorrington laughed pleasantly. 'Come, come,' he said, 'don't be frightened. I admire your cleverness, Mr Mallows, and I shall arrange everything pleasantly, as you will see. And as to the court plaster, if you'd rather not have it you needn't. You have another piece on now, I see. Why didn't you get them to paint it over at Clarkson's? They really did the face very well, though! And there again you were quite right. Such a man as yourself was likely to be recognized in such a place as Birmingham, and that would have been unfortunate for both of us—

both of us, I assure you. . . . Man alive, don't look as though I was going to cut your throat! I'm not, I assure you. You're a smart man of business, and I happen to have spotted a little operation of yours, that's all. I shall arrange easy terms for you. . . . Pull yourself together and talk business before the men come back. Here, sit on this bench.'

Mallows, staring amazedly in Dorrington's face, suffered himself to be led to a bench, and sat on it.

'Now,' said Dorrington, 'the first thing is a little matter of a hundred pounds. That was the reward you promised if I should discover who broke Gillett's arm last night. Well, I *have*. Do you happen to have any notes with you? If not, make it a cheque.'

'But—but—how—I mean who—who——'

'Tut, tut! Don't waste time, Mr Mallows. *Who*? Why, yourself, of course. I knew all about it before I left you last night, though it wasn't quite convenient to claim the reward then, for reasons you'll understand presently. Come, that little hundred.'

'But what—what proof have you? I'm not to be bounced like this, you know.' Mr Mallows was gathering his faculties again.

'Proof? Why, man alive, be reasonable! Suppose I have none—none at all? What difference does that make? Am I to walk out and tell your fellow directors where I have met you—here—or am I to have that hundred? More, am I to publish abroad that Mr Paul Mallows is the moving spirit in the rotten "Avalanche Bicycle Company"?'

'Well,' Mallows answered reluctantly, 'if you put it like that——'

'But I only put it like that to make you see things reasonably. As a matter of fact your connection with this new company is enough to bring your little performance with the iron chair near proof. But I got at it from the other side. See here—you're much too clumsy with your fingers, Mr Mallows. First you go and tear the tip of your middle finger opening your brougham door, and have to get court plaster from me. Then you let that court plaster get frayed at the edge, and you still keep it on. After that you execute your very successful chair operation. When the eyes of the others are following the bicycles you take the chair in the hand with the plaster on it, catching hold of it at the place where a rough, loose, square nut protrudes, and you pitch it on to the track so clumsily and nervously that the nut carries away the frayed thread of the court plaster with it. Here it is, you see, still in my pocket-book, where I put it last night by the light of the lantern; just a sticky black silk thread, that's all. I've only brought it to show you I'm playing a fair game with you. Of course I might easily have got a witness before I took the thread off the nut, if I had thought you were likely to fight the matter. But I knew you were not. You can't fight, you know, with this bogus company business known to me. So that I am only showing you this thread as an act of grace, to prove that I have stumped you with perfect fairness. And now the hundred. Here's a fountain pen, if you want one.'

'Well,' said Mallows glumly, 'I suppose I must, then.' He took the pen and wrote the cheque. Dorrington blotted it on the pad of his pocket-book and folded it away.

'So much for that!' he said. 'That's just a little preliminary, you understand. We've done these little things just as a guarantee of good faith—not necessarily for publication, though you must remember that as yet there's nothing to prevent it. I've done you a turn by finding out who upset those bicycles, as you so ardently wished me to do last night, and you've loyally fulfilled your part of the contract by paying the promised reward—though I must say that you haven't paid with all the delight and pleasure you spoke of at the time. But I'll forgive you that, and now that the little hors d'œuvre is disposed of, we'll proceed to serious business.'

Mallows looked uncomfortably glum.

'But you mustn't look so ashamed of yourself, you know,' Dorrington said, purposely misinterpreting his glumness. 'It's all business. You were disposed for a little side flutter, so to speak—a little speculation outside your regular business. Well, you mustn't be ashamed of that.'

'No,' Mallows observed, assuming something of his ordinarily ponderous manner; 'no, of course not. It's a little speculative deal. Everybody does it, and there's a deal of money going.'

'Precisely. And since everybody does it, and there is so much money going, you are only making your share.'

'Of course.' Mr Mallows was almost pompous by now.

'Of course.' Dorrington coughed slightly. 'Well now, do you know, I am exactly the same sort of man as yourself —if you don't mind the comparison. *I* am disposed for a little side flutter, so to speak—a little speculation outside my regular business. I also am not ashamed of it. And since everybody does it, and there is so much money going —why, *I* am thinking of making *my* share. So we are evidently a pair, and naturally intended for each other!'

Mr Paul Mallows here looked a little doubtful.

'See here, now,' Dorrington proceeded. 'I have lately taken it into my head to operate a little on the cycle share market. That was why I came round myself about that little spoke affair, instead of sending an assistant. I wanted to know somebody who understood the cycle trade, from whom I might get tips. You see I'm perfectly frank with you. Well, I have succeeded uncommonly well. And I want you to understand that I have gone every step of the way by fair work. I took nothing for granted, and I played the game fairly. When you asked me (as you had anxious reason to ask) if I had found anything, I told you there was nothing very big—and see what a little thing the thread was! Before I came away from the pavilion I made sure that you were really the only man there with black court plaster on his fingers. I had noticed the hands of every man but two, and I made an excuse of borrowing something to see those. I saw your thin pretence of suspecting the betting men, and I played up to it. I have had a telegraphic report on your Exeter works this morning—a deserted cloth mills with nothing on it of yours but a sign-board, and only a deposit of rent paid. *There* they referred to the works here. *Here* they referred to the works there. It was very clever, really! Also I have had a telegraphic report of your make-up adventure this morning. Clarkson does it marvellously, doesn't he? And, by the way, that telegram bringing you down to Birmingham was not from your confederate here, as perhaps you fancied. It was from me. Thanks for coming so promptly. I managed to get a quiet look round here just before you arrived, and on the whole the conclusion I come to as to the "Avalanche Bicycle and Tyre Company, Limited", is this: A clever man, whom it gives me great pleasure to know,' with a bow to Mallows, 'conceives the notion of offering the public the very rottenest cycle company ever planned, and all without appearing in it himself. He finds what little capital is required; his two or three confederates help to make up a board of directors, with one or two titled guinea-pigs, who know nothing of the company and care nothing, and the rest's easy. A professional racing man is employed to win races and make records, on machines which have been specially made by another firm (perhaps it was the "Indestructible", who knows?) to a private order, and afterwards decorated with the name and style of the bogus company on a transfer. For ordinary sale, bicycles of the "trade" description are bought—so much a hundred from the factors, and put your own name

on 'em. They come cheap, and they sell at a good price—
the profit pays all expenses and perhaps a bit over; and by
the time they all break down the company will be successfully floated, the money—the capital—will be divided, the
moving spirit and his confederates will have disappeared,
and the guinea-pigs will be left to stand the racket—if
there is a racket. And the moving spirit will remain un-
suspected, a man of account in the trade all the time!
Admirable! All the work to be done at the "works" is the
sticking on of labels and a bit of enamelling. Excellent, all
round! Isn't that about the size of your operations?'

'Well, yes,' Mallows answered, a little reluctantly, but
with something of modest pride in his manner, 'that was
the notion, since you speak so plainly.'

'And it shall be the notion. All—everything—shall be
as you have planned it, with one exception, which is this.
The moving spirit shall divide his plunder with me.'

'*You*? But—but—why, I gave you a hundred just now!'

'Dear, dear! Why will you harp so much on that vulgar
little hundred? That's settled and done with. That's our
little personal bargain in the matter of the lamentable
accident with the chair. We are now talking of bigger
business—not hundreds, but thousands, and not one of
them, but a lot. Come now, a mind like yours should be
wide enough to admit of a broad and large view of things.
If I refrain from exposing this charming scheme of yours
I shall be promoting a piece of scandalous robbery. Very
well then, I want my promotion money, in the regular way.
Can I shut my eyes and allow a piece of iniquity like this
to go on unchecked, without getting anything by way of
damages for myself? Perish the thought! When all expenses are paid, and the confederates are sent off with as
little as they will take, you and I will divide fairly, Mr
Mallows, respectable brothers in rascality. Mind, I might
say we'd divide to begin with, and leave you to pay

expenses, but I am always fair to a partner in anything of this sort. I shall just want a little guarantee, you know—it's safest in such matters as these; say a bill at six months for ten thousand pounds—which is very low. When a satisfactory division is made you shall have the bill back. Come—I have a bill-stamp ready, being so much convinced of your reasonableness as to buy it this morning, though it cost five pounds.'

'But that's nonsense—you're trying to impose. I'll give you anything reasonable—half is out of the question. What, after all the trouble and worry and risk that I've had?'

'Which would suffice for no more than to put you in gaol if I held up my finger!'

'But hang it, be reasonable! You're a mighty clever man, and you've got me on the hip, as I admit. Say ten per cent.'

'You're wasting time, and presently the men will be back. Your choice is between making half, or making none, and going to gaol into the bargain. Choose!'

'But just consider——'

'Choose!'

Mallows looked despairingly about him. 'But really,' he said, 'I want the money more than you think. I——'

'For the last time—choose!'

Mallow's despairing gaze stopped at the enamelling oven. 'Well, well,' he said, 'if I must, I must, I suppose. But I warn you, you may regret it.'

'Oh dear no, I'm not so pessimistic. Come, you wrote a cheque—now I'll write the bill. "Six months after date, pay to me or my order the sum of ten thousand pounds for value received"—excellent value too, *I* think. There you are!'

When the bill was written and signed, Mallows scribbled his acceptance with more readiness than might have been expected. Then he rose, and said with something of brisk cheerfulness in his tone, 'Well, that's done, and the least said the soonest mended. You've won it, and I won't grumble any more. I think I've done this thing pretty neatly, eh? Come and see the "works".'

Every other part of the place was empty of machinery. There were a good many finished frames and wheels, bought separately, and now in course of being fitted together for sale; and there were many more complete bicycles of cheap but showy make to which nothing needed to be done but to fix the red and gold 'transfer' of the 'Avalanche' company. Then Mallows opened the tall iron door of the enamelling oven.

'See this,' he said; 'this is the enamelling oven. Get in and look round. The frames and other different parts hang on the racks after the enamel is laid on, and all those gas jets are lighted to harden it by heat. Do you see that deeper part there by the back?—go closer.'

Dorrington felt a push at his back and the door was swung to with a bang, and the latch dropped. He was in the dark, trapped in a great iron chamber. 'I warned you,' shouted Mallows from without; 'I warned you you might regret it!' And instantly Dorrington's nostrils were filled with the smell of escaping gas. He realized his peril on the instant. Mallows had given him the bill with the idea of silencing him by murder and recovering it. He had pushed him into the oven and had turned on the gas. It was dark, but to light a match would mean death instantly, and without the match it must be death by suffocation and poison of gas in a very few minutes. To appeal to Mallows was useless—Dorrington knew too much. It would seem that at last a horribly-fitting retribution had overtaken Dorrington in death by a mode parallel to that which he and his creatures had prepared for others. Dorrington's victims had drowned in water—and now Dorrington himself was to drown in gas. The oven was of sheet iron, fastened by a latch in the centre. Dorrington flung himself desperately against the door, and it gave outwardly at the extreme bottom. He snatched a loose angle-iron with which his hand came in contact, dashed against the door once more, and thrust the iron through where it strained open. Then, with another tremendous plunge, he drove the door a little more outward and raised the angle-iron in the crack; then once more, and raised it again. He was near to losing his senses, when, with one more plunge, the catch of the latch, not designed for such treatment, suddenly gave way, the door flew open, and Dorrington, blue in the face, staring, stumbling and gasping, came staggering out into the fresher air, followed by a gush of gas.

Mallows had retreated to the rooms behind, and thither Dorrington followed him, gaining vigour and fury at every step. At sight of him the wretched Mallows sank in a corner, sighing and shivering with terror. Dorrington reached him and clutched him by the collar. There should be no more honour between these two thieves now. He would drag Mallows forth and proclaim him aloud; and he would keep that £10,000 bill. He hauled the struggling wretch across the room, tearing off the crêpe whiskers as he came, while Mallows supplicated and whined, fearing that it might be the other's design to imprison *him* in the enamelling oven. But at the door of the room against that containing the oven their progress came to an end, for the escaped gas had reached the lighted candle, and with one loud report the partition wall fell in, half burying Mallows where he lay, and knocking Dorrington over.

Windows fell out of the building, and men broke through the front gate, climbed into the ruined rooms and stopped the still escaping gas. When the two men and the boy returned, with the conspirator who had been in charge of the works, they found a crowd from the hardware and cycle factories thereabout, surveying with great interest the spectacle of the extrication of Mr Paul Mallows, managing director of the 'Indestructible Bicycle Company', from the broken bricks, mortar, bicycles and transfers of the 'Avalanche Bicycle and Tyre Company, Limited', and the preparations for carrying him to a surgeon's where his broken leg might be set. As for Dorrington, a crushed hat and a torn coat were all his hurts, beyond a few scratches. And in a couple of hours it was all over Birmingham, and spreading to other places, that the business of the 'Avalanche Bicycle and Tyre Company' consisted of sticking brilliant labels on factors' bicycles, bought in batches; for the whole thing was thrown open to the general gaze by the explosion. So that when, next day, Lant won the fifty miles race in London, he was greeted with ironical shouts of 'Gum on yer transfer!' 'Hi! mind your label!' 'Where did you steal that bicycle?' 'Sold yer shares?' and so forth.

Somehow the 'Avalanche Bicycle and Tyre Company, Limited', never went to allotment. It was said that a few people in remote and benighted spots, where news never came till it was in the history books, had applied for shares, but the bankers returned their money, doubtless to their extreme disappointment. It was found politic, also, that Mr Paul Mallows should retire from the directorate of the 'Indestructible Bicycle Company'—a concern which is still, I believe, flourishing exceedingly.

As for Dorrington, he had his hundred pounds reward. But the bill for £10,000 he never presented. Why, I do not altogether know, unless he found that Mr Mallow's financial position, as he had hinted, was not altogether so good as was supposed. At any rate, it was found among the notes and telegrams in this case in the Dorrington deed-box.

V

The Assyrian Rejuvenator

Clifford Ashdown

As six o'clock struck the procession of the un-dined began to stream beneath the electric arcade which graces the entrance to Cristiani's. The doors swung unceasingly; the mirrors no longer reflected a mere squadron of tables and erect serviettes; a hum of conversation now mingled with the clatter of knives and the popping of corks; and the brisk scurry of waiters' slippers replaced the stillness of the afternoon.

Although the restaurant had been crowded some time before he arrived, Mr Romney Pringle had secured his favourite seat opposite the feminine print after Gainsborough, and in the intervals of feeding listened to a selection from Mascagni through a convenient electrophone, price sixpence in the slot. It was a warm night for the time of year, a muggy spell having succeeded a week of biting north-east wind, and as the evening wore on the atmosphere grew somewhat oppressive, more particularly to those who had dined well. Its effects were not very visible on Pringle, whose complexion (a small port-wine mark on his right cheek its only blemish) was of that fairness which imparts to its fortunate possessor the air of youth until long past forty; especially in a man who shaves clean, and habitually goes to bed before two in the morning.

As the smoke from Pringle's havana wreathed upwards to an extractor, his eye fell, not for the first time, upon a diner at the next table. He was elderly, probably on the wrong side of sixty, but with his erect figure might easily have claimed a few years' grace, while the retired soldier spoke in his scrupulous neatness, and in the trim of a carefully tended moustache. He had finished his dinner some little time, but remained seated, studying a letter with an intentness more due to its subject than to its length, which Pringle could see was by no means excessive. At last, with a gesture almost equally compounded of weariness and disgust, he rose and was helped into his overcoat by a waiter, who held the door for him in the obsequious manner of his kind.

The languid attention which Pringle at first bestowed on his neighbour had by this time given place to a deeper interest, and as the swing-doors closed behind the old gentleman, he scarcely repressed a start, when he saw lying beneath the vacant table the identical letter which had received such careful study. His first impulse was to run after the old gentleman and restore the paper, but by this time he had disappeared, and the waiter being also invisible, Pringle sat down and read:

'The Assyrian Rejuvenator Co.,
  82, Barbican, E.C. April 5th
  'Dear Sir—We regret to hear of the failure of the "Rejuvenator" in your hands. This is possibly due to your not having followed the directions for its use sufficiently closely, but I must point out that we do not guarantee its infallible success. As it is an expensive preparation, we do not admit the justice of your contention that our charges are exorbitant. In

any case we cannot entertain your request to return the whole or any part of the fees. Should you act upon your threat to take proceedings for the recovery of the same, we must hold your good self responsible for any publicity which may follow your trial of the preparation.

Yours faithfully,
·   Henry Jacobs,
Secretary.

Lieut.-Col. Sandstream,
272, Piccadilly, W.'

To Pringle this businesslike communication hardly seemed to deserve so much consideration as Colonel Sandstream had given it, but having read and pondered it over afresh, he walked back to his chambers in Furnival's Inn.

He lived at No. 33, on the left as you enter from Holborn, and anyone who, scaling the stone stairs, reached the second floor, might observe on the entrance to the front set of chambers the legend, 'Mr Romney Pringle, Literary Agent'. According to high authority, the reason of being of the literary agent is to act as a buffer between the ravening publisher and his prey. But although a very fine oak bureau with capacious pigeon-holes stood conspicuously in Pringle's sitting-room, it was tenanted by no rolls of MS, or type-written sheets. Indeed, little or no business appeared to be transacted in the chambers. The buffer was at present idle, if it could be said to have ever worked! It was 'resting' to use the theatrical expression.

Mr Pringle was an early riser, and as nine o'clock chimed the next morning from the brass lantern-clock which ticked sedately on a mantel unencumbered by the usual litter of a bachelor's quarters, he had already spent some time in consideration of last night's incident, and a further study of the letter had only served thoroughly to arouse his curiosity, and decided him to investigate the affair of the mysterious 'Rejuvenator'. Unlocking a cupboard in the bottom of the bureau, he disclosed a regiment of bottles and jars. Sprinkling a few drops from one on to a hare's-foot, he succeeded, with a little friction, in entirely removing the port-wine mark from his cheek. Then from another phial he saturated a sponge and rubbed it into his eyebrows, which turned in the process from their original yellow to a jetty black. From a box of several, he selected a waxed moustache (that most facile article of disguise), and having attached it with a few drops of spirit-gum, covered his scalp with a black wig, which, as is commonly the case, remained an aggressive fraud in spite of the most assiduous adjustment. Satisfied with the completeness of his disguise, he sallied out in search of the offices of the 'Assyrian Rejuvenator', affecting a military bearing which his slim but tall and straight-backed figure readily enabled him to assume.

'My name is Parkins—Major Parkins,' said Pringle, as he opened the door of a mean-looking room on the second floor of No. 82, Barbican. He addressed an oleaginous-looking gentleman, whose curly locks and beard suggested the winged bulls of Nineveh, and who appeared to be the sole representative of the concern. The latter bowed politely, and handed him a chair.

'I have been asked,' Pringle continued, 'by a friend who saw your advertisement to call upon you for some further information.'

Now the subject of rejuvenation being a delicate one, especially where ladies are concerned, the business of the company was mainly transacted through the post. So seldom, indeed, did a client desire a personal interview, that the Assyrian-looking gentleman jumped to the conclusion that his visitor was interested in quite another matter.

'Ah yes! You refer to "Pelosia",' he said briskly. 'Allow me to read you an extract from the prospectus.'

And before Pringle could reply he proceeded to read from a small leaflet with unctuous elocution:

'Pelosia. The sovereign remedy of Mud has long been used with the greatest success in the celebrated baths of Schwalbach and Franzensbad. The proprietors of Pelosia having noted the beneficial effect which many of the lower animals derive from the consumption of earth with their food, have been led to investigate the internal uses of mud. The success which has crowned the treatment of some of the longest-standing cases of dyspepsia (the disease so characteristic of this neurotic age), has induced them to admit the world at large to its benefits. To thoroughly safeguard the public, the proprietors have secured the sole right to the alluvial deposits of a stream remote from human habitation, and consequently above any suspicion of contamination. Careful analysis has shown that the deposit in this particular locality, consisting of finely divided mineral particles, practically free from organic admixture, is calculated to give the most gratifying results. The proprietors are prepared to quote special terms for public institutions.'

'Many thanks,' said Pringle, as the other momentarily paused for breath; 'but I think you are under a slight misapprehension. I called on you with reference to the "Assyrian Rejuvenator". Have I mistaken the offices?'

'Pray excuse my absurd mistake! I am secretary of the "Assyrian Rejuvenator Company", who are also the proprietors of "Pelosia".' And in evident concern he regarded Pringle fixedly.

It was not the first time he had known a diffident person to assume an interest in the senility of an absent friend, and he mentally decided that Pringle's waxed moustache, its blue-blackness speaking loudly of hair-dye, together with the unmistakable wig, were evidence of the decrepitude for which his new customer presumably sought the Company's assistance.

'Ours, my dear sir,' he resumed, leaning back in his chair, and placing the tips of his fingers in apposition— 'Ours is a world-renowned specific for removing the ravages which time effects in the human frame. It is a secret which has been handed down for many generations in the family of the original proprietor. Its success is frequently remarkable, and its absolute failure is impossible. It is not a drug, it is not a cosmetic, yet it contains the properties of both. It is agreeable and soothing to use, and being best administered during the hours of sleep does not interfere with the ordinary avocations of every-day life. The price is so moderate—ten and sixpence, including the Government stamp—that it could only prove remunerative with an enormous sale. If you—ah, on behalf of your friend!— would care to purchase a bottle, I shall be most happy to explain its operation.'

Mr Pringle laid a half sovereign and a sixpence on the table, and the secretary, diving into a large packing-case which stood on one side, extracted a parcel. This contained a cardboard box adorned with a representation of Blake's preposterous illustration to 'The Grave', in which a centenarian on crutches is hobbling into a species of banker's strongroom with a rocky top, whereon is seated a youth clothed in nothing, and with an ecstatic expression.

'This,' said Mr Jacobs impressively, 'is the entire apparatus!' And he opened the box, displaying a moderate-sized phial and a spirit-lamp with a little tin dish attached. 'On retiring to rest, a teaspoonful of the contents of the bottle is poured into the receptacle above the lamp, which is then lighted, and the preparation being vaporized is inhaled by the patient. It is best to concentrate the thoughts on some object of beauty whilst the delicious aroma sooths the patient to sleep.'

'But how does it act?' inquired the Major a trifle impatiently.

'In this way,' replied the imperturbable secretary. 'Remember that the appearance of age is largely due to wrinkles; that is to say, to the skin losing its elasticity and fulness—so true is it that beauty is only skin-deep.' Here he laughed gaily. 'The joints grow stiff from loss of their natural tone, the figure stoops, and the vital organs decline their functions from the same cause. In a word, old age is due to a loss of *elasticity*, and that is the very property which the "Rejuvenator" imparts to the system, if inhaled for a few hours daily.'

Mr Pringle diplomatically succeeded in maintaining his gravity while the merits of the "Rejuvenator" were expounded, and it was not until he had bidden Mr Jacobs a courteous farewell, and was safely outside the office, that he allowed the fastening of his moustache to be disturbed by an expansive grin.

About nine o'clock the same evening the housekeeper of the Barbican offices was returning from market, her thoughts centred on the savoury piece of fried fish she was carrying home for supper.

'Mrs Smith?' said a man's voice behind her, as she produced her latch-key.

'My name's 'Odges,' she replied unguardedly, dropping the key in her agitation.

'You're the housekeeper, aren't you?' said the stranger, picking up the key and handing it to her politely.

'Lor', sir! You did give me a turn,' she faltered.

'Very sorry, I'm sure. I only want to know where I can find Mr Jacobs, of the "Assyrian Rejuvenator Company".'

'Well, sir, he told me I wasn't to give his address to anyone. Not that I know it either, sir, for I always send the letters to Mr Weeks.'

'I'll see you're not found fault with. I know he won't

mind your telling me.' A sovereign clinked against the latch-key in her palm.

For a second she hesitated, then her eye caught the glint of the gold, and she fell.

'All I know, sir, is that when Mr Jacobs is away I send the letters—and a rare lot there are—to Mr Newton Weeks, at the Northumberland Avenue Hotel.'

'Is he one of the firm?'

'I don't know, sir, but there's no one comes here but Mr Jacobs.'

'Thank you very much, and good night,' said the stranger; and he strode down Barbican, leaving Mrs Hodges staring at the coin in her hand as if doubting whether, like fairy gold, it might not disappear even as she gazed.

The next day Mr Jacobs received a letter at his hotel:

'April 7th

'Sir—My friend Col. Sandstream informs me he has communicated with the police, and has sworn an information against you in respect of the moneys you have obtained from him, as he alleges, by false pretences. Although I am convinced that his statements are true, a fact which I can more readily grasp after my interview with you today, I give you this warning in order that you may make your escape before it is too late. Do not misunderstand my motives; I have not the slightest desire to save you from the punishment you so richly deserve. I am simply anxious to rescue my old friend from the ridiculous position he will occupy before the world should he prosecute you.

Your obedient servant,
Joseph Parkins, Major.

Newton Weeks, Esq.,
Northumberland Avenue Hotel.'

Mr Jacobs read this declaration of war with very mixed feelings.

So his visitor of yesterday was the friend of Colonel

Sandstream! Obviously come to get up evidence against him. Knowing old dog, that Sandstream! But then how had they run him to earth? That looked as if the police had got their fingers in the pie. Mrs Hodges was discreet. She would never have given the address to any but the police. It was annoying, though, after all his precautions; seemed as if the game was really up at last. Well, it was bound to come some day, and he had been in tighter places before. He could hardly complain; the 'Rejuvenator' had been going very well lately. But suppose the whole thing was a plant—a dodge to intimidate him?

He read the letter through again. The writer had been careful to omit his address, but it seemed plausible enough on the face of it. Anyhow, whatever the major's real motive might he, he couldn't afford to neglect the warning, and the one clear thing was that London was an unhealthy place for him just at present. He would pack up, so as to be ready for all emergencies, and drive round to Barbican and reconnoitre. Then, if things looked fishy, he could go to Cannon Street and catch the 11.5 Continental. He'd show them that Harry Jacobs wasn't the man to be bluffed out of his claim!

Mr Jacobs stopped his cab some doors from the "Rejuvenator" office, and was in the act of alighting when he paused, spellbound at the apparition of Pringle. The latter was loitering outside No. 82, and as the cab drew up he ostentatiously consulted a large pocket-book, and glanced several times from its pages to the countenance of his victim as if comparing a description. Attired in a long overcoat, a bowler hat, and wearing thick boots of a constabulary pattern to the nervous imagination of Mr Jacobs, he afforded startling evidence of the police interest in the establishment; and this idea was confirmed when Pringle, as if satisfied with his scrutiny, drew a paper from the pocket-book and made a movement in his direction. Without waiting for further developments, Mr Jacobs retreated into the cab and hoarsely whispered through the trap-door, 'Cannon Street as hard as you can go!'

The cabman wrenched the horse's head round. He had been an interested spectator of the scene, and sympathised with the evident desire of his fare to escape what appeared to be the long arm of the law. At this moment a 'crawling' hansom came up, and was promptly hailed by Pringle.

'Follow that cab and don't lose it on any account!' he cried, as he stood on the step and pointed vigorously after the receding hansom.

While Mr Jacobs careered down Barbican, his cabman looked back in time to observe this expressive pantomime, and with the instinct of a true sportsman lashed the unfortunate brute into a hand-gallop. But the observant eye of a policeman checked this moderate exhibition of speed just as they were rounding the sharp corner into Aldersgate Street, and had not a lumbering railway van intervened Pringle would have caught him up and brought the farce to an awkward finish. But the van saved the situation. The moment's respite was all that the chase needed, and in response to the promises of largesse, frantically roared by Mr Jacobs through the trap-door, he was soon bounding and bumping over the wood pavement with Pringle well in the rear.

Then ensued a mad stampede down Aldersgate Street.

In and out, between the crowded files of vans and 'buses, the two cabs wound a zig-zag course; the horses slipping and skating over the greasy surface, or ploughing up the mud as their bits skidded them within inches of a collision. In vain did policemen roar to them to stop—the order fell on heedless ears. In vain did officious boys wave intimidating arms, or make futile grabs at the harness of the apparent runaways. Did a cart dart unexpectedly from out a side street, the inevitable disaster failed to come off.

Did an obstacle loom dead ahead of them, it melted into thin air as they approached. Triumphantly they piloted the narrowest of straits, and dashed unscathed into St Martin's-le-Grand.

There was a block in Newgate Street, and the cross traffic was stopped. Mr Jacobs' hansom nipped through a temporary gap, grazing the pole of an omnibus, and being lustily anathematised in the process. But Pringle's cabman, attempting to follow, was imperiously waved back by a policeman.

'No go, I'm afraid, sir!' was the man's comment, as they crossed into St Paul's Churchyard after a three minutes' wait. 'I can't see him nowhere.'

'Never mind,' said Pringle cheerfully. 'Go to Charing Cross telegraph office.'

There he sent the following message:

'To Mrs Hodges, 82, Barbican. Called away to country. Mr Weeks will take charge of office—Jacobs.'

About two the same afternoon, Pringle, wearing the wig and moustache of Major Parkins, rang the housekeeper's bell at 82.

'I'm Mr Weeks,' he stated, as Mrs Hodges emerged from the bowels of the earth. 'Mr Jacobs has had to leave town, and has asked me to take charge of the office.'

'Oh yes, sir! I've had a telegram from Mr Jacobs to say so. You know the way up, I suppose.'

'I think so. But Mr Jacobs forgot to send me the office key.'

'I'd better lend you mine, then, sir, till you can hear from Mr Jacobs.' She fumbled in her voluminous pocket. 'I hope nothing's the matter with him?'

'Oh dear no! He found he needed a short holiday, that's all,' Pringle reassured her, and taking the key from the confiding woman he climbed to the second floor.

Sitting down at the secretarial desk, he sent a quick glance round the office. A poor creature, that Jacobs, he reflected, for all his rascality, or he wouldn't have been scared so easily. And he drew a piece of wax from his pocket and took a careful impression of the key.

He had not been in possession of the 'Rejuvenator' offices for very long before he discovered that Mr Jacobs' desire to break out in a fresh place had proved abortive. It will be remembered that on the occasion of his interview with that gentleman, Mr Jacobs assumed that Pringle's visit had reference to 'Pelosia', whose virtues he extolled in a leaflet composed in his own very pronounced style. A large package in the office Pringle found to contain many thousands of these effusions, which had apparently been laid aside for some considerable time. From the absence in the daily correspondence of any inquiries thereafter, it was clear that the public had failed to realize the advantages of the internal administration of mud, so that Mr Jacobs had been forced to stick to the swindle that was already in existence. After all, the latter was a paying concern—eminently so! Besides, the patent-medicine trade is rather overdone.

The price of the 'Assyrian Rejuvenator' was such as to render the early cashing of remittances an easy matter. Ten-and-sixpence being a sum for which the average banker demurs to honour a cheque, the payments were usually made in postal orders; and Pringle acquired a larger faith in Carlyle's opinion of the majority of his fellow-creatures as he cashed the previous day's takings at the General Post Office on his way up to Barbican each morning. The business was indeed a flourishing one, and his satisfaction was only alloyed by the probability of some legal interference, at the instance of Colonel Sandstream, with the further operations of the Company. But for the present Fortune smiled, and Pringle continued energetically to despatch parcels of the 'Rejuvenator' in response to the daily shower of postal orders. In this indeed he had little trouble, for he had found many gross of parcels duly packed and ready for posting.

One day while engaged in the process, which had grown quite a mechanical one by that time, he listened absently to a slow but determined step which ascended the stairs and paused on the landing outside. Above, on the third floor, was an importer of cigars made in Germany, and the visitor evidently delayed the further climb until he had regained his wind. Presently, after a preliminary pant or two, he got under weigh again, but proceeded only as far as the 'Rejuvenator' door, to which he gave a peremptory thump, and, opening it, walked in without further ceremony.

There was no need for him to announce himself. Pringle recognized him at first glance, although he had never seen him since the eventful evening at Cristiani's restaurant.

'I'm Colonel Sandstream!' he growled, looking round him savagely.

'Delighted to see you, sir,' said Pringle with assurance. 'Pray be seated,' he added politely.

'Who am I speaking to?'

'My name is Newton Weeks. I am——'

'I don't want to see *you!*' interrupted the Colonel testily. 'I want to see the secretary of this concern. I've no time to waste either.'

'I regret to say that Mr Jacobs——'

'Ah, yes! That's the name. Where is he?' again interrupted the old gentleman.

'Mr Jacobs is at present out of town.'

'Well, I'm not going to run after him. When will he be here again?'

'It is quite impossible for me to tell. But I was just now going to say that as the managing director of the company I am also acting as secretary during Mr Jacobs' absence.'

'What do you say your name is?' demanded the other, still ignoring the chair which Pringle had offered him.

'Newton Weeks.'

'Newton Weeks,' repeated the Colonel, making a note of the name on the back of an envelope.

'Managing director,' added Pringle suavely.

'Well, Mr Weeks, if you represent the *company*—' this with a contemptuous glance from the middle of the room at his surroundings—'I've called with reference to a letter you've had the impertinence to send me.'

'What was the date of it?' inquired Pringle innocently.

'I don't remember!' snapped the Colonel.

'May I ask what was the subject of the correspondence?'

'Why, this confounded "Rejuvenator" of yours, of course!'

'You see we have a very large amount of correspondence concerning the "Rejuvenator", and I'm afraid unless you have the letter with you——'

'I've lost it or mislaid it somewhere.'

'That is unfortunate! Unless you can remember the contents I fear it will be quite impossible for *me* to do so.'

'I remember them well enough! I'm not likely to forget them in a hurry. I asked you to return me the money your "Rejuvenator", as you call it, has cost me, because it's been quite useless, and in your reply you not only refused absolutely, but hinted that I dare not prosecute you.'

As Pringle made no reply, he continued more savagely: 'Would you like to hear my candid opinion of you?'

'We are always pleased to hear the opinion of our clients.'

Pringle's calmness only appeared to exasperate the Colonel the more.

'Well, sir, you shall have it. I consider that letter the most impudent attempt at blackmail that I have ever heard of!' He ground out the words from between his clenched teeth in a voice of concentrated passion.

'Blackmail!' echoed Pringle, allowing an expression of horror to occupy his countenance.

'Yes, sir! Blackmail!' asseverated the Colonel, nodding his head vigorously.

'Of course,' said Pringle, with a deprecating gesture, 'I am aware that some correspondence has passed between us, but I cannot attempt to remember every word of it. At the same time, although you are pleased to put such an unfortunate construction upon it, I am sure there is some misunderstanding in the matter. I must positively decline to admit that there has been any attempt on the part of the company of such a nature as you allege.'

'Oh! so you don't admit it, don't you? Perhaps you won't admit taking pounds and pounds of my money for your absurd concoction, which hasn't done me the least little bit of good in the world—nor ever will! And perhaps you won't admit refusing to return me my money? Eh? Perhaps you won't admit daring me to take proceedings because it would show up what an ass I've been! Don't talk to me, sir! Haugh!'

'I'm really very sorry that this unpleasantness has arisen,' began Pringle, 'but——'

'Pleasant or unpleasant, sir, I'm going to stop your little game! I mislaid your letter or I'd have called upon you before this. As you're the managing director I'm better pleased to see you than your precious secretary. Anyhow, I've come to tell you that you're a set of swindlers! Of swindlers, sir!'

'I can make every allowance for your feelings,' said Pringle, drawing himself up with an air of pained dignity, 'but I regret to see a holder of His Majesty's commission so deficient in self-control.'

'Like your impertinence, sir!' vociferated the veteran. 'I'll let the money go, and I'll prosecute the pair of you, no matter what it costs me! Yes, you, and your rascally secretary too! I'll go and swear an information against you this very day!' He bounced out of the room, and explosively snorted downstairs.

Pringle followed in the rear, and reached the outer door in time to hear him exclaim, 'Mansion House Police Court,' to the driver of a motor-cab, in which he appropriately clanked and rumbled out of sight.

Returning upstairs, Pringle busied himself in making a bonfire of the last few days' correspondence. Then, collecting the last batch of postal orders, he proceeded to cash them at the General Post Office, and walked back to Furnival's Inn. After all, the farce couldn't have lasted much longer.

Arrived at Furnival's Inn, Pringle rapidly divested himself of the wig and moustache, and, assuming his official port-wine mark, became once more the unemployed literary agent.

It was now half-past one, and, after lunching lightly at a near restaurant, he lighted a cigar and strolled leisurely eastward.

By the time he reached Barbican three o'clock was reverberating from St Paul's. He entered the private bar of a tavern nearly opposite, and sat down by a window which commanded a view of No. 82.

As time passed and the quarters continued to strike in rapid succession, Pringle felt constrained to order further refreshment; and he was lighting a third cigar before his patience was rewarded. Happening to glance up at the second floor window, he caught a glimpse of a strange man engaged in taking a momentary survey of the street below.

The march of events had been rapid. He had evidently resigned the secretaryship not a moment too soon!

Not long after the strange face had disappeared from the window, a four-wheeled cab stopped outside the tavern, and an individual wearing a pair of large blue spectacles, and carrying a Gladstone bag, got out and carefully scrutinized the offices of the 'Rejuvenator'. Mr Jacobs, for it was he, did not intend to be caught napping this time.

At length, being satisfied with the normal appearance of the premises, he crossed the road, and to Pringle's intense amusement, disappeared into the house opposite. The spectator had not long to wait for the next act of the drama.

About ten minutes after Mr Jacobs' disappearance, the man who had looked out of the window emerged from the house and beckoned to the waiting cab. As it drew up at the door, a second individual came down the steps, fast-holding Mr Jacobs by the arm. The latter, in very crest-fallen guise, re-entered the vehicle, being closely followed by his captor; and the first man having taken his seat with them, the party adjourned to a destination as to which Pringle had no difficulty in hazarding a guess. Satisfying the barmaid, he sallied into the street. The 'Rejuvenator' offices seemed once more to be deserted, and the postman entered in the course of his afternoon round. Pringle walked a few yards up the street and then, crossing as the postman re-appeared, turned back and entered the house boldly. Softly mounting the stairs, he knocked at the door. There was no response. He knocked again more loudly, and finally turned the handle. As he expected, it was locked securely, and, satisfied that the coast was clear, he inserted his own replica of the key and entered. The books tumbled on the floor in confused heaps, the wide-open and empty drawers, and the overturned packing-cases, showed how thoroughly the place had been ransacked in the search for compromising evidence. But Pringle took no further interest in these things. The letter-box was the sole object of his attention. He tore open the batch of newly-delivered letters, and crammed the postal orders into his pockets; then, secreting the correspondence behind a rifled packing-case, he silently locked the door.

As he strolled down the street, on a last visit to the General Post Office, the two detectives passed him on their way back in quest of the 'Managing Director'.

VI

Madame Sara

L. T. Meade and Robert Eustace

Everyone in trade and a good many who are not have heard of Werner's Agency, the Solvency Inquiry Agency for all British trade. Its business is to know the financial condition of all wholesale and retail firms, from Rothschild's to the smallest sweetstuff shop in Whitechapel. I do not say that every firm figures on its books, but by methods of secret inquiry it can discover the status of any firm or individual. It is the great safeguard to British trade and prevents much fraudulent dealing.

Of this agency I, Dixon Druce, was appointed manager in 1890. Since then I have met queer people and seen strange sights, for men do curious things for money in this world.

It so happened that in June, 1899, my business took me to Madeira on an inquiry of some importance. I left the island on the 14th of the month by the *Norham Castle* for Southampton. I embarked after dinner. It was a lovely night, and the strains of the band in the public gardens of Funchal came floating across the star-powdered bay through the warm, balmy air. Then the engine bells rang to 'Full speed ahead', and, flinging a farewell to the fairest island on earth, I turned to the smoking-room in order to light my cheroot.

'Do you want a match, sir?'

The voice came from a slender, young-looking man who stood near the taffrail. Before I could reply he had struck one and held it out to me.

'Excuse me,' he said, as he tossed it overboard, 'but surely I am addressing Mr Dixon Druce?'

'You are, sir,' I said, glancing keenly back at him, 'but you have the advantage of me.'

'Don't you know me?' he responded, 'Jack Selby, Hayward's House, Harrow, 1879.'

'By Jove! so it is,' I cried.

Our hands met in a warm clasp, and a moment later I found myself sitting close to my old friend, who had fagged for me in the bygone days, and whom I had not seen from the moment when I said goodbye to the 'Hill' in the grey mist of a December morning twenty years ago. He was a boy of fourteen then, but nevertheless I recognised him. His face was bronzed and good-looking, his features refined. As a boy Selby had been noted for his grace, his well-shaped head, his clean-cut features; these characteristics still were his, and although he was now slightly past his first youth he was decidedly handsome. He gave me a quick sketch of his history.

'My father left me plenty of money,' he said, 'and The Meadows, our old family place, is now mine. I have a taste for natural history; that taste took me two years ago to South America. I have had my share of strange adventures, and have collected valuable specimens and trophies. I am now on my way home from Para, on the Amazon, having come by a Booth boat to Madeira and changed there to the Castle Line. But why all this talk about myself?' he added, bringing his deck chair a little nearer to mine. 'What about your history, old chap? Are you settled down with a wife and kiddies of your own, or is that dream of your school days fulfilled, and are you the owner of the best private laboratory in London?'

'As to the laboratory,' I said, with a smile, 'you must come and see it. For the rest I am unmarried. Are you?'

'I was married the day before I left Para, and my wife is on board with me.'

'Capital,' I answered. 'Let me hear all about it.'

'You shall. Her maiden name was Dallas; Beatrice Dallas. She is just twenty now. Her father was an Englishman and her mother a Spaniard; neither parent is living. She has an elder sister, Edith, nearly thirty years of age, unmarried, who is on board with us. There is also a step-brother, considerably older than either Edith or Beatrice. I met my wife last year in Para, and at once fell in love. I am the happiest man on earth. It goes without saying that I think her beautiful, and she is also very well off. The story of her wealth is a curious one. Her uncle on the mother's side was an extremely wealthy Spaniard, who made an enormous fortune in Brazil out of diamonds and minerals; he owned several mines. But it is supposed that his wealth turned his brain. At any rate, it seems to have done so as far as the disposal of his money went. He divided the yearly profits and interest between his nephew and his two nieces, but declared that the property itself should never be split up. He has left the whole of it to that one of the three who should survive the others. A perfectly insane arrangement, but not, I believe, unprecedented in Brazil.'

'Very insane,' I echoed. 'What was he worth?'

'Over two million sterling.'

'By Jove!' I cried, 'what a sum! But what about the half-brother?'

'He must be over forty years of age, and is evidently a bad lot. I have never seen him. His sisters won't speak to him or have anything to do with him. I understand that he is a great gambler; I am further told that he is at present in England, and, as there are certain technicalities to be gone through before the girls can fully enjoy their incomes, one of the first things I must do when I get home is to find him out. He has to sign certain papers, for we shan't be able to put things straight until we get his whereabouts. Some time ago my wife and Edith heard that he was ill, but dead or alive we must know all about him, and as quickly as possible.'

I made no answer, and he continued:

'I'll introduce you to my wife and sister-in-law tomorrow. Beatrice is quite a child compared to Edith, who acts towards her almost like a mother. Bee is a little beauty, so fresh and round and young-looking. But Edith is handsome, too, although I sometimes think she is as vain as a peacock. By the way, Druce, this brings me to another part of my story. The sisters have an acquaintance on board, one of the most remarkable women I have ever met. She goes by the name of Madame Sara, and knows London well. In fact, she confesses to having a shop in the Strand. What she has been doing in Brazil I do not know, for she keeps all her affairs strictly private. But you will be amazed when I tell you what her calling is.'

'What?' I asked.

'A professional beautifier. She claims the privilege of restoring youth to those who consult her. She also declares that she can make quite ugly people handsome. There is no doubt that she is very clever. She knows a little bit of everything, and has wonderful recipes with regard to medicines, surgery, and dentistry. She is a most lovely woman herself, very fair, with blue eyes, an innocent, childlike manner, and quantities of rippling gold hair. She openly confesses that she is very much older than she appears. She looks about five-and-twenty. She seems to have travelled all over the world, and says that by birth

she is a mixture of Indian and Italian, her father having
been Italian and her mother Indian. Accompanying her
is an Arab, a handsome, picturesque sort of fellow, who
gives her the most absolute devotion, and she is also
bringing back to England two Brazilians from Para. This
woman deals in all sorts of curious secrets, but principally
in cosmetics. Her shop in the Strand could, I fancy, tell
many a strange history. Her clients go to her there, and
she does what is necessary for them. It is a fact that she
occasionally performs small surgical operations, and there
is not a dentist in London who can vie with her. She confesses quite naively that she holds some secrets for making
false teeth cling to the palate that no one knows of. Edith
Dallas is devoted to her—in fact, her adoration amounts
to idolatry.'

'You give a very brilliant account of this woman,' I
said. 'You must introduce me tomorrow.'

'I will,' answered Jack, with a smile. 'I should like your
opinion of her. I am right glad I have met you, Druce, it is
like old times. When we get to London I mean to put up
at my town house in Eaton Square for the remainder of the
season. The Meadows shall be re-furnished, and Bee and I
will take up our quarters some time in August; then you
must come and see us. But I am afraid before I give myself up to mere pleasure I must find that precious brother-
in-law, Henry Joachim Silva.'

'If you have any difficulty apply to me,' I said. 'I can
put at your disposal, in an unofficial way, of course, agents
who would find almost any man in England, dead or alive.'

I then proceeded to give Selby a short account of my
own business.

'Thanks,' he said presently, 'that is capital. You are
the very man we want.'

The next morning after breakfast Jack introduced me to
his wife and sister-in-law. They were both foreign-looking,

but very handsome, and the wife in particular had a graceful and uncommon appearance.

We had been chatting about five minutes when I saw
coming down the deck a slight, rather small woman,
wearing a big sun hat.

'Ah, Madame,' cried Selby, 'here you are. I had the
luck to meet an old friend on board—Mr Dixon Druce—
and I have been telling him all about you. I should like
you to know each other. Druce, this lady is Madame Sara,
of whom I have spoken to you. Mr Dixon Druce—Madame
Sara.'

She bowed gracefully and then looked at me earnestly.
I had seldom seen a more lovely woman. By her side both
Mrs Selby and her sister seemed to fade into insignificance.
Her complexion was almost dazzlingly fair, her face refined
in expression, her eyes penetrating, clever, and yet with
the innocent, frank gaze of a child. Her dress was very
simple; she looked altogether like a young, fresh, and
natural girl.

As we sat chatting lightly and about commonplace topics,
I instinctively felt that she took an interest in me even
greater than might be expected upon an ordinary introduction. By slow degrees she so turned the conversation as to
leave Selby and his wife and sister out, and then as they
moved away she came a little nearer, and said in a low
voice:

'I am very glad we have met, and yet how odd this
meeting is! Was it really accidental?'

'I do not understand you,' I answered.

'I know who you are,' she said, lightly. 'You are the
manager of Werner's Agency; its business is to know the
private affairs of those people who would rather keep their
own secrets. Now, Mr Druce, I am going to be absolutely
frank with you. I own a small shop in the Strand—a per-
fumery shop—and behind those innocent-looking doors I

conduct the business which brings me in gold of the realm. Have you, Mr Druce, any objection to my continuing to make a livelihood in perfectly innocent ways?'

'None whatever,' I answered. 'You puzzle me by alluding to the subject.'

'I want you to pay my shop a visit when you come to London. I have been away for three or four months. I do wonders for my clients, and they pay me largely for my services. I hold some perfectly innocent secrets which I cannot confide to anybody. I have obtained them partly from the Indians and partly from the natives of Brazil. I have lately been in Para to inquire into certain methods by which my trade can be improved.'

'And your trade is—?' I said, looking at her with amusement and some surprise.

'I am a beautifier,' she said, lightly. She looked at me with a smile. 'You don't want me yet, Mr Druce, but the time may come when even you will wish to keep back the infirmities of years. In the meantime can you guess my age?'

'I will not hazard a guess,' I answered.

'And I will not tell you. Let it remain a secret. Meanwhile, understand that my calling is quite an open one, and I do hold secrets. I should advise you, Mr Druce, even in your professional capacity, not to interfere with them.'

The childlike expression faded from her face as she uttered the last words. There seemed to ring a sort of challenge in her tone. She turned away after a few moments and I rejoined my friends.

'You have been making acquaintance with Madame Sara, Mr Druce,' said Mrs Selby. 'Don't you think she is lovely?'

'She is one of the most beautiful women I have ever seen,' I answered, 'but there seems to be a mystery about her.'

'Oh, indeed there is,' said Edith Dallas, gravely.

'She asked me if I could guess her age,' I continued. 'I did not try, but surely she cannot be more than five-and-twenty.'

'No one knows her age,' said Mrs Selby, 'but I will tell you a curious fact, which, perhaps, you will not believe. She was bridesmaid at my mother's wedding thirty years ago. She declares that she never changes, and has no fear of old age.'

'You mean that seriously?' I cried. 'But surely it is impossible?'

'Her name is on the register, and my mother knew her well. She was mysterious then, and I think my mother got into her power, but of that I am not certain. Anyhow, Edith and I adore her, don't we, Edie?'

She laid her hand affectionately on her sister's arm. Edith Dallas did not speak, but her face was careworn. After a time she said slowly:

'Madame Sara is uncanny and terrible.'

There is, perhaps, no business imaginable—not even a lawyer's—that engenders suspicions more than mine. I hate all mysteries—both in persons and things. Mysteries are my natural enemies; I felt now that this woman was a distinct mystery. That she was interested in me I did not doubt, perhaps because she was afraid of me.

The rest of the voyage passed pleasantly enough. The more I saw of Mrs Selby and her sister the more I liked them. They were quiet, simple, and straightforward. I felt sure that they were both as good as gold.

We parted at Waterloo, Jack and his wife and her sister going to Jack's house in Eaton Square, and I returning to my quarters in St John's Wood. I had a house there, with a long garden, at the bottom of which was my laboratory, the laboratory that was the pride of my life, it being, I fondly considered, the best private laboratory in London. There I spent all my spare time making experiments and trying this chemical combination and the other, living in hopes of doing great things some day, for Werner's Agency was not to be the end of my career. Nevertheless, it interested me thoroughly, and I was not sorry to get back to my commercial conundrums.

The next day, just before I started to go to my place of business, Jack Selby was announced.

'I want you to help me,' he said. 'I have been already trying in a sort of general way to get information about my brother-in-law, but all in vain. There is no such person in any of the directories. Can you put me on the road to discovery?'

I said I could and would if he would leave the matter in my hands.

'With pleasure,' he replied. 'You see how we are fixed up. Neither Edith nor Bee can get money with any regularity until the man is found. I cannot imagine why he hides himself.'

'I will insert advertisements in the personal columns of the newspapers,' I said, 'and request anyone who can give information to communicate with me at my office. I will also give instructions to all the branches of my firm, as well as to my head assistants in London, to keep their eyes open for any news. You may be quite certain that in a week or two we shall know all about him.'

Selby appeared cheered at this proposal, and, having begged of me to call upon his wife and her sister as soon as possible, took his leave.

On that very day advertisements were drawn up and sent to several newspapers and inquiry agents; but week after week passed without the slightest result. Selby got very fidgety at the delay. He was never happy except in my presence, and insisted on my coming, whenever I had time, to his house. I was glad to do so, for I took an interest both in him and his belongings, and as to Madame Sara I could not get her out of my head. One day Mrs Selby said to me:

'Have you ever been to see Madame? I know she would like to show you her shop and general surroundings.'

'I did promise to call upon her,' I answered, 'but have not had time to do so yet.'

'Will you come with me tomorrow morning?' asked Edith Dallas, suddenly.

She turned red as she spoke, and the worried, uneasy expression became more marked on her face. I had noticed for some time that she had been looking both nervous and depressed. I had first observed this peculiarity about her on board the *Norham Castle*, but, as time went on, instead of lessening it grew worse. Her face for so young a woman was haggard; she started at each sound, and Madame Sara's name was never spoken in her presence without her evincing almost undue emotion.

'Will you come with me?' she said, with great eagerness.

I immediately promised, and the next day, about eleven o'clock, Edith Dallas and I found ourselves in a hansom driving to Madame Sara's shop. We reached it in a few minutes, and found an unpretentious little place wedged in between a hosier's on one side and a cheap print-seller's on the other. In the windows of the shop were pyramids of perfume bottles, with scintillating facet stoppers tied with coloured ribbons. We stepped out of the hansom and went indoors. Inside the shop were a couple of steps, which led to a door of solid mahogany.

'This is the entrance to her private house,' said Edith, and she pointed to a small brass plate, on which was engraved the name—'Madame Sara, Parfumeuse'.

Edith touched an electric bell and the door was immediately opened by a smartly-dressed page-boy. He looked at Miss Dallas as if he knew her very well, and said:

'Madame is within, and is expecting you, miss.'

He ushered us both into a quiet-looking room, soberly but handsomely furnished. He left us, closing the door. Edith turned to me.

'Do you know where we are?' she asked.

'We are standing at present in a small room just behind Madame Sara's shop,' I answered. 'Why are you so excited, Miss Dallas? What is the matter with you?'

'We are on the threshold of a magician's cave,' she replied. 'We shall soon be face to face with the most marvellous woman in the whole of London. There is no one like her.'

'And you—fear her?' I said, dropping my voice to a whisper.

She started, stepped back, and with great difficulty recovered her composure. At that moment the page-boy returned to conduct us through a series of small waiting-rooms, and we soon found ourselves in the presence of Madame herself.

'Ah!' she said, with a smile. 'This is delightful. You have kept your word, Edith, and I am greatly obliged to you. I will now show Mr Druce some of the mysteries of my trade. But understand, sir,' she added, 'that I shall not tell you any of my real secrets, only as you would like to know something about me you shall.'

'How can you tell I should like to know about you?' I asked.

She gave me an earnest glance which somewhat astonished me, and then she said:

'Knowledge is power; don't refuse what I am willing to give. Edith, you will not object to waiting here while I show Mr Druce through the rooms. First observe this room, Mr Druce. It is lighted only from the roof. When the door shuts it automatically locks itself, so that any intrusion from without is impossible. This is my sanctum sanctorum—a faint odour of perfume pervades the room. This is a hot day, but the room itself is cool. What do you think of it all?'

I made no answer. She walked to the other end and motioned to me to accompany her. There stood a polished oak square table, on which lay an array of extraordinary-looking articles and implements—stoppered bottles full of strange medicaments, mirrors, plane and concave, brushes, sprays, sponges, delicate needle-pointed instruments of bright steel, tiny lancets, and forceps. Facing this table was a chair, like those used by dentists. Above the chair hung electric lights in powerful reflectors, and lenses like bull's-eye lanterns. Another chair, supported on a glass pedestal, was kept there, Madame Sara informed me, for administering static electricity. There were dry-cell batteries for the continuous currents and induction coils for Faradic currents. There were also platinum needles for burning out the roots of hairs.

Madame took me from this room into another, where a still more formidable array of instruments was to be found. Here were a wooden operating table and chloroform and ether apparatus. When I had looked at everything, she turned to me.

'Now you know,' she said. 'I am a doctor—perhaps a quack. These are my secrets. By means of these I live and flourish.'

She turned her back on me and walked into the other room with the light, springy step of youth. Edith Dallas, white as a ghost, was waiting for us.

'You have done your duty, my child,' said Madame. 'Mr Druce has seen just what I want him to see. I am very much obliged to you both. We shall meet tonight at Lady Farringdon's "At Home". Until then, farewell.'

When we got into the street and were driving back again to Eaton Square, I turned to Edith.

'Many things puzzle me about your friend,' I said, 'but perhaps none more than this. By what possible means can a woman who owns to being the possessor of a shop obtain the entrée to some of the best houses in London? Why does Society open her doors to this woman, Miss Dallas?'

'I cannot quite tell you,' was her reply. 'I only know the fact that wherever she goes she is welcomed and treated with consideration, and wherever she fails to appear there is a universally expressed feeling of regret.'

I had also been invited to Lady Farringdon's reception that evening, and I went there in a state of great curiosity. There was no doubt that Madame interested me. I was not sure of her. Beyond doubt there was a mystery attached to her, and also, for some unaccountable reason, she wished both to propitiate and defy me. Why was this?

I arrived early, and was standing in the crush near the head of the staircase when Madame was announced. She wore the richest white satin and quantities of diamonds. I saw her hostess bend towards her and talk eagerly. I noticed Madame's reply and the pleased expression that crossed Lady Farringdon's face. A few minutes later a man with a foreign-looking face and long beard sat down before the grand piano. He played a light prelude and Madame Sara began to sing. Her voice was sweet and low, with an extraordinary pathos in it. It was the sort of voice that penetrates to the heart. There was an instant pause in the gay chatter. She sang amidst perfect silence, and when the song had come to an end there followed a furore of applause. I was just turning to say something to my nearest neighbour when I observed Edith Dallas, who was standing close by. Her eyes met mine; she laid her hand on my sleeve.

'The room is hot,' she said, half panting as she spoke. 'Take me out on the balcony.'

I did so. The atmosphere of the reception-rooms was

almost intolerable, but it was comparatively cool in the open air.

'I must not lose sight of her,' she said, suddenly.

'Of whom?' I asked, somewhat astonished at her words.

'Of Sara.'

'She is there,' I said. 'You can see her from where you stand.'

We happened to be alone. I came a little closer.

'Why are you afraid of her?' I asked.

'Are you sure that we shall not be heard?' was her answer.

'She terrifies me,' were her next words.

'I will not betray your confidence, Miss Dallas. Will you not trust me? You ought to give me a reason for your fears.'

'I cannot—I dare not; I have said far too much already. Don't keep me, Mr Druce. She must not find us together.'

As she spoke she pushed her way through the crowd, and before I could stop her was standing by Madame Sara's side.

The reception in Portland Place was, I remember, on the 26th of July. Two days later the Selbys were to give their final 'At Home' before leaving for the country. I was, of course, invited to be present, and Madame was also there. She had never been dressed more splendidly, nor had she ever before looked younger or more beautiful. Wherever she went all eyes followed her. As a rule her dress was simple, almost like what a girl would wear, but tonight she chose rich Oriental stuffs made of many colours, and absolutely glittering with gems. Her golden hair was studded with diamonds. Round her neck she wore turquoise and diamonds mixed. There were many younger women in the room, but not the youngest nor the fairest had a chance beside Madame. It was not mere beauty of appearance, it was charm—charm which carries all before it.

I saw Miss Dallas, looking slim and tall and pale, standing at a little distance. I made my way to her side. Before I had time to speak she bent towards me.

'Is she not divine?' she whispered. 'She bewilders and delights everyone. She is taking London by storm.'

'Then you are not afraid of her tonight?' I said.

'I fear her more than ever. She has cast a spell over me. But listen, she is going to sing again.'

I had not forgotten the song that Madame had given us at the Farringdons', and stood still to listen. There was a complete hush in the room. Her voice floated over the heads of the assembled guests in a dreamy Spanish song. Edith told me that it was a slumber song, and that Madame boasted of her power of putting almost anyone to sleep who listened to her rendering of it.

'She has many patients who suffer from insomnia,' whispered the girl, 'and she generally cures them with that song, and that alone. Ah! we must not talk; she will hear us.'

Before I could reply Selby came hurrying up. He had not noticed Edith. He caught me by the arm.

'Come just for a minute into this window, Dixon,' he said. 'I must speak to you. I suppose you have no news with regard to my brother-in-law?'

'Not a word,' I answered.

'To tell you the truth, I am getting terribly put out over the matter. We cannot settle any of our money affairs just because this man chooses to lose himself. My wife's lawyers wired to Brazil yesterday, but even his bankers do not know anything about him.'

'The whole thing is a question of time,' was my answer. 'When are you off to Hampshire?'

'On Saturday.'

As Selby said the last words he looked around him, then he dropped his voice.

'I want to say something else. The more I see—' he nodded towards Madame Sara—'the less I like her. Edith is getting into a very strange state. Have you not noticed it? And the worst of it is my wife is also infected. I suppose it is that dodge of the woman's for patching people up and making them beautiful. Doubtless the temptation is overpowering in the case of a plain woman, but Beatrice is beautiful herself and young. What can she have to do with cosmetics and complexion pills?'

'You don't mean to tell me that your wife has consulted Madame Sara as a doctor?'

'Not exactly, but she has gone to her about her teeth. She complained of toothache lately, and Madame's dentistry is renowned. Edith is constantly going to her for one thing or another, but then Edith is infatuated.'

As Jack said the last words he went over to speak to someone else, and before I could leave the seclusion of the window I perceived Edith Dallas and Madame Sara in earnest conversation together. I could not help overhearing the following words:

'Don't come to me tomorrow. Get into the country as soon as you can. It is far and away the best thing to do.'

As Madame spoke she turned swiftly and caught my eye. She bowed, and the peculiar look, the sort of challenge, she had given me before flashed over her face. It made me uncomfortable, and during the night that followed I could not get it out of my head. I remembered what Selby had said with regard to his wife and her money affairs. Beyond doubt he had married into a mystery—a mystery that Madame knew all about. There was a very big money interest, and strange things happen when millions are concerned.

The next morning I had just risen and was sitting at breakfast when a note was handed to me. It came by special messenger, and was marked 'Urgent'. I tore it open. These were its contents:

'My dear Druce, A terrible blow has fallen on us. My sister-in-law, Edith, was taken suddenly ill this morning at breakfast. The nearest doctor was sent for, but he could do nothing, as she died half an hour ago. Do come and see me, and if you know any very clever specialist bring him with you. My wife is utterly stunned by the shock. Yours, Jack Selby.'

I read the note twice before I could realize what it meant. Then I rushed out and, hailing the first hansom I met, said to the man:

'Drive to No. 192, Victoria Street, as quickly as you can.'

Here lived a certain Mr Eric Vandeleur, an old friend of mine and the police surgeon for the Westminster district, which included Eaton Square. No shrewder or sharper fellow existed than Vandeleur, and the present case was essentially in his province, both legally and professionally. He was not at his flat when I arrived, having already gone down to the court. Here I accordingly hurried, and was informed that he was in the mortuary.

For a man who, as it seemed to me, lived in a perpetual atmosphere of crime and violence, of death and coroners' courts, his habitual cheerfulness and brightness of manner were remarkable. Perhaps it was only the reaction from his work, for he had the reputation of being one of the most astute experts of the day in medical jurisprudence, and the most skilled analyst in toxicological cases on the Metropolitan Police staff. Before I could send him word that I wanted to see him I heard a door bang, and Vandeleur came hurrying down the passage, putting on his coat as he rushed along.

'Halloa!' he cried. 'I haven't seen you for ages. Do you want me?'

'Yes, very urgently,' I answered. 'Are you busy?'

'Head over ears, my dear chap. I cannot give you a moment now, but perhaps later on.'

'What is it? You look excited.'

'I have got to go to Eaton Square like the wind, but come along, if you like, and tell me on the way.'

'Capital,' I cried. 'The thing has been reported then? You are going to Mr Selby's, No. 34a; then I am going with you.'

He looked at me in amazement.

'But the case has only just been reported. What can you possibly know about it?'

'Everything. Let us take this hansom, and I will tell you as we go along.'

As we drove to Eaton Square I quickly explained the situation, glancing now and then at Vandeleur's bright, clean-shaven face. He was no longer Eric Vandeleur, the man with the latest club story and the merry twinkle in his blue eyes: he was Vandeleur the medical jurist, with a face like a mask, his lower jaw slightly protruding and features very fixed.

'The thing promises to be serious,' he replied, as I finished, 'but I can do nothing until after the autopsy. Here we are, and there is my man waiting for me; he has been smart.'

On the steps stood an official-looking man in uniform, who saluted.

'Coroner's officer,' explained Vandeleur.

We entered the silent, darkened house. Selby was standing in the hall. He came to meet us. I introduced him to Vandeleur, and he at once led us into the dining-room, where we found Dr Osborne, whom Selby had called in when the alarm of Edith's illness had been first given. Dr Osborne was a pale, under-sized, very young man. His face expressed considerable alarm. Vandeleur, however, managed to put him completely at his ease.

'I will have a chat with you in a few minutes, Dr Osborne,' he said; 'but first I must get Mr Selby's report. Will you please tell me, sir, exactly what occurred?'

'Certainly,' he answered. 'We had a reception here last night, and my sister-in-law did not go to bed until early morning; she was in bad spirits, but otherwise in her usual health. My wife went into her room after she was in bed, and told me later on that she had found Edith in hysterics, and could not get her to explain anything. We both talked about taking her to the country without delay. Indeed, our intention was to get off this afternoon.'

'Well?' said Vandeleur.

'We had breakfast about half-past nine, and Miss Dallas came down, looking quite in her usual health, and in apparently good spirits. She ate with appetite, and, as it happened, she and my wife were both helped from the same dish. The meal had nearly come to an end when she jumped up from the table, uttered a sharp cry, turned very pale, pressed her hand to her side, and ran out of the room. My wife immediately followed her. She came back again in a minute or two, and said that Edith was in violent pain, and begged of me to send for a doctor. Dr Osborne lives just round the corner. He came at once, but she died almost immediately after his arrival.'

'You were in the room?' asked Vandeleur, turning to Osborne.

'Yes,' he replied. 'She was conscious to the last moment, and died suddenly.'

'Did she tell you anything?'

'No, except to assure me that she had not eaten any food that day until she had come down to breakfast. After the death occurred I sent immediately to report the case, locked the door of the room where the poor girl's body is, and saw also that nobody touched anything on this table.'

Vandeleur rang the bell and a servant appeared. He

gave quick orders. The entire remains of the meal were collected and taken charge of, and then he and the coroner's officer went upstairs.

When we were alone Selby sank into a chair. His face was quite drawn and haggard.

'It is the horrible suddenness of the thing which is so appalling,' he cried. 'As to Beatrice, I don't believe she will ever be the same again. She was deeply attached to Edith. Edith was nearly ten years her senior, and always acted the part of mother to her. This is a sad beginning to our life. I can scarcely think collectedly.'

I remained with him a little longer, and then, as Vandeleur did not return, went back to my own house. There I could settle to nothing, and when Vandeleur rang me up on the telephone about six o'clock I hurried off to his rooms. As soon as I arrived I saw that Selby was with him, and the expression on both their faces told me the truth.

'This is a bad business,' said Vandeleur. 'Miss Dallas has died from swallowing poison. An exhaustive analysis and examination have been made, and a powerful poison, unknown to European toxicologists, has been found. This is strange enough, but how it has been administered is a puzzle. I confess, at the present moment, we are all nonplussed. It certainly was not in the remains of the breakfast, and we have her dying evidence that she took nothing else. Now, a poison with such appalling potency would take effect quickly. It is evident that she was quite well when she came to breakfast, and that the poison began to work towards the close of the meal. But how did she get it? This question, however, I shall deal with later on. The more immediate point is this. The situation is a serious one in view of the monetary issues and the value of the lady's life. From the aspects of the case, her undoubted sanity and her affection for her sister, we may almost exclude the idea of suicide. We must, therefore, call it murder. This harmless, innocent lady is struck down by the hand of an assassin, and with such devilish cunning that no trace or clue is left behind. For such an act there must have been some very powerful motive, and the person who designed and executed it must be a criminal of the highest order of scientific ability. Mr Selby has been telling me the exact financial position of the poor lady, and also of his own young wife. The absolute disappearance of the step-brother, in view of his previous character, is in the highest degree strange. Knowing, as we do, that between him and two million sterling there stood two lives—*one is taken!*'

A deadly sensation of cold seized me as Vandeleur uttered these last words. I glanced at Selby. His face was colourless and the pupils of his eyes were contracted, as though he saw something which terrified him.

'What happened once may happen again,' continued Vandeleur. 'We are in the presence of a great mystery, and I counsel you, Mr Selby, to guard your wife with the utmost care.'

These words, falling from a man of Vandeleur's position and authority on such matters, were sufficiently shocking for me to hear, but for Selby to be given such a solemn warning about his young and beautiful and newly-married wife, who was all the world to him, was terrible indeed. He leant his head on his hands.

'Mercy on us!' he muttered. 'Is this a civilized country when death can walk abroad like this, invisible, not to be avoided? Tell me, Mr Vandeleur, what I must do.'

'You must be guided by me,' said Vandeleur, 'and, believe me, there is no witchcraft in the world. I shall place a detective in your household immediately. Don't be alarmed; he will come to you in plain clothes and will simply act as a servant. Nevertheless, nothing can be done to your wife without his knowledge. As to you, Druce,' he continued, turning to me, 'the police are doing all they can to find this man Silva, and I ask you to help them with your big agency, and to begin at once. Leave your friend to me. Wire instantly if you hear news.'

'You may rely on me,' I said, and a moment later I had left the room.

As I walked rapidly down the street the thought of Madame Sara, her shop and its mysterious background, its surgical instruments, its operating-table, its induction coils, came back to me. And yet what could Madame Sara have to do with the present strange, inexplicable mystery?

The thought had scarcely crossed my mind before I heard a clatter alongside the kerb, and turning round I saw a smart open carriage, drawn by a pair of horses, standing there. I also heard my own name. I turned. Bending out of the carriage was Madame Sara.

'I saw you going by, Mr Druce. I have only just heard the news about poor Edith Dallas. I am terribly shocked and upset. I have been to the house, but they would not admit me. Have you heard what was the cause of her death?'

Madame's blue eyes filled with tears as she spoke.

'I am not at liberty to disclose what I have heard, Madame,' I answered, 'since I am officially connected with the affair.'

Her eyes narrowed. The brimming tears dried as though by magic. Her glance became scornful.

'Thank you,' she answered, 'your reply tells me that she did not die naturally. How very appalling! But I must not keep you. Can I drive you anywhere?'

'No, thank you.'

'Goodbye, then.'

She made a sign to the coachman, and as the carriage rolled away turned to look at me. Her face wore the defiant expression I had seen there more than once. Could she be connected with the affair? The thought came upon me with a violence that seemed almost conviction. Yet I had no reason for it—none.

To find Henry Joachim Silva was now my principal thought. My staff had instructions to make every possible inquiry, with large money rewards as incitements. The collateral branches of other agencies throughout Brazil were communicated with by cable, and all the Scotland Yard channels were used. Still there was no result. The newspapers took up the case; there were paragraphs in most of them with regard to the missing step-brother and the mysterious death of Edith Dallas. Then someone got hold of the story of the will, and this was retailed with many additions for the benefit of the public. At the inquest the jury returned the following verdict:

'We find that Miss Edith Dallas died from taking poison of unknown name, but by whom or how administered there is no evidence to say.'

This unsatisfactory state of things was destined to change quite suddenly. On the 6th of August, as I was seated in my office, a note was brought me by a private messenger. It was as follows:

'Norfolk Hotel, Strand.

'Dear Sir—I have just arrived in London from Brazil, and have seen your advertisements. I was about to insert one myself in order to find the whereabouts of my sisters. I am a great invalid and unable to leave my room. Can you come to see me at the earliest possible moment? Yours, Henry Joachim Silva.'

In uncontrollable excitement I hastily dispatched two telegrams, one to Selby and the other to Vandeleur, begging of them to be with me, without fail, as soon as possible. So the man had never been in England at all. The situation was more bewildering than ever. One thing, at least, was probable—Edith Dallas's death was not due to her stepbrother. Soon after half-past six Selby arrived, and Vandeleur walked in ten minutes later. I told them what had occurred and showed them the letter. In half an hour's time we reached the hotel, and on stating who I was we were shown into a room on the first floor by Silva's private servant. Resting in an armchair, as we entered, sat a man; his face was terribly thin. The eyes and cheeks were so sunken that the face had almost the appearance of a skull. He made no effort to rise when we entered, and glanced from one of us to the other with the utmost astonishment. I at once introduced myself and explained who we were. He then waved his hand for his man to retire.

'You have heard the news, of course, Mr Silva?' I said.

'News! What?' He glanced up to me and seemed to read something in my face. He started back in his chair.

'Good heavens,' he replied. 'Do you allude to my sisters? Tell me, quickly, are they alive?'

'Your elder sister died on the 29th of July, and there is every reason to believe that her death was caused by foul play.'

As I uttered these words the change that passed over his face was fearful to witness. He did not speak, but remained motionless. His claw-like hands clutched the arms of the chair, his eyes were fixed and staring, as though they would start from their hollow sockets, the colour of his skin was like clay. I heard Selby breathe quickly behind me, and Vandeleur stepped towards the man and laid his hand on his shoulder.

'Tell us what you know of this matter,' he said sharply.

Recovering himself with an effort, the invalid began in a tremulous voice:

'Listen closely, for you must act quickly. I am indirectly responsible for this fearful thing. My life has been a wild and wasted one, and now I am dying. The doctors tell me I cannot live a month, for I have a large aneurism of the heart. Eighteen months ago I was in Rio. I was living fast and gambled heavily. Among my fellow-gamblers was a man much older than myself. His name was José Aranjo. He was, if anything, a greater gambler than I. One night we played alone. The stakes ran high until they reached a big figure. By daylight I had lost to him nearly £200,000. Though I am a rich man in point of income under my uncle's will, I could not pay a twentieth part of that sum. This man knew my financial position, and, in addition to a sum of £5,000 paid down, I gave him a document. I must have been mad to do so. The document was this—it was duly witnessed and attested by a lawyer— that, in the event of my surviving my two sisters and thus inheriting the whole of my uncle's vast wealth, half a million should go to José Aranjo. I felt I was breaking up at the time, and the chances of my inheriting the money were small. Immediately after the completion of the document this man left Rio, and I then heard a great deal about him that I had not previously known. He was a man of the queerest antecedents, partly Indian, partly Italian. He had spent many years of his life amongst the Indians. I heard also that he was as cruel as he was clever, and possessed some wonderful secrets of poisoning unknown to the West. I thought a great deal about this, for I knew that by signing that document I had placed the lives of my two sisters between him and a fortune. I came to Para six weeks ago, only to learn that one of my sisters was married and that both had gone to England. Ill as I was, I determined to follow them in order to warn them. I also wanted to arrange matters with you, Mr Selby.'

'One moment, sir,' I broke in, suddenly. 'Do you happen to be aware if this man, José Aranjo, knew a woman calling herself Madame Sara?'

'Knew her?' cried Silva. 'Very well indeed, and so, for that matter, did I. Aranjo and Madame Sara were the best friends, and constantly met. She called herself a professional beautifier—was very handsome, and had secrets for the pursuing of her trade unknown even to Aranjo.'

'Good heavens!' I cried, 'and the woman is now in London. She returned here with Mrs Selby and Miss Dallas. Edith was very much influenced by her, and was constantly with her. There is no doubt in my mind that she is guilty. I have suspected her for some time, but I could not find a motive. Now the motive appears. You surely can have her arrested?'

Vandeleur made no reply. He gave me a strange look, then he turned to Selby.

'Has your wife also consulted Madame Sara?' he asked, sharply.

'Yes, she went to her once about her teeth, but has not been to the shop since Edith's death. I begged of her not to see the woman, and she promised me faithfully she would not do so.'

'Has she any medicines or lotions given to her by Madame Sara—does she follow any line of treatment advised by her?'

'No, I am certain on that point.'

'Very well. I will see your wife tonight in order to ask her some questions. You must both leave town at once. Go to your country house and settle there. I am quite serious when I say that Mrs Selby is in the utmost possible danger until after the death of her brother. We must leave you now, Mr Silva. All business affairs must wait for the present. It is absolutely necessary that Mrs Selby should leave London at once. Good night, sir. I shall give myself the pleasure of calling on you tomorrow morning.'

We took leave of the sick man. As soon as we got into the street Vandeleur stopped.

'I must leave it to you, Selby,' he said, 'to judge how much of this matter you tell to your wife. Were I you I would explain everything. The time for immediate action has arrived, and she is a brave and sensible woman. From this moment you must watch all the foods and liquids that she takes. She must never be out of your sight or out of the sight of some other trustworthy companion.'

'I shall, of course, watch my wife myself,' said Selby. 'But the thing is enough to drive one mad.'

'I will go with you to the country, Selby,' I said, suddenly.

'Ah!' cried Vandeleur, 'that is the best thing possible, and what I wanted to propose. Go, all of you, by an early train tomorrow.'

'Then I will be off home at once, to make arrangements,' I said. 'I will meet you, Selby, at Waterloo for the first train to Cronsmoor tomorrow.'

As I was turning away Vandeleur caught my arm.

'I am glad you are going with them,' he said. 'I shall write to you tonight re instructions. Never be without a loaded revolver. Good night.'

By 6.15 the next morning Selby, his wife, and I were in a reserved, locked, first-class compartment, speeding rapidly west. The servants and Mrs Selby's own special maid were in a separate carriage. Selby's face showed signs of a sleepless night, and presented a striking contrast to the fair, fresh face of the girl round whom this strange battle raged. Her husband had told her everything, and, though still suffering terribly from the shock and grief of her sister's death, her face was calm and full of repose.

A carriage was waiting for us at Cronsmoor, and by half-past nine we arrived at the old home of the Selbys, nestling amid its oaks and elms. Everything was done to make the home-coming of the bride as cheerful as circumstances would permit, but a gloom, impossible to lift, overshadowed

Selby himself. He could scarcely rouse himself to take the slightest interest in anything.

The following morning I received a letter from Vandeleur. It was very short, and once more impressed on me the necessity of caution. He said that two eminent physicians had examined Silva, and the verdict was that he could not live a month. Until his death precautions must be strictly observed.

The day was cloudless, and after breakfast I was just starting out for a stroll when the butler brought me a telegram. I tore it open; it was from Vandeleur.

'Prohibit all food until I arrive. Am coming down,' were the words. I hurried into the study and gave it to Selby. He read it and looked up at me.

'Find out the first train and go and meet him, old chap,' he said. 'Let us hope that this means an end of the hideous affair.'

I went into the hall and looked up the trains. The next arrived at Cronsmoor at 10.45. I then strolled round to the stables and ordered a carriage, after which I walked up and down on the drive. There was no doubt that something strange had happened. Vandeleur coming down so suddenly must mean a final clearing up of the mystery. I had just turned round at the lodge gates to wait for the carriage when the sound of wheels and of horses galloping struck on my ears. The gates were swung open, and Vandeleur in an open fly dashed through them. Before I could recover from my surprise he was out of the vehicle and at my side. He carried a small black bag in his hand.

'I came down by special train,' he said, speaking quickly. 'There is not a moment to lose. Come at once. Is Mrs Selby all right?'

'What do you mean?' I replied. 'Of course she is. Do you suppose that she is in danger?'

'Deadly,' was his answer. 'Come.'

We dashed up to the house together. Selby, who had heard our steps, came to meet us.

'Mr Vandeleur,' he cried. 'What is it? How did you come?'

'By special train, Mr Selby. And I want to see your wife at once. It will be necessary to perform a very trifling operation.'

'Operation!' he exclaimed.

'Yes; at once.'

We made our way through the hall and into the morning-room, where Mrs Selby was busily engaged reading and answering letters. She started up when she saw Vandeleur and uttered an exclamation of surprise.

'What has happened?' she asked.

Vandeleur went up to her and took her hand.

'Do not be alarmed,' he said, 'for I have come to put all your fears to rest. Now, please, listen to me. When you visited Madame Sara with your sister, did you go for medical advice?'

The colour rushed into her face.

'One of my teeth ached,' she answered. 'I went to her about that. She is, as I suppose you know, a most wonderful dentist. She examined the tooth, found that it required stopping, and got an assistant, a Brazilian, I think, to do it.'

'And your tooth has been comfortable ever since?'

'Yes, quite. She had one of Edith's stopped at the same time.'

'Will you kindly sit down and show me which was the tooth into which the stopping was put?'

She did so.

'This was the one,' she said, pointing with her finger to one in the lower jaw. 'What do you mean? Is there anything wrong?'

Vandeleur examined the tooth long and carefully. There

was a sudden rapid movement of his hand, and a sharp cry from Mrs Selby. With the deftness of long practice, and a powerful wrist, he had extracted the tooth with one wrench. The suddenness of the whole thing, startling as it was, was not so strange as his next movement.

'Send Mrs Selby's maid to her,' he said, turning to her husband; 'then come, both of you, into the next room.'

The maid was summoned. Poor Mrs Selby had sunk back in her chair, terrified and half fainting. A moment later Selby joined us in the dining-room.

'That's right,' said Vandeleur; 'close the door, will you?'

He opened his black bag and brought out several instruments. With one he removed the stopping from the tooth. It was quite soft and came away easily. Then from the bag he produced a small guinea-pig, which he requested me to hold. He pressed the sharp instrument into the tooth, and opening the mouth of the little animal placed the point on the tongue. The effect was instantaneous. The little head fell on to one of my hands—the guinea-pig was dead. Vandeleur was white as a sheet. He hurried up to Selby and wrung his hand.

'Thank heaven!' he said, 'I've been in time, but only just. Your wife is safe. This stopping would hardly have held another hour. I have been thinking all night over the mystery of your sister-in-law's death, and over every minute detail of evidence as to how the poison could have been administered. Suddenly the coincidence of both sisters having had their teeth stopped struck me as remarkable. Like a flash the solution came to me. The more I considered it the more I felt that I was right; but by what fiendish cunning such a scheme could have been conceived and executed is still beyond my power to explain. The poison is very like hyoscine, one of the worst toxic-alkaloids known, so violent in its deadly proportions that the amount that would go into a tooth would cause almost instant death. It has been kept in by a gutta-percha stopping, certain to come out within a month, probably earlier, and most probably during mastication of food. The person would die either immediately or after a very few minutes, and no one would connect a visit to the dentist with a death a month afterwards.'

What followed can be told in a very few words. Madame Sara was arrested on suspicion. She appeared before the magistrate, looking innocent and beautiful, and managed during her evidence completely to baffle that acute individual. She denied nothing, but declared that the poison must have been put into the tooth by one of the two Brazilians whom she had lately engaged to help her with her dentistry. She had her suspicions with regard to these men soon afterwards, and had dismissed them. She believed that they were in the pay of José Aranjo, but she could not tell anything for certain. Thus Madame escaped conviction. I was certain that she was guilty, but there was not a shadow of real proof. A month later Silva died, and Selby is now a double millionaire.

VII

The Submarine Boat

Clifford Ashdown

Tric-trac! tric-trac! went the black and white discs as the
players moved them over the backgammon board in
expressive justification of the French term for the game.
Tric-trac! They are indeed a nation of poets, reflected Mr
Pringle. Was not Teuf-teuf! for the motor-car a veritable
inspiration? And as he smoked, the not unmusical clatter
of the enormous wooden discs filled the atmosphere.

In these days of cookery not entirely based upon air-
tights—to use the expressive Americanism for tinned
meats—it is no longer necessary for the man who wishes
to dine, as distinguished from the mere feeding animal, to
furtively seek some restaurant in remote Soho, jealously
guarding its secret from his fellows. But Mr Pringle, in his
favourite study of human nature, was an occasional visitor
to the 'Poissonière' in Gerrard Street, and, the better to
pursue his researches, had always denied familiarity with
the foreign tongues he heard around him. The restaurant
was distinctly close—indeed, some might have called it
stuffy—and Pringle, though near a ventilator, thoughtfully
provided by the management, was fast being lulled into
drowsiness, when a man who had taken his seat with a
companion at the next table leaned across the intervening
gulf and addressed him.

'Nous ne vous dérangeons pas, monsieur?'

Pringle, with a smile of fatuous uncomprehending, bowed, but said never a word.

'Cochon d'Anglais, n'entendez-vous pas?'

'I'm afraid I do not understand,' returned Pringle, shaking his head hopelessly, but still smiling.

'Canaille! Faut-il que je vous tire le nez?' persisted the Frenchman, as, apparently still sceptical of Pringle's assurance, he added threats to abuse.

'I have known the English gentleman a long time, and without a doubt he does not understand French,' testified the waiter who had now come forward for orders. Satisfied by this corroboration of Pringle's innocence, the Frenchman bowed and smiled sweetly to him, and, ordering a bottle of Clos de Vougeot, commenced an earnest conversation with his neighbour.

By the time this little incident had closed, Pringle's drowsiness had given place to an intense feeling of curiosity. For what purpose could the Frenchman have been so insistent in disbelieving his expressed ignorance of the language? Why, too, had he striven to make Pringle betray himself by resenting the insults showered upon him? In a Parisian restaurant, as he knew, far more trivial affronts had ended in meetings in the Bois de Boulogne. Besides, cochon was an actionable term of opprobrium in France. The Frenchman and his companion had seated themselves at the only vacant table, also it was in a corner; Pringle, at the next, was the single person within ear-shot, and the Frenchman's extraordinary behaviour could only be due to a consuming thirst for privacy. Settling himself in an easy position, Pringle closed his eyes, and while appearing to resume his slumber, strained every nerve to discern the lightest word that passed at the next table. Dressed in the choicest mode of Piccadilly, the Frenchman bore himself with all the intolerable self-consciousness of the Boulevardier; but there was no trace of good-natured levity in the dark aquiline features, and the evil glint of the eyes recalled visions of an operatic Mephistopheles. His guest was unmistakably an Englishman of the bank-clerk type, who contributed his share of the conversation in halting Anglo-French, punctuated by nervous laughter as, with agonising pains, he dredged his memory for elusive colloquialisms.

Freely translated, this was what Pringle heard:

'So your people have really decided to take up the submarine, after all?'

'Yes; I am working out the details of some drawings in small-scale.'

'But are they from headquarters?'

'Certainly! Duly initialled and passed by the chief constructor.'

'And you are making——'

'Full working drawings.'

'There will be no code or other secret about them?'

'What I am doing can be understood by any naval architect.'

'Ah, an English one!'

'The measurements of course, are English, but they are easily convertible.'

'You could do that?'

'Too dangerous! Suppose a copy in metric scale were found in my possession! Besides, any draughtsman could reduce them in an hour or two.'

'And when can you let me have it?'

'In about two weeks.'

'Impossible! I shall not be here.'

'Unless something happens to let me get on with it quickly, I don't see how I can do it even then. I am never sufficiently free from interruption to take tracings; there are far too many eyes upon me. The only chance I have is to spoil the thing as soon as I have the salient points worked out on it, and after I have pretended to destroy it, smuggle it home; then I shall have to take elaborate notes every day and work out the details from them in the evening. It is simply impossible for me to attempt to take a finished drawing out of the yard, and, as it is, I don't quite see my way to getting the spoilt one out—they look so sharply after spoilt drawings.'

'Two weeks you say, then?'

'Yes; and I shall have to sit up most nights copying the day's work from my notes to do it.'

'Listen! In a week I must attend at the Ministry of Marine in Paris, but our military attaché is my friend. I can trust him; he shall come down to you.'

'What, at Chatham? Do you wish to ruin me?' A smile from the Frenchman. 'No; it must be in London, where no one knows me.'

'Admirable! My friend will be better able to meet you.'

'Very well, as soon as I am ready I will telegraph to you.'

'Might not the address of the embassy be remarked by the telegraph officials? Your English post-office is charmingly unsuspicious, but we must not risk anything.'

'Ah, perhaps so. Well, I will come up to London and telegraph to you from here. But your representative— will he be prepared for it?'

'I will warn him to expect it in fourteen days.' He made an entry in his pocket-book. 'How will you sign the message?'

'Gustave Zédé,' suggested the Englishman, sniggering for the first and only time.

'Too suggestive. Sign yourself "Pauline", and simply add the time.'

'"Pauline", then. Where shall the rendezvous be?'

'The most public place we can find.'

'Public?'

'Certainly. Some place where everyone will be too much occupied with his own affairs to notice you. What say you to your Nelson's column? There you can wait in a way we shall agree upon.'

'It would be a difficult thing for me to wear a disguise.'

'All disguises are clumsy unless one is an expert. Listen! You shall be gazing at the statue with one hand in your breast—so.'

'Yes; and I might hold a "Baedeker" in my other hand.'

'Admirable, my friend! You have the true spirit of an artist,' sneered the Frenchman.

'Your representative will advance and say to me, "Pauline", and the exchange can be made without another word.'

'Exchange?'

'I presume your Government is prepared to pay me handsomely for the very heavy risks I am running in this matter,' said the Englishman stiffly.

'Pardon, my friend! How imbecile of me! I am authorised to offer you ten thousand francs.'

A pause, during which the Englishman made a calculation on the back of an envelope.

'That is four hundred pounds,' he remarked, tearing the envelope into carefully minute fragments. 'Far too little for such a risk.'

'Permit me to remind you, my friend, that you came in search of me, or rather of those I represent. You have something to sell? Good! But it is customary for the merchant to display his wares first.'

'I pledge myself to give you copies of the working drawings made for the use of the artificers themselves. I have already met you oftener than is prudent. As I say, you offer too little.'

'Should the drawings prove useless to us, we should, of course, return them to your Admiralty, explaining how they came into our possession.' There was an unpleasant smile beneath the Frenchman's waxed moustache as he spoke. 'What sum do you ask?'

'Five hundred pounds in small notes—say, five pounds each.'

'That is—what do you say? Ah, twelve thousand five hundred francs! Impossible! My limit is twelve thousand.'

To this the Englishman at length gave an ungracious consent, and after some adroit compliments beneath which the other sought to bury his implied threat, the pair rose from the table. Either by accident or design, the Frenchman stumbled over the feet of Pringle, who, with his long legs stretching out from under the table, his head bowed and his lips parted, appeared in a profound slumber. Opening his eyes slowly, he feigned a lifelike yawn, stretched his arms, and gazed lazily around, to the entire satisfaction of the Frenchman, who, in the act of parting with his companion, was watching him from the door.

Calling for some coffee, Pringle lighted a cigarette, and reflected with a glow of indignant patriotism upon the sordid transaction he had become privy to. It is seldom that public servants are in this country found ready to betray their trust—with all honour be it recorded of them! But there ever exists the possibility of some under-paid official succumbing to the temptation at the command of the less scrupulous representatives of foreign powers, whose actions in this respect are always ignored officially by their superiors. To Pringle's somewhat cynical imagination, the sordid huckstering of a dockyard draughtsman with a French naval attaché appealed as corroboration of Walpole's famous principle, and as he walked homewards to Furnival's Inn, he determined, if possible, to turn his discovery to the mutual advantage of his country and himself—especially the latter.

During the next few days Pringle elaborated a plan of

taking up a residence at Chatham, only to reject it as he had done many previous ones. Indeed, so many difficulties presented themselves to every single course of action, that the tenth day after found him strolling down Bond Street in the morning without having taken any further step in the matter. With his characteristic fastidious neatness in personal matters, he was bound for the Piccadilly establishment of the chief and, for West-Enders, the only firm of hatters in London.

'Breton Stret, do you noh?' said a voice suddenly. And Pringle, turning, found himself accosted by a swarthy foreigner.

'Bruton Street, n'est-ce pas?' Pringle suggested.

'Mais oui, Brrruten Stret, monsieur!' was the reply in faint echo of the English syllables.

'Le voila! à droite,' was Pringle's glib direction. Politely raising his hat in response to the other's salute, he was about to resume his walk when he noticed that the Frenchman had been joined by a companion, who appeared to have been making similar inquiries. The latter started and uttered a slight exclamation on meeting Pringle's eye. The recognition was mutual—it was the French attaché! As he hurried down Bond Street, Pringle realised with acutest annoyance that his deception at the restaurant had been unavailing, while he must now abandon all hope of a counter-plot for the honour of his country, to say nothing of his own profit. The port-wine mark on his right cheek was far too conspicuous for the attaché not to recognise him by it, and he regretted his neglect to remove it as soon as he had decided to follow up the affair. Forgetful of all beside, he walked on into Piccadilly, and it was not until he found himself more than half-way back to his chambers that he remembered the purpose for which he had set out; but matters of greater moment now claimed his attention, and he endeavoured by the brisk exercise to work off some of the chagrin with which he was consumed. Only as he reached the Inn and turned into the gateway did it occur to him that he had been culpably careless in thus going straight homeward. What if he had been followed? Never in his life had he shown such disregard of ordinary precautions. Glancing back, he just caught a glimpse of a figure which seemed to whip behind the corner of the gateway. He retraced his steps and looked out into Holborn. There, in the very act of retreat, and still but a few feet from the gate, was the attaché himself. Cursing the persistence of his own folly, Pringle dived through the arch again, and determined that the Frenchman should discover no more that day he turned nimbly to the left and ran up his own stairway before the pursuer could have time to re-enter the Inn.

The most galling reflection was his absolute impotence in the matter. Through lack of the most elementary foresight he had been fairly run to earth, and could see no way of ridding himself of this unwelcome attention. To transfer his domicile, to tear himself up by the roots as it were, was out of the question; and as he glanced around him, from the soft carpets and luxurious chairs to the warm, distempered walls with their old prints above the dado of dwarf bookcases, he felt that the pang of severance from the refined associations of his chambers would be too acute. Besides, he would inevitably be tracked elsewhere. He would gain nothing by the transfer. One thing at least was absolutely certain—the trouble which the Frenchman was taking to watch him showed the importance he attached to Pringle's discovery. But this again only increased his disgust with the ill-luck which had met him at the very outset. After all, he had done nothing illegal, however contrary it might be to the code of ethics, so that if it pleased them the entire French legation might continue to watch him till the Day of Judgment, and, consoling himself with this reflection, he philosophically dismissed the matter from his mind.

It was nearing six when he again left the Inn for Pagani's, the Great Portland Street restaurant which he much affected; instead of proceeding due west, he crossed Holborn intending to bear round by way of the Strand and Regent Street, and so get up an appetite. In Staple Inn he paused a moment in the further archway. The little square, always reposeful amid the stress and turmoil of its environment, seemed doubly so this evening, its eighteenth-century calm so welcome after the raucous thoroughfare. An approaching footfall echoed noisily, and as Pringle moved from the shadow of the narrow wall the newcomer hesitated and stopped, and then made the circuit of the square, scanning the doorways as if in search of a name. The action was not unnatural, and twenty-four hours earlier Pringle would have thought nothing of it, but after the events of the morning he endowed it with a personal interest, and, walking on, he ascended the steps into Southampton Buildings and stopped by a hoarding. As he looked back he was rewarded by the sight of a man stealthily emerging from the archway and making his way up the steps, only to halt as he suddenly came abreast of Pringle. Although his face was unfamiliar, Pringle could only conclude that the man was following him, and all doubt was removed when, having walked along the street and turning about at the entrance to Chancery Lane, he saw the spy had resumed the chase and was now but a few yards back. Pringle, as a philosopher, felt more inclined to laughter than resentment at this ludicrous espionage. In a spirit of mischief, he pursued his way to the Strand at a tortoise-like crawl, halting as if doubtful of his way at every corner, and staring into every shop whose lights still invited customers. Once or twice he even doubled back, and passing quite close to the man, had several opportunities of examining him. He was

quite unobtrusive, even respectable-looking; there was
nothing of the foreigner about him, and Pringle shrewdly
conjectured that the attaché, wearied of sentry-go had
turned it over to some English servant on whom he could
rely.

Thus shepherded, Pringle arrived at the restaurant,
from which he only emerged after a stay maliciously prolonged over each item of the menu, followed by the smoking
of no fewer than three cigars of a brand specially lauded
by the proprietor. With a measure of humanity diluting
his malice, he was about to offer the infallibly exhausted
sentinel some refreshment when he came out, but as the
man was invisible, Pringle started for home, taking much
the same route as before, and calmly debating whether or
no the cigars he had just sampled would be a wise investment; nor until he had reached Southampton Buildings
and the sight of the hoarding recalled the spy's discomfiture, did he think of looking back to see if he were still
followed. All but the main thoroughfares were by this time
deserted, and although he shot a keen glance up and down
Chancery Lane, now clear of all but the most casual traffic,
not a soul was anywhere near him. By a curious psycho-
logical process Pringle felt inclined to resent the man's
absence. He had begun to regard him almost in the light
of a body-guard, the private escort of some eminent
politician. Besides, the whole incident was pregnant with
possibilities appealing to his keenly intellectual sense of
humour, and as he passed the hoarding, he peered into its
shadow with the half-admitted hope that his attendant
might be lurking in the depths. Later on he recalled how,
as he glanced upwards, a man's figure passed like a shadow
from a ladder to an upper platform of the scaffold. The
vision, fleeting and unsubstantial, had gone almost before
his retina had received it, but the momentary halt was to
prove his salvation. Even as he turned to walk on, a cataract

of planks, amid scaffold-poles and a chaos of loose bricks, crashed on the spot he was about to traverse; a stray beam, more erratic in its descent, caught his hat, and, telescoping it, glanced off his shoulder, bearing him to the ground, where he lay dazed by the sudden uproar and half-choked by the cloud of dust. Rapid and disconcerting as was the event, he remembered afterwards a dim and spectral shape approaching through the gloom. In a dreamy kind of way he connected it with that other shadow-figure he had seen high up on the scaffold, and as it bent over him he recognized the now familiar features of the spy. But other figures replaced the first, and, when helped to his feet, he made futile search for it amid the circle of faces gathered round him. He judged it an hallucination. By the time he had undergone a tentative dust-down, he was sufficiently collected to acknowledge the sympathetic congratulations of the crowd and to decline the homeward escort of a constable.

In the privacy of his chambers, his ideas began to clarify. Events arranged themselves in logical sequence, and the spectres assumed more tangible form. A single question dwarfed all others. He asked himself, 'Was the cataclysm such an accident as it appeared?' And as he surveyed the battered ruins of his hat, he began to realise how nearly had he been the victim of a murderous vendetta!

When he arose the next morning, he scarcely needed the dilapidated hat to remind him of the events of yesterday. Normally a sound and dreamless sleeper, his rest had been a series of short snatches of slumber interposed between longer spells of rumination. While he marvelled at the intensity of malice which he could no longer doubt pursued him—a vindictiveness more natural to a mediaeval Italian state than to this present-day metropolis—he bitterly regretted the fatal curiosity which had brought him to such an extremity. By no means deficient in the grosser forms of physical courage, his sense that in the game which was being played his adversaries, as unscrupulous as they were crafty, held all the cards, and above all, that their espionage effectually prevented him filling the gaps in the plot which he had as yet only half-discovered, was especially galling to his active and somewhat neurotic temperament. Until yesterday he had almost decided to drop the affair of the Restaurant 'Poissonière' but now, after what he firmly believed to be a deliberate attempt to assassinate him, he realized the desperate situation of a duellist with his back to a wall—having scarce room to parry, he felt the prick of his antagonist's rapier deliberately goading him to an incautious thrust. Was he regarded as the possessor of a dangerous secret? Then it behoved him to strike, and that without delay.

Now that he was about to attack, a disguise was essential; and reflecting how lamentably he had failed through the absence of one hitherto, he removed the port-wine mark from his right cheek with his customary spirit-lotion, and blackened his fair hair with a few smart applications of a preparation from his bureau. It was with a determination to shun any obscure streets or alleys, and especially all buildings in course of erection, that he started out after his usual light breakfast. At first he was doubtful whether he was being followed or not, but after a few experimental turns and doublings he was unable to single out any regular attendant of his walk; either his disguise had proved effectual, or his enemies imagined that the attempt of last night had been less innocent in its results.

Somewhat soothed by this discovery, Pringle had gravitated towards the Strand and was nearing Charing Cross, when he observed a man cross from the station to the opposite corner carrying a brown paper roll. With his thoughts running in the one direction, Pringle in a flash recognised the dockyard draughtsman. Could he be even

now on his way to keep the appointment at Nelson's
Column? Had he been warned of Pringle's discovery, and
so expedited his treacherous task? And thus reflecting,
Pringle determined at all hazards to follow him. The
draughtsman made straight for the telegraph office. It
was now the busiest time of the morning, most of the little
desks were occupied by more or less glib message-writers,
and the draughtsman had found a single vacancy at the
far end when Pringle followed him in and reached over his
shoulder to withdraw a form from the rack in front of him.
Grabbing three or four, Pringle neatly spilled them upon
the desk, and with an abject apology hastily gathered
them up together with the form the draughtsman was
employed upon. More apologies, and Pringle, seizing a
suddenly vacant desk, affected to compose a telegram of
his own. The draughtsman's message had been short, and
(to Pringle) exceptionally sweet, consisting as it did of the
three words—'Four-thirty, Pauline'. The address Pringle
had not attempted to read—he knew that already. The
moment the other left Pringle took up a sheaf of forms,
and, as if they had been the sole reason of his visit, hurried
out of the office and took a hansom back to Furnival's Inn.

Here his first care was to fold some newspapers into a
brown-paper parcel resembling the one carried by the
draughtsman as nearly as he remembered it, and having
cut a number of squares of stiff tissue paper, he stuffed an
envelope with them and pondered over a cigarette the most
difficult stage of his campaign. Twice had the draughtsman
seen him. Once at the restaurant, in his official guise as the
sham literary agent, with smooth face, fair hair, and the
fugitive port-wine mark staining his right cheek; again
that morning, with blackened hair and unblemished face.
True, he might have forgotten the stranger at the restaurant;
on the other hand, he might not—and Pringle was then
(as always) steadfastly averse to leaving anything to chance.

Besides, in view of this sudden journey to London, it was very likely that he had received warning of Pringle's discovery. Lastly, it was more than probable that the spy was still on duty, even though he had failed to recognise Pringle that morning. The matter was clinched by a single glance at the Venetian mirror above the mantel, which reflected a feature he had overlooked—his now blackened hair. Nothing remained for him but to assume a disguise which should impose on both the spy and the draughtsman, and after some thought he decided to make up as a Frenchman of the South, and to pose as a servant of the French embassy. Reminiscent of the immortal Tartarin, his ready bureau furnished him with a stiff black moustache and some specially stout horsehair to typify the stubbly beard of that hero. When, at almost a quarter to four, he descended into the Inn with the parcel in his hand, a Baedeker and the envelope of tissues in his pocket, a cab was just setting down, and impulsively he chartered it as far as Exeter Hall. Concealed in the cab, he imagined he would the more readily escape observation, and by the time he alighted, flattered himself that any pursuit had been baffled. As he discharged the cab, however, he noticed a hansom draw up a few paces in the rear, whilst a man got out and began to saunter westward behind him. His suspicions alert, although the man was certainly a stranger, Pringle at once put him to the test by entering Romano's and ordering a small whisky. After a decent delay, he emerged, and his pulse quickened when he saw a couple of doors off the same man staring into a shop window! Pringle walked a few yards back, and then crossed to the opposite side of the street, but although he dodged at infinite peril through a string of omnibuses, he was unable to shake off his satellite, who, with unswerving persistence, occupied the most limited horizon whenever he looked back.

For almost the first time in his life, Pringle began to

despair. The complacent regard of his own precautions
had proved but a fool's paradise. Despite his elaborate
disguise, he must have been plainly recognisable to his
enemies, and he began to ask himself whether it was not
useless to struggle further. As he paced slowly on, an in-
definable depression stole over him. He thought of the
heavy price so nearly exacted for his interposition. Resentment surged over him at the memory, and his hand clenched
on the parcel. The contact furnished the very stimulus he
required. The instrument of settling such a score was in his
hands, and rejecting his timorous doubts, he strode on,
determined to make one bold and final stroke for vengeance.
The shadows had lengthened appreciably, and the quarter
chiming from near St Martin's warned him that there was
no time to lose—the spy must be got rid of at any cost.
Already could he see the estuary of the Strand, with the
Square widening beyond; on his right loomed the tunnel
of the Lowther Arcade, with its vista of juvenile delights.
The sight was an inspiration. Darting in, he turned off
sharp to the left into an artist's repository, with a double
entrance to the Strand and the Arcade, and, softly closing
the door, peeped through the palettes and frames which
hung upon the glass. Hardly had they ceased swinging to
his movement when he had the satisfaction of seeing the
spy, the scent already cold, rush furiously up the Arcade,
his course marked by falling toys and the cries of the out-
raged stall-keepers. Turning, Pringle made the purchase of
a sketching-block, the first thing handy, and then passed
through the door which gave on the Strand. At the post-
office he stopped to survey the scene. A single policeman
stood by the eastward base of the column, and the people
scattered round seemed but ordinary wayfarers, but just
across the maze of traffic was a spectacle of intense interest
to him. At the quadrant of the Grand Hotel, patrolling
aimlessly in front of the shops, at which he seemed too

perturbed to stare for more than a few seconds at a time, the draughtsman kept palpitating vigil until the clock should strike the half-hour of his treason. True to the Frenchman's advice, he sought safety in a crowd, avoiding the desert of the square until the last moment.

It wanted two minutes to the half-hour when Pringle opened his Baedeker, and thrusting one hand into his breast, examined the statue and coil of rope erected to the glory of our greatest hero. 'Pauline!' said a voice, with the musical inflection unattainable by any but a Frenchman. Beside him stood a slight, neatly dressed young man, with close-cropped hair, and a moustache and imperial, who cast a significant look at the parcel. Pringle immediately held it towards him, and the dark gentleman producing an envelope from his breast-pocket, the exchange was effected in silence. With bows and a raising of hats they parted, while Big Ben boomed on his eight bells.

The attaché's representative had disappeared some minutes beyond the westernmost lion before the draughts-man appeared from the opposite direction, his uncertain steps intermitted by frequent halts and nervous backward glances. With his back to the National Gallery he produced a Baedeker and commenced to stare up at the monument, withdrawing his eyes every now and then to cast a shame-faced look to right and left. In his agitation the draughts-man had omitted the hand-in-the-breast attitude, and even as Pringle advanced to his side and murmured 'Pauline', his legs (almost stronger than his will) seemed to be urging him to a flight from the field of dishonour. With tremulous eagerness he thrust a brown paper parcel into Pringle's hands, and, snatching the envelope of tissue slips, rushed across the road and disappeared in the bar of the Grand Hotel.

Pringle turned to go, but was confronted by a revolver, and as his eye traversed the barrel and met that of its owner,

he recognised the Frenchman to whom he had just sold the
bundle of newspapers. Dodging the weapon, he tried to
spring into the open, but a restraining grip on each elbow
held him in the angle of the plinth, and turning ever so
little Pringle found himself in custody of the man whom
he had last seen in full cry up the Lowther Arcade. No
constable was anywhere near, and even casual passengers
walked unheeding by the nook, so quiet was the progress
of this little drama. Lowering his revolver, the dark gentleman picked up the parcel which had fallen from Pringle
in the struggle. He opened it with delicacy, partially withdrew some sheets of tracing paper, which he intently
examined, and then placed the whole in an inner pocket,
and giving a sign to the spy to loose his grasp, he spoke
for the first time.

'May I suggest, sir,' he said in excellent English with
the slightest foreign accent, 'may I suggest that in future
you do not meddle with what cannot possibly concern you?
These documents have been bought and sold, and although
you have been good enough to act as intermediary in the
transaction, I can assure you we were under no necessity
of calling on you for your help.' Here his tone hardened,
and, speaking with less calmness, the accent became more
noticeable. 'I discovered your impertinence in selling me
a parcel of worthless papers very shortly after I left you.
Had you succeeded in the attempt you appear to have
planned so carefully, it is possible you might have lived
long enough to regret it—perhaps not! I wish you good
day, sir.' He bowed, as did his companion, and Pringle,
walking on, turned up by the corner of the Union Club.

Dent's clock marked twenty minutes to five, and Pringle
reflected how much had been compressed into the last
quarter of an hour. True, he had not prevented the sale of
his country's secrets; on the other hand—he pressed the
packet which held the envelope of notes. Hailing a cab,

he was about to step in, when, looking back, at the nook between the lions he saw a confused movement about the spot. The two men he had just left were struggling with a third, who, brandishing a handful of something white, was endeavouring, with varying success, to plant his fist on divers areas of their persons. He was the draughtsman. A small crowd, which momentarily increased, surrounded them, and as Pringle climbed into the hansom two policemen were seen to penetrate the ring and impartially lay hands upon the three combatants.

VIII

The Secret of the Fox Hunter

William Le Queux

It happened three winters ago. Having just returned from
Stuttgart, where I had spent some weeks at the Marquardt
in the guise I so often assumed, that of Monsieur Gustav
Dreux, commercial traveller, of Paris, and where I had
been engaged in watching the movements of two persons
staying in the hotel, a man and a woman, I was glad to be
back again in Bloomsbury to enjoy the ease of my arm-
chair and pipe.

I was much gratified that I had concluded a very difficult
piece of espionage, and having obtained the information
I sought, had been able to place certain facts before my
Chief, the Marquess of Macclesfield, which had very
materially strengthened his hands in some very delicate
diplomatic negotiations with Germany. Perhaps the most
exacting position in the whole of British diplomacy is the
post of Ambassador at Berlin, for the Germans are at once
our foes, as well as our friends, and are at this moment
only too ready to pick a quarrel with us from motives of
jealousy which may have serious results.

The war cloud was still hovering over Europe; hence a
swarm of spies, male and female, were plotting, scheming,

and working in secret in our very midst. The reader would be amazed if he could but glance at a certain red-bound book, kept under lock and key at the Foreign Office, in which are registered the names, personal descriptions and other facts concerning all the known foreign spies living in London and in other towns in England.

But active as are the agents of our enemies, so also are we active in the opposition camp. Our Empire has such tremendous responsibilities that we cannot now depend upon mere birth, wealth and honest dealing, but must call in shrewdness, tact, subterfuge and the employment of secret agents in order to combat the plots of those ever seeking to accomplish England's overthrow.

Careful student of international affairs that I was, I knew that trouble was brewing in China. Certain confidential despatches from our Minister in Pekin had been shown to me by the Marquess, who, on occasion, flattered me by placing implicit trust in me, and from them I gathered that Russia was at work in secret to undermine our influence in the Far East.

I knew that the grave, kindly old statesman was greatly perturbed by the grim shadows that were slowly rising, but when we consulted on the day after my return from Stuttgart, his lordship was of opinion that at present I had not sufficient ground upon which to institute inquiries.

'For the present, Drew,' he said, 'we must watch and wait. There is war in the air—first at Pekin, and then in Europe. But we must prevent it at all costs. Huntley leaves for Pekin tonight with despatches in which I have fully explained the line which Sir Henry is to follow. Hold yourself in readiness, for you may have to return to Germany or Russia tomorrow. We cannot afford to remain long in the dark. We must crush any alliance between Petersburg and Berlin.'

'A telegram to my rooms will bring me to your lordship at any moment,' was my answer.

'Ready to go anywhere—eh, Drew?' he smiled; and then, after a further chat, I left Downing Street and returned to Bloomsbury.

Knowing that for at least a week or two I should be free, I left my address with Boyd, and went down to Cotterstock, in Northamptonshire, to stay with my old friend of college days, George Hamilton, who rented a hunting-box and rode with the Fitzwilliam Pack.

I had had a long-standing engagement with him to go down and get a few runs with the hounds, but my constant absence abroad had always prevented it until then. Of course none of my friends knew my real position at the Foreign Office. I was believed to be an attaché.

Personally, I am extremely fond of riding to hounds, therefore, when that night I sat at dinner with George, his wife, and the latter's cousin, Beatrice Graham, I was full of expectation of some good runs. An English country house, with its old oak, old silver and air of solidity, is always delightful to me after the flimsy gimcracks of Continental life. The evening proved a very pleasant one. Never having met Beatrice Graham before, I was much attracted by her striking beauty. She was tall and dark, about twenty-two, with a remarkable figure which was shown to advantage by her dinner-gown of turquoise blue. So well did she talk, so splendidly did she sing Dupont's 'Jeune Fille', and so enthusiastic was she regarding hunting, that, before I had been an hour with her, I found myself thoroughly entranced.

The meet, three days afterwards, was at Wansford, that old-time hunting centre by the Nene, about six miles distant, and as I rode at her side along the road through historic Fotheringhay and Nassington, I noticed what a splendid horsewoman she was. Her dark hair was coiled tightly behind, and her bowler hat suited her face admirably while her habit fitted as though it had been moulded to her figure. In her mare's tail was a tiny piece of scarlet silk to warn others that she was a kicker.

At Wansford, opposite the old Haycock, once a hunting inn in the old coaching days, but now Lord Chesham's hunting-box, the gathering was a large one. From the great rambling old house servants carried glasses of sloe gin to all who cared to partake of his lordship's hospitality, while every moment the meet grew larger and the crowd of horses and vehicles more congested.

George had crossed to chat with the Master, Mr George Fitzwilliam, who had just driven up and was still in his overcoat, therefore I found myself alone with my handsome companion, who appeared to be most popular everywhere. Dozens of men and women rode up to her and exchanged greetings, the men more especially, until at last Barnard, the huntsman, drew his hounds together, the word was given, and they went leisurely up the hill to draw the first cover.

The morning was one of those damp cold ones of mid-February; the frost had given and everyone expected a good run, for the scent would be excellent. Riding side by side with my fair companion, we chatted and laughed as we went along, until, on reaching the cover, we drew up with the others and halted while hounds went in.

The first cover was, however, drawn blank, but from the second a fox went away straight for Elton, and soon the hounds were in full cry after him and we followed at a gallop. After a couple of miles more than half the field was left behind, still we kept on, until of a sudden, and without effort, my companion took a high hedge and was cutting across the pastures ere I knew that she had left the road. That she was a straight rider I at once saw, and I must confess that I preferred the gate to the hedge and ditch which she had taken so easily.

Half an hour later the kill took place near Haddon Hall, and of the half dozen in at the death Beatrice Graham was one.

When I rode up, five minutes afterwards, she smiled at me. Her face was a trifle flushed by hard riding, yet her hair was in no way awry, and she declared that she had thoroughly enjoyed that tearing gallop.

Just, however, as we sat watching Barnard cut off the brush, a tall, rather good-looking man rode up, having apparently been left just as I had. As he approached I noticed that he gave my pretty friend a strange look, almost as of warning, while she on her part, refrained from acknowledging him. It was as though he had made her some secret sign which she had understood.

But there was a further fact that puzzled me greatly.

I had recognized in that well-turned-out hunting man someone whom I had had distinct occasion to recollect. At first I failed to recall the man's identity, but when I did, a few moments later, I sat regarding his retreating figure like one in a dream. The horseman who rode with such military bearing was none other than the renowned spy, one of the cleverest secret agents in the world, Otto Krempelstein, Chief of the German Secret Service.

That my charming little friend knew him was apparent. The slightest quiver in his eyelids and the almost imperceptible curl of his lip had not passed me unnoticed. There was some secret between them, of what nature I, of course, knew not. But all through that day my eyes were ever open to re-discover the man whose ingenuity and cunning had so often been in competition with my own. Twice I saw him again, once riding with a big, dark-haired man in pink, on a splendid bay and followed by a groom with a second horse, and on the second occasion, at the edge of

Stockhill Wood while we were waiting together he galloped past us, but without the slightest look of recognition.

'I wonder who that man is?' I remarked casually, as soon as he was out of hearing.

'I don't know,' was her prompt reply. 'He's often out with the hounds—a foreigner, I believe. Probably he's one of those who come to England for the hunting season. Since the late Empress of Austria came here to hunt, the Fitzwilliam has always been a favourite pack with the foreigners.'

I saw that she did not intend to admit that she had any knowledge of him. Like all women, she was a clever diplomatist. But he had made a sign to her—a sign of secrecy.

Did Krempelstein recognize me, I wondered? I could not think so, because we had never met face to face. He had once been pointed out to me in the Wilhelmstrasse in Berlin by one of our secret agents who knew him, and his features had ever since been graven on my memory.

That night, when I sat alone with my friend George, I learned from him that Mr Graham, his wife's uncle, had lived a long time on the Continent as manager to a large commercial firm, and that Beatrice had been born in France and had lived there a good many years. I made inquiries regarding the foreigners who were hunting that season with the Fitzwilliam, but he, with an Englishman's prejudice, declared that he knew none of them, and didn't want to know them.

The days passed and we went to several meets together—at Apethorpe, at Castor Hanglands, at Laxton Park and other places, but I saw no more of Krempelstein. His distinguished-looking friend, however, I met on several occasions, and discovered that his name was Baron Stern, a wealthy Viennese, who had taken a hunting-box near Stoke Doyle, and had as friend a young man named Percival, who was frequently out with the hounds.

But the discovery there of Krempelstein had thoroughly

aroused my curiosity. He had been there for some distinct purpose, without a doubt. Therefore I made inquiry of Kersch, one of our secret agents in Berlin, a man employed in the Ministry of Foreign Affairs, and from him received word that Krempelstein was back in Berlin, and further warning me that something unusual was on foot in England.

This aroused me at once to activity. I knew that Krempelstein and his agents were ever endeavouring to obtain the secrets of our guns, our ships, and our diplomacy with other nations, and I therefore determined that on this occasion he should not succeed. However much I admired Beatrice Graham, I now knew that she had lied to me, and that she was in all probability his associate. So I watched her carefully, and when she went out for a stroll or a ride, as she often did, I followed her.

How far I was justified in this action does not concern me. I had quite unexpectedly alighted upon certain suspicious facts, and was determined to elucidate them. The only stranger she met was Percival. Late one afternoon, just as dusk was deepening into night, she pulled up her mare beneath the bare black trees while crossing Burghley Park, and after a few minutes was joined by the young foreigner, who, having greeted her, chatted for a long time in a low, earnest tone, as though giving her directions. She seemed to remonstrate with him, but at the place I was concealed I was unable to distinguish what was said. I saw him, however, hand her something, and then, raising his hat, he turned his horse and galloped away down the avenue in the opposite direction.

I did not meet her again until I sat beside her at the dinner-table that night, and then I noticed how pale and anxious she was, entirely changed from her usual sweet, light-hearted self.

She told me that she had ridden into Stamford for exercise, but told me nothing of the clandestine meeting.

How I longed to know what the young foreigner had given her. Whatever it was, she kept it a close secret to herself.

More than once I felt impelled to go to her room in her absence and search her cupboards, drawers and travelling trunks. My attitude towards her was that of a man fallen entirely in love, for I had discovered that she was easily flattered by a little attention.

I was searching for some excuse to know Baron Stern, but often for a week he never went to the meets. It was as though he purposely avoided me. He was still at Weldon Lodge, near Stoke Doyle, for George told me that he had met him in Oundle only two days before.

Three whole weeks went by, and I remained just as puzzled as ever. Beatrice Graham was, after all, a most delightful companion, and although she was to me a mystery, yet we had become excellent friends.

One afternoon, just as I entered the drawing-room where she stood alone, she hurriedly tore up a note, and threw the pieces on the great log fire. I noticed one tiny piece about an inch square remained unconsumed, and managed, half an hour later, to get possession of it.

The writing upon it was, I found, in German, four words in all, which, without context, conveyed to me no meaning.

On the following night Mrs Hamilton and Beatrice remained with us in the smoking-room till nearly eleven o'clock, and at midnight I bade my host good night, and ascended the stairs to retire. I had been in my room about half an hour when I heard stealthy footsteps. In an instant the truth flashed upon me. It was Beatrice on her way downstairs.

Quickly I slipped on some things and noiselessly followed my pretty fellow-guest through the drawing-room out across the lawn and into the lane beyond. White mists had risen from the river, and the low roaring of the weir prevented her hearing my footsteps behind her. Fearing lest

I should lose her I kept close behind, following her across several grass fields until she came to Southwick Wood, a dark, deserted spot, away from road or habitation.

Her intention was evidently to meet someone, so when, presently, she halted beneath a clump of high black firs, I also took shelter a short distance away.

She sat on the fallen trunk of a tree and waited in patience. Time went on, and so cold was it that I became chilled to the bones. I longed for a pipe, but feared that the smell of tobacco or the light might attract her. Therefore I was compelled to crouch and await the clandestine meeting.

She remained very quiet. Not a dead leaf was stirred; not a sound came from her direction. I wondered why she waited in such complete silence.

Nearly two hours passed, when, at last, cramped and half frozen, I raised myself in order to peer into the darkness in her direction.

At first I could see no one, but, on straining my eyes, I saw, to my dismay, that she had fallen forward from the tree trunk, and was lying motionless in a heap upon the ground.

I called to her, but received no reply. Then rising, I walked to the spot, and in dismay threw myself on my knees and tried to raise her. My hand touched her white cheek. It was as cold as stone.

Next instant I undid her fur cape and bodice, and placed my hand upon her heart. There was no movement.

Beatrice Graham was dead.

The shock of the discovery held me spellbound. But when, a few moments later, I aroused myself to action, a difficult problem presented itself. Should I creep back to my room and say nothing, or should I raise the alarm, and admit that I had been watching her? My first care was to search the unfortunate girl's pocket, but I found nothing save a handkerchief and purse.

Then I walked back, and, regardless of the consequences, gave the alarm.

It is unnecessary here to describe the sensation caused by the discovery, or of how we carried the body back to the house. Suffice it to say that we called the doctor, who could find no mark of violence, or anything to account for death.

And yet she had expired suddenly, without a cry.

One feature, however, puzzled the doctor—namely, that her left hand and arm were much swollen, and had turned almost black, while the spine was curved—a fact which aroused a suspicion of some poison akin to strychnia.

From the very first, I held a theory that she had been secretly poisoned, but with what motive I could not imagine.

A post-mortem examination was made by three doctors on the following day, but, beyond confirming the theory I held, they discovered nothing.

On the day following, a few hours before the inquest, I was recalled to the Foreign Office by telegraph, and that same afternoon sat with the Marquess of Macclesfield in his private room receiving his instructions.

An urgent despatch from Lord Rockingham, our Ambassador at Petersburg, made it plain that an alliance had been proposed by Russia to Germany, the effect of which would be to break British power in the Far East. His Excellency knew that the terms of the secret agreement had been settled, and all that remained was its signature. Indeed, it would have already been signed save for opposition in some quarters unknown, and while that opposition existed I might gain time to ascertain the exact terms of the proposed alliance—no light task in Russia, be it said, for police spies exist there in thousands, and my disguise had always to be very carefully thought out whenever I passed the frontier at Wirballen.

The Marquess urged upon me to put all our secret machinery in motion in order to discover the terms of the proposed agreement, and more particularly as regards the extension of Russian influence in Manchuria.

'I know well the enormous difficulties of the inquiry,' his lordship said; 'but recollect, Drew, that in this matter you may be the means of saving the situation in the Far East. If we gain knowledge of the truth, we may be able to act promptly and effectively. If not—well—' and the grey-headed statesman shrugged his shoulders expressively without concluding the sentence.

Full of regret that I was unable to remain at Cotterstock and sift the mystery surrounding Beatrice Graham's death, I left London that night for Berlin, where, on the following evening, I called upon our secret agent, Kersch, who lived in a small but comfortable house at Teltow, one of the suburbs of the German capital. He occupied a responsible position in the German Foreign Office, but, having expensive tastes and a penchant for cards, was not averse to receiving British gold in exchange for the confidential information with which he furnished us from time to time.

I sat with him, discussing the situation for a long time. It was true, he said, that a draft agreement had been prepared and placed before the Tzar and the Kaiser, but it had not yet been signed. He knew nothing of the clauses, however, as they had been prepared in secret by the Minister's own hand, neither could he suggest any means of obtaining knowledge of them.

My impulse was to go on next day to Petersburg. Yet somehow I felt that I might be more successful in Germany than in Russia, so resolved to continue my inquiries.

'By the way,' the German said, 'you wrote me about Krempelstein. He has been absent a great deal lately, but

I had no idea he had been to England. Can he be interested in the same matter on which you are now engaged?'

'Is he now in Berlin?' I inquired eagerly.

'I met him at Boxhagen three days ago. He seems extremely active just now.'

'Three days ago!' I echoed. 'You are quite certain of the day?' I asked him this because, if his statement were true, it was proved beyond doubt that the German spy had no hand in the unfortunate girl's death.

'I am quite certain,' was his reply. 'I saw him entering the station on Monday morning.'

At eleven o'clock that same night, I called at the British Embassy and sat for a long time with the Ambassador in his private room. His Excellency told me all he knew regarding the international complication which the Marquess, sitting in Downing Street, had foreseen weeks ago, but could make no suggestion as to my course of action. The war clouds had gathered undoubtedly, and the signing of the agreement between our enemies would cause it at once to burst over Europe. The crisis was one of the most serious in English history.

One fact puzzled us both, just as it puzzled our Chief at home—namely, if the agreement had been seen and approved by both Emperors, why was it not signed? Whatever hitch had occurred, it was more potent than the will of the two most powerful monarchs in Europe.

On my return to the hotel I scribbled a hasty note and sent it by messenger to the house of the Imperial Chancellor's son in Charlottenburg. It was addressed to Miss Maud Baines, the English governess of the Count's children, who, I may as well admit, was in our employ. She was a young, ingenuous and fascinating little woman. She had, at my direction, acted as governess in many of the great families in France, Russia and Germany, and was now in the employ of the Chancellor's son, in order to have opportunity of keeping a watchful eye on the great statesman himself.

She kept the appointment next morning at an obscure café near the Behrenstrasse. She was a neatly dressed, rather petite person, with a face that entirely concealed her keen intelligence and marvellous cunning.

As she sat at the little table with me, I told her in low tones of the object of my visit to Berlin, and sought her aid.

'A serious complication has arisen. I was about to report to you through the Embassy,' was her answer. 'Last night the Chancellor dined with us, and I overheard him discussing the affair with his son as they sat alone smoking after the ladies had left. I listened at the door and heard the Chancellor distinctly say that the draft treaty had been stolen.'

'Stolen!' I gasped. 'By whom?'

'Ah! that's evidently the mystery—a mystery for us to fathom. But the fact that somebody else is in possession of the intentions of Germany and Russia against England, believed to be a secret, is no doubt the reason why the agreement has not been signed.'

'Because it is no longer secret!' I suggested. 'Are you quite certain you've made no mistake?'

'Quite,' was her prompt answer. 'You can surely trust me after the intricate little affairs which I have assisted you in unravelling? When may I return to Gloucester to see my friends?'

'Soon, Miss Baines—as soon as this affair is cleared up. But tell me, does the Chancellor betray any fear of awkward complications when the secret of the proposed plot against England is exposed?'

'Yes. The Prince told his son in confidence that his only fear was of England's retaliation. He explained that, as far as was known, the secret document, after being put before the Tzar and approved, mysteriously disappeared.

Every inquiry was being made by the confidential agents of Russia and Germany, and further, he added, that even his trusted Krempelstein was utterly nonplussed.'

Mention of Krempelstein brought back to me the recollection of the tragedy in rural England.

'You've done us a great service, Miss Baines,' I said. 'This information is of highest importance. I shall telegraph in cipher at once to Lord Macclesfield. Do you, by any chance, happen to know a young lady named Graham?' I inquired, recollecting that the deceased woman had lived in Germany for several years.

She responded in the negative, whereupon I drew from my pocket a snap-shot photograph, which I had taken of one of the meets of hounds at Wansford, and handing it to her inquired if she recognized any of the persons in it.

Having carefully examined it, she pointed to Baron Stern, whom I had taken in the act of lighting a cigarette, and exclaimed—

'Why! that's Colonel Davidoff, who was secretary to Prince Obolenski when I was in his service. Do you know him?'

'No,' I answered. 'But he has been hunting in England as Baron Stern, of Vienna. This man is his friend,' I added, indicating Percival.

'And that's undoubtedly a man whom you know well by repute—Moore, Chief of the Russian Secret Service in England. He came to Prince Obolenski's once, when he was in Petersburg, and the Princess told me who he was.'

Unfortunately, I had not been able to include Beatrice in the group, therefore I had only her description to place before the clever young woman, who had, on so many occasions, gained knowledge of secrets where I and my agents had failed. Her part was always a difficult one to play, but she was well paid, was a marvellous linguist, and for patience and cunning was unequalled.

I described her as minutely as I could, but still she had no knowledge of her. She remained thoughtful a long time, and then observed:

'You have said that she apparently knew Moore? He has, I know, recently been back in Petersburg, therefore they may have met there. She may be known. Why not seek for traces of her in Russia?'

It seemed something of a wild-goose chase, yet with the whole affair shrouded in mystery and tragedy as it was, I was glad to adopt any suggestion that might lead to a solution of the enigma. The reticence of Mrs Hamilton regarding her cousin, and the apparent secret association of the dead girl with those two notorious spies, had formed a problem which puzzled me almost to the point of madness.

The English governess told me where in Petersburg I should be likely to find either the two Russian agents, Davidoff or Moore, who had been posing in England for some unknown purpose as hunting men of means; therefore I left by the night mail for the Russian capital. I put up at a small, and not overclean hotel, in preference to the Europe, and, compelled to carefully conceal my identity, I at once set about making inquiries in various quarters, whether the two men had returned to Russia. They had, and had both had long interviews, two days before, with General Zouboff, Chief of the Secret Service, and with the Russian Foreign Minister.

At the Embassy, and in various English quarters, I sought trace of the woman whose death was such a profound mystery, but all in vain. At last I suddenly thought of another source of information as yet untried—namely, the register of the English Charity in Petersburg, and on searching it, I found, to my complete satisfaction, that about six weeks before Beatrice Graham applied to the administration, and was granted money to take her back to England. She was the daughter, it was registered, of a

Mr Charles Graham, the English manager of a cotton mill in Moscow, who had been killed by an accident, and had left her penniless. For some months she had tried to earn her own living, in a costumier's shop in the Newski, and, not knowing Russian sufficiently well, had been discharged. Before her father's death she had been engaged to marry a young Englishman, whose name was not given, but who was said to be tutor to the children of General Vraski, Governor-General of Warsaw.

The information was interesting, but carried me no further, therefore I set myself to watch the two men who had travelled from England to consult the Tzar's chief adviser. Aided by two Russians, who were in British pay, I shadowed them day and night for six days, until, one evening, I followed Davidoff down to the railway station, where he took a ticket for the frontier. Without baggage I followed him, for his movements were of a man who was escaping from the country. He passed out across the frontier, and went on to Vienna, and thence direct to Paris, where he put up at the Hotel Terminus, Gare St Lazare.

Until our arrival at the hotel he had never detected that I was following him, but on the second day in Paris we came face to face in the large central hall, used as a reading room. He glanced at me quickly, but whether he recognized me as the companion of Beatrice Graham in the hunting field I have no idea. All I know is that his movements were extremely suspicious, and that I invoked the aid of all three of our Secret Agents in Paris to keep watch on him, just as had been done in Petersburg.

On the fourth night of our arrival in the French capital I returned to the hotel about midnight, having dined at the Café Americain with Greville, the naval attaché at the Embassy. In washing my hands prior to turning in, I received a nasty scratch on my left wrist from a pin which a careless laundress had left in the towel. There was a little blood, but I tied my handkerchief around it, and, tired out, lay down and was soon asleep.

Half an hour afterwards, however, I was aroused by an excruciating pain over my whole left side, a strange twitching of the muscles of my face and hands, and a contraction of the throat which prevented me from breathing or crying out.

I tried to rise and press the electric bell for assistance, but could not. My whole body seemed entirely paralysed. Then the ghastly truth flashed upon me, causing me to break out into a cold sweat.

That pin had been placed there purposely. I had been poisoned and in the same manner as Beatrice Graham!

I recollect that my heart seemed to stop, and my nails clenched themselves in the palms in agony. Then next moment I knew no more.

When I recovered consciousness, Ted Greville, together with a tall, black-bearded man named Delisle, who was in the confidential department of the Quai d'Orsay and who often furnished us with information—at a very high figure, be it said—were standing by my bedside, while a French doctor was leaning over the foot rail watching me.

'Thank heaven you're better, old chap!' Greville exclaimed. 'They thought you were dead. You've had a narrow squeak. How did it happen?'

'That pin!' I cried, pointing to the towel.

'What pin?' he asked.

'Mind! don't touch the towel,' I cried. 'There's a pin in it—a pin that's poisoned! That Russian evidently came here in my absence and very cunningly laid a deathtrap for me.'

'You mean Davidoff,' chimed in the Frenchman. 'When, m'sieur, the doctor has left the room I can tell you something in confidence.'

The doctor discreetly withdrew, and then our spy said:

'Davidoff has turned traitor to his own country. I have discovered that the reason of his visit here is because he has in his possession the original draft of a proposed secret agreement between Russia and Germany against England, and is negotiating for its sale to us for one hundred thousand francs. He had a secret interview with our Chief last night at his private house in the Avenue des Champs Elysées.'

'Then it is he who stole it, after it had the Tzar's approval!' I cried, starting up in bed, aroused at once to action by the information. 'Has he disposed of it to France?'

'Not yet. It is still in his possession.'

'And he is here?'

'No. He has hidden himself in lodgings in the Rue Lafayette, No. 247, until the Foreign Minister decides whether he shall buy the document.'

'And the name by which he is known there?'

'He is passing as a Greek named Geunadios.'

'Keep a strict watch on him. He must not escape,' I said. 'He has endeavoured to murder me.'

'A watch is being kept,' was the Frenchman's answer, as, exhausted, I sank again upon the pillow.

Just before midnight I entered the traitor's room in the Rue Lafayette, and when he saw me he fell back with blanched face and trembling hands.

'No doubt my presence here surprises you,' I said, 'but I may as well at once state my reason for coming here. I want a certain document which concerns Germany and your own country—the document which you have stolen to sell to France.'

'What do you mean, m'sieur?' he asked, with an attempted hauteur.

'My meaning is simple. I require that document, otherwise I shall give you into the hands of the police for attempted murder. The Paris police will detain you until

[211]

the police of Petersburg apply for your extradition as a traitor. You know what that means—Schusselburg.'

Mention of that terrible island fortress, dreaded by every Russian, caused him to quiver. He looked me straight in the face, and saw determination written there, yet he was unyielding, and refused for a long time to give the precious document into my hands. I referred to his stay at Stoke Doyle, and spoke of his friendship with the spy Moore, so that he should know that I was aware of the truth, until at last he suggested a bargain with me, namely, that in exchange for the draft agreement against England I should preserve silence and permit him to return to Russia.

To this course I acceded, and then the fellow took from a secret cavity of his travelling bag a long official envelope, which contained the innocent-looking paper, which would, if signed, have destroyed England's prestige in the Far East. He handed it to me, the document for which he hoped to obtain one hundred thousand francs, and in return I gave him his liberty to go back to Russia unmolested.

Our parting was the reverse of cordial, for undoubtedly he had placed in my towel the pin which had been steeped in some subtle and deadly poison, and then escaped from the hotel, in the knowledge that I must sooner or later become scratched and fall a victim.

I had had a very narrow escape it was true, but I did not think so much of my good fortune in regaining my life as the rapid delivery of the all-important document into Lord Macclesfield's hands, which I effected at noon next day.

My life had been at stake, for I afterwards found that a second man had been his accomplice, but happily I had succeeded in obtaining possession of the actual document, the result being that England acted so promptly and vigorously that the situation was saved, and the way was, as you know, opened for the Anglo-Japanese Treaty, which, to the discomfiture of Germany, was effected a few months later.

Nearly two years have gone by since then, and it was only the other day, by mere accident, that I made a further discovery which explained the death of the unfortunate Beatrice Graham.

A young infantry lieutenant, named Bellingham, having passed in Russian, had some four years before entered our Secret Service, and been employed in Russia on certain missions. A few days ago, on his return to London, after performing a perilous piece of espionage on the Russo-German frontier, he called upon me in Bloomsbury, and in course of conversation, mentioned that about two years ago, in order to get access to certain documents relating to the Russian mobilisation scheme for her western frontier, he acted as tutor to the sons of the Governor-General of Warsaw.

In an instant a strange conjecture flashed across my mind.

'Am I correct in assuming that you knew a young English lady in Russia named Graham—Beatrice Graham?'

He looked me straight in the face, open-mouthed in astonishment, yet I saw that a cloud of sadness overshadowed him instantly.

'Yes,' he said. 'I knew her. Our meeting resulted in a terrible tragedy. Owing to the position I hold I have been compelled to keep the details to myself—although it is the tragedy of my life.'

'How? Tell me,' I urged sympathetically.

'Ah!' he sighed, 'it is a strange story. We met in Petersburg, where she was employed in a shop in the Newski. I loved her, and we became engaged. Withholding nothing from her I told her who I was and the reason I was in the service of the Governor-General. At once, instead of

despising me as a spy, she became enthusiastic as an English-
woman, and declared her readiness to assist me. She was
looking forward to our marriage, and saw that if I could
effect a big coup my position would at once be improved,
and we could then be united.'

He broke off, and remained silent for a few moments,
looking blankly down into the grey London street. Then
he said,

'I explained to her the suspicion that Germany and
Russia were conspiring in the Far East, and told her that
a draft treaty was probably in existence, and that it was a
document of supreme importance to British interests. Judge
my utter surprise when, a week later, she came to me with
the actual document which she said she had managed to
secure from the private cabinet of Prince Korolkoff,
director of the private Chancellerie of the Emperor, to
whose house she had gone on a commission to the Princess.
Truly she had acted with a boldness and cleverness that
were amazing. Knowing the supreme importance of the
document, I urged her to leave Russia at once, and conceal
herself with friends in England, taking care always that
the draft treaty never left her possession. This plan she
adopted, first, however, placing herself under the protection
of the English charity, thus allaying any suspicions that
the police might entertain.

'Poor Beatrice went to stay with her cousin, a lady
named Hamilton, in Northamptonshire, but the instant the
document was missed the Secret Services of Germany and
Russia were at once agog, and the whole machinery was
set in motion, with the result that two Russian agents—
an Englishman named Moore, and a Russian named
Davidoff—as well as Krempelstein, chief of the German
Service, had suspicions, and followed her to England with
the purpose of obtaining re-possession of the precious
document. For some weeks they plotted in vain, although

both the German and the Englishman succeeded in getting on friendly terms with her.

'She telegraphed to me, asking how she should dispose of the document, fearing to keep it long in her possession, but not being aware of the desperate character of the game, I replied that there was nothing to be feared. I was wrong,' he cried, bitterly. 'I did not recognize the vital importance of the information; I did not know that Empires were at stake. The man Davidoff, who posed as a wealthy Austrian Baron, had by some means discovered that she always carried the precious draft concealed in the bodice of her dress, therefore he had recourse to a dastardly ruse. From what I have since discovered he one day succeeded in concealing in the fur of her cape a pin impregnated with a certain deadly arrow poison unknown to toxicologists. Then he caused to be dispatched from London a telegram purporting to come from me, urging her to meet me in secret at a certain spot on that same night. In eager expectation the poor girl went forth to meet me, believing I had returned unexpectedly from Russia, but in putting on her cape, she tore her finger with the poisoned pin. While waiting for me the fatal paralysis seized her, and she expired, after which Davidoff crept up, secured the missing document and escaped. His anxiety to get hold of it was to sell it at a high price to a foreign country, nevertheless he was compelled first to return to Russia and report. No one knew that he actually held the draft, for to Krempelstein, as well as to Moore, my poor love's death was believed to be due to natural causes, while Davidoff, on his part, took care to so arrange matters, that his presence at the spot where poor Beatrice expired could never be proved. The spies therefore left England reluctantly after the tragedy, believing that the document, if ever possessed by my unfortunate love, had passed out of her possession into unknown hands.'

'And what of the assassin Davidoff now?' I inquired.

'I have avenged her death,' answered Bellingham with set teeth. 'I gave information to General Zouboff of the traitor's attempted sale of the draft treaty to France, with the result that the court martial has condemned him to incarceration for life in the cells below the lake at Schusselburg.'

IX

The Mysterious Death on the Underground Railway

The Baroness Orczy

It was all very well for Mr Richard Frobisher (of the London Mail) to cut up rough about it. Polly did not altogether blame him.

She liked him all the better for that frank outburst of manlike ill-temper which, after all said and done, was only a very flattering form of masculine jealousy.

Moreover, Polly distinctly felt guilty about the whole thing. She had promised to meet Dickie—that is Mr Richard Frobisher—at two o'clock sharp outside the Palace Theatre, because she wanted to go to a Maud Allan matinée, and because he naturally wished to go with her.

But at two o'clock sharp she was still in Norfolk Street, Strand, inside an A.B.C. shop, sipping cold coffee opposite a grotesque old man who was fiddling with a bit of string.

How could she be expected to remember Maud Allan or the Palace Theatre, or Dickie himself for a matter of that? The man in the corner had begun to talk of that mysterious death on the Underground Railway, and Polly had lost count of time, of place, and circumstance.

She had gone to lunch quite early, for she was looking forward to the matinée at the Palace.

The old scarecrow was sitting in his accustomed place when she came into the A.B.C. shop, but he had made no remark all the time that the young girl was munching her scone and butter. She was just busy thinking how rude he was not even to have said 'Good morning', when an abrupt remark from him caused her to look up.

'Will you be good enough,' he said suddenly, 'to give me a description of the man who sat next to you just now, while you were having your cup of coffee and scone.'

Involuntarily Polly turned her head towards the distant door, through which a man in a light overcoat was even now quickly passing. That man had certainly sat at the next table to hers, when she first sat down to her coffee and scone; he had finished his luncheon—whatever it was— a moment ago, had paid at the desk and gone out. The incident did not appear to Polly as being of the slightest consequence.

Therefore she did not reply to the rude old man, but shrugged her shoulders, and called to the waitress to bring her bill.

'Do you know if he was tall or short, dark or fair?' continued the man in the corner, seemingly not the least disconcerted by the young girl's indifference. 'Can you tell me at all what he was like?'

'Of course I can,' rejoined Polly impatiently, 'but I don't see that my description of one of the customers of an A.B.C. shop can have the slightest importance.'

He was silent for a minute, while his nervous fingers fumbled about in his capacious pockets in search of the inevitable piece of string. When he had found this necessary 'adjunct to thought', he viewed the young girl again through his half-closed lids, and added maliciously:

'But supposing it were of paramount importance that

you should give an accurate description of a man who sat next to you for half an hour today, how would you proceed?'

'I should say that he was of medium height——'

'Five foot eight, nine, or ten?' he interrupted quietly.

'How can one tell to an inch or two?' rejoined Polly crossly. 'He was between colours.'

'What's that?' he inquired blandly.

'Neither fair nor dark—his nose—'

'Well, what was his nose like? Will you sketch it?'

'I am not an artist. His nose was fairly straight—his eyes—'

'Were neither dark nor light—his hair had the same striking peculiarity—he was neither short nor tall—his nose was neither aquiline nor snub—' he recapitulated sarcastically.

'No,' she retorted; 'he was just ordinary looking.'

'Would you know him again—say tomorrow, and among a number of other men who were "neither tall nor short, dark nor fair, aquiline nor snub-nosed", etc.?'

'I don't know—I might—he was certainly not striking enough to be specially remembered.'

'Exactly,' he said, while he leant forward excitedly, for all the world like a Jack-in-the-box let loose. 'Precisely; and you are a journalist—call yourself one, at least—and it should be part of your business to notice and describe people. I don't mean only the wonderful personage with the clear Saxon features, the fine blue eyes, the noble brow and classic face, but the ordinary person—the person who represents ninety out of every hundred of his own kind—the average Englishman, say, of the middle classes, who is neither very tall nor very short, who wears a moustache which is neither fair nor dark, but which masks his mouth, and a top hat which hides the shape of his head and brow, a man, in fact, who dresses like hundreds of his fellow-creatures, moves like them, speaks like them, has no peculiarity.

'Try to describe *him*, to recognize him, say a week hence, among his other eighty-nine doubles; worse still, to swear his life away, if he happened to be implicated in some crime, wherein *your* recognition of him would place the halter round his neck.

'Try that, I say, and having utterly failed you will more readily understand how one of the greatest scoundrels unhung is still at large, and why the mystery on the Underground Railway was never cleared up.

'I think it was the only time in my life that I was seriously tempted to give the police the benefit of my own views upon the matter. You see, though I admire the brute for his cleverness, I did not see that his being unpunished could possibly benefit anyone.

'In these days of tubes and motor traction of all kinds, the old-fashioned "best, cheapest, and quickest route to City and West End" is often deserted, and the good old Metropolitan Railway carriages cannot at any time be said to be over-crowded. Anyway, when that particular train steamed into Aldgate at about 4 p.m. on March 18th last, the first-class carriages were all but empty.

'The guard marched up and down the platform looking into all the carriages to see if anyone had left a halfpenny evening paper behind for him, and opening the door of one of the first-class compartments, he noticed a lady sitting in the further corner, with her head turned away towards the window, evidently oblivious of the fact that on this line Aldgate is the terminal station.

'"Where are you for, lady?"' he said.

'The lady did not move, and the guard stepped into the carriage, thinking that perhaps the lady was asleep. He touched her arm lightly and looked into her face. In his own poetic language, he was "struck all of a 'eap". In the glassy eyes, the ashen colour of the cheeks, the rigidity of the head, there was the unmistakable look of death.

'Hastily the guard, having carefully locked the carriage door, summoned a couple of porters, and sent one of them off to the police-station, and the other in search of the station-master.

'Fortunately at this time of day the up platform is not very crowded, all the traffic tending westward in the afternoon. It was only when an inspector and two police constables, accompanied by a detective in plain clothes and a medical officer, appeared upon the scene, and stood round a first-class railway compartment, that a few idlers realized that something unusual had occurred, and crowded round, eager and curious.

'Thus it was that the later editions of the evening papers, under the sensational heading, "Mysterious Suicide on the Underground Railway", had already an account of the extraordinary event. The medical officer had very soon come to the decision that the guard had not been mistaken, and that life was indeed extinct.

'The lady was young, and must have been very pretty before the look of fright and horror had so terribly distorted her features. She was very elegantly dressed, and the more frivolous papers were able to give their feminine readers a detailed account of the unfortunate woman's gown, her shoes, hat and gloves.

'It appears that one of the latter, the one on the right hand, was partly off, leaving the thumb and wrist bare. That hand held a small satchel, which the police opened, with a view to the possible identification of the deceased, but which was found to contain only a little loose silver, some smelling-salts, and a small empty bottle, which was handed over to the medical officer for purposes of analysis.

'It was the presence of that small bottle which had caused the report to circulate freely that the mysterious case on the Underground Railway was one of suicide. Certain it was that neither about the lady's person, nor in the appearance of the railway carriage, was there the slightest sign of struggle or even of resistance. Only the look in the poor woman's eyes spoke of sudden terror, of the rapid vision of an unexpected and violent death, which probably only lasted an infinitesimal fraction of a second, but which had left its indelible mark upon the face, otherwise so placid and so still.

'The body of the deceased was conveyed to the mortuary. So far, of course, not a soul had been able to identify her, or to throw the slightest light upon the mystery which hung around her death.

'Against that, quite a crowd of idlers—genuinely interested or not—obtained admission to view the body, on the pretext of having lost or mislaid a relative or a friend. At about 8.30 p.m. a young man, very well dressed, drove up to the station in a hansom, and sent in his card to the superintendent. It was Mr Hazeldene, shipping agent, of 11, Crown Lane, E.C., and No. 19, Addison Row, Kensington.

'The young man looked in a pitiable state of mental distress; his hand clutched nervously a copy of the St James's Gazette, which contained the fatal news. He said very little to the superintendent except that a person who was very dear to him had not returned home that evening.

'He had not felt really anxious until half an hour ago, when suddenly he thought of looking at his paper. The description of the deceased lady, though vague, had terribly alarmed him. He had jumped into a hansom, and now begged permission to view the body, in order that his worst fears might be allayed.

'You know what followed, of course,' continued the man in the corner, 'the grief of the young man was truly pitiable. In the woman lying there in a public mortuary before him, Mr Hazeldene had recognized his wife.

'I am waxing melodramatic,' said the man in the corner,

who looked up at Polly with a mild and gentle smile, while his nervous fingers vainly endeavoured to add another knot on the scrappy bit of string with which he was continually playing, 'and I fear that the whole story savours of the penny novelette, but you must admit, and no doubt you remember, that it was an intensely pathetic and truly dramatic moment.

'The unfortunate young husband of the deceased lady was not much worried with questions that night. As a matter of fact, he was not in a fit condition to make any coherent statement. It was at the coroner's inquest on the following day that certain facts came to light, which for the time being seemed to clear up the mystery surrounding Mrs Hazeldene's death, only to plunge that same mystery, later on, into denser gloom than before.

'The first witness at the inquest was, of course, Mr Hazeldene himself. I think everyone's sympathy went out to the young man as he stood before the coroner and tried to throw what light he could upon the mystery. He was well-dressed, as he had been the day before, but he looked terribly ill and worried, and no doubt the fact that he had not shaved gave his face a careworn and neglected air.

'It appears that he and the deceased had been married some six years or so, and that they had always been happy in their married life. They had no children. Mrs Hazeldene seemed to enjoy the best of health till lately, when she had had a slight attack of influenza, in which Dr Arthur Jones had attended her. The doctor was present at this moment, and would no doubt explain to the coroner and the jury whether he thought that Mrs Hazeldene had the slightest tendency to heart disease, which might have had a sudden and fatal ending.

'The coroner was, of course, very considerate to the bereaved husband. He tried by circumlocution to get at the point he wanted, namely, Mrs Hazeldene's mental condition lately. Mr Hazeldene seemed loath to talk about this. No doubt he had been warned as to the existence of the small bottle found in his wife's satchel.

'"It certainly did seem to me at times", he at last reluctantly admitted, "that my wife did not seem quite herself. She used to be very gay and bright, and lately I often saw her in the evening sitting, as if brooding over some matters, which evidently she did not care to communicate to me."

'Still the coroner insisted, and suggested the small bottle.

'"I know, I know", replied the young man, with a short, heavy sigh. "You mean—the question of suicide—I cannot understand it at all—it seems so sudden and so terrible—she certainly had seemed listless and troubled lately—but only at times—and yesterday morning, when I went to business, she appeared quite herself again, and I suggested that we should go to the opera in the evening. She was delighted, I know, and told me she would do some shopping, and pay a few calls in the afternoon."

'"Do you know at all where she intended to go when she got into the Underground Railway?"

'"Well, not with certainty. You see, she may have meant to get out at Baker Street, and go down to Bond Street to do her shopping. Then, again, she sometimes goes to a shop in St Paul's Churchyard, in which case she would take a ticket to Aldersgate Street; but I cannot say."

'"Now, Mr Hazeldene", said the coroner at last very kindly, "will you try to tell me if there was anything in Mrs Hazeldene's life which you know of, and which might in some measure explain the cause of the distressed state of mind, which you yourself had noticed? Did there exist any financial difficulty which might have preyed upon Mrs Hazeldene's mind; was there any friend—to whose intercourse with Mrs Hazeldene—you—er—at any time took exception? In fact", added the coroner, as if thankful that he had got over an unpleasant moment, "can you give me the slightest indication which would tend to confirm the suspicion that the unfortunate lady, in a moment of mental anxiety or derangement, may have wished to take her own life?"

'There was silence in the court for a few moments. Mr Hazeldene seemed to everyone there present to be labouring under some terrible moral doubt. He looked very pale and wretched, and twice attempted to speak before he at last said in scarcely audible tones:

'"No; there were no financial difficulties of any sort. My wife had an independent fortune of her own—she had no extravagant tastes——"

'"Nor any friend you at any time objected to?" insisted the coroner.

'"Nor any friend, I—at any time objected to", stammered the unfortunate young man, evidently speaking with an effort.

'I was present at the inquest,' resumed the man in the corner, after he had drunk a glass of milk and ordered another, 'and I can assure you that the most obtuse person there plainly realized that Mr Hazeldene was telling a lie. It was pretty plain to the meanest intelligence that the unfortunate lady had not fallen into a state of morbid dejection for nothing, and that perhaps there existed a third person who could throw more light on her strange and sudden death than the unhappy, bereaved young widower.

'That the death was more mysterious even than it had at first appeared became very soon apparent. You read the case at the time, no doubt, and must remember the excitement in the public mind caused by the evidence of the two doctors. Dr Arthur Jones, the lady's usual medical man, who had attended her in a last very slight illness, and who had seen her in a professional capacity fairly recently, declared most emphatically that Mrs Hazeldene suffered from no organic complaint which could possibly have been the cause of sudden death. Moreover, he had assisted Mr Andrew Thornton, the district medical officer, in making a post mortem examination, and together they had come to the conclusion that death was due to the action of prussic acid, which had caused instantaneous failure of the heart, but how the drug had been administered neither he nor his colleague were at present able to state.

'"Do I understand, then, Dr Jones, that the deceased died, poisoned with prussic acid?"

'"Such is my opinion", replied the doctor.

'"Did the bottle found in her satchel contain prussic acid?"

'"It had contained some at one time, certainly".

'"In your opinion, then, the lady caused her own death by taking a dose of that drug?"

'"Pardon me, I never suggested such a thing: the lady died poisoned by the drug, but how the drug was administered we cannot say. By injection of some sort, certainly. The drug certainly was not swallowed; there was not a vestige of it in the stomach."

'"Yes," added the doctor in reply to another question from the coroner, "death had probably followed the injection in this case almost immediately; say within a couple of minutes, or perhaps three. It was quite possible that the body would not have more than one quick and sudden convulsion, perhaps not that; death in such cases is absolutely sudden and crushing."

'I don't think that at the time anyone in the room realized how important the doctor's statement was, a statement, which, by the way, was confirmed in all its details by the district medical officer, who had conducted the post mortem. Mrs Hazeldene had died suddenly from an injection of prussic acid, administered no one knew

how or when. She had been travelling in a first-class railway carriage in a busy time of the day. That young and
elegant woman must have had singular nerve and coolness
to go through the process of a self-inflicted injection of a
deadly poison in the presence of perhaps two or three other
persons.

'Mind you, when I say that no one there realized the
importance of the doctor's statement at that moment, I
am wrong; there were three persons, who fully understood
at once the gravity of the situation, and the astounding
development which the case was beginning to assume.

'Of course, I should have put myself out of the question,'
added the weird old man, with that inimitable self-conceit
peculiar to himself. 'I guessed then and there in a moment
where the police were going wrong, and where they would
go on going wrong until the mysterious death on the Underground Railway had sunk into oblivion, together with
the other cases which they mismanage from time to
time.

'I said there were three persons who understood the
gravity of the two doctors' statements—the other two
were, firstly, the detective who had originally examined
the railway carriage, a young man of energy and plenty of
misguided intelligence, the other was Mr Hazeldene.

'At this point the interesting element of the whole
story was first introduced into the proceedings, and this
was done through the humble channel of Emma Funnel,
Mrs Hazeldene's maid, who, as far as was known then,
was the last person who had seen the unfortunate lady
alive and had spoken to her.

'"Mrs Hazeldene lunched at home," explained Emma,
who was shy, and spoke almost in a whisper; "she seemed
well and cheerful. She went out at about half-past three,
and told me she was going to Spence's, in St Paul's Churchyard to try on her new tailor-made gown. Mrs Hazeldene

had meant to go there in the morning, but was prevented as Mr Errington called."

'"Mr Errington?" asked the coroner casually. "Who is Mr Errington?"

'But this Emma found difficult to explain. Mr Errington was—Mr Errington, that's all.

'"Mr Errington was a friend of the family. He lived in a flat in the Albert Mansions. He very often came to Addison Row, and generally stayed late."

'Pressed still further with questions, Emma at last stated that latterly Mrs Hazeldene had been to the theatre several times with Mr Errington, and that on those nights the master looked very gloomy, and was very cross.

'Recalled, the young widower was strangely reticent. He gave forth his answers very grudgingly, and the coroner was evidently absolutely satisfied with himself at the marvellous way in which, after a quarter of an hour of firm yet very kind questionings, he had elicited from the witness what information he wanted.

'Mr Errington was a friend of his wife. He was a gentleman of means, and seemed to have a great deal of time at his command. He himself did not particularly care about Mr Errington, but he certainly had never made any observations to his wife on the subject.

'"But who is Mr Errington?" repeated the coroner once more. "What does he do? What is his business or profession?"

'"He has no business or profession."

'"What is his occupation, then?"

'"He has no special occupation. He has ample private means. But he has a great and very absorbing hobby."

'"What is that?"

'"He spends all his time in chemical experiments, and is, I believe, as an amateur, a very distinguished toxicologist."

'Did you ever see Mr Errington, the gentleman so closely connected with the mysterious death on the Underground Railway?' asked the man in the corner as he placed one or two of his little snapshot photos before Miss Polly Burton.

'There he is, to the very life. Fairly good-looking, a pleasant face enough, but ordinary, absolutely ordinary.

'It was this absence of any peculiarity which very nearly, but not quite, placed the halter round Mr Errington's neck.

'But I am going too fast, and you will lose the thread. The public, of course, never heard how it actually came about that Mr Errington, the wealthy bachelor of Albert Mansions, of the Grosvenor, and other young dandies' clubs, one fine day found himself before the magistrates at Bow Street, charged with being concerned in the death of Mary Beatrice Hazeldene, late of No. 19, Addison Row.

'I can assure you both press and public were literally flabbergasted. You see, Mr Errington was a well-known and very popular member of a certain smart section of London society. He was a constant visitor at the opera, the race-course, the Park, and the Carlton, he had a great many friends, and there was consequently quite a large attendance at the police court that morning. What had happened was this:

'After the very scrappy bits of evidence which came to light at the inquest, two gentlemen bethought themselves that perhaps they had some duty to perform towards the State and the public generally. Accordingly they had come forward offering to throw what light they could upon the mysterious affair on the Underground Railway.

'The police naturally felt that their information, such as it was, came rather late in the day, but as it proved of paramount importance, and the two gentlemen, moreover, were of undoubtedly good position in the world, they were thankful for what they could get, and acted accordingly; they accordingly brought Mr Errington up before the magistrate on a charge of murder.

'The accused looked pale and worried when I first caught sight of him in the court that day, which was not to be wondered at, considering the terrible position in which he found himself. He had been arrested at Marseilles, where he was preparing to start for Colombo.

'I don't think he realized how terrible his position was until later in the proceedings, when all the evidence relating to the arrest had been heard, and Emma Funnel had repeated her statement as to Mr Errington's call at 19, Addison Row, in the morning, and Mrs Hazeldene starting off for St Paul's Churchyard at 3.30 in the afternoon. Mr Hazeldene had nothing to add to the statements he had made at the coroner's inquest. He had last seen his wife alive on the morning of the fatal day. She had seemed very well and cheerful.

'I think everyone present understood that he was trying to say as little as possible that could in any way couple his deceased wife's name with that of the accused.

'And yet, from the servant's evidence, it undoubtedly leaked out that Mrs Hazeldene, who was young, pretty, and evidently fond of admiration, had once or twice annoyed her husband by her somewhat open, yet perfectly innocent flirtation with Mr Errington.

'I think everyone was most agreeably impressed by the widower's moderate and dignified attitude. You will see his photo there, among this bundle. That is just how he appeared in court. In deep black, of course, but without any sign of ostentation in his mourning. He had allowed his beard to grow lately, and wore it closely cut in a point.

'After his evidence, the sensation of the day occurred. A tall, dark-haired man, with the word "City" written metaphorically all over him, had kissed the book, and was waiting to tell the truth, and nothing but the truth.

'He gave his name as Andrew Campbell, head of the firm of Campbell & Co., brokers, of Throgmorton Street.

'In the afternoon of March 18th Mr Campbell, travelling on the Underground Railway, had noticed a very pretty woman in the same carriage as himself. She had asked him if she was in the right train for Aldersgate. Mr Campbell replied in the affirmative, and then buried himself in the Stock Exchange quotations of his evening paper.

'At Gower Street, a gentleman in a tweed suit and bowler hat got into the carriage, and took a seat opposite the lady. She seemed very much astonished at seeing him, but Mr Campbell did not recollect the exact words she said.

'The two talked to one another a good deal, and certainly the lady appeared animated and cheerful. Witness took no notice of them; he was very much engrossed in some calculations, and finally got out at Farringdon Street. He noticed that the man in the tweed suit also got out close behind him, having shaken hands with the lady, and said in a pleasant way: "Au revoir! Don't be late tonight". Mr Campbell did not hear the lady's reply, and soon lost sight of the man in the crowd.

'Everyone was on tenter-hooks, and eagerly waiting for the palpitating moment when witness would describe and identify the man who last had seen and spoken to the unfortunate woman, within five minutes probably of her strange and unaccountable death.

'Personally I knew what was coming before the Scotch stockbroker spoke. I could have jotted down the graphic and lifelike description he would give of a probable murderer. It would have fitted equally well the man who sat and had luncheon at this table just now; it would certainly have described five out of every ten young Englishmen you know.

'The individual was of medium height, he wore a

moustache which was not very fair nor yet very dark, his hair was between colours. He wore a bowler hat, and a tweed suit—and—and—that was all—Mr Campbell might perhaps know him again, but then again, he might not— he was not paying much attention—the gentleman was sitting on the same side of the carriage as himself—and he had his hat on all the time. He himself was busy with his newspaper—yes—he might know him again—but he really could not say.

'Mr Andrew Campbell's evidence was not worth very much, you will say. No, it was not in itself, and would not have justified any arrest were it not for the additional statements made by Mr James Verner, manager of Messrs Rodney & Co., colour printers.

'Mr Verner is a personal friend of Mr Andrew Campbell, and it appears that at Farringdon Street, where he was waiting for his train, he saw Mr Campbell get out of a first-class railway carriage. Mr Verner spoke to him for a second, and then, just as the train was moving off, he stepped into the same compartment which had just been vacated by the stockbroker and the man in the tweed suit. He vaguely recollects a lady sitting in the opposite corner to his own, with her face turned away from him, apparently asleep, but he paid no special attention to her. He was like nearly all business men when they are travelling—engrossed in his paper. Presently a special quotation interested him; he wished to make a note of it, took out a pencil from his waistcoat pocket, and seeing a clean piece of paste-board on the floor, he picked it up, and scribbled on it the memo-randum, which he wished to keep. He then slipped the card into his pocket-book.'

'"It was only two or three days later", added Mr Verner in the midst of breathless silence, "that I had occasion to refer to these same notes again.

'"In the meanwhile the papers had been full of the

[232]

mysterious death on the Underground Railway, and the names of those connected with it were pretty familiar to me. It was, therefore, with much astonishment that on looking at the paste-board which I had casually picked up in the railway carriage I saw the name on it, "Frank Errington"."

'There was no doubt that the sensation in court was almost unprecedented. Never since the days of the Fenchurch Street mystery, and the trial of Smethurst, had I seen so much excitement. Mind you, I was not excited—I knew by now every detail of that crime as if I had committed it myself. In fact, I could not have done it better, although I have been a student of crime for many years now. Many people there—his friends, mostly—believed that Errington was doomed. I think he thought so, too, for I could see that his face was terribly white, and he now and then passed his tongue over his lips, as if they were parched.

'You see he was in the awful dilemma—a perfectly natural one, by the way—of being absolutely incapable of proving an alibi. The crime—if crime there was—had been committed three weeks ago. A man about town like Mr Frank Errington might remember that he spent certain hours of a special afternoon at his club, or in the Park, but it is very doubtful in nine cases out of ten if he can find a friend who could positively swear as to having seen him there. No! no! Mr Errington was in a tight corner, and he knew it. You see, there were—besides the evidence—two or three circumstances which did not improve matters for him. His hobby in the direction of toxicology, to begin with. The police had found in his room every description of poisonous substances, including prussic acid.

'Then, again, that journey to Marseilles, the start for Colombo, was, though perfectly innocent, a very unfortunate one. Mr Errington had gone on an aimless voyage, but the public thought that he had fled, terrified at his own crime. Sir Arthur Inglewood, however, here again displayed his marvellous skill on behalf of his client by the masterly way in which he literally turned all the witnesses for the Crown inside out.

'Having first got Mr Andrew Campbell to state positively that in the accused he certainly did *not* recognize the man in the tweed suit, the eminent lawyer, after twenty minutes' cross-examination, had so completely upset the stock-broker's equanimity that it is very likely he would not have recognized his own office-boy.

'But through all his flurry and all his annoyance Mr Andrew Campbell remained very sure of one thing; namely, that the lady was alive and cheerful, and talking pleasantly with the man in the tweed suit up to the moment when the latter, having shaken hands with her, left her with a pleasant "Au revoir! Don't be late tonight". He had heard neither scream nor struggle, and in his opinion, if the individual in the tweed suit had administered a dose of poison to his companion, it must have been with her own knowledge and free will; and the lady in the train most emphatically neither looked nor spoke like a woman pre-pared for a sudden and violent death.

'Mr James Verner, against that, swore equally positively that he had stood in full view of the carriage door from the moment that Mr Campbell got out until he himself stepped into the compartment, that there was no one else in that carriage between Farringdon Street and Aldgate, and that the lady, to the best of his belief, had made no movement during the whole of that journey.

'No; Frank Errington was *not* committed for trial on the capital charge', said the man in the corner with one of his sardonic smiles, 'thanks to the cleverness of Sir Arthur Inglewood, his lawyer. He absolutely denied his identity with the man in the tweed suit, and swore he had not seen

Mrs Hazeldene since eleven o'clock in the morning of that fatal day. There was no proof that he had; moreover, according to Mr Campbell's opinion, the man in the tweed suit was in all probability not the murderer. Common sense would not admit that a woman could have a deadly poison injected into her without her knowledge, while chatting pleasantly to her murderer.

'Mr Errington lives abroad now. He is about to marry. I don't think any of his real friends for a moment believed that he committed the dastardly crime. The police think they know better. They do know this much, that it could not have been a case of suicide, that if the man who undoubtedly travelled with Mrs Hazeldene on that fatal afternoon had no crime upon his conscience he would long ago have come forward and thrown what light he could upon the mystery.

'As to who that man was, the police in their blindness have not the faintest doubt. Under the unshakable belief that Errington is guilty they have spent the last few months in unceasing labour to try and find further and stronger proofs of his guilt. But they won't find them, because there are none. There are no positive proofs against the actual murderer, for he was one of those clever blackguards who think of everything, foresee every eventuality, who know human nature well and can foretell exactly what evidence will be brought against them, and act accordingly.

'This blackguard from the first kept the figure, the personality, of Frank Errington before his mind. Frank Errington was the dust which the scoundrel threw metaphorically in the eyes of the police, and you must admit that he succeeded in blinding them—to the extent even of making them entirely forget the one simple little sentence, overheard by Mr Andrew Campbell, and which was, of course, the clue to the whole thing—the only slip the cunning rogue made—"Au revoir! Don't be late tonight".

Mrs Hazeldene was going that night to the opera with her husband.

'You are astonished?' he added with a shrug of the shoulders, 'you do not see the tragedy yet, as I have seen it before me all along. The frivolous young wife, the flirtation with the friend?—all a blind, all pretence. I took the trouble which the police should have taken immediately, of finding out something about the finances of the Hazeldene ménage. Money is in nine cases out of ten the keynote to a crime.

'I found that the will of Mary Beatrice Hazeldene had been proved by the husband, her sole executor, the estate being sworn at £15,000. I found out, moreover, that Mr Edward Sholto Hazeldene was a poor shipper's clerk when he married the daughter of a wealthy builder in Kensington —and then I made note of the fact that the disconsolate widower had allowed his beard to grow since the death of his wife.

'There's no doubt that he was a clever rogue,' added the strange creature, leaning excitedly over the table, and peering into Polly's face. 'Do you know how that deadly poison was injected into the poor woman's system? By the simplest of all means, one known to every scoundrel in Southern Europe. A ring—yes! a ring, which has a tiny hollow needle capable of holding a sufficient quantity of prussic acid to have killed two persons instead of one. The man in the tweed suit shook hands with his fair companion—probably she hardly felt the prick, not sufficiently in any case to make her utter a scream. And, mind you, the scoundrel had every facility, through his friendship with Mr Errington, of procuring what poison he required, not to mention his friend's visiting card. We cannot gauge how many months ago he began to try and copy Frank Errington in his style of dress, the cut of his moustache, his general appearance, making the change probably so gradual, that no one in his own entourage would notice it. He selected for his model a man his own height and build, with the same coloured hair.'

'But there was the terrible risk of being identified by his fellow-traveller in the Underground,' suggested Polly.

'Yes, there certainly was that risk; he chose to take it, and he was wise. He reckoned that several days would in any case elapse before that person, who, by the way, was a business man absorbed in his newspaper, would actually see him again. The great secret of successful crime is to study human nature,' added the man in the corner, as he began looking for his hat and coat. 'Edward Hazeldene knew it well.'

'But the ring?'

'He may have bought that when he was on his honeymoon,' he suggested with a grim chuckle; 'the tragedy was not planned in a week, it may have taken years to mature. But you will own that there goes a frightful scoundrel unhung. I have left you his photograph as he was a year ago, and as he is now. You will see he has shaved his beard again, but also his moustache. I fancy he is a friend now of Mr Andrew Campbell.'

He left Miss Polly Burton wondering, not knowing what to believe.

And that is why she missed her appointment with Mr Richard Frobisher (of the London Mail) to go and see Maud Allan dance at the Palace Theatre that afternoon.

X

The Moabite Cipher

R. Austin Freeman

A large and motley crowd lined the pavements of Oxford
Street as Thorndyke and I made our way leisurely eastward. Floral decorations and drooping bunting announced
one of those functions inaugurated from time to time by a
benevolent Government for the entertainment of fashionable loungers and the relief of distressed pick-pockets. For
a Russian Grand Duke, who had torn himself away, amidst
valedictory explosions, from a loving if too demonstrative
people, was to pass anon on his way to the Guildhall; and
a British Prince, heroically indiscreet, was expected to
occupy a seat in the ducal carriage.

Near Rathbone Place Thorndyke halted and drew my
attention to a smart-looking man who stood lounging in a
doorway, cigarette in hand.

'Our old friend Inspector Badger,' said Thorndyke. 'He
seems mightily interested in that gentleman in the light
overcoat. How d'ye do, Badger?' for at this moment the
detective caught his eye and bowed. 'Who is your friend?'

'That's what I want to know, sir,' replied the inspector.
'I've been shadowing him for the last half-hour, but I can't
make him out, though I believe I've seen him somewhere.
He don't look like a foreigner, but he has got something
bulky in his pocket, so I must keep him in sight until the

Duke is safely past. I wish,' he added gloomily, 'these beastly Russians would stop at home. They give us no end of trouble.'

'Are you expecting any—occurrences, then?' asked Thorndyke.

'Bless you, sir,' exclaimed Badger, 'the whole route is lined with plain-clothes men. You see, it is known that several desperate characters followed the Duke to England, and there are a good many exiles living here who would like to have a rap at him. Hallo! What's he up to now?'

The man in the light overcoat had suddenly caught the inspector's too inquiring eye, and forthwith dived into the crowd at the edge of the pavement. In his haste he trod heavily on the foot of a big, rough-looking man, by whom he was in a moment hustled out into the road with such violence that he fell sprawling face downwards. It was an unlucky moment. A mounted constable was just then backing in upon the crowd, and before he could gather the meaning of the shout that arose from the bystanders, his horse had set down one hind-hoof firmly on the prostrate man's back.

The inspector signalled to a constable, who forthwith made a way for us through the crowd; but even as we approached the injured man, he rose stiffly and looked round with a pale, vacant face.

'Are you hurt?' Thorndyke asked gently, with an earnest look into the frightened, wondering eyes.

'No, sir,' was the reply; 'only I feel queer—sinking—just here.'

He laid a trembling hand on his chest, and Thorndyke still eyeing him anxiously, said in a low voice to the inspector: 'Cab or ambulance, as quickly as you can.'

A cab was led round from Newman Street, and the injured man put into it. Thorndyke, Badger, and I entered, and we drove off up Rathbone Place. As we proceeded, our patient's face grew more and more ashen, drawn, and anxious; his breathing was shallow and uneven, and his teeth chattered slightly. The cab swung round into Goodge Street, and then—suddenly, in the twinkling of an eye—there came a change. The eyelids and jaw relaxed, the eyes became filmy, and the whole form subsided into the corner in a shrunken heap, with the strange gelatinous limpness of a body that is dead as a whole, while its tissues are still alive.

'God save us! The man's dead!' exclaimed the inspector in a shocked voice—for even policemen have their feelings. He sat staring at the corpse, as it nodded gently with the jolting of the cab, until we drew up inside the courtyard of the Middlesex Hospital, when he got out briskly, with suddenly renewed cheerfulness, to help the porter to place the body on the wheeled couch.

'We shall know who he is now, at any rate,' said he, as we followed the couch to the casualty-room. Thorndyke nodded unsympathetically. The medical instinct in him was for the moment stronger than the legal.

The house surgeon leaned over the couch, and made a rapid examination as he listened to our account of the accident. Then he straightened himself up and looked at Thorndyke.

'Internal haemorrhage, I expect,' said he. 'At any rate, he's dead, poor beggar!—as dead as Nebuchadnezzar. Ah! here comes a bobby; it's his affair now.'

A sergeant came into the room, breathing quickly, and looked in surprise from the corpse to the inspector. But the latter, without loss of time, proceeded to turn out the dead man's pockets, commencing with the bulky object that had first attracted his attention; which proved to be a brown-paper parcel tied up with red tape.

'Pork-pie, begad!' he exclaimed with a crestfallen air as he cut the tape and opened the package. 'You had better go through his other pockets, sergeant.'

The small heap of odds and ends that resulted from this process tended, with a single exception, to throw little light on the man's identity; the exception being a letter, sealed, but not stamped, addressed in an exceedingly illiterate hand to Mr Adolf Schonberg, 213, Greek Street, Soho.

'He was going to leave it by hand, I expect,' observed the inspector, with a wistful glance at the sealed envelope. 'I think I'll take it round myself, and you had better come with me, sergeant.'

He slipped the letter into his pocket, and, leaving the sergeant to take possession of the other effects, made his way out of the building.

'I suppose, Doctor,' he said as we crossed into Berners Street, 'you are not coming our way? Don't want to see Mr Schonberg, h'm?'

Thorndyke reflected for a moment. 'Well, it isn't very far, and we may as well see the end of the incident. Yes; let us go together.'

No. 213, Greek Street, was one of those houses that irresistibly suggest to the observer the idea of a church organ, either jamb of the doorway being adorned with a row of brass bell-handles corresponding to the stop-knobs.

These the sergeant examined with the air of an expert musician, and having, as it were, gauged the capacity of the instrument, selected the middle knob on the right-hand side and pulled it briskly; whereupon a first-floor window was thrown up and a head protruded. But it afforded us a momentary glimpse only, for, having caught the sergeant's upturned eye, it retired with surprising precipitancy, and before we had time to speculate on the apparition, the street door was opened and a man emerged. He was about to close the door after him when the inspector interposed.

'Does Mr Adolf Schonberg live here?'

The new-comer, a very typical Jew of the red-haired

type, surveyed us thoughtfully through his gold-rimmed spectacles as he repeated the name.

'Schonberg—Schonberg? Ah, yes! I know. He lives on the third floor. I saw him go up a short time ago. Third floor back;' and indicating the open door with a wave of the hand, he raised his hat and passed into the street.

'I suppose we had better go up,' said the inspector, with a dubious glance at the row of bell-pulls. He accordingly started up the stairs, and we all followed in his wake.

There were two doors at the back on the third floor, but as the one was open, displaying an unoccupied bedroom, the inspector rapped smartly on the other. It flew open almost immediately, and a fierce-looking little man confronted us with a hostile stare.

'Well?' said he.

'Mr Adolf Schonberg?' inquired the inspector.

'Well? What about him?' snapped our new acquaintance.

'I wished to have a few words with him,' said Badger.

'Then what the deuce do you come banging at my door for?' demanded the other.

'Why, doesn't he live here?'

'No. First floor front,' replied our friend, preparing to close the door.

'Pardon me,' said Thorndyke, 'but what is Mr Schonberg like? I mean——'

'Like?' interrupted the resident. 'He's like a blooming Sheeny, with a carroty beard and gold giglamps!' and, having presented this impressionist sketch, he brought the interview to a definite close by slamming the door and turning the key.

With a wrathful exclamation, the inspector turned towards the stairs, down which the sergeant was already clattering in hot haste, and made his way back to the ground floor, followed, as before, by Thorndyke and me. On the doorstep we found the sergeant breathlessly interrogating a smartly-dressed youth, whom I had seen alight from a hansom as we entered the house, and who now stood with a notebook tucked under his arm, sharpening a pencil with deliberate care.

'Mr James saw him come out, sir,' said the sergeant. 'He turned up towards the Square.'

'Did he seem to hurry?' asked the inspector.

'Rather,' replied the reporter. 'As soon as you were inside he went off like a lamplighter. You won't catch him now.'

'We don't want to catch him,' the detective rejoined gruffly; then, backing out of earshot of the eager pressman, he said in a lower tone: 'That was Mr Schonberg beyond a doubt, and it is clear that he has some reason for making himself scarce; so I shall consider myself justified in opening that note.'

He suited the action to the word, and, having cut the envelope open with official neatness, drew out the enclosure.

'My hat!' he exclaimed, as his eye fell upon the contents. 'What in creation is this? It isn't shorthand, but what the deuce is it?'

He handed the document to Thorndyke, who, having held it up to the light and felt the paper critically, proceeded to examine it with keen interest. It consisted of a single half-sheet of thin notepaper, both sides of which were covered with strange, crabbed characters, written with a brownish-black ink in continuous lines, without any spaces to indicate the divisions into words; and, but for the modern material which bore the writing, it might have been a portion of some ancient manuscript or forgotten codex.

'What do you make of it, Doctor?' inquired the inspector anxiously, after a pause, during which Thorndyke had scrutinized the strange writing with knitted brows.

'Not a great deal,' replied Thorndyke. 'The character

is the Moabite or Phoenician—primitive Semitic, in fact—
and reads from right to left. The language I take to be
Hebrew. At any rate, I can find no Greek words, and I see
here a group of letters which *may* form one of the few
Hebrew words that I know—the word badim, "lies". But
you had better get it deciphered by an expert.'

'If it is Hebrew,' said Badger, 'we can manage it all
right. There are plenty of Jews at our disposal.'

'You had much better take the paper to the British
Museum,' said Thorndyke, 'and submit it to the keeper of
the Phoenician antiquities for decipherment.'

Inspector Badger smiled a foxy smile as he deposited
the paper in his pocket-book. 'We'll see what we can make
of it ourselves first,' he said; 'but many thanks for your
advice, all the same, Doctor. No, Mr James, I can't give
you any information just at present; you had better apply
at the hospital.'

'I suspect,' said Thorndyke, as we took our way homewards, 'that Mr James has collected enough material for
his purpose already. He must have followed us from the
hospital, and I have no doubt that he has his report, with
"full details", mentally arranged at this moment. And I
am not sure that he didn't get a peep at the mysterious
paper, in spite of the inspector's precautions.'

'By the way,' I said, 'what do you make of the document?'

'A cipher, most probably,' he replied. 'It is written in
the primitive Semitic alphabet, which, as you know, is
practically identical with primitive Greek. It is written
from right to left, like the Phoenician, Hebrew, and
Moabite, as well as the earliest Greek, inscriptions. The
paper is common cream-laid notepaper, and the ink is
ordinary indelible Chinese ink, such as is used by draughts-
men. Those are the facts, and without further study of the
document itself, they don't carry us very far.'

'Why do you think it is a cipher rather than a document in straightforward Hebrew?'

'Because it is obviously a secret message of some kind. Now, every educated Jew knows more or less Hebrew, and, although he is able to read and write only the modern square Hebrew character, it is so easy to transpose one alphabet into another that the mere language would afford no security. Therefore, I expect that, when the experts translate this document, the translation or transliteration will be a mere farrago of unintelligible nonsense. But we shall see, and meanwhile the facts that we have offer several interesting suggestions which are well worth consideration.'

'As, for instance—?'

'Now, my dear Jervis,' said Thorndyke, shaking an admonitory forefinger at me, 'don't, I pray you, give way to mental indolence. You have these few facts that I have mentioned. Consider them separately and collectively, and in their relation to the circumstances. Don't attempt to suck my brain when you have an excellent brain of your own to suck.'

On the following morning the papers fully justified my colleague's opinion of Mr James. All the events which had occurred, as well as a number that had not, were given in the fullest and most vivid detail, a lengthy reference being made to the paper 'found on the person of the dead anarchist,' and 'written in a private shorthand or cryptogram.'

The report concluded with the gratifying—though untrue —statement that 'in this intricate and important case the police have wisely secured the assistance of Dr John Thorndyke, to whose acute intellect and vast experience the portentous cryptogram will doubtless soon deliver up its secret.'

'Very flattering,' laughed Thorndyke, to whom I read the extract on his return from the hospital, 'but a little awkward if it should induce our friends to deposit a few trifling mementoes in the form of nitro-compounds on our main staircase or in the cellars. By the way, I met Superintendent Miller on London Bridge. The "cryptogram", as Mr James calls it, has set Scotland Yard in a mighty ferment.'

'Naturally. What have they done in the matter?'

'They adopted my suggestion, after all, finding that they could make nothing of it themselves, and took it to the British Museum. The Museum people referred them to Professor Poppelbaum, the great palæographer, to whom they accordingly submitted it.'

'Did he express any opinion about it?'

'Yes, provisionally. After a brief examination, he found it to consist of a number of Hebrew words sandwiched between apparently meaningless groups of letters. He furnished the Superintendent off-hand with a translation of the words, and Miller forthwith struck off a number of hectograph copies of it, which he has distributed among the senior officials of his department; so that at present—' here Thorndyke gave vent to a soft chuckle '—Scotland Yard is engaged in a sort of missing word—or, rather, missing sense—competition. Miller invited me to join in the sport, and to that end presented me with one of the hectograph copies on which to exercise my wits, together with a photograph of the document.'

'And shall you?' I asked.

'Not I,' he replied, laughing. 'In the first place I have not been formally consulted, and consequently am a passive, though interested spectator. In the second place, I have a theory of my own which I shall test if the occasion arises. But if you would like to take part in the competition, I am authorized to show you the photograph and the translation. I will pass them on to you, and I wish you joy of them.'

R. Austin Freeman

He handed me the photograph and a sheet of paper that he had just taken from his pocket-book, and watched me with grim amusement as I read out the first few lines.

The Cipher.

'Woe, city, lies, robbery, prey, noise, whip, rattling, wheel, horse, chariot, day, darkness, gloominess, clouds, darkness, morning, mountain, people, strong, fire, them, flame.'

[247]

'It doesn't look very promising at first sight,' I remarked. 'What is the Professor's theory?'

'His theory—provisionally, of course—is that the words form the message, and the groups of letters represent mere filled-up spaces between the words.'

'But surely,' I protested, 'that would be a very transparent device.'

Thorndyke laughed. 'There is a childlike simplicity about it,' said he, 'that is highly attractive—but discouraging. It is much more probable that the words are dummies, and that the letters contain the message. Or, again, the solution may lie in an entirely different direction. But listen! Is that cab coming here?'

It was. It drew up opposite our chambers, and a few moments later a brisk step ascending the stairs heralded a smart rat-tat at our door. Flinging open the latter, I found myself confronted by a well-dressed stranger, who, after a quick glance at me, peered inquisitively over my shoulder into the room.

'I am relieved, Dr Jervis,' said he, 'to find you and Dr Thorndyke at home, as I have come on somewhat urgent professional business. My name,' he continued, entering in response to my invitation, 'is Barton, but you don't know me, though I know you both by sight. I have come to ask you if one of you—or, better still, both—could come to-night and see my brother.'

'That,' said Thorndyke, 'depends on the circumstances and on the whereabouts of your brother.'

'The circumstances,' said Mr Barton, 'are, in my opinion, highly suspicious, and I will place them before you—of course, in strict confidence.'

Thorndyke nodded and indicated a chair.

'My brother,' continued Mr Barton, taking the proffered seat, 'has recently married for the second time. His age is fifty-five, and that of his wife twenty-six, and I may say that the marriage has been—well, by no means a success. Now, within the last fortnight, my brother has been attacked by a mysterious and extremely painful infection of the stomach, to which his doctor seems unable to give a name. It has resisted all treatment hitherto. Day by day the pain and distress increase, and I feel that, unless something decisive is done, the end cannot be far off.'

'Is the pain worse after taking food?' inquired Thorndyke.

'That's just it!' exclaimed our visitor. 'I see what is in your mind, and it has been in mine, too; so much so that I have tried repeatedly to obtain samples of the food that he is taking. And this morning I succeeded.' Here he took from his pocket a wide-mouthed bottle, which, disengaging from its paper wrappings, he laid on the table. 'When I called, he was taking his breakfast of arrowroot, which he complained had a gritty taste, supposed by his wife to be due to the sugar. Now I had provided myself with this bottle, and during the absence of his wife, I managed unobserved to convey a portion of the arrowroot that he had left into it, and I should be greatly obliged if you would examine it, and tell me if this arrowroot contains anything that it should not.'

He pushed the bottle across to Thorndyke, who carried it to the window, and, extracting a small quantity of the contents with a glass rod, examined the pasty mass with the aid of a lens; then, lifting the bell-glass cover from the microscope, which stood on its table by the window, he smeared a small quantity of the suspected matter on to a glass slip, and placed it on the stage of the instrument.

'I observe a number of crystalline particles in this,' he said, after a brief inspection, 'which have the appearance of arsenious acid.'

'Ah!' ejaculated Mr Barton, 'just what I feared. But are you certain?'

'No,' replied Thorndyke; 'but the matter is easily tested.'

He pressed the button of the bell that communicated with the laboratory, a summons that brought the laboratory assistant from his lair with characteristic promptitude.

'Will you please prepare a Marsh's apparatus, Polton,' said Thorndyke.

'I have a couple ready, sir,' replied Polton.

'Then pour the acid into one and bring it to me, with a tile.'

As his familiar vanished silently, Thorndyke turned to Mr Barton.

'Supposing we find arsenic in this arrowroot, as we probably shall, what do you want us to do?'

'I want you to come and see my brother,' replied our client.

'Why not take a note from me to his doctor?'

'No, no; I want you to come—I should like you both to come—and put a stop at once to this dreadful business. Consider! It's a matter of life and death. You won't refuse! I beg you not to refuse me your help in these terrible circumstances.'

'Well,' said Thorndyke, as his assistant reappeared, 'let us first see what the test has to tell us.'

Polton advanced to the table, on which he deposited a small flask, the contents of which were in a state of brisk effervescence, a bottle labelled "calcium hypochloride", and a white porcelain tile. The flask was fitted with a safety-funnel and a glass tube drawn out to a fine jet, to which Polton cautiously applied a lighted match. Instantly there sprang from the jet a tiny, pale violet flame. Thorndyke now took the tile, and held it in the flame for a few seconds, when the appearance of the surface remained unchanged save for a small circle of condensed moisture. His next proceeding was to thin the arrowroot with distilled water until it was quite fluid, and then pour a small quantity into the funnel. It ran slowly down the tube into the flask, with the bubbling contents of which it became speedily mixed. Almost immediately a change began to appear in the character of the flame, which from a pale violet turned gradually to a sickly blue, while above it hung a faint cloud of white smoke. Once more Thorndyke held the tile above the jet, but this time no sooner had the pallid flame touched the cold surface of the porcelain, than there appeared on the latter a glistening black stain.

'That is pretty conclusive,' observed Thorndyke, lifting the stopper out of the reagent bottle, 'but we will apply the final test.' He dropped a few drops of the hypochloride solution on to the tile, and immediately the black stain faded away and vanished. 'We can now answer your question, Mr Barton,' said he, replacing the stopper as he turned to our client. 'The specimen that you brought us certainly contains arsenic, and in very considerable quantities.'

'Then,' exclaimed Mr Barton, starting from his chair, 'you will come and help me to rescue my brother from this dreadful peril. Don't refuse me, Dr Thorndyke, for mercy's sake, don't refuse.'

Thorndyke reflected for a moment.

'Before we decide,' said he, 'we must see what engagements we have.'

With a quick, significant glance at me, he walked into the office, whither I followed in some bewilderment, for I knew that we had no engagements for the evening.

'Now, Jervis,' said Thorndyke, as he closed the office door, 'what are we to do?'

'We must go, I suppose,' I replied. 'It seems a pretty urgent case.'

'It does,' he agreed. 'Of course, the man may be telling the truth, after all.'

'You don't think he is, then?'

'No. It is a plausible tale, but there is too much arsenic in that arrowroot. Still, I think I ought to go. It is an ordinary professional risk. But there is no reason why you should put your head into the noose.'

'Thank you,' said I, somewhat huffily. 'I don't see what risk there is, but if any exists I claim the right to share it.'

'Very well,' he answered with a smile, 'we will both go. I think we can take care of ourselves.'

He re-entered the sitting-room, and announced his decision to Mr Barton, whose relief and gratitude were quite pathetic.

'But,' said Thorndyke, 'you have not yet told us where your brother lives.'

'Rexford,' was the reply—'Rexford, in Essex. It is an out-of-the-way place, but if we catch the seven-fifteen train from Liverpool Street, we shall be there in an hour and a half.'

'And as to the return? You know the trains, I suppose?'

'Oh yes,' replied our client; 'I will see that you don't miss your train back.'

'Then I will be with you in a minute,' said Thorndyke; and taking the still-bubbling flask, he retired to the laboratory, whence he returned in a few minutes carrying his hat and overcoat.

The cab which had brought our client was still waiting, and we were soon rattling through the streets towards the station, where we arrived in time to furnish ourselves with dinner-baskets and select our compartment at leisure.

During the early part of the journey our companion was in excellent spirits. He despatched the cold fowl from the basket and quaffed the rather indifferent claret with as much relish as if he had not had a single relation in the world, and after dinner he became genial to the verge of hilarity. But, as time went on, there crept into his manner a certain anxious restlessness. He became silent and preoccupied, and several times furtively consulted his watch.

'The train is confoundedly late!' he exclaimed irritably. 'Seven minutes behind time already!'

'A few minutes more or less are not of much consequence,' said Thorndyke.

'No of course not; but still—Ah, thank heaven, here we are!'

He thrust his head out of the off-side window, and gazed eagerly down the line; then, leaping to his feet, he bustled out on to the platform while the train was still moving. Even as we alighted a warning bell rang furiously on the up-platform, and as Mr Barton hurried us through the empty booking-office to the outside of the station, the rumble of the approaching train could be heard above the noise made by our own train moving off.

'My carriage doesn't seem to have arrived yet,' exclaimed Mr Barton, looking anxiously up the station approach. 'If you will wait here a moment, I will go and make inquiries.'

He darted back into the booking-hall and through it on to the platform, just as the up-train roared into the station. Thorndyke followed him with quick but stealthy steps, and peering out of the booking-office door, watched his proceedings; then he turned and beckoned to me.

'There he goes,' said he, pointing to an iron foot-bridge that spanned the line; and, as I looked, I saw, clearly defined against the dim night sky, a flying figure racing towards the 'up' side.

It was hardly two-thirds across when the guard's whistle sang out its shrill warning.

'Quick, Jervis,' exclaimed Thorndyke; 'she's off!'

He leaped down on to the line, whither I followed instantly, and, crossing the rails, we clambered up together

on to the foot-board opposite an empty first-class compartment. Thorndyke's magazine knife, containing, among
other implements, a railway-key, was already in his hand.
The door was speedily unlocked, and, as we entered,
Thorndyke ran through and looked out on to the platform.

'Just in time!' he exclaimed. 'He is in one of the forward
compartments.'

He relocked the door, and, seating himself, proceeded
to fill his pipe.

'And now,' said I, as the train moved out of the station,
'perhaps you will explain this little comedy.'

'With pleasure,' he replied, 'if it needs any explanation.
But you can hardly have forgotten Mr James's flattering
remarks in his report of the Greek Street incident, clearly
giving the impression that the mysterious document was
in my possession. When I read that, I knew I must look
out for some attempt to recover it, though I hardly expected such promptness. Still, when Mr Barton called
without credentials or appointment, I viewed him with
some suspicion. That suspicion deepened when he wanted
us both to come. It deepened further when I found an
impossible quantity of arsenic in his sample, and it gave
place to certainty when, having allowed him to select the
trains by which we were to travel, I went up to the laboratory and examined the time-table; for I then found that
the last train for London left Rexford ten minutes after we
were due to arrive. Obviously this was a plan to get us both
safely out of the way while he and some of his friends ransacked our chambers for the missing documents.'

'I see; and that accounts for his extraordinary anxiety
at the lateness of the train. But why did you come, if you
knew it was a "plant"?'

'My dear fellow,' said Thorndyke, 'I never miss an
interesting experience if I can help it. There are possibilities
in this, too, don't you see?'

'But supposing his friends have broken into our chambers already?'

'That contingency has been provided for; but I think they will wait for Mr Barton—and us.'

Our train, being the last one up, stopped at every station, and crawled slothfully in the intervals, so that it was past eleven o'clock when we reached Liverpool Street. Here we got out cautiously, and, mingling with the crowd, followed the unconscious Barton up the platform, through the barrier, and out into the street. He seemed in no special hurry, for, after pausing to light a cigar, he set off at an easy pace up New Broad Street.

Thorndyke hailed a hansom, and, motioning me to enter, directed the cabman to drive to Clifford's Inn Passage.

'Sit well back,' said he, as we rattled away up New Broad Street. 'We shall be passing our gay deceiver presently—in fact, there he is, a living, walking illustration of the folly of underrating the intelligence of one's adversary.'

At Clifford's Inn Passage we dismissed the cab, and, retiring into the shadow of the dark, narrow alley, kept an eye on the gate of Inner Temple Lane. In about twenty minutes we observed our friend approaching on the south side of Fleet Street. He halted at the gate, plied the knocker, and after a brief parley with the night-porter vanished through the wicket. We waited yet five minutes more, and then, having given him time to get clear of the entrance we crossed the road.

The porter looked at us with some surprise.

'There's a gentleman just gone down to your chambers, sir,' said he. 'He told me you were expecting him.'

'Quite right,' said Thorndyke, with a dry smile. 'I was. Good night.'

We slunk down the lane, past the church, and through the gloomy cloisters, giving a wide berth to all lamps and lighted entries, until, emerging into Paper Buildings, we crossed at the darkest part to King's Bench Walk, where Thorndyke made straight for the chambers of our friend Anstey, which were two doors above our own.

'Why are we coming here?' I asked, as we ascended the stairs.

But the question needed no answer when we reached the landing, for through the open door of our friend's chambers I could see in the darkened room Anstey himself with two uniformed constables and a couple of plain-clothes men.

'There has been no signal yet, sir,' said one of the latter, whom I recognized as a detective-sergeant of our division.

'No,' said Thorndyke, 'but the M.C. has arrived. He came in five minutes before us.'

'Then,' exclaimed Anstey, 'the hall will open shortly, ladies and gents. The boards are waxed, the fiddlers are tuning up, and——'

'Not quite so loud, if you please, sir,' said the sergeant. 'I think there is somebody coming up Crown Office Row.'

The ball had, in fact, opened. As we peered cautiously out of the open window, keeping well back in the darkened room, a stealthy figure crept out of the shadow, crossed the road, and stole noiselessly into the entry of Thorndyke's chambers. It was quickly followed by a second figure, and then by a third, in which I recognized our elusive client.

'Now listen for the signal,' said Thorndyke. 'They won't waste time. Confound that clock!'

The soft-voiced bell of the Inner Temple clock, mingling with the harsher tones of St Dunstan's and the Law Courts, slowly tolled out the hour of midnight; and as the last reverberations were dying away, some metallic object, apparently a coin, dropped with a sharp clink on to the pavement under our window.

At the sound the watchers simultaneously sprang to their feet.

'You two go first,' said the sergeant, addressing the uniformed men, who thereupon stole noiselessly, in their rubber-soled boots, down the stone stairs and along the pavement. The rest of us followed, with less attention to silence, and as we ran up to Thorndyke's chambers, we were aware of quick but stealthy footsteps on the stairs above.

'They've been at work, you see,' whispered one of the constables, flashing his lantern on to the iron-bound outer door of our sitting-room, on which the marks of a large jemmy were plainly visible.

The sergeant nodded grimly, and, bidding the constables to remain on the landing, led the way upwards.

As we ascended, faint rustlings continued to be audible from above, and on the second-floor landing we met a man descending briskly, but without hurry, from the third. It was Mr Barton, and I could not but admire the composure with which he passed the two detectives. But suddenly his glance fell on Thorndyke, and his composure vanished. With a wild stare of incredulous horror, he halted as if petrified; then he broke away and raced furiously down the stairs, and a moment later a muffled shout and the sound of a scuffle told us that he had received a check. On the next flight we met two more men, who, more hurried and less self-possessed, endeavoured to push past; but the sergeant barred the way.

'Why, bless me!' exclaimed the latter, 'it's Moakey; and isn't that Tom Harris?'

'It's all right, sergeant,' said Moakey plaintively, striving to escape from the officer's grip. 'We've come to the wrong house, that's all.'

The sergeant smiled indulgently. 'I know,' he replied. 'But you're always coming to the wrong house, Moakey; and now you're just coming along with me to the right house.'

He slipped his hand inside his captive's coat, and

adroitly fished out a large, folding jemmy; whereupon the discomforted burglar abandoned all further protest.

On our return to the first-floor, we found Mr Barton sulkily awaiting us, handcuffed to one of the constables, and watched by Polton with pensive disapproval.

'I needn't trouble you tonight, Doctor,' said the sergeant, as he marshalled his little troop of captors and captives. 'You'll hear from us in the morning. Good night, sir.'

The melancholy procession moved off down the stairs, and we retired into our chambers with Anstey to smoke a last pipe.

'A capable man, that Barton,' observed Thorndyke— 'ready, plausible, and ingenious, but spoilt by prolonged contact with fools. I wonder if the police will perceive the significance of this little affair.'

'They will be more acute than I am if they do,' said I.

'Naturally,' interposed Anstey, who loved to "cheek" his revered senior, 'because there isn't any. It's only Thorndyke's bounce. He is really in a deuce of a fog himself.'

However this may have been, the police were a good deal puzzled by the incident, for, on the following morning, we received a visit from no less a person than Superintendent Miller, of Scotland Yard.

'This is a queer business,' said he, coming to the point at once—'this burglary, I mean. Why should they want to crack your place, right here in the Temple, too? You've got nothing of value here, have you? No "hard stuff", as they call it, for instance?'

'Not so much as a silver teaspoon,' replied Thorndyke, who had a conscientious objection to plate of all kinds.

'It's odd,' said the superintendent, 'deuced odd. When we got your note, we thought these anarchist idiots had mixed you up with the case—you saw the papers, I suppose —and wanted to go through your rooms for some reason.

We thought we had our hands on the gang, instead of which we find a party of common crooks that we're sick of the sight of. I tell you, sir, it's annoying when you think you've hooked a salmon, to bring up a blooming eel.'

'It must be a great disappointment,' Thorndyke agreed, suppressing a smile.

'It is,' said the detective. 'Not but what we're glad enough to get these beggars, especially Halkett, or Barton, as he calls himself—a mighty slippery customer is Halkett, and mischievous, too—but we're not wanting any disappointments just now. There was that big jewel job in Piccadilly, Taplin and Horne's; I don't mind telling you that we've not got the ghost of a clue. Then there's this anarchist affair. We're all in the dark there, too.'

'But what about the cipher?' asked Thorndyke.

'Oh, hang the cipher!' exclaimed the detective irritably. 'This Professor Poppelbaum may be a very learned man, but he doesn't help *us* much. He says the document is in Hebrew, and he has translated it into Double Dutch. Just listen to this!' He dragged out of his pocket a bundle of papers, and, dabbing down a photograph of the document before Thorndyke, commenced to read the Professor's report.

'"The document is written in the characters of the well-known inscription of Mesha, King of Moab." (Who the devil's he? Never heard of him. Well known, indeed!) "The language is Hebrew, and the words are separated by groups of letters, which are meaningless, and obviously introduced to mislead and confuse the reader. The words themselves are not strictly consecutive, but, by the interpolation of certain other words, a series of intelligible sentences is obtained, the meaning of which is not very clear, but is no doubt allegorical. The method of decipherment is shown in the accompanying tables, and the full rendering suggested on the enclosed sheet. It is to be noted that the writer of this document was apparently quite unacquainted with the Hebrew language, as appears from the absence of any grammatical construction." That's the Professor's report, Doctor, and here are the tables showing how he worked it out. It makes my head spin to look at 'em.'

He handed to Thorndyke a bundle of ruled sheets, which my colleague examined attentively for a while, and then passed on to me.

'This is very systematic and thorough,' said he. 'But now let us see the final result at which he arrives.'

'It may be all very systematic,' growled the superintendent, sorting out his papers, 'but I tell you, sir, it's all BOSH!' The latter word he jerked out viciously, as he slapped down on the table the final product of the Professor's labours. 'There,' he continued, 'that's what he calls the "full rendering", and I reckon it'll make your hair curl. It might be a message from Bedlam.'

Analysis of the cipher with transliteration into modern square Hebrew characters with a translation into English. N.B. The cipher reads from right to left.

	Space	Word	Space	Word	Space	Word
Moabite						
Hebrew		בַּדִּים		עִיר		אוֹי
Translation		LIES		CITY		WOE
Moabite						
Hebrew		קוֹל		טֶרֶף		גֵּזֶל
Translation		NOISE		PREY		ROBBERY
Moabite						
Hebrew		אוֹפָן		רַעַשׁ		שׁוֹט
Translation		WHEEL		RATTLING		WHIP
Moabite						
Hebrew		יוֹם		מֶרְכָּבָה		סוּס
Translation		DAY		CHARIOT		HORSE

The Professor's Analysis.

Thorndyke took up the first sheet, and as he compared the constructed renderings with the literal translation, the ghost of a smile stole across his usually immovable countenance.

'The meaning is certainly a little obscure,' he observed, 'though the reconstruction is highly ingenious; and, moreover, I think the Professor is probably right. That is to say, the words which he has supplied are probably the omitted parts of the passages from which the words of the cryptogram were taken. What do you think, Jervis?'

He handed me the two papers, of which one gave the actual words of the cryptogram, and the other a suggested reconstruction, with omitted words supplied. The first read:

'Woe	city	lies	robbery	prey
noise	whip	rattling	wheel	horse
chariot	day	darkness	gloominess	
cloud	darkness	morning	mountain	
people	strong	fire	them	flame.'

Turning to the second paper, I read out the suggested rendering:

'"Woe *to the bloody* city! *It is full of* lies *and* robbery; *the* prey *departeth not. The* noise *of a* whip, *and the noise of the* rattling *of the* wheel*s, and of the prancing* horse*s, and of the jumping* chariot*s.*

'"*A* day *of* darkness *and of* gloominess, *a day of* cloud*s, and of thick* darkness, *as the* morning *spread upon the* mountain*s, a great* people *and a* strong.

'"*A* fire *devoureth before* them, *and behind them a* flame *burneth.*"'

Here the first sheet ended, and, as I laid it down, Thorndyke looked at me inquiringly.

'There is a good deal of reconstruction in proportion to

the original matter,' I objected. 'The Professor has "sup-plied" more than three-quarters of the final rendering.'

'Exactly,' burst in the superintendent; 'it's all Professor and no cryptogram.'

'Still, I think the reading is correct,' said Thorndyke, 'As far as it goes, that is.'

'Good Lord!' exclaimed the dismayed detective. 'Do you mean to tell me, sir, that that balderdash is the real meaning of the thing?'

'I don't say that,' replied Thorndyke. 'I say it is correct as far as it goes; but I doubt its being the solution of the cryptogram.'

'Have you been studying that photograph that I gave you?' demanded Miller, with sudden eagerness.

'I have looked at it,' said Thorndyke evasively, 'but I should like to examine the original if you have it with you.'

'I have,' said the detective. 'Professor Poppelbaum sent it back with the solution. You can have a look at it, though I can't leave it with you without special authority.'

He drew the document from his pocket-book and handed it to Thorndyke, who took it over to the window and scrutinized it closely. From the window he drifted into the adjacent office, closing the door after him; and presently the sound of a faint explosion told me that he had lighted the gas-fire.

'Of course,' said Miller, taking up the translation again, 'this gibberish is the sort of stuff you might expect from a parcel of crack-brained anarchists; but it doesn't seem to mean anything.'

'Not to us,' I agreed; 'but the phrases may have some pre-arranged significance. And then there are the letters between the words. It is possible that they may really form a cipher.'

'I suggested that to the Professor,' said Miller, 'but he wouldn't hear of it. He is sure they are only dummies.'

'I think he is probably mistaken, and so, I fancy, does my colleague. But we shall hear what he has to say presently.'

'Oh, I know what he will say,' growled Miller. 'He will put the thing under the microscope, and tell us who made the paper, and what the ink is composed of, and then we shall be just where we were.' The superintendent was evidently deeply depressed.

We sat for some time pondering in silence on the vague sentences of the Professor's translation, until, at length, Thorndyke reappeared, holding the document in his hand. He laid it quietly on the table by the officer, and then inquired:

'Is this an official consultation?'

'Certainly,' replied Miller. 'I was authorized to consult you respecting the translation, but nothing was said about the original. Still, if you want it for further study, I will get it for you.'

'No, thank you,' said Thorndyke. 'I have finished with it. My theory turned out to be correct.'

'Your theory?' exclaimed the superintendent, eagerly. 'Do you mean to say——?'

'And, as you are consulting me officially, I may as well give you this.'

He held out a sheet of paper, which the detective took from him and began to read.

'What is this?' he asked, looking up at Thorndyke with a puzzled frown. 'Where did it come from?'

'It is the solution of the cryptogram,' replied Thorndyke.

The detective re-read the contents of the paper, and, with the frown of perplexity deepening, once more gazed at my colleague.

'This is a joke, sir; you are fooling me,' he said sulkily.

'Nothing of the kind,' answered Thorndyke. 'That is the genuine solution.'

'But it's impossible!' exclaimed Miller. 'Just look at it, Dr Jervis.'

I took the paper from his hand, and, as I glanced at it, I had no difficulty in understanding his surprise. It bore a short inscription in printed Roman capitals, thus:

'THE PICKERDILLEY STUF IS UP THE CHIMBLY 416 WARDOUR STREET 2ND FLOUR BACK IT WAS HID BECOS OF OLD MOAKEYS JOOD MOAKEY IS A BLITER.'

'Then that fellow wasn't an anarchist at all?' I exclaimed.

'No,' said Miller. 'He was one of Moakey's gang. We suspected Moakey of being mixed up with that job, but we couldn't fix it on him. By Jove!' he added, slapping his thigh, 'if this is right, and I can lay my hands on the loot! Can you lend me a bag, doctor? I'm off to Wardour Street this very moment.'

We furnished him with an empty suitcase, and, from the window, watched him making for Mitre Court at a smart double.

'I wonder if he will find the booty,' said Thorndyke. 'It depends on whether the hiding-place was known to more than one of the gang. Well, it has been a quaint case, and instructive, too. I suspect our friend Barton and the evasive Schonberg were the collaborators who produced that curiosity of literature.'

'May I ask how you deciphered the thing?' I said. 'It didn't appear to take long.'

'It didn't. It was merely a matter of testing a hypothesis; and you ought not to have to ask that question,' he added, with mock severity, 'seeing that you had what turns out to have been all the necessary facts, two days ago. But I will prepare a document and demonstrate to you tomorrow morning.'

'So Miller was successful in his quest,' said Thorndyke, as we smoked our morning pipes after breakfast. 'The "entire swag", as he calls it, was "up the chimbly", undisturbed.'

He handed me a note which had been left, with the empty suitcase, by a messenger, shortly before, and I was about to read it when an agitated knock was heard at our door. The visitor, whom I admitted, was a rather haggard and dishevelled elderly gentleman, who, as he entered, peered inquisitively through his concave spectacles from one of us to the other.

'Allow me to introduce myself, gentlemen,' said he. 'I am Professor Poppelbaum.'

Thorndyke bowed and offered a chair.

'I called yesterday afternoon,' our visitor continued, 'at Scotland Yard, where I heard of your remarkable decipherment and of the convincing proof of its correctness. Thereupon I borrowed the cryptogram, and have spent the entire night studying it, but I cannot connect your solution with any of the characters. I wonder if you would do me the great favour of enlightening me as to your method of decipherment, and so save me further sleepless nights? You may rely on my discretion.'

'Have you the document with you?' asked Thorndyke.

The Professor produced it from his pocket-book, and passed it to my colleague.

'You observe, Professor,' said the latter, 'that this is a laid paper, and has no water-mark?'

'Yes, I noticed that.'

'And that the writing is in indelible Chinese ink?'

'Yes, yes,' said the savant impatiently; 'but it is the inscription that interests me, not the paper and ink.'

'Precisely,' said Thorndyke. 'Now, it was the ink that interested me when I caught a glimpse of the document three days ago. "Why", I asked myself, "should anyone use this troublesome medium"—for this appears to be stick ink—"when good writing ink is to be had?" What advantages has Chinese ink over writing ink? It has several advantages as a drawing ink, but for writing purposes it has only one: it is quite unaffected by wet. The obvious inference, then, was that this document was, for some reason, likely to be exposed to wet. But this inference instantly suggested another, which I was yesterday able to put to the test—thus.'

He filled a tumbler with water, and, rolling up the document, dropped it in. Immediately there began to appear on it a new set of characters of a curious grey colour. In a few seconds Thorndyke lifted out the wet paper, and held it up to the light, and now there was plainly visible an inscription in transparent lettering, like a very distinct water-mark. It was in printed Roman capitals, written across the other writing, and read:

'The Pickerdilly stuf is up the chimbly 416 Wardour St 2nd flour back it was hid becos of old Moakeys jood moakey is a bliter.'

The Professor regarded the inscription with profound disfavour.

'How do you suppose this was done?' he asked gloomily.

'I will show you,' said Thorndyke. 'I have prepared a piece of paper to demonstrate the process to Dr Jervis. It is exceedingly simple.'

He fetched from the office a small plate of glass, and a photographic dish in which a piece of thin notepaper was soaking in water.

'This paper,' said Thorndyke, lifting it out and laying it on the glass, 'has been soaking all night, and is now quite pulpy.'

He spread a dry sheet of paper over the wet one, and on the former wrote heavily with a hard pencil, 'Moakey is a bliter'. On lifting the upper sheet, the writing was seen to be transferred in a deep grey to the wet paper, and when the latter was held up to the light the inscription stood out clear and transparent as if written with oil.

'When this dries,' said Thorndyke, 'the writing will completely disappear, but it will reappear whenever the paper is again wetted.'

The Professor nodded.

'Very ingenious,' said he—'a sort of artificial palimpsest, in fact. But I do not understand how that illiterate man could have written in the difficult Moabite script.'

'He did not,' said Thorndyke. 'The "cryptogram" was probably written by one of the leaders of the gang, who, no doubt, supplied copies to the other members to use instead of blank paper for secret communications. The object of the Moabite writing was evidently to divert attention from the paper itself, in case the communication fell into the wrong hands, and I must say it seems to have answered its purpose very well.'

The Professor started, stung by the sudden recollection of his labours.

'Yes,' he snorted; 'but I am a scholar, sir, not a policeman. Every man to his trade.'

He snatched up his hat, and with a curt 'Good morning', flung out of the room in dudgeon.

Thorndyke laughed softly.

'Poor Professor!' he murmured. 'Our playful friend Barton has much to answer for.'

XI

The Woman in the Big Hat

The Baroness Orczy

Lady Molly always had the idea that if the finger of Fate had pointed to Mathis' in Regent Street, rather than to Lyons', as the most advisable place for us to have a cup of tea that afternoon, Mr Culledon would be alive at the present moment.

My dear lady is quite sure—and needless to say that I share her belief in herself—that she would have anticipated the murderer's intentions, and thus prevented one of the most cruel and callous of crimes which were ever perpetrated in the heart of London.

She and I had been to a matinée of 'Trilby', and were having tea at Lyons', which is exactly opposite Mathis' Vienna café in Regent Street. From where we sat we commanded a view of the street and of the café, which had been very crowded during the last hour.

We had lingered over our toasted muffin until past six, when our attention was drawn to the unusual commotion which had arisen both outside and in the brilliantly lighted place over the road.

We saw two men run out of the doorway, and return a minute or two later in company with a policeman. You know what is the inevitable result of such a proceeding in London. Within three minutes a crowd had collected outside Mathis'. Two or three more constables had already assembled, and had some difficulty in keeping the entrance clear of intruders.

But already my dear lady, keen as a pointer on the scent, had hastily paid her bill, and, without waiting to see if I followed her or not, had quickly crossed the road, and the next moment her graceful form was lost in the crowd.

I went after her, impelled by curiosity, and presently caught sight of her in close conversation with one of our own men. I have always thought that Lady Molly must have eyes at the back of her head, otherwise how could she have known that I stood behind her now? Anyway, she beckoned to me, and together we entered Mathis', much to the astonishment and anger of the less fortunate crowd.

The usually gay little place was indeed sadly transformed. In one corner the waitresses, in dainty caps and aprons, had put their heads together, and were eagerly whispering to one another whilst casting furtive looks at the small group assembled in front of one of those pretty alcoves, which, as you know, line the walls all round the big tea-room at Mathis'.

Here two of our men were busy with pencil and notebook, whilst one fair-haired waitress, dissolved in tears, was apparently giving them a great deal of irrelevant and confused information.

Chief Inspector Saunders had, I understood, been already sent for; the constables, confronted with this extraordinary tragedy, were casting anxious glances towards the main entrance, whilst putting the conventional questions to the young waitress.

And in the alcove itself, raised from the floor of the room by a couple of carpeted steps, the cause of all this commotion, all this anxiety, and all these tears, sat huddled up on a chair, with arms lying straight across the marble-topped table, on which the usual paraphernalia of afternoon tea still lay scattered about. The upper part of the body, limp, backboneless, and awry, half propped up against the wall, half falling back upon the outstretched arms, told quite plainly its weird tale of death.

Before my dear lady and I had time to ask any questions, Saunders arrived in a taxicab. He was accompanied by the medical officer, Dr Townson, who at once busied himself with the dead man, whilst Saunders went up quickly to Lady Molly.

'The chief suggested sending for you,' he said quickly; 'he was phoning you when I left. There's a woman in this case, and we shall rely on you a good deal.'

'What has happened?' asked my dear lady, whose fine eyes were glowing with excitement at the mere suggestion of work.

'I have only a few stray particulars,' replied Saunders, 'but the chief witness is that yellow-haired girl over there. We'll find out what we can from her directly Dr Townson has given us his opinion.'

The medical officer, who had been kneeling beside the dead man, now rose and turned to Saunders. His face was very grave.

'The whole matter is simple enough, so far as I am concerned,' he said. 'The man has been killed by a terrific dose of morphia—administered, no doubt, in this cup of chocolate,' he added, pointing to a cup in which there still lingered the cold dregs of the thick beverage.'

'But when did this occur?' asked Saunders, turning to the waitress.

'I can't say,' she replied, speaking with obvious nervousness. 'The gentleman came in very early with a lady, somewhere about four. They made straight for this alcove.

The place was just beginning to fill, and the music had begun.'

'And where is the lady now?'

'She went off almost directly. She had ordered tea for herself and a cup of chocolate for the gentleman, also muffins and cakes. About five minutes afterwards, as I went past their table, I heard her say to him, "I am afraid I must go now, or Jay's will be closed, but I'll be back in less than half an hour. You'll wait for me, won't you?"'

'Did the gentleman seem all right then?'

'Oh, yes,' said the waitress. 'He had just begun to sip his chocolate, and merely said "S'long" as she gathered up her gloves and muff and then went out of the shop.'

'And she has not returned since?'

'No.'

'When did you first notice there was anything wrong with this gentleman?' asked Lady Molly.

'Well,' said the girl with some hesitation, 'I looked at him once or twice as I went up and down, for he certainly seemed to have fallen all of a heap. Of course, I thought that he had gone to sleep, and I spoke to the manageress about him, but she thought that I ought to leave him alone for a bit. Then we got very busy, and I paid no more attention to him, until about six o'clock, when most afternoon tea customers had gone, and we were beginning to get the tables ready for dinners. Then I certainly did think there was something wrong with the man. I called to the manageress, and we sent for the police.'

'And the lady who was with him at first, what was she like? Would you know her again?' queried Saunders.

'I don't know,' replied the girl; 'you see, I have to attend to such crowds of people of an afternoon, I can't notice each one. And she had on one of those enormous mushroom hats; no one could have seen her face—not more than her chin—unless they looked right under the hat.'

'Would you know the hat again?' asked Lady Molly.

'Yes—I think I should,' said the waitress. 'It was black velvet and had a lot of plumes. It was enormous,' she added, with a sigh of admiration and of longing for the monumental headgear.

During the girl's narrative one of the constables had searched the dead man's pockets. Among other items, he had found several letters addressed to Mark Culledon, Esq., some with an address in Lombard Street, others with one in Fitzjohn's Avenue, Hampstead. The initials M.C., which appeared both in the hat and on the silver mount of a letter-case belonging to the unfortunate gentleman, proved his identity beyond a doubt.

A house in Fitzjohn's Avenue does not, somehow suggest a bachelor establishment. Even whilst Saunders and the other men were looking through the belongings of the deceased, Lady Molly had already thought of his family—children, perhaps a wife, a mother—who could tell?

What awful news to bring to an unsuspecting, happy family, who might even now be expecting the return of father, husband, or son, at the very moment when he lay murdered in a public place, the victim of some hideous plot or feminine revenge!

As our amiable friends in Paris would say, it jumped to the eyes that there was a woman in the case—a woman who had worn a gargantuan hat for the obvious purpose of remaining unidentifiable when the question of the unfortunate victim's companion that afternoon came up for solution. And all these facts to put before an expectant wife or an anxious mother!

As, no doubt, you have already foreseen, Lady Molly took the difficult task on her own kind shoulders. She and I drove together to Lorbury House, Fitzjohn's Avenue, and on asking of the manservant who opened the door if his mistress were at home, we were told that Lady Irene Culledon was in the drawing-room.

Mine is not a story of sentiment, so I am not going to dwell on that interview, which was one of the most painful moments I recollect having lived through.

Lady Irene was young—not five-and-twenty, I should say—petite and frail-looking, but with a quiet dignity of manner which was most impressive. She was Irish, as you know, the daughter of the Earl of Athyville, and, it seems, had married Mr Mark Culledon in the teeth of strenuous opposition on the part of her family, which was as penniless as it was aristocratic, whilst Mr Culledon had great prospects and a splendid business, but possessed neither ancestors nor high connections. She had only been married six months, poor little soul, and from all accounts must have idolized her husband.

Lady Molly broke the news to her with infinite tact, but there it was! It was a terrific blow—wasn't it?—to deal to a young wife—now a widow; and there was so little that a stranger could say in these circumstances. Even my dear lady's gentle voice, her persuasive eloquence, her kindly words, sounded empty and conventional in the face of such appalling grief.

2

Of course, everyone expected that the inquest would reveal something of the murdered man's inner life—would, in fact, allow the over-eager public to get a peep into Mr Mark Culledon's secret orchard, wherein walked a lady who wore abnormally large velvet hats, and who nourished in her heart one of those terrible grudges against a man which can only find satisfaction in crime.

Equally, of course, the inquest revealed nothing that the public did not already know. The young widow was extremely reticent on the subject of her late husband's life, and the servants had all been fresh arrivals when the young couple, just home from their honeymoon, organized their new household at Lorbury House.

There was an old aunt of the deceased—a Mrs Steinberg —who lived with the Culledons, but who at the present moment was very ill. Someone in the house—one of the younger servants, probably—very foolishly had told her every detail of the awful tragedy. With positively amazing strength, the invalid thereupon insisted on making a sworn statement, which she desired should be placed before the coroner's jury. She wished to bear solemn testimony to the integrity of her late nephew, Mark Culledon, in case the personality of the mysterious woman in the big hat suggested to evilly disposed minds any thoughts of scandal.

'Mark Culledon was the one nephew whom I loved,' she stated with solemn emphasis. 'I have shown my love for him by bequeathing to him the large fortune which I inherited from the late Mr Steinberg. Mark was the soul of honour, or I should have cut him out of my will as I did my other nephews and nieces. I was brought up in a Scotch home, and I hate all this modern fastness and smartness, which are only other words for what I call profligacy.'

Needless to say, the old lady's statement, solemn though it was, was of no use whatever for the elucidation of the mystery which surrounded the death of Mr Mark Culledon. But as Mrs Steinberg had talked of 'other nephews', whom she had cut out of her will in favour of the murdered man, the police directed inquiries in those various quarters.

Mr Mark Culledon certainly had several brothers and sisters, also cousins, who at different times—usually for some peccadillo or other—seemed to have incurred the wrath of the strait-laced old lady. But there did not appear to have been any ill-feeling in the family owing to this. Mrs Steinberg was sole mistress of her fortune. She might just as well have bequeathed it in toto to some hospital as to one particular nephew whom she favoured, and the various relations were glad, on the whole, that the money was going to remain in the family rather than be cast abroad.

The mystery surrounding the woman in the big hat deepened as the days went by. As you know, the longer the period of time which elapses between a crime and the identification of the criminal, the greater chance the latter has of remaining at large.

In spite of strenuous efforts and close questionings of every one of the employees at Mathis', no one could give a very accurate description of the lady who had tea with the deceased on that fateful afternoon.

The first glimmer of light on the mysterious occurrence was thrown, about three weeks later, by a young woman named Katherine Harris, who had been parlourmaid at Lorbury House when first Mr and Lady Irene Culledon returned from their honeymoon.

I must tell you that Mrs Steinberg had died a few days after the inquest. The excitement had been too much for her enfeebled heart. Just before her death she had deposited £250 with her banker, which sum was to be paid over to any person giving information which would lead to the apprehension and conviction of the murderer of Mr Mark Culledon.

This offer had stimulated everyone's zeal, and, I presume, had aroused Katherine Harris to a realization of what had all the while been her obvious duty.

Lady Molly saw her in the chief's private office, and had much ado to disentangle the threads of the girl's confused narrative. But the main point of Harris's story was that a foreign lady had once called at Lorbury House, about a week after the master and mistress had returned from their honeymoon. Lady Irene was out at the time, and Mr Culledon saw the lady in his smoking-room.

'She was a very handsome lady,' explained Harris, 'and was beautifully dressed.'

'Did she wear a large hat?' asked the chief.

'I don't remember if it was particularly large,' replied the girl.

'But you remember what the lady was like?' suggested Lady Molly.

'Yes, pretty well. She was very, very tall, and very good-looking.'

'Would you know her again if you saw her?' rejoined my dear lady.

'Oh, yes; I think so,' was Katherine Harris's reply.

Unfortunately, beyond this assurance the girl could say nothing very definite. The foreign lady seems to have been closeted with Mr Culledon for about an hour, at the end of which time Lady Irene came home.

The butler being out that afternoon it was Harris who let her mistress in, and as the latter asked no questions, the girl did not volunteer the information that her master had a visitor. She went back to the servants' hall, but five minutes later the smoking-room bell rang, and she had to run up again. The foreign lady was then in the hall alone, and obviously waiting to be shown out. This Harris did, after which Mr Culledon came out of his room, and, in the girl's own graphic words, 'he went on dreadful'.

'I didn't know I 'ad done anything so very wrong,' she explained, 'but the master seemed quite furious, and said I wasn't a proper parlour-maid, or I'd have known that visitors must not be shown in straight away like that. I ought to have said that I didn't know if Mr Culledon was in; that I would go and see. Oh, he did go on at me!' continued Katherine Harris, volubly. 'And I suppose he complained to the mistress, for she give me notice the next day.'

'And you have never seen the foreign lady since?' concluded Lady Molly.

'No; she never come while I was there.'

'By the way, how did you know she was foreign? Did she speak like a foreigner?'

'Oh, no,' replied the girl. 'She did not say much—only asked for Mr Culledon—but she looked French like.'

This unanswerable bit of logic concluded Katherine's statement. She was very anxious to know whether, if the foreign lady was hanged for murder, she herself would get the £250.

On Molly's assurance that she certainly would, she departed in apparent content.

3

'Well! we are no nearer than we were before,' said the chief, with an impatient sigh, when the door had closed behind Katherine Harris.

'Don't you think so?' rejoined Lady Molly, blandly.

'Do you consider that what we have heard just now has helped us to discover who was the woman in the big hat?' retorted the chief, somewhat testily.

'Perhaps not,' replied my dear lady, with her sweet smile; 'but it may help us to discover who murdered Mr Culledon.'

With which enigmatical statement she effectually silenced the chief, and finally walked out of his office, followed by her faithful Mary.

Following Katherine Harris's indications, a description of the lady who was wanted in connection with the murder of Mr Culledon was very widely circulated, and within two days of the interview with the ex-parlour-maid another very momentous one took place in the same office.

Lady Molly was at work with the chief over some reports, whilst I was taking shorthand notes at a side desk, when a card was brought in by one of the men, and the next moment, without waiting either for permission to enter or to be more formally announced, a magnificent apparition literally sailed into the dust-covered little back office, filling it with an atmosphere of Parma violets and Russia leather.

I don't think that I had ever seen a more beautiful woman in my life. Tall, with a splendid figure and perfect carriage, she vaguely reminded me of the portraits one sees of the late Empress of Austria. This lady was, moreover, dressed to perfection, and wore a large hat adorned with a quantity of plumes.

The chief had instinctively risen to greet her, whilst Lady Molly, still and placid was eyeing her with a quizzical smile.

'You know who I am, sir,' began the visitor as soon as she had sunk gracefully into a chair; 'my name is on that card. My appearance, I understand, tallies exactly with that of a woman who is supposed to have murdered Mark Culledon.'

She said this so calmly, with such perfect self-possession, that I literally gasped. The chief, too, seemed to have been metaphorically lifted off his feet. He tried to mutter a reply.

'Oh, don't trouble yourself, sir!' she interrupted him, with a smile. 'My landlady, my servant, my friends have all read the description of the woman who murdered Mr Culledon. For the past twenty-four hours I have been watched by your police, therefore I come to you of my own accord, before they came to arrest me in my flat. I am not too soon, am I?' she asked, with that same cool indifference which was so startling, considering the subject of her conversation.

She spoke English with a scarcely perceptible foreign accent, but I quite understood what Katherine Harris had meant when she said that the lady looked 'French like'. She certainly did not look English, and when I caught sight of her name on the card, which the chief had handed to Lady Molly, I put her down at once as Viennese. Miss Elizabeth Lowenthal had all the charm, the grace, the elegance, which one associates with Austrian women more than with those of any other nation.

No wonder the chief found it difficult to tell her that, as a matter of fact, the police were about to apply for a warrant that very morning for her arrest on a charge of wilful murder.

'I know—I know,' she said, seeming to divine his thoughts; 'but let me tell you at once, sir, that I did not murder Mark Culledon. He treated me shamefully, and I would willingly have made a scandal just to spite him; he had become so respectable and strait-laced. But between scandal and murder there is a wide gulf. Don't you think so, madam?' she added, turning for the first time towards Lady Molly.

'Undoubtedly,' replied my dear lady, with the same quizzical smile.

'A wide gulf which, no doubt, Miss Elizabeth Lowenthal will best be able to demonstrate to the magistrate to-morrow,' rejoined the chief, with official sternness of manner.

I thought that, for the space of a few seconds, the lady lost her self-assurance at this obvious suggestion—the bloom on her cheeks seemed to vanish, and two hard lines appeared between her fine eyes. But, frightened or not, she quickly recovered herself, and said quietly:

'Now, my dear sir, let us understand one another. I came here for that express purpose. I take it that you don't want your police to look ridiculous any more than I want a scandal. I don't want detectives to hang about round my flat, questioning my neighbours and my servants. They would soon find out that I did not murder Mark Culledon, of course; but the atmosphere of the police would hang round me, and I—I prefer Parma violets,' she added, raising a daintily perfumed handkerchief to her nose.

'Then you have come to make a statement?' asked the chief.

'Yes,' she replied; 'I'll tell you all I know. Mr Culledon was engaged to marry me; then he met the daughter of an earl, and thought he would like her better as a wife than a simple Miss Lowenthal. I suppose I should be considered an undesirable match for a young man who has a highly respectable and snobbish aunt, who would leave him all her money only on the condition that he made a suitable marriage. I have a voice, and I came over to England two years ago to study English, so that I might sing in oratorio at the Albert Hall. I met Mark on the Calais–Dover boat, when he was returning from a holiday abroad. He fell in love with me, and presently he asked me to be his wife. After some demur, I accepted him; we became engaged, but he told me that our engagement must remain a secret, for he had an old aunt from whom he had great expectations, and who might not approve of his marrying a foreign girl, who was without connections and a professional singer. From that moment I mistrusted him, nor was I very astonished when gradually his affection for me seemed to cool. Soon after he informed me quite callously that he had changed his mind, and was going to marry some swell English lady. I didn't care much, but I wanted to punish him by making a scandal, you understand. I went to his house just to worry him, and finally I decided to bring an action for breach of promise against him. It would have upset him, I know; no doubt his aunt would have cut him out of her will. That is all I wanted, but I did not care enough about him to murder him.'

Somehow her tale carried conviction. We were all of us obviously impressed. The chief alone looked visibly disturbed, and I could read what was going on in his mind.

'As you say, Miss Lowenthal,' he rejoined, 'the police would have found all this out within the next few hours. Once your connection with the murdered man was known to us, the record of your past and his becomes an easy one to peruse. No doubt, too,' he added insinuatingly, 'our men would soon have been placed in possession of the one undisputable proof of your complete innocence with regard to that fateful afternoon spent at Mathis' café.'

'What is that?' she queried blandly.

'An alibi.'

'You mean, where I was during the time that Mark was being murdered in a tea shop?'

'Yes,' said the chief.

'I was out for a walk,' she replied quietly.

'Shopping, perhaps?'

'No.'

'You met someone who would remember the circumstance—or your servants could say at what time you came in?'

'No,' she repeated dryly; 'I met no-one, for I took a brisk walk on Primrose Hill. My two servants could only say that I went out at three o'clock that afternoon and returned after five.'

There was silence in the little office for a moment or two. I could hear the scraping of the pen with which the chief was idly scribbling geometrical figures on his blotting pad.

Lady Molly was quite still. Her large, luminous eyes were fixed on the beautiful woman who had just told us her strange story, with its unaccountable sequel, its mystery which had deepened with the last phrase which she had uttered. Miss Lowenthal, I felt sure, was conscious of her peril. I am not sufficiently a psychologist to know whether it was guilt or merely fear which was distorting the handsome features now, hardening the face and causing the lips to tremble.

[281]

Lady Molly scribbled a few words on a scrap of paper, which she then passed over to the chief. Miss Lowenthal was making visible efforts to steady her nerves.

'That is all I have to tell you,' she said, in a voice which sounded dry and harsh. 'I think I will go home now.'

But she did not rise from her chair, and seemed to hesitate as if fearful lest permission to go were not granted her.

To her obvious astonishment—and, I must add, to my own—the chief immediately rose and said, quite urbanely:

'I thank you very much for the helpful information which you have given me. Of course, we may rely on your presence in town for the next few days, may we not?'

She seemed greatly relieved, and all at once resumed her former charm of manner and elegance of attitude. The beautiful face was lit up by a smile.

The chief was bowing to her in quite a foreign fashion, and in spite of her visible reassurance she eyed him very intently. Then she went up to Lady Molly and held out her hand.

My dear lady took it without an instant's hesitation. I, who knew that it was the few words hastily scribbled by Lady Molly which had dictated the chief's conduct with regard to Miss Lowenthal, was left wondering whether the woman I loved best in all the world had been shaking hands with a murderess.

4

No doubt you will remember the sensation which was caused by the arrest of Miss Lowenthal, on a charge of having murdered Mr Mark Culledon, by administering morphia to him in a cup of chocolate at Mathis' cafe in Regent Street.

The beauty of the accused, her undeniable charm of manner, the hitherto blameless character of her life, all tended to make the public take violent sides either for or against her, and the usual budget of amateur correspondence, suggestions, recriminations and advice poured into the chief's office in titanic proportions.

I must say that, personally, all my sympathies went out to Miss Lowenthal. As I have said before, I am no psychologist, but I had seen her in the original interview at the office, and I could not get rid of an absolutely unreasoning certitude that the beautiful Viennese singer was innocent.

The magistrate's court was packed, as you may well imagine, on that first day of the inquiry; and, of course, sympathy with the accused went up to fever pitch when she staggered into the dock, beautiful still, despite the ravages caused by horror, anxiety, fear, in face of the deadly peril in which she stood.

The magistrate was most kind to her; her solicitor was unimpeachably assiduous; even our fellows, who had to give evidence against her, did no more than their duty, and were as lenient in their statements as possible.

Miss Lowenthal had been arrested in her flat by Danvers, accompanied by two constables. She had loudly protested her innocence all along, and did so still, pleading 'Not guilty' in a firm voice.

The great points in favour of the arrest were, firstly, the undoubted motive of disappointment and revenge against a faithless sweetheart, then the total inability to prove any kind of alibi, which, under the circumstances, certainly added to the appearance of guilt.

The question of where the fatal drug was obtained was more difficult to prove. It was stated that Mr Mark Culledon was director of several important companies, one of which carried on business as wholesale druggists.

Therefore it was argued that the accused, at different times and under some pretext or other, had obtained drugs from Mr Culledon himself. She had admitted to having visited the deceased at his office in the City, both before and after his marriage.

Miss Lowenthal listened to all this evidence against her with a hard, set face, as she did also to Katherine Harris's statement about her calling on Mr Culledon at Lorbury House, but she brightened up visibly when the various attendants at Mathis' café were placed in the box.

A very large hat belonging to the accused was shown to the witnesses, but, though the police upheld the theory that this was the headgear worn by the mysterious lady at the café on that fatal afternoon, the waitresses made distinctly contradictory statements with regard to it.

Whilst one girl swore that she recognized the very hat, another was equally positive that it was distinctly smaller than the one she recollected, and when the hat was placed on the head of Miss Lowenthal, three out of the four witnesses positively refused to identify her.

Most of these young women declared that though the accused, when wearing the big hat, looked as if she might have been the lady in question, yet there was a certain something about her which was different.

With that vagueness which is a usual and highly irritating characteristic of their class, the girls finally parried every question by refusing to swear positively either for or against the identity of Miss Lowenthal.

'There's something that's different about her somehow,' one of the waitresses asserted positively.

'What is it that's different?' asked the solicitor for the accused, pressing his point.

'I can't say,' was the perpetual, maddening reply.

Of course the poor young widow had to be dragged into the case, and here, I think, opinions and even expressions of sympathy were quite unanimous.

The whole tragedy had been inexpressibly painful to her, of course, and now it must have seemed doubly so. The scandal which had accumulated round her late husband's name must have added the poignancy of shame to that of grief. Mark Culledon had behaved as callously to the girl whom clearly he had married from interested, family motives, as he had to the one whom he had heartlessly cast aside.

Lady Irene, however, was most moderate in her statements. There was no doubt that she had known of her husband's previous entanglement with Miss Lowenthal, but apparently had not thought fit to make him accountable for the past. She did not know that Miss Lowenthal had threatened a breach of promise action against her husband.

Throughout her evidence she spoke with absolute calm and dignity, and looked indeed a strange contrast, in her closely fitting tailor-made costume of black serge and tiny black toque, to the more brilliant woman who stood in the dock.

The two great points in favour of the accused were, firstly, the vagueness of the witnesses who were called to identify her, and, secondly, the fact that she had undoubtedly begun proceedings for breach of promise against the deceased. Judging by the latter's letters to her, she would have had a splendid case against him, which fact naturally dealt a severe blow to the theory as to motive for the murder.

On the whole, the magistrate felt that there was not a sufficiency of evidence against the accused to warrant his committing her for trial; he therefore discharged her, and, amid loud applause from the public, Miss Lowenthal left the court a free woman.

Now, I know that the public did loudly, and, to my mind, very justly, blame the police for that arrest, which was denounced as being as cruel as it was unjustifiable. I felt as strongly as anybody on the subject, for I knew that the prosecution had been instituted in defiance of Lady

Molly's express advice, and in distinct contradiction to the evidence which she had collected. When, therefore, the chief again asked my dear lady to renew her efforts in that mysterious case, it was small wonder that her enthusiasm did not respond to his anxiety. That she would do her duty was beyond a doubt, but she had very naturally lost her more fervent interest in the case.

The mysterious woman in the big hat was still the chief subject of leading articles in the papers, coupled with that of the ineptitude of the police who could not discover her. There were caricatures and picture post-cards in all the shop windows of a gigantic hat covering the whole figure of its wearer, only the feet and a very long and pointed chin, protruding from beneath the enormous brim. Below was the device, 'Who is she? Ask the police?'

One day—it was the second since the discharge of Miss Lowenthal—my dear lady came into my room beaming. It was the first time I had seen her smile for more than a week, and already I had guessed what it was that had cheered her.

'Good news, Mary,' she said gaily. 'At last I've got the chief to let me have a free hand. Oh, dear! what a lot of argument it takes to extricate that man from the tangled meshes of red tape!'

'What are you going to do?' I asked.

'Prove that my theory is right as to who murdered Mark Culledon,' she replied seriously; 'and as a preliminary we'll go and ask his servants at Lorbury House a few questions.'

It was then three o'clock in the afternoon. At Lady Molly's bidding, I dressed somewhat smartly, and together we went off in a taxi to Fitzjohn's Avenue.

Lady Molly had written a few words on one of her cards, urgently requesting an interview with Lady Irene Culledon. This she handed over to the man-servant who opened the door at Lorbury House. A few moments later we were sitting in the cosy boudoir. The young widow, high-bred and dignified in her tight-fitting black gown, sat opposite to us, her white hands folded demurely before her, her small head, with its very close coiffure, bent in closest attention towards Lady Molly.

'I most sincerely hope, Lady Irene,' began my dear lady, in her most gentle and persuasive voice, 'that you will look with all possible indulgence on my growing desire —shared, I may say, by all my superiors at Scotland Yard— to elucidate the mystery which still surrounds your late husband's death.'

Lady Molly paused, as if waiting for encouragement to proceed. The subject must have been extremely painful to the young widow; nevertheless she responded quite gently:

'I can understand that the police wish to do their duty in the matter; as for me, I have done all, I think, that could be expected of me. I am not made of iron, and after that day in the police court—'

She checked herself, as if afraid of having betrayed more emotion than was consistent with good breeding, and concluded more calmly:

'I cannot do any more.'

'I fully appreciate your feelings in the matter,' said Lady Molly, 'but you would not mind helping me—would you—in a passive way, if you could, by some simple means, further the cause of justice?'

'What is it you want me to do?' asked Lady Irene.

'Only to allow me to ring for two of your maids and to ask them a few questions. I promise you that they shall not be of such a nature as to cause you the slightest pain.'

For a moment I thought that the young widow hesitated, then, without a word, she rose and rang the bell.

'Which of my servants did you wish to see?' she asked,

[287]

turning to my dear lady as soon as the butler entered in answer to the bell.

'Your own maid and your parlour-maid, if I may,' replied Lady Molly.

Lady Irene gave the necessary orders, and we all sat expectant and silent until, a minute or two later, two girls entered the room. One wore a cap and apron, the other, in neat black dress and dainty lace collar, was obviously the lady's maid.

'This lady,' said their mistress, addressing the two girls, 'wishes to ask you a few questions. She is a representative of the police, so you had better do your best to satisfy her with your answers.'

'Oh!' rejoined Lady Molly pleasantly—choosing not to notice the tone of acerbity with which the young widow had spoken, nor the unmistakable barrier of hostility and reserve which her words had immediately raised between the young servants and the 'representative of the police'— 'what I am going to ask these two young ladies is neither very difficult nor very unpleasant. I merely want their kind help in a little comedy which will have to be played this evening, in order to test the accuracy of certain statements made by one of the waitresses at Mathis' tea shop with regard to the terrible tragedy which has darkened this house. You will do that much, will you not?' she added, speaking directly to the maids.

No one can be so winning or so persuasive as my dear lady. In a moment I saw the girls' hostility melting before the sunshine of Lady Molly's smile.

'We'll do what we can, ma'am,' said the maid.

'That's a brave, good girl!' replied my lady. 'You must know that the chief waitress at Mathis' has, this very morning, identified the woman in the big hat who, we all believe, murdered your late master. Yes!' she continued, in response to a gasp of astonishment which seemed to go round the room like a wave, 'the girl seems quite positive, both as regards the hat and the woman who wore it. But, of course, one cannot allow a human life to be sworn away without bringing every possible proof to bear on such a statement, and I am sure that everyone in this house will understand that we don't want to introduce strangers more than we can help into this sad affair, which already has been bruited abroad too much.'

She paused a moment; then, as neither Lady Irene nor the maids made any comment, she continued:

'My superiors at Scotland Yard think it their duty to try and confuse the witness as much as possible in her act of identification. They desire that a certain number of ladies wearing abnormally large hats should parade before the waitress. Among them will be, of course, the one whom the girl has already identified as being the mysterious person who had tea with Mr Culledon at Mathis' that afternoon.

'My superiors can then satisfy themselves whether the waitress is or is not so sure of her statement that she invariably picks out again and again one particular individual amongst a number of others or not.'

'Surely,' interrupted Lady Irene, dryly, 'you and your superiors do not expect my servants to help in such a farce?'

'We don't look upon such a proceeding as a farce, Lady Irene,' rejoined Lady Molly, gently. 'It is often resorted to in the interests of an accused person, and we certainly would ask the co-operation of your household.'

'I don't see what they can do.'

But the two girls did not seem unwilling. The idea appealed to them, I felt sure; it suggested an exciting episode, and gave promise of variety in their monotonous lives.

'I am sure both these young ladies possess fine big hats,' continued Lady Molly with an encouraging smile.

'I should not allow them to wear ridiculous headgear,' retorted Lady Irene, sternly.

'I have the one your ladyship wouldn't wear and threw away,' interposed the young parlour-maid. 'I put it together again with the scraps I found in the dusthole.'

There was just one instant of absolute silence, one of those magnetic moments when Fate seems to have dropped the spool on which she was spinning the threads of a life, and is just stooping in order to pick it up.

Lady Irene raised a black-bordered handkerchief to her lips, then said quietly:

'I don't know what you mean, Mary. I never wear big hats.'

'No, my lady,' here interposed the lady's maid; 'but Mary means the one you ordered at Sanchia's and only wore the once—the day you went to that concert.'

'Which day was that?' asked Lady Molly, blandly.

'Oh! I couldn't forget that day,' ejaculated the maid; 'her ladyship came home from the concert—I had undressed her, and she told me that she would never wear her big hat again—it was too heavy. That same day Mr Culledon was murdered.'

'That hat would answer our purpose very well,' said Lady Molly, quite calmly. 'Perhaps Mary will go and fetch it, and you had better go and help her put it on.'

The two girls went out of the room without another word, and there were we three women left facing one another, with that awful secret, only half-revealed, hovering in the air like an intangible spectre.

'What are you going to do, Lady Irene?' asked Lady Molly, after a moment's pause, during which I literally could hear my own heart beating, whilst I watched the rigid figure of the widow in deep black crepe, her face set and white, her eyes fixed steadily on Lady Molly.

'You can't prove it!' she said defiantly.

'I think we can,' rejoined Lady Molly, simply; 'at any rate, I mean to try. I have two of the waitresses from Mathis' outside in a cab, and I have already spoken to the attendant who served you at Sanchia's, an obscure milliner in a back street near Portland Road. We know that you were at great pains there to order a hat of certain dimensions and to your own minute description; it was a copy of one you had once seen Miss Lowenthal wear when you met her at your late husband's office. We can prove that meeting, too. Then we have your maid's testimony that you wore that same hat once, and once only, the day, presumably, that you went out to a concert—a statement which you will find it difficult to substantiate—and also the day on which your husband was murdered.'

'Bah! the public will laugh at you!' retorted Lady Irene, still defiantly. 'You would not dare to formulate so monstrous a charge!'

'It will not seem monstrous when justice has weighed in the balance the facts which we can prove. Let me tell you a few of these, the result of careful investigation. There is the fact that you knew of Mr Culledon's entanglement with Miss Elizabeth Lowenthal, and did your best to keep it from old Mrs Steinberg's knowledge, realizing that any scandal round her favourite nephew would result in the old lady cutting him—and therefore you—out of her will. You dismissed a parlour-maid for the sole reason that she had been present when Miss Lowenthal was shown into Mr Culledon's study. There is the fact that Mrs Steinberg had so worded her will that, in the event of her nephew dying before her, her fortune would devolve on you; the fact that, with Miss Lowenthal's action for breach of promise against your husband, your last hope of keeping the scandal from the old lady's ears had effectually vanished. You saw the fortune eluding your grasp; you feared Mrs Steinberg would alter her will. Had you found the means,

[291]

and had you dared, would you not rather have killed the old lady? But discovery would have been certain. The other crime was bolder and surer. You have inherited the old lady's millions, for she never knew of her nephew's earlier peccadilloes.

'All this we can state and prove, and the history of the hat, bought, and worn one day only, that same memorable day, and then thrown away.'

A loud laugh interrupted her—a laugh that froze my very marrow.

'There is one fact you have forgotten, my lady of Scotland Yard,' came in sharp, strident accents from the black-robed figure, which seemed to have become strangely spectral in the fast gathering gloom which had been enveloping the luxurious little boudoir. 'Don't omit to mention the fact that the accused took the law into her own hands.'

And before my dear lady and I could rush to prevent her, Lady Irene Culledon had conveyed something—we dared not think what—to her mouth.

'Find Danvers quickly, Mary!' said Lady Molly, calmly. 'You'll find him outside. Bring a doctor back with you.'

Even as she spoke Lady Irene, with a cry of agony, fell senseless in my dear lady's arms.

The doctor, I may tell you, came too late. The unfortunate woman evidently had a good knowledge of poisons. She had been determined not to fail; in case of discovery, she was ready and able to mete out justice to herself.

I don't think the public ever knew the real truth about the woman in the big hat. Interest in her went the way of all things. Yet my dear lady had been right from beginning to end. With unerring precision she had placed her dainty finger on the real motive and the real perpetrator of the crime—the ambitious woman who had married solely for money, and meant to have that money even at the cost of one of the most dastardly murders that have ever darkened the criminal annals of this country.

I asked Lady Molly what it was that first made her think of Lady Irene as the possible murderess. No one else for a moment had thought her guilty.

'The big hat,' replied my dear lady with a smile. 'Had the mysterious woman at Mathis' been tall, the waitresses would not, one and all, have been struck by the abnormal size of the hat. The wearer must have been petite, hence the reason that under a wide brim only the chin would be visible. I at once sought for a small woman. Our fellows did not think of that, because they are men.'

You see how simple it all was!

XII

The Horse of the Invisible

William Hope Hodgson

I had that afternoon received an invitation from Carnacki. When I reached his place I found him sitting alone. As I came into the room he rose with a perceptibly stiff move-ment and extended his left hand. His face seemed to be badly scarred and bruised and his right hand was bandaged. He shook hands and offered me his paper, which I refused. Then he passed me a handful of photographs and returned to his reading.

Now, that is just Carnacki. Not a word had come from him and not a question from me. He would tell us all about it later. I spent about half an hour looking at the photo-graphs which were chiefly 'snaps' (some by flashlight) of an extraordinarily pretty girl; though in some of the photo-graphs it was wonderful that her prettiness was so evident for so frightened and startled was her expression that it was difficult not to believe that she had been photographed in the presence of some imminent and overwhelming danger.

The bulk of the photographs were of interiors of different rooms and passages and in every one the girl might be seen, either full length in the distance or closer, with perhaps little more than a hand or arm or portion of the head or dress included in the photograph. All of these had evidently been taken with some definite aim that did not have for its first purpose the picturing of the girl, but obviously of her surroundings and they made me very curious, as you can imagine.

Near the bottom of the pile, however, I came upon something *definitely* extraordinary. It was a photograph of the girl standing abrupt and clear in the great blaze of a flashlight, as was plain to be seen. Her face was turned a little upward as if she had been frightened suddenly by some noise. Directly above her, as though half-formed and coming down out of the shadows, was the shape of a single, enormous hoof.

I examined this photograph for a long time without understanding it more than that it had probably to do with some queer case in which Carnacki was interested.

When Jessop, Arkright and Taylor came in Carnacki quietly held out his hand for the photographs which I returned in the same spirit and afterwards we all went in to dinner. When we had spent a quiet hour at the table we pulled our chairs round and made ourselves snug and Carnacki began:

'I've been North,' he said, speaking slowly and painfully between puffs at his pipe. 'Up to Hisgins of East Lancashire. It has been a pretty strange business all round, as I fancy you chaps will think, when I have finished. I knew before I went, something about the "horse story", as I have heard it called; but I never thought of it coming my way, somehow. Also I know *now* that I never considered it seriously—in spite of my rule always to keep an open mind. Funny creatures, we humans!

'Well, I got a wire asking for an appointment, which of course told me that there was some trouble. On the date I fixed old Captain Hisgins himself came up to see me. He told me a great many new details about the horse story; though naturally I had always known the main points and understood that if the first child were a girl, that girl would be haunted by the Horse during her courtship.

'It is, as you can see already, an extraordinary story and though I have always known about it, I have never thought it to be anything more than an old-time legend, as I have already hinted. You see, for seven generations the Hisgins family have had men children for their first-born and even the Hisgins themselves have long considered the tale to be little more than a myth.

'To come to the present, the eldest child of the reigning family is a girl and she has been often teased and warned in jest by her friends and relations that she is the first girl to be the eldest for seven generations and that she would have to keep her men friends at arm's length or go into a nunnery if she hoped to escape the haunting. And this, I think, shows us how thoroughly the tale had grown to be considered as nothing worthy of the least serious thought. Don't you think so?

'Two months ago Miss Hisgins became engaged to Beaumont, a young Naval Officer, and on the evening of the very day of the engagement, before it was even formally announced, a most extraordinary thing happened which resulted in Captain Hisgins making the appointment and my ultimately going down to their place to look into the thing.

'From the old family records and papers that were entrusted to me I found that there could be no possible doubt that prior to something like a hundred and fifty years ago there were some very extraordinary and disagreeable coincidences, to put the thing in the least emotional way. In the whole of the two centuries prior to that date there were five first-born girls out of a total of seven generations of the family. Each of these girls grew up to maidenhood and each became engaged, and each one died during the period of engagement, two by suicide, one by falling from a window, one from a "broken heart" (presumably heart failure, owing to sudden shock through fright). The fifth girl was killed one evening in the park round the house; but just how, there seemed to be no *exact* knowledge; only that there was an impression that she had been kicked by a horse. She was dead when found.

'Now, you see, all of these deaths might be attributed in a way—even the suicides—to natural causes, I mean as distinct from supernatural. You see? Yet, in every case the maidens had undoubtedly suffered some extraordinary and terrifying experiences during their various courtships; for in all of the records there was mention either of the neighing of an unseen horse or of the sounds of an invisible horse galloping, as well as many other peculiar and quite inexplicable manifestations. You begin to understand now, I think, just how extraordinary a business it was that I was asked to look into.

'I gathered from one account that the haunting of the girls was so constant and horrible that two of the girls' lovers fairly ran away from their lady-loves. And I think it was this, more than anything else that made me feel that there had been something more in it than a mere succession of uncomfortable coincidences.

'I got hold of these facts before I had been many hours in the house and after this I went pretty carefully into the details of the thing that happened on the night of Miss Hisgins' engagement to Beaumont. It seems that as the two of them were going through the big lower corridor, just after dusk and before the lamps had been lighted, there had been a sudden, horrible neighing in the corridor, close to them. Immediately afterward Beaumont received a tremendous blow or kick which broke his right forearm. Then the rest of the family and the servants came running

to know what was wrong. Lights were brought and the
corridor and, afterwards, the whole house searched, but
nothing unusual was found.

'You can imagine the excitement in the house and the
half incredulous, half believing talk about the old legend.
Then, later, in the middle of the night the old Captain was
waked by the sound of a great horse galloping round and
round the house.

'Several times after this both Beaumont and the girl said
that they had heard the sounds of hoofs near to them after
dusk, in several of the rooms and corridors.

'Three nights later Beaumont was waked by a strange
neighing in the night-time seeming to come from the
direction of his sweetheart's bedroom. He ran hurriedly
for her father and the two of them raced to her room. They
found her awake and ill with sheer terror, having been
awakened by the neighing, seemingly close to her bed.

'The night before I arrived, there had been a fresh
happening and they were all in a frightfully nervy state,
as you can imagine.

'I spent most of the first day, as I have hinted, in getting
hold of details; but after dinner I slacked off and played
billiards all the evening with Beaumont and Miss Hisgins.
We stopped about ten o'clock and had coffee and I got
Beaumont to give me full particulars about the thing that
had happened the evening before.

'He and Miss Hisgins had been sitting quietly in her
aunt's boudoir whilst the old lady chaperoned them, behind a book. It was growing dusk and the lamp was at her
end of the table. The rest of the house was not yet lit as the
evening had come earlier than usual.

'Well, it seems that the door into the hall was open and
suddenly the girl said: "H'sh! what's that?"

'They both listened and then Beaumont heard it—the
sound of a horse outside of the front door.

'"Your father?" he suggested, but she reminded him that her father was not riding.

'Of course they were both ready to feel queer, as you can suppose, but Beaumont made an effort to shake this off and went into the hall to see whether anyone was at the entrance. It was pretty dark in the hall and he could see the glass panels of the inner draught-door, clear-cut in the darkness of the hall. He walked over to the glass and looked through into the drive beyond, but there was nothing in sight.

'He felt nervous and puzzled and opened the inner door and went out on to the carriage-circle. Almost directly afterward the great hall door swung to with a crash behind him. He told me that he had a sudden awful feeling of having been trapped in some way—that is how he put it. He whirled round and gripped the door handle, but something seemed to be holding it with a vast grip on the other side. Then, before he could be fixed in his mind that this was so, he was able to turn the handle and open the door.

'He paused a moment in the doorway and peered into the hall, for he had hardly steadied his mind sufficiently to know whether he was really frightened or not. Then he heard his sweetheart blow him a kiss out of the greyness of the big, unlit hall and he knew that she had followed him from the boudoir. He blew her a kiss back and stepped inside the doorway, meaning to go to her. And then, suddenly, in a flash of sickening knowledge he knew that it was not his sweetheart who had blown him that kiss. He knew that something was trying to tempt him alone into the darkness and that the girl had never left the boudoir. He jumped back and in the same instant of time he heard the kiss again, nearer to him. He called out at the top of his voice: "Mary, stay in the boudoir. Don't move out of the boudoir until I come to you." He heard her call something in reply from the boudoir and then he had struck a clump of a dozen or so matches and was holding them above his head and looking round the hall. There was no one in it, but even as the matches burned out there came the sounds of a great horse galloping down the empty drive.

'Now you see, both he and the girl had heard the sounds of the horse galloping; but when I questioned more closely I found that the aunt had heard nothing, though it is true she is a bit deaf, and she was further back in the room. Of course, both he and Miss Hisgins had been in an extremely nervous state and ready to hear anything. The door might have been slammed by a sudden puff of wind owing to some inner door being opened; and as for the grip on the handle, that may have been nothing more than the sneck catching.

'With regard to the kisses and the sounds of the horse galloping, I pointed out that these might have seemed ordinary enough sounds, if they had been only cool enough to reason. As I told him, and as he knew, the sounds of a horse galloping carry a long way on the wind so that what he had heard might have been nothing more than a horse being ridden some distance away. And as for the kiss, plenty of quiet noises—the rustle of a paper or a leaf—have a somewhat similar sound, especially if one is in an overstrung condition and imagining things.

'I finished preaching this little sermon on common-sense versus hysteria as we put out the lights and left the billiard room. But neither Beaumont nor Miss Hisgins would agree that there had been any fancy on their parts.

'We had come out of the billiard room by this time and were going along the passage and I was still doing my best to make both of them see the ordinary, commonplace possibilities of the happening, when what killed my pig, as the saying goes, was the sound of a hoof in the dark billiard room we had just left.

'I felt the "creep" come on me in a flash, up my spine

and over the back of my head. Miss Hisgins whooped like a child with the whooping-cough and ran up the passage, giving little gasping screams. Beaumont, however, ripped round on his heels and jumped back a couple of yards. I gave back too, a bit, as you can understand.

'"There it is," he said in a low, breathless voice. "Perhaps you'll believe now."

'"There's certainly something," I whispered, never taking my gaze off the closed door of the billiard room.

'"H'sh!" he muttered. "There it is again."

'There was a sound like a great horse pacing round and round the billiard room with slow, deliberate steps. A horrible cold fright took me so that it seemed impossible to take a full breath, you know the feeling, and then I saw we must have been walking backwards for we found ourselves suddenly at the opening of the long passage.

'We stopped there and listened. The sounds went on steadily with a horrible sort of deliberateness, as if the brute were taking a sort of malicious gusto in walking about all over the room which we had just occupied. Do you understand just what I mean?

'Then there was a pause and a long time of absolute quiet except for an excited whispering from some of the people down in the big hall. The sound came plainly up the wide stairway. I fancy they were gathered round Miss Hisgins, with some notion of protecting her.

'I should think Beaumont and I stood there, at the end of the passage, for about five minutes, listening for any noise in the billiard room. Then I realized what a horrible funk I was in and I said to him: "I'm going to see what's there."

'"So'm I," he answered. He was pretty white, but he had heaps of pluck. I told him to wait one instant and I made a dash into my bedroom and got my camera and flashlight. I slipped my revolver into my right-hand pocket and a knuckle-duster over my left fist, where it was ready and yet would not stop me from being able to work my flashlight.

'Then I ran back to Beaumont. He held out his hand to show me that he had his pistol and I nodded, but whispered to him not to be too quick to shoot, as there might be some silly practical joking at work, after all. He had got a lamp from a bracket in the upper hall which he was holding in the crook of his damaged arm, so that we had a good light. Then we went down the passage towards the billiard room and you can imagine that we were a pretty nervous couple.

'All this time there had not been a sound, but abruptly when we were within perhaps a couple of yards of the door we heard the sudden clumping of a hoof on the solid parquet floor of the billiard room. In the instant afterward it seemed to me that the whole place shook beneath the ponderous hoof falls of some huge thing, *coming towards the door*. Both Beaumont and I gave back a pace or two, and then realized and hung on to our courage, as you might say, and waited. The great tread came right up to the door and then stopped and there was an instant of absolute silence, except that so far as I was concerned, the pulsing in my throat and temples almost deafened me.

'I dare say we waited quite half a minute and then came the further restless clumping of a great hoof. Immediately afterward the sounds came right on as if some invisible thing passed through the closed door and the ponderous tread was upon us. We jumped, each of us, to our side of the passage and I know that I spread myself stiff against the wall. The clungk clunck, clungk clunck, of the great hoof falls passed right between us and slowly and with deadly deliberateness, down the passage. I heard them through a haze of blood-beats in my ears and temples and my body was extraordinarily rigid and pringling and I was horribly breathless. I stood for a little time like this, my head turned so that I could see up the passage. I was conscious only that there was a hideous danger abroad. Do you understand?

'And then, suddenly, my pluck came back to me. I was aware that the noise of the hoof-beats sounded near the other end of the passage. I twisted quickly and got my camera to bear and snapped off the flashlight. Immediately afterward, Beaumont let fly a storm of shots down the passage and began to run, shouting: "It's after Mary. Run! Run!"

'He rushed down the passage and I after him. We came out on the main landing and heard the sound of a hoof on the stairs and after that, nothing. And from thence onward, nothing.

'Down below us in the big hall I could see a number of the household round Miss Hisgins, who seemed to have fainted and there were several of the servants clumped together a little way off, staring up at the main landing and no one saying a single word. And about some twenty steps up the stairs was the old Captain Hisgins with a drawn sword in his hand where he had halted, just below the last hoof-sound. I think I never saw anything finer than the old man standing there between his daughter and that infernal thing.

'I daresay you can understand the queer feeling of horror I had at passing that place on the stairs where the sounds had ceased. It was as if the monster were still standing there, invisible. And the peculiar thing was that we never heard another sound of the hoof, either up or down the stairs.

'After they had taken Miss Hisgins to her room I sent word that I should follow, so soon as they were ready for me. And presently, when a message came to tell me that I could come any time, I asked her father to give me a hand with my instrument box and between us we carried it into the girl's bedroom. I had the bed pulled well out into the middle of the room, after which I erected the electric pentacle round the bed.

'Then I directed that lamps should be placed round the room, but that on no account must any light be made within the pentacle; neither must anyone pass in or out. The girl's mother I had placed within the pentacle and directed that her maid should sit without, ready to carry any message so as to make sure that Mrs Hisgins did not have to leave the pentacle. I suggested also that the girl's father should stay the night in the room and that he had better be armed.

'When I left the bedroom I found Beaumont waiting outside the door in a miserable state of anxiety. I told him what I had done and explained to him that Miss Hisgins was probably perfectly safe within the "protection"; but that in addition to her father remaining the night in the room, I intended to stand guard at the door. I told him that I should like him to keep me company, for I knew that he could never sleep, feeling as he did, and I should not be sorry to have a companion. Also, I wanted to have him under my own observation, for there was no doubt but that he was actually in greater danger in some ways than the girl. At least, that was my opinion and is still, as I think you will agree later.

'I asked him whether he would object to my drawing a pentacle round him for the night and got him to agree, but I saw that he did not know whether to be superstitious about it or to regard it more as a piece of foolish mumming; but he took it seriously enough when I gave him some particulars about the Black Veil case, when young Aster died. You remember, he said it was a piece of silly superstition and stayed outside. Poor devil!

'The night passed quietly enough until a little while before dawn when we both heard the sounds of a great

horse galloping round and round the house, just as old
Captain Hisgins had described it. You can imagine how
queer it made me feel and directly afterward, I heard
someone stir within the bedroom. I knocked at the door,
for I was uneasy, and the Captain came. I asked whether
everything was right; to which he replied yes, and immediately asked me whether I had heard the sounds of the
galloping, so that I knew he had heard them also. I suggested that it might be well to leave the bedroom door
open a little until the dawn came in, as there was certainly
something abroad. This was done and he went back into
the room, to be near his wife and daughter.

'I had better say here that I was doubtful whether there
was any value in the "Defense" about Miss Hisgins, for
what I term the "personal-sounds" of the manifestation
were so extraordinarily material that I was inclined to
parallel the case with that one of Harford's where the hand
of the child kept materialising within the pentacle and
patting the floor. As you will remember, that was a hideous
business.

'Yet, as it chanced, nothing further happened and so
soon as daylight had fully come we all went off to bed.

'Beaumont knocked me up about midday and I went
down and made breakfast into lunch. Miss Hisgins was
there and seemed in very fair spirits, considering. She told
me that I had made her feel almost safe for the first time
for days. She told me also that her cousin, Harry Parsket,
was coming down from London and she knew that he
would do anything to help fight the ghost. And after that
she and Beaumont went out into the grounds to have a
little time together.

'I had a walk in the grounds myself and went round the
house, but saw no traces of hoof-marks and after that I
spent the rest of the day making an examination of the
house, but found nothing.

'I made an end of my search before dark and went to my room to dress for dinner. When I got down the cousin had just arrived and I found him one of the nicest men I have met for a long time. A chap with a tremendous amount of pluck, and the particular kind of man I like to have with me in a bad case like the one I was on.

'I could see that what puzzled him most was our belief in the genuineness of the haunting and I found myself almost wanting something to happen, just to show him how true it was. As it chanced, something did happen, with a vengeance.

'Beaumont and Miss Hisgins had gone out for a stroll just before the dusk and Captain Hisgins asked me to come into his study for a short chat whilst Parsket went upstairs with his traps, for he had no man with him.

'I had a long conversation with the old Captain in which I pointed out that the "haunting" had evidently no particular connection with the house, but only with the girl herself and that the sooner she was married, the better, as it would give Beaumont a right to be with her at all times and further than this, it might be that the manifestations would cease if the marriage were actually performed.

'The old man nodded agreement to this, especially to the first part and reminded me that three of the girls who were said to have been "haunted" had been sent away from home and met their deaths whilst away. And then in the midst of our talk there came a pretty frightening interruption, for all at once the old butler rushed into the room, most extraordinarily pale:

'"Miss Mary, sir! Miss Mary, sir!" he gasped. "She's screaming . . . out in the Park, sir! And they say they can hear the Horse——"

'The Captain made one dive for a rack of arms and snatched down his old sword and ran out, drawing it as he ran. I dashed out and up the stairs, snatched my camera-flashlight and a heavy revolver, gave one yell at Parsket's door: "The Horse!" and was down and into the grounds.

'Away in the darkness there was a confused shouting and I caught the sounds of shooting, out among the scattered trees. And then, from a patch of blackness to my left, there burst suddenly an infernal gobbling sort of neighing. Instantly I whipped round and snapped off the flashlight. The great light blazed out momentarily, showing me the leaves of a big tree close at hand, quivering in the night breeze, but I saw nothing else and then the ten-fold blackness came down upon me and I heard Parsket shouting a little way back to know whether I had seen anything.

'The next instant he was beside me and I felt safer for his company, for there was some incredible thing near to us and I was momentarily blind because of the brightness of the flashlight. "What was it? What was it?" he kept repeating in an excited voice. And all the time I was staring into the darkness and answering, mechanically, "I don't know. I don't know."

'There was a burst of shouting somewhere ahead and then a shot. We ran towards the sounds, yelling to the people not to shoot; for in the darkness and panic there was this danger also. Then there came two of the game-keepers, racing hard up the drive with their lanterns and guns; and immediately afterward a row of lights dancing towards us from the house, carried by some of the men-servants.

'As the lights came up I saw we had come close to Beaumont. He was standing over Miss Hisgins and he had his revolver in his hand. Then I saw his face and there was a great wound across his forehead. By him was the Captain, turning his naked sword this way and that, and peering into the darkness; a little behind him stood the old butler, a battle-axe from one of the arm-stands in the hall in his hands. Yet there was nothing strange to be seen anywhere.

'We got the girl into the house and left her with her mother and Beaumont, whilst a groom rode for a doctor. And then the rest of us, with four other keepers, all armed with guns and carrying lanterns, searched round the home-park. But we found nothing.

'When we got back we found that the doctor had been. He had bound up Beaumont's wound, which luckily was not deep, and ordered Miss Hisgins straight to bed. I went upstairs with the Captain and found Beaumont on guard outside of the girl's door. I asked him how he felt and then, so soon as the girl and her mother were ready for us, Captain Hisgins and I went into the bedroom and fixed the pentacle again round the bed. They had already got lamps about the room and after I had set the same order of watching as on the previous night, I joined Beaumont outside of the door.

'Parsket had come up while I had been in the bedroom and between us we got some idea from Beaumont as to what had happened out in the Park. It seems that they were coming home after their stroll from the direction of the West Lodge. It had got quite dark and suddenly Miss Hisgins said: "Hush!" and came to a standstill. He stopped and listened, but heard nothing for a little. Then he caught it—the sound of a horse, seemingly a long way off, galloping towards them over the grass. He told the girl that it was nothing and started to hurry her towards the house, but she was not deceived, of course. In less than a minute they heard it quite close to them in the darkness and they started running. Then Miss Hisgins caught her foot and fell. She began to scream and that is what the butler heard. As Beaumont lifted the girl he heard the hoofs come thudding right at him. He stood over her and fired all five chambers of his revolver right at the sounds. He told us that he was sure he saw something that looked like an enormous horse's head, right upon him in the light of the last flash of his pistol. Immediately afterwards he was struck a tremendous blow which knocked him down and then the Captain and the butler came running up, shouting. The rest, of course, we knew.

'About ten o'clock the butler brought us up a tray, for which I was very glad, as the night before I had got rather hungry. I warned Beaumont, however, to be very particular not to drink any spirits and I also made him give me his pipe and matches. At midnight I drew a pentacle round him and Parsket and I sat one on each side of him, but outside the pentacle, for I had no fear that there would be any manifestation made against anyone except Beaumont or Miss Hisgins.

'After that we kept pretty quiet. The passage was lit by a big lamp at each end so that we had plenty of light and we were all armed, Beaumont and I with revolvers and Parsket with a shot-gun. In addition to my weapon I had my camera and flashlight.

'Now and again we talked in whispers and twice the Captain came out of the bedroom to have a word with us. About half past one we had all grown very silent and suddenly, about twenty minutes later, I held up my hand, silently; for there seemed to be a sound of galloping out in the night. I knocked on the bedroom door for the Captain to open it and when he came I whispered to him that we thought we heard the Horse. For some time we stayed, listening, and both Parsket and the Captain thought they heard it; but now I was not so sure, neither was Beaumont. Yet afterwards, I thought I heard it again.

'I told Captain Hisgins I thought he had better go back into the bedroom and leave the door a little open and this he did. But from that time onward we heard nothing and presently the dawn came in and we all went very thankfully to bed.

'When I was called at lunch-time I had a little surprise,

for Captain Hisgins told me that they had held a family council and had decided to take my advice and have the marriage without a day's more delay than possible. Beaumont was already on his way to London to get a special License and they hoped to have the wedding next day.

'This pleased me, for it seemed the sanest thing to be done in the extraordinary circumstances and meanwhile I should continue my investigations; but until the marriage was accomplished, my chief thought was to keep Miss Hisgins near to me.

'After lunch I thought I would take a few experimental photographs of Miss Hisgins and her *surroundings*. Sometimes the camera sees things that would seem very strange to normal human eyesight.

'With this intention and partly to make an excuse to keep her in my company as much as possible, I asked Miss Hisgins to join me in my experiments. She seemed glad to do this and I spent several hours with her, wandering all over the house, from room to room and whenever the impulse came I took a flashlight of her and the room or corridor in which we chanced to be at the moment.

After we had gone right through the house in this fashion, I asked her whether she felt sufficiently brave to repeat the experiments in the cellars. She said yes, and so I rooted out Captain Hisgins and Parsket, for I was not going to take her even into what you might call artificial darkness without help and companionship at hand.

'When we were ready we went down into the wine cellar, Captain Hisgins carrying a shot-gun and Parsket a specially prepared background and a lantern. I got the girl to stand in the middle of the cellar whilst Parsket and the Captain held out the background behind her. Then I fired off the flashlight, and we went into the next cellar where we repeated the experiment.

'Then in the third cellar, a tremendous, pitch-dark

place, something extraordinary and horrible manifested itself. I had stationed Miss Hisgins in the centre of the place, with her father and Parsket holding the background, as before. When all was ready and just as I pressed the trigger of the "flash", there came in the cellar that dreadful, gobbling neighing that I had heard out in the Park. It seemed to come from somewhere above the girl and in the glare of the sudden light I saw that she was staring tensely upward, but at no visible thing. And then in the succeeding comparative darkness, I was shouting to the Captain and Parsket to run Miss Hisgins out into the daylight.

'This was done instantly and I shut and locked the door afterwards making the First and Eighth signs of the Saaamaaa Ritual opposite to each post and connecting them across the threshold with a triple line.

'In the meanwhile Parsket and Captain Hisgins carried the girl to her mother and left her there, in a half-fainting condition whilst I stayed on guard outside of the cellar door, feeling pretty horrible for I knew that there was some disgusting thing inside, and along with this feeling there was a sense of half-ashamedness, rather miserable, you know, because I had exposed Miss Hisgins to the danger.

'I had got the Captain's shot-gun and when he and Parsket came down again they were each carrying guns and lanterns. I could not possibly tell you the utter relief of spirit and body that came to me when I heard them coming, but just try to imagine what it was like, standing outside of that cellar. Can you?

'I remember noticing, just before I went to unlock the door, how white and ghastly Parsket looked and the old Captain was grey-looking and I wondered whether my face was like theirs. And this, you know, had its own distinct effect upon my nerves, for it seemed to bring the beastliness

[311]

of the thing bash down on to me in a fresh way. I know it was only sheer will power that carried me up to the door and made me turn the key.

'I paused one little moment and then with a nervy jerk sent the door wide open and held my lantern over my head. Parsket and the Captain came one on each side of me and held up their lanterns, but the place was absolutely empty. Of course, I did not trust to a casual look of this kind, but spent several hours with the help of the two others in sounding every square foot of the floor, ceiling and walls.

'Yet, in the end I had to admit that the place itself was absolutely normal and so we came away. But I sealed the door and outside, opposite each door-post I made the First and Last signs of the Saaamaaa Ritual, joined them as before, with a triple line. Can you imagine what it was like, searching that cellar?

'When we got upstairs I inquired very anxiously how Miss Hisgins was and the girl came out herself to tell me that she was all right and that I was not to trouble about her, or blame myself, as I told her I had been doing.

'I felt happier then and went off to dress for dinner and after that was done, Parsket and I took one of the bath-rooms to develop the negatives that I had been taking. Yet none of the plates had anything to tell us until we came to the one that was taken in the cellar. Parsket was developing and I had taken a batch of the fixed plates out into the lamplight to examine them.

'I had just gone carefully through the lot when I heard a shout from Parsket and when I ran to him he was looking at a partly-developed negative which he was holding up to the red lamp. It showed the girl plainly, looking upward as I had seen her, but the thing that astonished me was the shadow of an enormous hoof, right above her, as if it were coming down upon her out of the shadows. And you know,

I had run her bang into that danger. That was the thought that was chief in my mind.

'As soon as the developing was complete I fixed the plate and examined it carefully in a good light. There was no doubt about it at all, the thing above Miss Hisgins was an enormous, shadowy hoof. Yet I was no nearer to coming to any definite knowledge and the only thing I could do was to warn Parsket to say nothing about it to the girl for it would only increase her fright, but I showed the thing to her father for I considered it right that he should know.

'That night we took the same precautions for Miss Hisgins' safety as on the two previous nights and Parsket kept me company; yet the dawn came in without anything unusual having happened and I went off to bed.

'When I got down to lunch I learnt that Beaumont had wired to say that he would be in soon after four; also that a message had been sent to the Rector. And it was generally plain that the ladies of the house were in a tremendous fluster.

'Beaumont's train was late and he did not get home until five, but even then the Rector had not put in an appearance and the butler came in to say that the coachman had returned without him as he had been called away unexpectedly. Twice more during the evening the carriage was sent down, but the clergyman had not returned and we had to delay the marriage until the next day.

'That night I arranged the "Defense" round the girl's bed and the Captain and his wife sat up with her as before. Beaumont, as I expected, insisted on keeping watch with me and he seemed in a curiously frightened mood; not for himself, you know, but for Miss Hisgins. He had a horrible feeling he told me, that there would be a final, dreadful attempt on his sweetheart that night.

'This, of course, I told him was nothing but nerves; yet really, it made me feel very anxious; for I have seen too

much not to know that under such circumstances a pre-
monitory *conviction* of impending danger is not necessarily
to be put down entirely to nerves. In fact, Beaumont was
so simply and earnestly convinced that the night would
bring some extraordinary manifestation that I got Parsket
to rig up a long cord from the wire of the butler's bell, to
come along the passage handy.

'To the butler himself I gave directions not to undress
and to give the same order to two of the footmen. If I rang
he was to come instantly, with the footmen, carrying
lanterns and the lanterns were to be kept ready lit all night.
If for any reason the bell did not ring and I blew my
whistle, he was to take that as a signal in the place of the
bell.

'After I had arranged all these minor details I drew a
pentacle about Beaumont and warned him very particularly
to stay within it, whatever happened. And when this was
done, there was nothing to do but wait and pray that the
night would go as quietly as the night before.

'We scarcely talked at all and by about one a.m. we
were all very tense and nervous so that at last Parsket got
up and began to walk up and down the corridor to steady
himself a bit. Presently I slipped off my pumps and joined
him and we walked up and down, whispering occasionally
for something over an hour, until in turning I caught my
foot in the bell-cord and went down on my face; but without hurting myself or making a noise.

'When I got up Parsket nudged me.

'"Did you notice that the bell never rang?" he whispered.

'"Jove!" I said, "you're right."

'"Wait a minute," he answered. "I'll bet it's only a
kink somewhere in the cord." He left his gun and slipped
along the passage and taking the top lamp, tiptoed away
into the house, carrying Beaumont's revolver ready in his

right hand. He was a plucky chap, I remember thinking then, and again, later.

'Just then Beaumont motioned to me for absolute quiet. Directly afterwards I heard the thing for which he listened —the sound of a horse galloping, out in the night. I think that I may say I fairly shivered. The sound died away and left a horrible, desolate, eerie feeling in the air, you know. I put my hand out to the bell-cord, hoping that Parsket had got it clear. Then I waited, glancing before and behind.

'Perhaps two minutes passed, full of what seemed like an almost unearthly quiet. And then, suddenly, down the corridor at the lighted end there sounded the clumping of a great hoof and instantly the lamp was thrown down with a tremendous crash and we were in the dark. I tugged hard on the cord and blew the whistle; then I raised my snap-shot and fired the flashlight. The corridor blazed into brilliant light, but there was nothing, and then the darkness fell like thunder. I heard the Captain at the bedroom-door and shouted to him to bring out a lamp, *quick*; but instead something started to kick the door and I heard the Captain shouting within the bedroom and then the screaming of the women. I had a sudden horrible fear that the monster had got into the bedroom, but in the same inst t from up the corridor there came abruptly the vile, gobbling neighing that we had heard in the park and the cellar. I blew the whistle again and groped blindly for the bell-cord, shouting to Beaumont to stay in the Pentacle, whatever happened. I yelled again to the Captain to bring out a lamp and there came a smashing sound against the bedroom door. Then I had my matches in my hand, to get some light before that incredible, unseen Monster was upon us.

'The match scraped on the box and flared up dully and in the same instant I heard a faint sound behind me. I whipped round in a kind of mad terror and saw something in the light of the match—a monstrous horse-head close to Beaumont.

'"Look out, Beaumont!" I shouted in a sort of scream. "It's behind you!"

'The match went out abruptly and instantly there came the huge bang of Parsket's double-barrel (both barrels at once), fired evidently single-handed by Beaumont close to my ear, as it seemed. I caught a momentary glimpse of the great head in the flash and of an enormous hoof amid the belch of fire and smoke seeming to be descending upon Beaumont. In the same instant I fired three chambers of my revolver. There was the sound of a dull blow and then that horrible, gobbling neigh broke out close to me. I fired twice at the sound. Immediately afterward something struck me and I was knocked backwards. I got on to my knees and shouted for help at the top of my voice. I heard the women screaming behind the closed door of the bedroom and was dully aware that the door was being smashed from the inside, and directly afterwards I knew that Beaumont was struggling with some hideous thing near to me. For an instant I held back, stupidly, paralysed with funk and then, blindly and in a sort of rigid chill of goose-flesh I went to help him, shouting his name. I can tell you, I was nearly sick with the naked fear I had on me. There came a little, choking scream out of the darkness, and at that I jumped forward into the dark. I gripped a vast, furry ear. Then something struck me another great blow, knocking me sick. I hit back, weak and blind and gripped with my other hand at the incredible thing. Abruptly I was dimly aware of a tremendous crash behind me and a great burst of light. There were other lights in the passage and a noise of feet and shouting. My hand-grips were torn from the thing they held; I shut my eyes stupidly and heard a loud yell above me and then a heavy blow, like a butcher chopping meat and then something fell upon me.

'I was helped to my knees by the Captain and the butler. On the floor lay an enormous horse-head out of which protruded a man's trunk and legs. On the wrists were fixed great hoofs. It was the monster. The Captain cut something with the sword that he held in his hand and stooped and lifted off the mask, for that is what it was. I saw the face then of the man who had worn it. It was Parsket. He had a bad wound across the forehead where the Captain's sword had bit through the mask. I looked bewilderedly from him to Beaumont, who was sitting up, leaning against the wall of the corridor. Then I stared at Parsket again.

'"By Jove!" I said at last, and then I was quiet for I was so ashamed for the man. You can understand, can't you? And he was opening his eyes. And you know, I had grown so to like him.

'And then, you know, just as Parsket was getting back his wits and looking from one to the other of us and beginning to remember, there happened a strange and incredible thing. For from the end of the corridor there sounded, suddenly, the clumping of a great hoof. I looked that way and then instantly at Parsket and saw a horrible fear in his face and eyes. He wrenched himself round, weakly, and stared in mad terror up the corridor to where the sound had been, and the rest of us stared, in a frozen group. I remember vaguely half sobs and whispers from Miss Hisgins' bedroom, all the while that I stared frightenedly up the corridor.

'The silence lasted several seconds and then, abruptly, there came again the clumping of the great hoof, away at the end of the corridor. And immediately afterward the clungk, clunk—clungk, clunk of mighty hoofs coming down the passage towards us.

'Even then, you know, most of us thought it was some mechanism of Parsket's still at work and we were in the queerest mixture of fright and doubt. I think everyone looked at Parsket. And suddenly the Captain shouted out:

'"Stop this damned fooling at once. Haven't you done enough?"

'For my part, I was now frightened for I had a *sense* that there was something horrible and wrong. And then Parsket managed to gasp out:

'"It's not me! My God! It's not me! My God! It's not me."

'And then, you know, it seemed to come home to everyone in an instant that there was really some dreadful thing coming down the passage. There was a mad rush to get away and even old Captain Hisgins gave back with the butler and the footmen. Beaumont fainted outright, as I found afterwards, for he had been badly mauled. I just flattened back against the wall, kneeling as I was, too stupid and dazed even to run. And almost in the same instant the ponderous hoof-falls sounded close to me and seeming to shake the solid floor as they passed. Abruptly the great sounds ceased and I knew in a sort of sick fashion that the thing had halted opposite to the door of the girl's bedroom. And then I was aware that Parsket was standing rocking in the doorway with his arms spread across, so as to fill the doorway with his body. Parsket was extraordinarily pale and the blood was running down his face from the wound in his forehead; and then I noticed that he seemed to be looking at something in the passage with a peculiar, desperate, fixed, incredibly masterful gaze. But there was really nothing to be seen. And suddenly the clungk, clunk—clungk, clunk recommenced and passed onward down the passage. In the same moment Parsket pitched forward out of the doorway on to his face.

'There were shouts from the huddle of men down the passage and the two footmen and the butler simply ran, carrying their lanterns, but the Captain went against the side-wall with his back and put the lamp he was carrying over his head. The dull tread of the Horse went past him, and left him unharmed and I heard the monstrous hoof-falls going away and away through the quiet house and after that a dead silence.

'Then the Captain moved and came towards us, very slow and shaky and with an extraordinarily grey face.

'I crept towards Parsket and the Captain came to help me. We turned him over and, you know, I knew in a moment that he was dead; but you can imagine what a feeling it sent through me.

'I looked at the Captain and suddenly he said:

'"That—That—That—" and I know that he was trying to tell me that Parsket had stood between his daughter and whatever it was that had gone down the passage. I stood up and steadied him, though I was not very steady myself. And suddenly his face began to work and he went down on to his knees by Parsket and cried like some shaken child. Then the women came out of the doorway of the bedroom and I turned away and left him to them, whilst I went over to Beaumont.

'That is practically the whole story and the only thing that is left to me is to try to explain some of the puzzling parts, here and there.

'Perhaps you have seen that Parsket was in love with Miss Hisgins and this fact is the key to a good deal that was extraordinary. He was doubtless responsible for some portions of the "haunting"; in fact I think for nearly everything, but, you know, I can prove nothing and what I have to tell you is chiefly the result of deduction.

'In the first place, it is obvious that Parsket's intention was to frighten Beaumont away and when he found that he could not do this, I think he grew so desperate that he really intended to kill him. I hate to say this, but the facts force me to think so.

'I am quite certain that it was Parsket who broke Beaumont's arm. He knew all the details of the so-called "Horse Legend", and got the idea to work upon the old story for his own end. He evidently had some method of slipping in and out of the house, probably through one of the many French windows, or possibly he had a key to one or two of the garden doors, and when he was supposed to be away, he was really coming down on the quiet and hiding somewhere in the neighbourhood.

'The incident of the kiss in the dark hall I put down to sheer nervous imaginings on the part of Beaumont and Miss Hisgins, yet I must say that the sound of the horse outside of the front door is a little difficult to explain away. But I am still inclined to keep to my first idea on this point, that there was nothing really unnatural about it.

'The hoof-sounds in the billiard-room and down the passage were done by Parsket from the floor below by bumping up against the panelled ceiling with a block of wood tied to one of the window-hooks. I proved this by an examination which showed the dents in the wood-work.

'The sounds of the horse galloping round the house were possibly made also by Parsket, who must have had a horse tied up in the plantation near by, unless, indeed, he made the sounds himself, but I do not see how he could have gone fast enough to produce the illusion. In any case, I don't feel perfect certainty on this point. I failed to find any hoof marks, as you remember.

'The gobbling neighing in the park was a ventriloquial achievement on the part of Parsket and the attack out there on Beaumont was also by him, so that when I thought he was in his bedroom, he must have been outside all the time and joined me after I ran out of the front door. This is almost probable. I mean that Parsket was the cause, for if it had been something more serious he would certainly have given up his foolishness, knowing that there was no longer any need for it. I cannot imagine how he escaped being shot, both then and in the last mad action of which I have just told you. He was enormously without fear of any kind for himself as you can see.

'The time when Parsket was with us, when we thought we heard the Horse galloping round the house, we must have been deceived. No one was very sure, except, of course, Parsket, who would naturally encourage the belief.

'The neighing in the cellar is where I consider there came the first suspicion into Parsket's mind that there was something more at work than his sham-haunting. The neighing was done by him in the same way that he did it in the park; but when I remember how ghastly he looked, I feel sure that the sounds must have had some infernal quality added to them which frightened the man himself. Yet, later, he would persuade himself that he had been getting fanciful. Of course, I must not forget that the effect upon Miss Hisgins must have made him feel pretty miserable.

'Then, about the clergyman being called away, we found afterwards that it was a bogus errand, or, rather, call and it is apparent that Parsket was at the bottom of this, so as to get a few more hours in which to achieve his end and what that was, a very little imagination will show you; for he had found that Beaumont would not be frightened away. I hate to think this, but I'm bound to. Anyway, it is obvious that the man was temporarily a bit off his normal balance. Love's a queer disease!

'Then, there is no doubt at all but that Parsket left the cord to the butler's bell hitched somewhere so as to give him an excuse to slip away naturally to clear it. This also gave him the opportunity to remove one of the passage lamps. Then he had only to smash the other and the passage was in utter darkness for him to make the attempt on Beaumont.

'In the same way, it was he who locked the door of the bedroom and took the key (it was in his pocket). This prevented the Captain from bringing a light and coming to the rescue. But Captain Hisgins broke down the door with the heavy fender-curb and it was his smashing the door that sounded so confusing and frightening in the darkness of the passage.

'The photograph of the monstrous hoof above Miss Hisgins in the cellar is one of the things that I am less sure about. It might have been faked by Parsket, whilst I was out of the room, and this would have been easy enough, to anyone who knew how. But, you know, it does not look like a fake. Yet, there is as much evidence of probability that it was faked, as against; and the thing is too vague for an examination to help to a definite decision so that I will express no opinion, one way or the other. It is certainly a horrible photograph.

'And now I come to that last, dreadful thing. There has been no further manifestation of anything abnormal, so that there is an extraordinary uncertainty in my conclusions. If we had not heard those last sounds and if Parsket had not shown that enormous sense of fear, the whole of this case could be explained in the way in which I have shown. And, in fact, as you have seen, I am of the opinion that almost all of it can be cleared up, but I see no way of going past the thing we heard at the last and the fear that Parsket showed.

'His death—no, that proves nothing. At the inquest it was described somewhat untechnically as due to heart-spasm. That is normal enough and leaves us quite in the dark as to whether he died because he stood between the girl and some incredible thing of monstrosity.

'The look on Parsket's face and the thing he called out when he heard the great hoof-sounds coming down the passage seem to show that he had the sudden realization of what before then may have been nothing more than a horrible suspicion. And his fear and appreciation of some tremendous danger approaching was probably more keenly real even than mine. And then he did the one fine, great thing!'

'And the cause?' I said. 'What caused it?'

Carnacki shook his head.

'God knows,' he answered, with a peculiar, sincere reverence. 'If that thing was what it seemed to be one might suggest an explanation which would not offend one's reason, but which may be utterly wrong. Yet I have thought, though it would take a long lecture on Thought Induction to get you to appreciate my reasons, that Parsket had produced what I might term a kind of "induced haunting", a kind of induced simulation of his mental conceptions due to his desperate thoughts and broodings. It is impossible to make it clearer in a few words.'

'But the old story!' I said. 'Why may not there have been something in *that*?'

'There may have been something in it,' said Carnacki. 'But I do not think it had anything to do with *this*. I have not clearly thought out my reasons , yet; but later I may be able to tell you why I think so.'

'And the marriage? And the cellar—was there anything found there?' asked Taylor.

'Yes, the marriage was performed that day in spite of the tragedy,' Carnacki told us. 'It was the wisest thing to do—considering the things that I cannot explain. Yes, I had the floor of that big cellar up, for I had a feeling I might find something there to give me some light. But there was nothing.

'You know, the whole thing is tremendous and

extraordinary. I shall never forget the look on Parsket's face. And afterwards the disgusting sounds of those great hoofs going away through the quiet house.'

Carnacki stood up:

'Out you go!' he said in friendly fashion, using the recognized formula.

And we went presently out into the quiet of the Embankment, and so to our homes.

XIII

The Game Played in the Dark

Ernest Bramah

'It's a funny thing, sir,' said Inspector Beedel, regarding Mr Carrados with the pensive respect that he always extended towards the blind amateur, 'it's a funny thing, but nothing seems to go on abroad now but what you'll find some trace of it here in London if you take the trouble to look.'

'In the right quarter,' contributed Carrados.

'Why, yes,' agreed the inspector. 'But nothing comes of it nine times out of ten, because it's no one's particular business to look here or the thing's been taken up and finished from the other end. I don't mean ordinary murders or single-handed burglaries, of course, but—' a modest ring of professional pride betrayed the quiet enthusiast—'real First-Class Crimes.'

'The State Antonio Five per cent. Bond Coupons?' suggested Carrados.

'Ah, you are right, Mr Carrados.' Beedel shook his head sadly, as though perhaps on that occasion someone ought to have looked. 'A man has a fit in the inquiry office of the Agent-General for British Equatoria, and two hundred and fifty thousand pounds' worth of faked securities is the result in Mexico. Then look at that jade fylfot charm pawned for one-and-three down at the Basin and the use that could have been made of it in the Kharkov "ritual murder" trial.'

'The West Hampstead Lost Memory puzzle and the Baripur bomb conspiracy that might have been smothered if one had known.'

'Quite true, sir. And the three children of that Chicago millionaire—Cyrus V. Bunting, wasn't it?—kidnapped in broad daylight outside the New York Lyric and here, three weeks later, the dumb girl who chalked the wall at Charing Cross. I remember reading once in a financial article that every piece of foreign gold had a string from it leading to Threadneedle Street. A figure of speech, sir, of course, but apt enough, I don't doubt. Well, it seems to me that every big crime done abroad leaves a finger-print here in London—if only, as you say, we look in the right quarter.'

'And at the right moment,' added Carrados. 'The time is often the present; the place the spot beneath our very noses. We take a step and the chance has gone forever.'

The inspector nodded and contributed a weighty mono-syllable of sympathetic agreement. The most prosaic of men in the pursuit of his ordinary duties, it nevertheless subtly appealed to some half-dormant streak of vanity to have his profession taken romantically when there was no serious work on hand.

'No; perhaps not "for ever" in one case in a thousand, after all,' amended the blind man thoughtfully. 'This perpetual duel between the Law and the Criminal has sometimes appeared to me in the terms of a game of cricket, inspector. Law is in the field; the Criminal at the wicket. If Law makes a mistake—sends down a loose ball or drops a catch—the Criminal scores a little or has another lease of life. But if *he* makes a mistake—if he lets a straight ball pass or spoons towards a steady man—he is done for. His mistakes are fatal; those of the Law are only temporary and retrievable.'

'Very good, sir,' said Mr Beedel, rising—the conversation had taken place in the study at The Turrets, where Beedel had found occasion to present himself—'very apt indeed. I must remember that. Well, sir, I only hope that this "Guido the Razor" lot will send a catch in our direction.'

The "this" delicately marked Inspector Beedel's instinctive contempt for Guido. As a craftsman he was compelled, on his reputation, to respect him, and he had accordingly availed himself of Carrados's friendship for a confabulation. As a man—he was a foreigner: worse, an Italian, and if left to his own resources the inspector would have opposed to his sinuous flexibility, those rigid, essentially Britannia-metal, methods of the force that strike the impartial observer as so ponderous, so amateurish and conventional, and, it must be admitted, often so curiously and inexplicably successful.

The offence that had circuitously brought 'il Rasojo' and his 'lot' within the cognizance of Scotland Yard outlines the kind of story that is discreetly hinted at by the society paragraphist of the day, politely disbelieved by the astute reader, and then at last laid indiscreetly bare in all its details by the inevitable princessly 'Recollections' of a generation later. It centred round an impending royal marriage in Vienna, a certain jealous 'Countess X' (here you have the discretion of the paragrapher), and a document or two that might be relied upon (the aristocratic biographer will impartially sum up the contingencies) to play the deuce with the approaching nuptials. To procure the evidence of these papers the Countess enlisted the services of Guido, as reliable a scoundrel as she could probably have selected for the commission. To a certain point—to the abstraction of the papers, in fact—he succeeded, but it was with pursuit close upon his heels. There was that disadvantage in employing a rogue to do work that implicated roguery, for whatever moral right the Countess had to the property, her accomplice had no legal right whatever to his liberty. On half-a-dozen charges at least he could be arrested on sight in as many capitals of Europe. He slipped out of Vienna by the Nordbahn with his destination known, resourcefully stopped the express outside Czaslau and got away across to Chrudim. By this time the game and the moves were pretty well understood in more than one keenly interested quarter. Diplomacy supplemented justice and the immediate history of Guido became that of a fox hunted from covert to covert with all the familiar earths stopped against him. From Pardubitz he passed on to Glatz, reached Breslau and went down the Oder to Stettin. Out of the liberality of his employer's advances he had ample funds to keep going, and he dropped and rejoined his accomplices as the occasion ruled. A week's harrying found him in Copenhagen, still with no time to spare, and he missed his purpose there. He crossed to Malmö by ferry, took the connecting night train to Stockholm and the same morning sailed down the Saltsjon, ostensibly bound for Obo, intending to cross to Reval and so get back to central Europe by the less frequented routes. But in this move again luck was against him and receiving warning just in time, and by the mysterious agency that had so far protected him, he contrived to be dropped from the steamer by boat among the islands of the crowded Archipelago, made his way to Helsingfors and within forty-eight hours was back again on the Frihaven with pursuit for the moment blinked and a breathing-time to the good.

To appreciate the exact significance of these wanderings it is necessary to recall the conditions. Guido was not zig-zagging a course about Europe in an aimless search for the picturesque, still less inspired by any love of the melodramatic. To him every step was vital, each tangent or rebound the necessary outcome of his much-badgered plans. In his pocket reposed the papers for which he had run grave risks. The price agreed upon for the service was sufficiently lavish to make the risks worth taking time after time; but in order to communicate the transaction it was necessary that the booty should be put into his employer's hand. Half-way across Europe that employer was waiting with such patience as she could maintain, herself watched and shadowed at every step. The Countess X was sufficiently exalted to be personally immune from the high-handed methods of her country's secret service, but every approach to her was tapped. The problem was for Guido to earn a long enough respite to enable him to communicate his position to the Countess and for her to go or to reach him by a trusty hand. Then the whole fabric of intrigue could fall to pieces, but so far Guido had been kept successfully on the run and in the meanwhile time was pressing.

'They lost him after the Hutola,' Beedel reported, in explaining the circumstances to Max Carrados. 'Three days later they found that he'd been back again in Copenhagen but by that time he'd flown. Now they're without a trace except the inference of these "Orange peach blossom" agonies in *The Times*. But the Countess has gone hurriedly to Paris; and Lafayard thinks it all points to London.'

'I suppose the Foreign Office is anxious to oblige just now?'

'I expect so, sir,' agreed Beedel, 'but, of course, my instructions don't come from that quarter. What appeals to *us* is that it would be a feather in our caps—they're still a little sore up at the Yard about Hans the Piper.'

'Naturally,' assented Carrados. 'Well, I'll see what I can do if there is real occasion. Let me know anything, and, if you see your chance yourself, come round for a talk if you like on—today's Wednesday?—I shall be in at any rate on Friday evening.'

Without being a precisian, the blind man was usually exact in such matters. There are those who hold that an engagement must be kept at all hazard; men who would miss a death-bed message in order to keep literal faith with a beggar. Carrados took lower, if more substantial ground. 'My word,' he sometimes had occasion to remark, 'is subject to contingencies, like everything else about me. If I make a promise it is conditional on nothing which seems more important arising to counteract it. That, among men of sense, is understood.' And, as it happened, something did occur on this occasion.

He was summoned to the telephone just before dinner on Friday evening to receive a message personally. Greatorex, his secretary, had taken the call, but came in to say that the caller would give him nothing beyond his name—Brebner. The name was unknown to Carrados, but such incidents were not uncommon, and he proceeded to comply.

'Yes,' he responded; 'I am Max Carrados speaking. What is it?'

'Oh, it is you, sir, is it? Mr Brickwell told me to get to you direct.'

'Well, you are all right. Brickwell? Are you the British Museum?'

'Yes. I am Brebner in the Chaldean Art Department. They are in a great stew here. We have just found out that someone has managed to get access to the second Inner Greek Room and looted some of the cabinets there. It is all a mystery as yet.'

'What is missing?' asked Carrados.

'So far we can only definitely speak of about six trays of Greek coins—a hundred to a hundred and twenty, roughly.'

'Important?'

The line conveyed a caustic bark of tragic amusement.

'Why, yes, I should say so. The beggar seems to have

known his business. All fine specimens of the best period. Syracuse—Messana—Croton—Amphipolis.   Eumenes— Evainetos—Kimons. The chief quite wept.'

Carrados groaned. There was not a piece among them that he had not handled lovingly.

'What are you doing?' he demanded.

'Mr Brickwell has been to Scotland Yard, and, on advice, we are not making it public as yet. We don't want a hint of it dropped anywhere, if you don't mind, sir.'

'That will be all right.'

'It was for that reason that I was to speak with you personally. We are notifying the chief dealers and likely collectors to whom the coins, or some of them, may be offered at once if it is thought that we haven't found it out yet. Judging from the expertness displayed in the selection, we don't think that there is any danger of the lot being sold to a pawnbroker or a metal-dealer, so that we are running very little real risk in not advertising the loss.'

'Yes; probably it is as well,' replied Carrados. 'Is there anything that Mr Brickwell wishes me to do?'

'Only this, sir; if you are offered a suspicious lot of Greek coins, or hear of them, would you have a look—I mean ascertain whether they are likely to be ours, and if you think they are communicate with us and Scotland Yard at once?'

'Certainly,' replied the blind man. 'Tell Mr Brickwell that he can rely on me if any indication comes my way. Convey my regrets to him and tell him that I feel the loss quite as a personal one. . . . I don't think that you and I have met as yet, Mr Brebner?'

'No, sir,' said the voice diffidently, 'but I have looked forward to the pleasure. Perhaps this unfortunate business will bring me an introduction.'

'You are very kind,' was Carrados's acknowledgement of the compliment. 'Any time. . . . I was going to say that perhaps you don't know my weakness, but I have spent many pleasant hours over your wonderful collection. That ensures the personal element. Goodbye.'

Carrados was really disturbed by the loss although his concern was tempered by the reflection that the coins would inevitably in the end find their way back to the Museum. That their restitution might involve ransom to the extent of several thousand pounds was the least poignant detail of the situation. The one harrowing thought was that the booty might, through stress or ignorance, find its way into the melting-pot. That dreadful contingency, remote but insistent, was enough to affect the appetite of the blind enthusiast.

He was expecting Inspector Beedel, who would be full of his own case, but he could not altogether dismiss the aspects of possibility that Brebner's communication opened before his mind. He was still concerned with the chances of destruction and a very indifferent companion for Greatorex, who alone sat with him, when Parkinson presented himself. Dinner was over but Carrados had remained rather longer than his custom, smoking his mild Turkish cigarette in silence.

'A lady wishes to see you, sir. She said you would not know her name, but that her business would interest you.'

The form of message was sufficiently unusual to take the attention of both men.

'You don't know her, of course, Parkinson?' inquired his master.

For just a second the immaculate Parkinson seemed tongue-tied. Then he delivered himself in his most ceremonial strain.

'I regret to say that I cannot claim the advantage, sir,' he replied.

'Better let me tackle her, sir,' suggested Greatorex with easy confidence. 'It's probably a sub.'

The sportive offer was declined by a smile and a shake of the head. Carrados turned to his attendant.

'I shall be in the study, Parkinson. Show her there in three minutes. You stay and have another cigarette, Greatorex. By that time she will either have gone or have interested me.'

In three minutes' time Parkinson threw open the study door.

'The lady, sir,' he announced.

Could he have seen, Carrados would have received the impression of a plainly, almost dowdily, dressed young woman of buxom figure. She wore a light veil, but it was ineffective in concealing the unattraction of the face beneath. The features were swart and the upper lip darkened with the more than incipient moustache of the southern brunette. Worse remained, for a disfiguring rash had assailed patches of her skin. As she entered she swept the room and its occupant with a quiet but comprehensive survey.

'Please take a chair, madame. You wished to see me?'

The ghost of a demure smile flickered about her mouth as she complied, and in that moment her face seemed less uncomely. Her eye lingered for a moment on a cabinet above the desk, and one might have noticed that her eye was very bright. Then she replied.

'You are Signor Carrados, in—in the person?'

Carrados made his smiling admission and changed his position a fraction—possibly to catch her curiously pitched voice the better.

'The great collector of the antiquities?'

'I do collect a little,' he admitted guardedly.

'You will forgive me, Signor, if my language is not altogether good. When I live at Naples with my mother we let boardings, chiefly to Inglish and Amerigans. I pick up the words, but since I marry and go to live in Calabria my

Inglish has gone all red—no, no, you say, rusty. Yes,
that's it; quite rusty.'

'It is excellent,' said Carrados. 'I am sure that we shall
understand one another perfectly.'

The lady shot a penetrating glance, but the blind man's
expression was merely suave and courteous. Then she
continued:

'My husband is of name Ferraja—Michele Ferraja. We
have a vineyard and a little property near Forenzana.'
She paused to examine the tips of her gloves for quite an
appreciable moment. 'Signor,' she burst out, with some
vehemence, 'the laws of my country are not good at all.'

'From what I hear on all sides,' said Carrados, 'I am
afraid that your country is not alone.'

'There is at Forenzana a poor labourer, Gian Verde of
name,' continued the visitor, dashing volubly into her
narrative, 'He is one day digging in the vineyard, the
vineyard of my husband, when his spade strikes itself
upon an obstruction. "Aha," says Gian, "what have we
here?" and he goes down upon his knees to see. It is an oil
jar of red earth, Signor, such as was anciently used, and in
it is filled with silver money.

'Gian is poor but he is wise. Does he call upon the
authorities? No, no; he understands that they are all
corrupt. He carries what he has found to my husband for
he knows him to be a man of great honour.

'My husband also is of brief decision. His mind is made
up. "Gian," he says, "keep your mouth shut. This will be
to your ultimate profit." Gian understands, for he can
trust my husband. He makes a sign of mutual implication.
Then he goes back to the spade digging.

'My husband understands a little of these things but
not enough. We go to the collections of Messina and Naples
and even Rome and there we see other pieces of silver
money, similar, and learn that they are of great value.

They are of different sizes but most would cover a lira and of the thickness of two. On the one side imagine the great head of a pagan deity; on the other—oh, so many things I cannot remember what.' A gesture of circumferential despair indicated the hopeless variety of design.

'A biga or quadriga of mules?' suggested Carrados. 'An eagle carrying off a hare, a figure flying with a wreath, a trophy of arms? Some of those perhaps?'

'Si, si bene,' cried Madame Ferraja. 'You understand, I perceive, Signor. We are very cautious, for on every side is extortion and unjust law. See, it is even forbidden to take these things out of the country, yet if we try to dispose of them at home they will be seized and we punished, for they are tesoro trovado, what you call treasure troven and belonging to the State—these coins which the industry of Gian discovered and which had lain for so long in the ground of my husband's vineyard.'

'So you brought them to England?'

'Si, Signor. It is spoken of as a land of justice and rich nobility who buy these things at the highest prices. Also my speaking a little of the language would serve us here.'

'I suppose you have the coins for disposal then? You can show them to me?'

'My husband retains them. I will take you, but you must first give parola d'onore of an English Signor not to betray us, or to speak of the circumstance to another.'

Carrados had already foreseen this eventuality and decided to accept it. Whether a promise exacted on the plea of treasure trove would bind him to respect the despoilers of the British Museum was a point for subsequent consideration. Prudence demanded that he should investigate the offer at once and to cavil over Madame Farraja's conditions would be fatal to that object. If the coins were, as there seemed little reason to doubt, the proceeds of the robbery, a modest ransom might be the safest way of preserving irreplaceable treasures, and in that case Carrados could offer his services as the necessary intermediary.

'I give you the promise you require, Madame,' he accordingly declared.

'It is sufficient,' assented Madame. 'I will now take you to the spot. It is necessary that you alone should accompany me, for my husband is so distraught in this country, where he understands not a word of what is spoken, that his poor spirit would cry "We are surrounded!" if he saw two strangers approach the house. Oh, he is become most dreadful in his anxiety, my husband. Imagine only, he keeps on the fire a cauldron of molten lead and he would not hesitate to plunge into it this treasure and obliterate its existence if he imagined himself endangered.'

'So,' speculated Carrados inwardly. 'A likely precaution for a simple vine-grower of Calabria! Very well,' he assented aloud. 'I will go with you alone. Where is the place?'

Madame Ferraja searched in the ancient purse that she discovered in her rusty handbag and produced a scrap of paper.

'People do not understand sometimes my way of saying it,' she explained. 'Sette, Herringbone——'

'May I—?' said Carrados, stretching out his hand. He took the paper and touched the writing with his finger-tips. 'Oh yes, 7 Heronsbourne Place. That is on the edge of Heronsbourne Park, is it not?' He transferred the paper casually to his desk as he spoke and stood up. 'How did you come, Madame Ferraja?'

Madame Ferraja followed the careless action with a discreet smile that did not touch her voice.

'By motor bus—first one then another, inquiring at every turning. Oh, but it was interminable,' sighed the lady.

'My driver is off for the evening—I did not expect to be

going out—but I will 'phone up a taxi and it will be at the gate as soon as we are.' He dispatched the message and then, turning to the house telephone, switched on to Greatorex.

'I'm just going round to Heronsbourne Park,' he explained. 'Don't stay, Greatorex, but if anyone calls expecting to see me, you can say that I don't anticipate being away more than an hour.'

Parkinson was hovering about the hall. With quite novel officiousness he pressed upon his master a succession of articles that were not required. Over this usually complacent attendant the unattractive features of Madame Ferraja appeared to exercise a stealthy fascination, for a dozen times the lady detected his eyes questioning her face and a dozen times he looked guiltily away again. But his incongruities could not delay for more than a few minutes the opening of the door.

'I do not accompany you, sir?' he inquired, with the suggestion plainly tendered in his voice that it would be much better if he did.

'Not this time, Parkinson.'

'Very well, sir. Is there any particular address to which we can telephone in case you are required, sir?'

'Mr Greatorex has instructions.'

Parkinson stood aside, his resources exhausted. Madame Ferraja laughed a little mockingly as they walked down the drive.

'Your man-servant thinks I may eat you, Signor Carrados,' she declared vivaciously.

Carrados, who held the key of his usually exact attendant's perturbation—for he himself had recognized in Madame Ferraja the angelic Nina Brun, of the Sicilian tetradrachm incident, from the moment she opened her mouth—admitted to himself the humour of her audacity. But it was not until half-an-hour later that enlightenment rewarded Parkinson. Inspector Beedel had just arrived and was speaking with Greatorex when the conscientious valet, who had been winnowing his memory in solitude, broke in upon them, more distressed than either had ever seen him in his life before, and with the breathless introduction: 'It was the ears, sir! I have her ears at last!' poured out his tale of suspicion, recognition and his present fears.

In the meanwhile the two objects of his concern had reached the gate as the summoned taxicab drew up.

'Seven Heronsbourne Place,' called Carrados to the driver.

'No, no,' interposed the lady, with decision, 'let him stop at the beginning of the street. It is not far to walk. My husband would be on the verge of distraction if he thought in the dark that it was the arrival of the police—who knows?'

'Brackedge Road, opposite the end of Heronsbourne Place,' amended Carrados.

Heronsbourne Place had the reputation, among those who were curious in such matters, of being the most re-clusive residential spot inside the four-mile circle. To earn that distinction it was, needless to say, a cul-de-sac. It bounded one side of Heronsbourne Park but did not at any point of its length give access to that pleasance. It was entirely devoted to unostentatious little houses something between the villa and the cottage, some detached and some in pairs, but all possessing the endowment of larger, more umbrageous gardens than can generally be secured within the radius. The local house agent described them as 'delightfully old-world' or 'completely modernized' according to the requirement of the applicant.

The cab was dismissed at the corner and Madame Ferraja guided her companion along the silent and deserted way. She had begun to talk with renewed animation, but her ceaseless chatter only served to emphasize to Carrados the one fact that it was contrived to disguise.

'I am not causing you to miss the house with looking after me—No. 7, Madame Ferraja?' he interposed.

'No, certainly,' she replied readily. 'It is a little further. The numbers are from the other end. But we are there. Ecco!'

She stopped at a gate and opened it, still guiding him. They passed into a garden, moist and sweet-scented with the distillate odours of a dewy evening. As she turned to relatch the gate the blind man endeavoured politely to anticipate her. Between them his hat fell to the ground.

'My clumsiness,' he apologized, recovering it from the step. 'My old impulses and my present helplessness, alas, Madame Ferraja!'

'One learns prudence by experience,' said Madame sagely. She was scarcely to know, poor lady, that even as she uttered this trite aphorism, under cover of darkness and his hat, Mr Carrados had just ruined his signet ring by blazoning a golden '7' upon her garden step to establish its identity if need be. A cul-de-sac that numbered from the closed end seemed to demand some investigation.

'Seldom,' he replied to her remark. 'One goes on taking risks. So we are there?'

Madame Ferraja had opened the front door with a latch-key. She dropped the latch and led Carrados forward along the narrow hall. The room they entered was at the back of the house, and from the position of the road it therefore overlooked the park. Again the door was locked behind them.

'The celebrated Mr Carrados!' announced Madame Ferraja with a sparkle of triumph in her voice. She waved her hand towards a lean, dark man who had stood beside the door as they entered. 'My husband.'

'Beneath our poor roof in the most fraternal manner,'

commented the dark man, in the same derisive spirit. 'But it is wonderful.'

'The even more celebrated Monsieur Dompierre, unless I am mistaken?' retorted Carrados blandly. 'I bow on our first real meeting.'

'You knew!' exclaimed the Dompierre of the earlier incident incredulously. 'Stoker, you were right and I owe you a hundred lire. Who recognized you, Nina?'

'How should I know?' demanded the real Madame Dompierre crossly. 'This blind man himself, by chance.'

'You pay a poor compliment to your charming wife's personality to imagine that one could forget her so soon,' put in Carrados. 'And you a Frenchman, Dompierre!'

'You knew, Monsieur Carrados,' reiterated Dompierre, 'and yet you ventured here. You are either a fool or a hero.'

'An enthusiast—it is the same thing as both,' interposed the lady. 'What did I tell you? What did it matter if he recognized? You see?'

'Surely you exaggerate, Monsieur Dompierre,' contributed Carrados. 'I may yet pay tribute to your industry. Perhaps I regret the circumstance and the necessity but I am here to make the best of it. Let me see the things Madame has spoken of and then we can consider the detail of their price, either for myself or on behalf of others.'

There was no immediate reply. From Dompierre came a saturnine chuckle and from Madame Dompierre a titter that accompanied a grimace. For one of the rare occasions in his life Carrados found himself wholly out of touch with the atmosphere of the situation. Instinctively he turned his face towards the other occupant of the room, the man addressed as 'Stoker', whom he knew to be standing near the window.

'This unfortunate business *has* brought me an introduction,' said a familiar voice.

For one dreadful moment the universe stood still round

Carrados. Then, with the crash and grind of overwhelming mental tumult, the whole strategy revealed itself, like the sections of a gigantic puzzle falling into place before his eyes.

There had been no robbery at the British Museum! That plausible concoction was as fictitious as the intentionally transparent tale of treasure trove. Carrados recognized now how ineffective the one device would have been without the other in drawing him—how convincing the two together—and while smarting at the humiliation of his plight he could not restrain a dash of admiration at the ingenuity—the accurately conjectured line of inference— of the plot. It was again the familiar artifice of the cunning pitfall masked by the clumsily contrived trap just beyond it. And straightway into it he had blundered!

'And this,' continued the same voice, 'is Carrados, Max Carrados, upon whose perspicuity a government—only the present government, let me in justice say—depends to outwit the undesirable alien! My country; O my country!'

'Is it really Monsieur Carrados?' inquired Dompierre in polite sarcasm. 'Are you sure, Nina, that you have not brought a man from Scotland Yard instead?'

'Basta! he is here; what more do you want? Do not mock the poor sightless gentleman,' answered Madame Dompierre, in doubtful sympathy.

'That is exactly what I was wondering,' ventured Carrados mildly. 'I am here—what more do you want? Perhaps you, Mr Stoker—?'

'Excuse me. "Stoker" is a mere colloquial appellation based on a trifling incident of my career in connection with a disabled liner. The title illustrates the childish weakness of the criminal classes for nicknames, together with their pitiable baldness of invention. My real name is Montmorency, Mr Carrados—Eustace Montmorency.'

'Thank you, Mr Montmorency,' said Carrados gravely.

'We are on opposite sides of the table here tonight, but I should be proud to have been with you in the stokehold of the Benvenuto.'

'That was pleasure,' muttered the Englishman. 'This is business.'

'Oh, quite so,' agreed Carrados. 'So far I am not exactly complaining. But I think it is high time to be told—and I address myself to you—why I have been decoyed here and what your purpose is.'

Mr Montmorency turned to his accomplice.

'Dompierre,' he remarked, with great clearness, 'why the devil is Mr Carrados kept standing?'

'Ah, oh, heaven!' exclaimed Madame Dompierre with tragic resignation, and flung herself down on a couch.

'Scusi,' grinned the lean man, and with burlesque grace he placed a chair for their guest's acceptance.

'Your curiosity is natural,' continued Mr Montmorency, with a cold eye towards Dompierre's antics, 'although I really think that by this time you ought to have guessed the truth. In fact, I don't doubt that you have guessed, Mr Carrados, and that you are only endeavouring to gain time. For that reason—because it will perhaps convince you that we have nothing to fear—I don't mind obliging you.'

'Better hasten,' murmured Dompierre uneasily.

'Thank you, Bill,' said the Englishman, with genial effrontery. 'I won't fail to report your intelligence to the Rasojo. Yes, Mr Carrados, as you have already conjectured, it is the affair of the Countess X to which you owe this inconvenience. You will appreciate the compliment that underlies your temporary seclusion, I am sure. When circumstances favoured our plans and London became the inevitable place of meeting, you and you alone stood in the way. We guessed that you would be consulted and we frankly feared your intervention. You were consulted. We know that Inspector Beedel visited you two days ago and he has no other case in hand. Your quiescence for just three days had to be obtained at any cost. So here you are.'

'I see,' assented Carrados. 'And having got me here, how do you propose to keep me?'

'Of course that detail has received consideration. In fact we secured this furnished house solely with that in view. There are three courses before us. The first, quite pleasant, hangs on your acquiescence. The second, more drastic, comes into operation if you decline. The third—but really, Mr Carrados, I hope you won't oblige me even to discuss the third. You will understand that it is rather objectionable for me to contemplate the necessity of two able-bodied men having to use even the smallest amount of physical compulsion towards one who is blind and helpless. I hope you will be reasonable and accept the inevitable.'

'The inevitable is the one thing that I invariably accept,' replied Carrados. 'What does it involve?'

'You will write a note to your secretary explaining that what you have learned at 7 Heronsbourne Place makes it necessary for you to go immediately abroad for a few days. By the way, Mr Carrados, although this is Heronsbourne Place it is *not* No. 7.'

'Dear, dear me,' sighed the prisoner. 'You seem to have had me at every turn, Mr Montmorency.'

'An obvious precaution. The wider course of giving you a different street altogether we rejected as being too risky in getting you here. To continue: To give conviction to the message you will direct your man Parkinson to follow by the first boat-train tomorrow, with all the requirements for a short stay, and put up at Mascot's, as usual, awaiting your arrival there.'

'Very convincing,' agreed Carrados. 'Where shall I be in reality?'

'In a charming though rather isolated bungalow on the

south coast. Your wants will be attended to. There is a boat. You can row and fish. You will be run down by motor car and brought back to your own gate. It's really very pleasant for a few days. I've often stayed there myself.'

'Your recommendation carries weight. Suppose, for the sake of curiosity, that I decline?'

'You will still go there but your treatment will be commensurate with your behaviour. The car to take you is at this moment waiting in a convenient spot on the other side of the park. We shall go down the garden at the back, cross the park, and put you into the car—anyway.'

'And if I resist?'

The man whose pleasantry it had been to call himself Eustace Montmorency shrugged his shoulders.

'Don't be a fool,' he said tolerantly. 'You know who you are dealing with and the kind of risks we run. If you call out or endanger us at a critical point we shall not hesitate to silence you effectively.'

The blind man knew that it was no idle threat. In spite of the cloak of humour and fantasy thrown over the proceedings, he was in the power of coolly desperate men. The window was curtained and shuttered against sight and sound, the door behind him locked. Possibly at that moment a revolver threatened him; certainly weapons lay within reach of both his keepers.

'Tell me what to write,' he asked, with capitulation in his voice.

Dompierre twirled his moustache in relieved approval. Madame laughed from her place on the couch and picked up a book, watching Montmorency over the cover of its pages. As for that gentleman, he masked his satisfaction by the practical business of placing on the table before Carrados the accessories of the letter.

'Put into your own words the message that I outlined just now.'

'Perhaps to make it altogether natural I had better write on a page of the notebook that I always use,' suggested Carrados.

'Do you wish to make it natural?' demanded Montmorency with latent suspicion.

'If the miscarriage of your plan is to result in my head being knocked—yes, I do,' was the reply.

'Good!' chuckled Dompierre, and sought to avoid Mr Montmorency's cold glance by turning on the electric table-lamp for the blind man's benefit. Madame Dompierre laughed shrilly.

'Thank you, Monsieur,' said Carrados, 'you have done quite right. What is light to you is warmth to me—heat, energy, inspiration. Now to business.'

He took out the pocket-book he had spoken of and leisurely proceeded to flatten it down upon the table before him. As his tranquil, pleasant eyes ranged the room meanwhile it was hard to believe that the shutters of an impenetrable darkness lay between them and the world. They rested for a moment on the two accomplices who stood beyond the table, picked out Madame Dompierre lolling on the sofa on his right, and measured the proportions of the long, narrow room. They seemed to note the positions of the window at the one end and the door almost at the other, and even to take into account the single pendent electric light which up till then had been the sole illuminant.

'You prefer pencil?' asked Montmorency.

'I generally use it for casual purposes. But not,' he added, touching the point critically, 'like this.'

Alert for any sign of retaliation, they watched him take an insignificant penknife from his pocket and begin to trim the pencil. Was there in his mind any mad impulse to force conclusions with that puny weapon? Dompierre worked his face into a fiercer expression and touched reassuringly the handle of his knife. Montmorency looked on

[345]

for a moment, then, whistling softly to himself, turned his back on the table and strolled towards the window, avoiding Madame Nina's pursuant eye.

Then, with overwhelming suddenness, it came, and in its form altogether unexpected.

Carrados had been putting the last strokes to the pencil, whittling it down upon the table. There had been no hasty movement, no violent act to give them warning; only the little blade had pushed itself nearer and nearer to the electric light cord lying there . . . and suddenly and instantly the room was plunged into absolute darkness.

'To the door, Dom!' shouted Montmorency in a flash. 'I am at the window. Don't let him pass and we are all right.'

'I am here,' responded Dompierre from the door.

'He will not attempt to pass,' came the quiet voice of Carrados from across the room. 'You are now all exactly where I want you. You are both covered. If either moves an inch, I fire—and remember that I shoot by sound, not sight.'

'But—but what does it mean?' stammered Montmorency, above the despairing wail of Madame Dompierre.

'It means that we are now on equal terms—three blind men in a dark room. The numerical advantage that you possess is counterbalanced by the fact that you are out of your element—I am in mine.'

'Dom,' whispered Montmorency across the dark space, 'strike a match. I have none.'

'I would not, Dompierre, if I were you,' advised Carrados, with a short laugh. 'It might be dangerous.' At once his voice seemed to leap into a passion. 'Drop that matchbox,' he cried. 'You are standing on the brink of your grave, you fool! Drop it, I say; let me hear it fall.'

A breath of thought—almost too short to call a pause —then a little thud of surrender sounded from the carpet by the door. The two conspirators seemed to hold their breath.

'That is right.' The placid voice once more resumed its sway. 'Why cannot things be agreeable? I hate to have to shout, but you seem far from grasping the situation yet. Remember that I do not take the slightest risk. Also please remember, Mr Montmorency, that the action even of a hair-trigger automatic scrapes slightly as it comes up. I remind you of that for your own good, because if you are so ill-advised as to think of trying to pot me in the dark, that noise gives me a fifth of a second start of you. Do you by any chance know Zinghi's in Mercer Street?'

'The shooting gallery?' asked Mr Montmorency a little sulkily.

'The same. If you happen to come through this alive and are interested you might ask Zinghi to show you a target of mine that he keeps. Seven shots at twenty yards, the target indicated by four watches, none of them so loud as the one you are wearing. He keeps it as a curiosity.'

'I wear no watch,' muttered Dompierre, expressing his thought aloud.

'No, Monsieur Dompierre, but you wear a heart, and that not on your sleeve,' said Carrados. 'Just now it is quite as loud as Mr Montmorency's watch. It is more central too—I shall not have to allow any margin. That is right; breath naturally'—for the unhappy Dompierre had given a gasp of apprehension. 'It does not make any difference to me, and after a time holding one's breath becomes really painful.'

'Monsieur,' declared Dompierre earnestly, 'there was no intention of submitting you to injury, I swear. This English-man did but speak within his hat. At the most extreme you would have been but bound and gagged. Take care: killing is a dangerous game.'

'For you—not for me,' was the bland rejoinder. 'If you

kill me you will be hanged for it. If I kill you I shall be honourably acquitted. You can imagine the scene—the sympathetic court—the recital of your villainies—the story of my indignities. Then with stumbling feet and groping hands the helpless blind man is led forward to give evidence. Sensation! No, no, it isn't really fair but I can kill you both with absolute certainty and Providence will be saddled with all the responsibility. Please don't fidget with your feet, Monsieur Dompierre. I know that you aren't moving but one is liable to make mistakes.'

'Before I die,' said Montmorency—and for some reason laughed unconvincingly in the dark—'before I die, Mr Carrados, I should really like to know what has happened to the light. That, surely, isn't Providence?'

'Would it be ungenerous to suggest that you are trying to gain time? You ought to know what has happened. But as it may satisfy you that I have nothing to fear from delay, I don't mind telling you. In my hand was a sharp knife—contemptible, you were satisfied, as a weapon; beneath my nose the "flex" of the electric lamp. It was only necessary for me to draw the one across the other and the system was short-circuited. Every lamp on that fuse is cut off and in the distributing-box in the hall you will find a burned-out wire. You, perhaps—but Monsieur Dompierre's experience in plating ought to have put him up to simple electricity.'

'How did you know that there is a distributing-box in the hall?' asked Dompierre, with dull resentment.

'My dear Dompierre, why beat the air with futile questions?' replied Max Carrados. 'Whatever does it matter? Have it in the cellar if you like.'

'True,' interposed Montmorency. 'The only thing that need concern us now——'

'But it is in the hall—nine feet high,' muttered Dompierre in bitterness. 'Yet he, this blind man——'

'The only thing that need concern us,' repeated the Englishman, severely ignoring the interruption, 'is what you intend doing in the end, Mr Carrados?'

'The end is a little difficult to foresee,' was the admission. 'So far, I am all for maintaining the status quo. Will the first grey light of morning find us still in this impasse? No, for between us we have condemned the room to eternal darkness. Probably about daybreak Dompierre will drop off to sleep and roll against the door. I, unfortunately, mistaking his intention, will send a bullet through—Pardon, Madame, I should have remembered—but pray don't move.'

'I protest, Monsieur——'

'Don't protest; just sit still. Very likely it will be Mr Montmorency who will fall off to sleep the first after all.'

'Then we will anticipate that difficulty,' said the one in question, speaking with renewed decision. 'We will play the last hand with our cards upon the table if you like. Nina, Mr Carrados will not injure you whatever happens— be sure of that. When the moment comes you will rise——'

'One word,' put in Carrados with determination. 'My position is precarious and I take no risks. As you say, I cannot injure Madame Dompierre, and you two men are therefore my hostages for her good behaviour. If she rises from the couch you, Dompierre, fall. If she advances another step Mr Montmorency follows you.'

'Do nothing rash, carissima,' urged her husband, with passionate solicitude. 'You might get hit in place of me. We will yet find a better way.'

'You dare not, Mr Carrados!' flung out Montmorency, for the first time beginning to show signs of wear in this duel of the temper. 'He dare not, Dompierre. In cold blood and unprovoked! No jury would acquit you!'

'Another who fails to do you justice, Madame Nina,' said the blind man, with ironic gallantry. 'The action might be a little high-handed, one admits, but when you, appropriately clothed and in your right complexion, stepped into the witness-box and I said: "Gentlemen of the jury, what is my crime? That I made Madame Dompierre a widow!" can you doubt their gratitude and my acquittal? Truly my countrymen are not all bats or monks, Madame.' Dompierre was breathing with perfect freedom now, while from the couch came the sounds of stifled emotion, but whether the lady was involved in a paroxysm of sobs or of laughter it might be difficult to swear.

*　*　*

It was perhaps an hour after the flourish of the introduction with which Madame Dompierre had closed the door of the trap upon the blind man's entrance.

The minutes had passed but the situation remained unchanged, though the ingenuity of certainly two of the occupants of the room had been tormented into shreds to discover a means of turning it to their advantage. So far the terrible omniscience of the blind man in the dark and the respect for his marksmanship with which his coolness had inspired them, dominated the group. But one strong card yet remained to be played, and at last the moment came upon which the conspirators had pinned their despairing hopes.

There was the sound of movement in the hall outside, not the first about the house, but towards the new complication Carrados had been strangely unobservant. True, Montmorency had talked rather loudly, to carry over the dangerous moments. But now there came an unmistakable step and to the accomplices it could only mean one thing. Montmorency was ready on the instant.

'Down, Dom!' he cried, 'throw yourself down! Break in, Guido. Break in the door. We are held up!'

There was an immediate response. The door, under the

pressure of a human battering-ram, burst open with a crash. On the threshold the intruders—four or five in number—stopped starkly for a moment, held in astonishment by the extraordinary scene that the light from the hall, and of their own bull's-eyes, revealed.

Flat on their faces, to present the least possible surface to Carrados's aim, Dompierre and Montmorency lay extended beside the window and behind the door. On the couch, with her head buried beneath the cushions, Madame Dompierre sought to shut out the sight and sound of violence. Carrados—Carrados had not moved, but with arms resting on the table and fingers placidly locked together he smiled benignly on the new arrivals. His attitude, compared with the extravagance of those around him, gave the impression of a complacent modern deity presiding over some grotesque ceremonial of pagan worship.

'So, Inspector, you could not wait for me, after all?' was his greeting.

Sources

1. Max Pemberton: *Jewel Mysteries I Have Known*. (Ward, Lock & Bowden, 1894)
2. Arthur Morrison: *Chronicles of Martin Hewitt*. (Ward, Lock & Bowden, 1895)
3. Guy Boothby: *A Prince of Swindlers*. (Ward, Lock n.d.) First published in Pearson's Magazine Jan. to July 1897.
4. Arthur Morrison: *The Dorrington Deed-Box*. (Ward, Lock n.d. [1897])
5. Clifford Ashdown: *The Adventures of Romney Pringle*. (Ward, Lock, 1902) First published in Cassell's Magazine June to November 1902.
6. L. T. Meade and Robert Eustace: *The Sorceress of the Strand*. (Ward, Lock, 1903) First published in The Strand Magazine October 1902–March 1903.
7. Clifford Ashdown: *Further Adventures of Romney Pringle*. (Cassell's Magazine June to November 1903) Not previously published in book form.
8. William Le Queux: *Secrets of the Foreign Office*. (Hutchinson, 1903)
9. Baroness Orczy: *The Old Man in the Corner*. (Greening, 1909) First published in the Royal Magazine in 1901 and 1902.
10. R. Austin Freeman: *John Thorndyke's Cases*. (Chatto & Windus, 1909)
11. Baroness Orczy: *Lady Molly of Scotland Yard*. (Cassell, 1910)
12. William Hope Hodgson: *Carnacki the Ghost-Finder*. (Eveleigh Nash, 1913)
13. Ernest Bramah: *Max Carrados*. (Methuen, 1914)

Other Pantheon mystery titles in paperback
you are sure to enjoy include:

CRIME ON HER MIND:
Fifteen Stories of Female Sleuths from the Victorian Era to the Forties
edited and with introductions
by Michele Slung $6.95 paperback

and

THE PANTHEON INTERNATIONAL

CRIME SERIES

THE POISON ORACLE
THE LIVELY DEAD
by Peter Dickinson

A KILLING KINDNESS
by Reginald Hill

THE FALSE INSPECTOR DEW
by Peter Lovesey

CUBAN PASSAGE by Norman Lewis

THE BLOOD OF AN ENGLISHMAN
THE CATERPILLAR COP
THE STEAM PIG
by James McClure

LAIDLAW by William McIlvanney

SCAPEGOAT by Poul Ørum

THE EURO-KILLERS
by Julian Rathbone

MURDER ON THE THIRTY-FIRST FLOOR
by Per Wahlöö

all $2.95 paperback